.OUR L

The
North Pole
*

Eureka

GREENLAND

Pond
Inlet

Labrador

Québec

Lawrence R.

New York

sallusautigiq

lying)

vaa = she

er

1300

SEVEN DREAMS

Also by William T. Vollmann

YOU BRIGHT AND RISEN ANGELS
THE RAINBOW STORIES
THE ICE-SHIRT
THIRTEEN STORIES AND THIRTEEN EPITAPHS
WHORES FOR GLORIA
FATHERS AND CROWS
BUTTERFLY STORIES

SEVEN DREAMS
A Book of North American Landscapes

by

WILLIAM T. VOLLMANN

VIKING

SEVEN DREAMS

ABOUT OUR CONTINENT
IN THE DAYS OF
THE RIFLEMEN

Unthawing the Multi-Frozen Breeches of
Starvation Guns
in the
Black-Mooned Days of Winter
Whose
Heroes
(Aiming Straight or Wide),
Smoothbored the Northwest Passage,
CHECKED THE RAMPAGES OF WHALES,
Relocated the Esquimaux;
Who discovered
Gold,
Who
WERE RIGHT ON THE MONEY;
Who had
SYPHILIS;
Who
Invented the Repeaters!

As Disassembled From
Diverse Gauges

by

WILLIAM T. VOLLMANN

(Known in This World as
"WILLIAM THE BLIND")

VIKING
Published by the Penguin Group
Penguin Books USA Inc., 375 Hudson Street, New York, New York 10014, U.S.A.
Penguin Books Ltd, 27 Wrights Lane, London W8 5TZ, England
Penguin Books Australia Ltd, Ringwood, Victoria, Australia
Penguin Books Canada Ltd, 10 Alcorn Avenue, Toronto, Ontario, Canada M4V 3B2
Penguin Books (N.Z.) Ltd, 182–190 Wairau Road, Auckland 10, New Zealand

Penguin Books Ltd, Registered Offices:
Harmondsworth, Middlesex, England

First published in 1994 by Viking Penguin, a division of Penguin Books USA Inc.

1 3 5 7 9 10 8 6 4 2

Copyright © William T. Vollmann, 1994
All rights reserved

The "Rifle-Text" section of this book first appeared in *Conjunctions* magazine. The final
"King William Island" section first appeared in *The Review of Contemporary Fiction.*

LIBRARY OF CONGRESS CATALOGING IN PUBLICATION DATA
Vollmann, William T.
The rifles/ William T. Vollmann.
p.   cm.—(Seven dreams, a book of North American landscapes; v. 6)
ISBN 0-670-84856-5
1. Arctic regions—Discovery and exploration—British—Fiction.
2. Franklin, John, Sir, 1786–1847—Fiction.   3. Inuit—Northwest Territories—Fiction.
4. Explorers—Arctic regions—Fiction.   5. Northwest Passage—Fiction.
I. Title.   II. Series: Vollmann, William T.   Seven dreams; v. 6.
PS3572.O395R54   1994
813'.54—dc20   93-31577

Printed in the United States of America
Set in Garamond

SIXTH DREAM
The Rifles

Are not the days of my life few? Let me alone, that I may find a little comfort before I go whence I shall not return, to the land of gloom and darkness, to the land of gloom and chaos, where light is as darkness.

Job 10.20–2

For ꓔꓲ

Contents

The reader is encouraged to use the Chronology and Glossary only as needed while reading *Seven Dreams*. The first gives context to characters and events in the text. The second defines and gives the origin of every word which may be unfamiliar. As for the Source Notes, they may be ignored or skimmed; their function is to record my starting points, which may interest travelers in other directions.

List of Maps

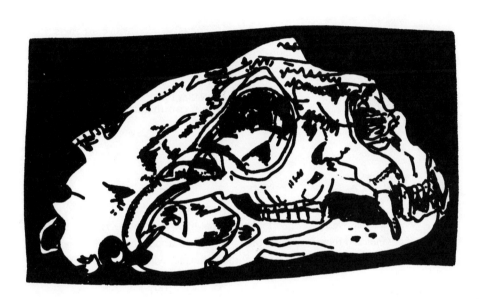

Another rule we followed was never to kill an animal that we were not going to use for food or clothing.

BARNABAS PIRYUAQ, 1986

Well, in those high latitudes we found such quantities of seals and walruses that we simply did not know what to do with them. There were thousands and thousands lying there; we walked among them and hit them on the head, and laughed heartily at the abundance which God had created.

JAN WELZL, 1933

Rifle-Text

The Quest for Polar Treasures 1933
A Historical Note

Walking south and south on Cornwallis Island with the sea always just over a little gravel ridge, and the sun a bright white disk of glare in the cloud-wall, you went wandering across a hard plain of stones, tan stones and grey stones, and the sea was just one more ridge away, a gentle waist-high ridge of stones, and over the ridge the plain continued and there was another ridge at the horizon with the sea just behind it and you crossed a very shallow wind-blown finger of water, stepping from stone to stone, and there were pieces of musk-ox bone in the water and the island curled its arms out around the sea ahead like two blue snow-streaked islands and the sea was just ahead and you went over another ridge and another and there were shells rubbed rough and white by the gravel that they lay on, and little pools whose banks were cushioned with algae three inches thick and you saw the feather of an Arctic tern rolled tight around itself by the wind and the sea was pure and greenish-grey and translucent before you and there was ice floating in it like the chondrocrania of sharks, and you came down onto the beach and it was still rocks, flat slabs of limestone, grey or sulphur-yellow; and the sea was emerald and drift-ice bobbed in it and there were bubbles and tunnels in those floes, which were shaped like ships and rams' heads and camels, and they rode the waves in herds and the water was so pure and clear and full of light that at 8:15 at night the sun was to the south, and in its track the ice was the color of the sea.

You were happy to be there, I know, but you remembered how the island had tricked you all the way, dangling ocean and ocean and ocean just in front of your face for so long, and although this place of ship-shaped icebergs was a paradise of sorts you suspected that other illusions and deceptions might beset you in this mirrorless house of mirrors. Indeed, just as it had happened with the seashore, so it happened with the source of the river that you followed inland past the little

pools where the Inuk girl said people liked to bathe (and it was sunny and hot because you were under a blue sky-hole although there were occasional flurries of snow on this mid-August day); for after half a dozen hours of walking the river had already narrowed enough so that if you picked your way you could cross it dry-shod and you were sure that the next day or the next would surely bring you to whatever snowbank or glacier it sprang from, so you walked with idiotic confidence alongside it, ascending low ridge-mounds of mud and hardpacked gravel, with an occasional yellow flower watching you from the barest possible place, nodding at you in the wind (its petals were cushioned on fuzzy hairs, and inside its golden cup a six-pointed star of sepals rested on blackness); and between the ridge-mounds were little dry gorges or sometimes streamlets running from snowbanks; and as you followed the river and the ridges everything was so low around you that you felt on top of the world. Days began to go by. Passing through a low gorge between two facing icebanks, stumbling upon the points of loose stone blocks, you saw that the ridge-walls that chilled you on either side were lowering, too, so that soon they must end and the source of the river would become apparent: a lake, a glacier, a great snowdrift – but when you turned the bend you saw only that same icy little creek flowing meaninglessly, and beyond, other ridge-walls rising; and you knew that you would have to follow the river up many more valleys . . . The gravel-ridges were endless. They were all around you like the waves of that Arctic Ocean that you had tried to reach; now you were in the middle of it and there was nothing else but its rising falling insidiousness; nevertheless you insisted on following your stream to its origin; you were determined to come to someplace definite. Sometimes the riverbed would widen, and the loose and painted gravel so weary and painful to your feet would give way for a space to sedimentary shelves and ledges studded with fossil snail shells and clam shells that were no different from the ones that lay scattered among the gravel all across the xxx square miles of the island, and here the river made more pools which might have been the ones that the Inuk girl had told you about, but you were never going to find that out, either. Sometimes there were cairns on the ridgetops, and the fallen ruins of stone houses. Sometimes great blocks of stone had shattered into bricks on the hillside; you picked your way down them as if down ruined stairs. A little before midnight on the third day, you reached a plain of rocks spewed up from the permafrost: – thin slabs on edge like decks of cards, and rocks with holes in them, and rocks like skulls. Here at last you found the source of your river, a pool of water that seemed eerily to float on the gravel, water from nowhere, of a transparent brownish color. The pool was sheared almost in two by a long gravel bank, behind which glowed the pink clouds of midnight, reddening the

water just a little, and west of the clouds the sky was sulphur-yellow behind
another ridge. As you watched, the clouds blew away, and the pool became the
color of molten sulphur. – So you had reached it finally! – You climbed the
gravel bank (and now you were high enough to see a second ridge to the west,
beyond which a tube of beautiful orange light had been squeezed upon the blade
of a third ridge, and the field of cloud above was yellow and glowing). You
looked at the pool. It curved around east and north and west, and a stream ran
into it. You were not at a definite place after all. But *now*, after another mile, the
real source became evident – a long thin brown lake behind a rust-colored ridge
– and the clouds were glowing orange there and the sky was striped blue and
yellow, and it was a mild windless midnight; and the rocks were fractured so
that perfect disks had fallen out of them – and then you discovered a stream two
feet wide that fed your latest lake; the rocks in it looked blue and green, and you
followed it up a flat plain of stepping stones, and at the summit of a little mound
of rocks was something that might or might not be a ruin (after the stone disks
you would believe anything). It was a rectangular open room, walled with
block-fractured rocks. Inside were square posts of the same brick, dividing it
into ten chambers not much more than knee-high. You heard the maddening
trickle of the stream and pressed on, finding a rock like a witch's head, and the
western light made the stream purple and orange. You came to another lake,
whose shore was paved with white slabs (and the sky was barred yellow, red
and orange). But *that* was not the source of the river, either. You arrived at
the shore of a wide, grey, ankle-deep lake, over which a single bird twittered.
Bands of muted color rippled across that lake. It flowed steadily in the cool
breeze you barely felt. Black rocks stuck up in it like birds. The water was pure
and good to drink. Two birds chased you, screaming through the sky. And you
went over another little rise and there was a lake whose waters rippled black
and blue and orange and silver, and there was a jet-black ridge behind it
topped with blue clouds, and the lake went on and on and on and there
was another lake behind it and streams ran out of that lake in all directions
and at last you understood that the river you had followed had no one source;
that these lakes were from permafrost melt; the whole island was permafrost;
when you were on the island you were in a world of rivers that came from
everywhere.

Still you had not learned your lesson. You thought to orient yourself. There was
snow everywhere now, a light snow that showed the pebbly texture of the

ground like stubble, and hung on the ridge across the river in flaking white scales. The sky was cloudy, although there were still patches of blue, and a chilly wind blew. The temperature was just below freezing. You could cross the river and go up onto one of the ridge-mounds, and suddenly you found yourself on a high round plate of a world extending as far as you could see in every direction, and instantly the river that you had come from and every other river vanished in the low featureless undulations of that plain and the clouds made another grey world-plate above your head; but to the south you saw a low mound of gravel upthrust from the gravel-pavement, so you walked toward it and after a quarter-hour you had reached it. Because it was only twenty feet high (when you first saw it you thought maybe it was a hundred), you climbed it, and then suddenly you could see clammy blue sea-bays to the south and east, and snow-valleys and river-tracks, and the blue cliffs of a headland sugared with snow, and purple clouds snowing far away; and it was all thanks to the mound that you saw these things, but you felt disconcerted; this center of things was not what you had expected. There was nothing wrong with anything, but you could not place yourself anywhere. Everything was below you and in the wrong direction. The wind blew numbingly cold, and a fog began to seep up onto the plain so that you saw that if you stayed there very long you would be well and truly lost, and then you might die, so you went back to your river while you could still locate it and descended tricked and bewildered . . .

It was to this island that Levi Nungaq and his family were moved by the *Qaallunaat*★ in 1955. Thirty-three years later, Levi sat drinking his coffee. He was sixty-three now, and a town had grown up around him. He looked out of the window of Minnie Allakariallak's kitchen and saw it, but his eyes were half-closed. Outside, it was now another autumn night in Resolute, with lights gleaming from the little boxes of houses and streetlights glowing yellow on the snow and a purple sky fixed with a single unwinking star, the light on Signal Hill. A boy in a dark parka went hurrying down the street, hunched against the wind, and then he was out of sight. – Old Levi lifted his coffee mug and swallowed. He had a ruddy face. His arms were crossed on his chest. When he began to speak, you saw that he was missing a lower tooth. He spoke slowly, clasping his hands. It was hard to tell whether he was calm or sad.

Elizabeth Allakariallak, the interpreter, sat beside him, looking at his face.

★ Literally, "the people with bushy eyebrows." Canadian Inuktitut word for white people.

Resolute

North Camp
Sewage lagoon
Slug Lake
Wrecked plane
Airstrip
Char Lake
Meretta Lake
BEACON
Mid Camp
Resolute Lake
Tear drop Lake
AIR BEACON
RESOLUTE BAY
Sight Pt.
Old Thule ruins

ᖃᐅᓱᐃᑦᑐᖅ

Mecham River (which has no source)

Signal Hill
Resolute town (= South Camp)
NAVIGATION LIGHTS

Cornwallis

Prospect Hills

Island

BEACON
Prospect Pt.

BARROW STRAIT

To Griffith Island

To Beechey Island →

SCALE OF MILES

Sometimes, when her children cried, she heated some frozen French fries in the oven or gave one of them the breast. She was a young woman whose round glasses gave her a somewhat owlish appearance.

In 1953 it was said that a family would be moving from northern Québec to the Northwest Territories. The first family that was moved here came in that year. Back in northern Québec, in Inukjuak, they used to communicate by letter, to see how the first family was doing here. They used to get a reply that it seemed okay.

He inclined his head; his eyes were half-closed; he caressed the tablecloth.

So when they were here, they lived for two years. In the year 'fifty-four they were told that they'd be moving back in two years if they didn't like it here.

He stroked the tablecloth. He was not looking at anything.

So after the two years went by, craving to see the rest of the family in northern Québec, they were ready to return to where they came from. So when they requested that they wanted to go back since the two years passed, they were told: "You should ask your relatives to come here since the town of Resolute is going to be established."

Elizabeth looked at him silently, with one arm on the table. The corners of her mouth were tight in concentration as she listened. A pretty gold cross hung at her throat.

So what happened was after D.I.N. Day★ *they told them they should get their families there. Levi's brother was one of the first family from 'fifty-three,* Elizabeth said. *Levi didn't really wanna come here; my parents didn't really wanna come here, but because his brother was stuck here and he couldn't leave him, they had to come here. At that time, one of the difficulties they had, they assumed anytime a white guy told them what to do, they thought they had to do it. So, RCMP†* got those people. In 'fifty-five his family moved in here. They didn't really hesitate to do that; they thought they'd be back in two years.*

❈ ❈ ❈

He was twenty-eight years then; he had four children. When he was seventeen years, in 1942, there was a World War II, or was it a World War I? There was a war between Canadian and German. He remembers the time they started and the time they stopped. It's like that now, remembering the time before the ship.

❈ ❈ ❈

Most upset for Levi was leaving and not knowing exactly where he was going. All he knew was that he was going to Resolute. The people who explained all this didn't explain. That was all the RCMP said. Then they were traveling. They had to stop at a lot of communities on the way. Every time, they were not allowed to land; they had to stay on the boat. The kids used to cry every time they saw an island, because they wanted to get onto the shore. They were traveling almost one month then. Finally, when they reached Arctic Bay,‡ they let the mens only go to the land. In Arctic Bay they felt that now that they were long distance now, they wouldn't be able to return anyways.

★ Department of Indian and Native Affairs Day.

† Royal Canadian Mounted Police.

‡ Arctic Bay is on the Borden Peninsula at the northern tip of Baffin Island. At this point the relocatees would have been about four-fifths of the way from Inukjuak to Resolute.

He remembers the time they were really hungry on the ship. They were craving to eat some meat. They had some meals on the ship, but it wasn't making them feel any fuller; it wasn't what they were used to. Levi never used to sit inside a ship. So he used to walk around, and he used to met with this RCMP who was assisting them. RCMP told him, "You're moving to a place where there's a lot of game." – The worst part that he'll never forget, that he can't forget, is when it was really stormy with strong winds. They were really seasick. That week they hardly ate that time. They were hungry, and it was the worst. But for my mother the hardest thing was the craving for fish, and having to part with another family that they took away on another boat in the middle of the ocean; they took them to Grise Fiord.

How did this island look to you when you first saw it from the ship? Did the land look ugly to you?

The old man gazed out the window. Softly, as if he did not want to scare it, he stroked the tablecloth.

When he looked at it, he says he was looking at just gravel, no moss, nothing like in northern Québec. He wondered, coming from a nice hot weather season to a cold weather place like this, he wondered how he was going to survive. Only shelter that they had to use was a canvas tent for each family. Used to be a lot of ice here. The boat that brought them, the C. D. Howe, it dropped them off in the bay here and then it was stuck in the ice about one month. They arrived in fall. It's fall now, but it was colder here when he first came. The summer's longer now. They had to be here in their tent from fall through winter. There were six in his family, all in that tent. Finally in summer, they collected scraps of plywood and things like that in South Camp to make a shelter.

Outside the window, the snowy street looked greenish, but the sky was black. Sleet sifted against the house. In the morning there would be another pale sunrise, as pure as a sapphire, that would last for hours; darkness had come to Resolute only a week or so before, but already the sun was becoming hesitant. The sun would not warm you; as soon as you went outside the wind would sting your nose and cheeks. There would be a white glow behind the ridge east of town, where the fog reflected the snow; there always was. Behind it, where your river had misled you and your ridges had confounded you a month before, hung a greyness like lead turned to light. Then, slowly, slowly, it would begin to get dark again. If you were outside the wind might howl like a wolf and even as you heard it howling from one direction you'd feel it pushing you from another. Freezing fog squeezed you and wiped its wet sleet on you. Your boots and drinking water froze every night like your frozen river with all its frozen lakes. The wind chilled you everywhere it could and pushed at your tent so that you had to throw big rocks inside to hold it down and your socks were frozen against your numb white feet and there was hardly any snow on the ground because it was mainly whirling busily in the wind, stinging your face and blowing in long trails that streamed across the ground like the wakes of sharks. You were at latitude 74° 40′ north, a few hundred miles from the Pole.

When they got into Resolute they were in difficulty getting game. There were no birds around or fish or anything to hunt. They were not used to the area. They were craving for the meat they had down there. The meat they used to have in northern Québec was ptarmigans, ducks, geese and fish. They were mostly starving, because they were not used to what was here. The only thing they could eat was polar bear meat and walrus meat. In northern Québec they were used to seal meat, a different kind. This kind of seal up here was a rich kind. They used to get sick. There was no death from hunger, but they used to be very skinny, very skinny bones from starving and craving to see their relatives for so many years.

In northern Québec they used to have kayaks and boats. In here they didn't have that much. Nothing to make them out of.

They brought their rifles with them – .303s and .30-.30s. RCMP allowed that. They still had their bullets. They used to buy them from the store in northern Québec. They got two bullets for one sealskin in trade in northern Québec. That was the same everywhere there was a Hudson's Bay. It was hard when a family ran out of bullets.

The white people were very cooperative; they were really nice to them. But it was the time the RCMP kept them apart. They were nice, but RCMP told them not to go near them. – Levi raised his arm and beamed. His black eyes sparkled. He grinned with his white teeth; he touched his tongue to the roof of his mouth. — *He used to go anywhere he wanted to go, right? He was just telling me about the place that he used to go to. That white man there used to be either a weatherman or a telecommunication. When the RCMP was asleep, Levi used to sneak in there and carve and make friends. He still doesn't know why the RCMP kept them apart.*

He remembers every morning, RCMP would be checking the camp. RCMP used to ask them if anyone had been visiting the whites and no one responded. When he found out that people had been visiting, he smelled them and put his fingers in their mouth to see if they had anything. Every time they go out hunting, when they return, the RCMP would check their load on sleds to see if they caught anything. When they came back from hunting and didn't catch anything, he would be mad at them. Very disappointed in them.

All through the years it broke a lot of families. He feels personally, himself, he blames himself for damaging his children because their life is destroyed. He blames himself for coming up here. He knows us kids is hurt, too. He feels if only he had stayed down in northern Québec his children would be a lot nicer. In northern Québec they call each other by their relations, like angajuga, aniga.★ *Here, they call each other by name. That hurts his children.*

At the time he came here he had four children. The younger ones are the ones that are hurt. Five younger children were born here and raised. They didn't know much about his parents and how the older ones used to live. They're not the same as the older ones.

Has the government ever offered to take them back to Inukjuak?

They haven't. Not until now. Last year or this year, it's been a talk whether they want to go back or not. There's a family in Grise Fiord that has already moved.†

★ Names that establish family relations. *Angajuga* means "my older sibling of the same sex"; *aniga* (used only if the speaker is female) means "my brother." There are many such words in Canadian Inuktitut.

† Mr. Nungaq was finally able to return to Inukjuak in the following year.

He knows now that around this island there's a lot of oil and gas. In his belief, that's the reason why he's here. They wanted to save this island for sovereignty for Canada. Otherwise Norway would have taken it over. But he doesn't know for sure. Nobody ever told him why they brought him here.

Up at North Camp where the administrative buildings were, the Coast Guard's radio operator had a different explanation for the existence of Resolute. – It was the Americans, he said. They wanted to keep a *friendly* eye on the *friendly* Russian neighbor to the north, no? – and he nudged you in the ribs. – So the Americans built this town in 1947, he said. All these Quonset huts around here, the Americans built them. Later they turned them over to Canada. But these old buildings are too close to the runway. In two years they're going to tear them all down. – You cast your *friendly* eye along the gravel road that led away from the airport, sometimes interrupted by construction ditches, and went on between the long red and yellow sheds where Environment Canada and the RCMP and the Coast Guard administered things – these would be torn down, then – and if you took a right after that to the yellow shed of the post office you

were then free to take another right just short of the sewage lagoon where you lived in your tent just over the rise from the wrecked plane in the spongy tundra where fuselage articulated horribly and creaked and swung in the wind, and twisted jagged pieces of the plane lay scattered across the ground, which was stony and grey, and a fog rose on the sea like a white line of burning magnesium and came closer, painfully white and bright, until it covered everything and there was only the wind; then you could begin walking back in the direction you had come, past crates of steel with a stenciled **2** for Resolute on them resting in the frozen mud of a new construction site – how ugly and senseless this tearing down and putting up! – the big ship had brought them, and if you kept going almost as far as the Narwhal Hotel you got to the Hudson's Bay Company where an Inuk girl sat bleakly behind the counter, her hair wrapped in a bandanna, and white men from the big ship came in wearing hats and pea jackets and laughing shyly at the funny Resolute T-shirts for sale and hoping that the pack-ice wasn't coming in yet because they still had to get out two days from now when the work was done. They were bound for Arctic Bay. Behind you, in the direction that you had originally gone, was the road east; a mile down it was the satellite dish of Environment Canada's Mid-Camp as they called it; they got a picture of the atmosphere from their polar satellite every hour and forty-five minutes; and then the road went on into the fog and wind for another three miles or so, past Lake Resolute, which was no longer potable thanks to the discharge from the sewage lagoon; and then came South Camp and then the village. But the village was not so frequently visited by the people at North Camp. Everyone seemed to be working fourteen-hour days, and if you said that the weather was good today they'd say: Yeah, better than *yesterday! Yesterday* it thawed so we couldn't *work!*   – Jacinthe, the other radio operator, said that some people never left North Camp; whether it was stormy or it was a pleasant snowy morning, the sky slate-grey with thunder-blue shadows, everything was the same; – the radar fanned itself in perfect stillness, and the office people yawned over their computers at half-past seven while the coffee perked, and the workmen welded and hammered; in three weeks a new building stood where there had been bare ground. If the shape of the town changed, if the old Quonset sheds that had been off limits to Levi and the other Inuit were torn down, would anyone notice? You read in a magazine that there was talk of putting up a plaque in Resolute to commemorate the brave services of those Inuit pioneers who established Canadian sovereignty on Cornwallis Island once and for all – a hard job, but someone had to do it in 1955, while the man from the RCMP kept his *friendly* eye on things. – Of course it was not so bad here. You remembered a

day in August when it was foggy and sleet struck the front of your jacket with
little ringing sounds and then a blue hole in the clouds opened wider and wider,
like the rainbow ring that you had seen around the sun on the day before the
mist had poured down from the ridges like some cold glaring-white liquid; and
now the blue hole got bigger and the sun came out and it was exactly 32°F and
you could see across the river valley again to the low brown ridge of gravel with
the blue sky behind; and the wind was chilly and between the rocks grew green
wet ribbons of tundra and the Arctic was so beautiful that all at once you knew
that you could live and die here. Snowdrifts lay steeply against that ridge,
corrugated by wind and rain, and the river flowed down the sand in dark blue
braids. No bird sang; no sound of life was heard, but a little black spider crawled
feebly in a warm spot on the mud. So you were happy and confident and set out
to find the source of your river; it would be around the next bend or the next,
just as Levi Nungaq's brother would be home in Inukjuak in two years or if not
then *definitely* two years after that.

Maybe life is a process of trading hopes for memories. When the snow was deep
in September maybe you did not remember very much. But you did remember,
I am sure, how many flat rocks of a sulphurous color there were which had been
shattered into slabs stacked neatly one against the next like the slices of a loaf of
bread; you could pick up a book of these slabs and turn their livid-yellow pages
in your hands, reading the words of lichen-dots and listening to the moaning of
the wind; then, if you chose, you could skip the pages into some Arctic lake one
by one, and watch them smash into two as they struck the water, sink, and lie
shimmering among the greenish rocks, and the water rippled over them in the
wind, as if trying to turn them, but they would never turn or be together again.
– All books are like this; they stand shoulder to shoulder in the library stacks;
perhaps they are "popular" at first, perhaps not, but eventually they stand
anonymous, unread, forgotten; and that is how it should be, for that is how it is
with lives. – I recall a book that most certainly remains intact, unrippled, unrifled;
it is called *The Quest for Polar Treasures*. It speaks of the devil-fish, "the terror of
all Polar men," that stands on four rows of legs and has bat-ears; it rolls on men
and crushes them to death. It tells of a meteor twelve feet across embedded in
the ice, whose core is half dross, half pure brass. It recounts the tale of the
Kaminerorov Expedition of 1903, when twenty-five men were drowned by a
monstrous wave; for a monument the survivors stood up one of their frozen

comrades in the snow, with a gun in his hand. – It is all lies, and quite interesting.
I am sure that any plaque in commemoration of Levi's thirty-three years in
Resolute would be the same. Let us read our histories and grin just as the sky
grinned chilly and humorless in a blue slit between the clouds.

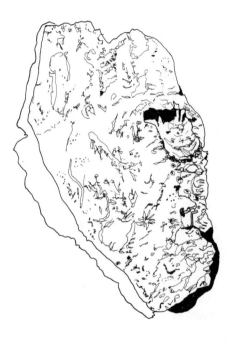

WITCH-HEAD ROCK, CORNWALLIS ISLAND

The Rifles

In those days, there were still plenty of walrus, since Norwegian hunters could get full cargoes on more accessible shores further west . . . Some 500 skins were taken at the cost of about 2,000 walrus, for all were shot in the water and many sank.

R. N. Rudnose Brown, 1923

During the last few years the catch has been unprofitable, only a few whales having been seen.

Franz Boas, 1888

1
King William Island
ᐱᖃᖅᑕᖅ

Two Men
1948, 1848

Pain, I came to feel, might well prove to be the sole proof of the
persistence of consciousness within the flesh . . .

YUKIO MISHIMA, *Sun and Steel* (1970)

A man was hunting a seal. He stood waiting on the hard cold sea. Half
a mile out from the shore, a plate of ice had buckled and riven in two; in
this lead a thin crust of new ice had formed, as delicate as a girl's skin, and
here the man stood, watching a round hole that was smaller than his
thumbnail. This was where the seal came to breathe. The man stood very
still. He knew that the seal would hear if he even wiggled his toes in his boots.
He waited for a long time, gazing at the hole and listening. He was holding a
rifle.

At last he heard the sound of rippling water. The seal was swimming
toward him. He waited. A little jet of water spurted from the hole, and still he
waited. The water was being displaced by the seal's body. Then he heard the
seal breathe. But it was only the first breath. The man knew that sometimes
seals listened from below the ice for danger, exhaling instead of inhaling; the
first breath was not necessarily a true breath. But then the seal breathed again.
The man pulled the trigger. There was a sound of the shot, and a thrashing
noise. The seal grunted in agony, and that was the last breath.

For the first time the man leaned forward and saw the seal that he had
killed. The water beneath the blowhole was red. The man chopped the hole
wider and pulled the dead seal out. There was a small hole in the seal's head
where the .22 magnum had gone in, and a larger one where it had gone out.
He had shot very well. The man was happy. Kneeling in the bloody snow, he

began peeling away the skin. He cut out the steaming meat. He shouted joyously, and a little boy came running. The boy laughed and put his foot on the dead seal and kicked it. The man cut off a piece of seal liver and gave it to his son smiling.

Not far away, another man was waiting. Here the sky was grey, with a bar of yellow glare low on the horizon. The fjord, too, was grey. Ice had just begun to form on it in earnest – steely grey ice, with the beginnings of pressure ridges already rising between its flat plates. In places it was thick enough to support a man's weight. In other places it could not bear the touch of a pebble, for as yet it was only half frozen. In the middle ran a broad channel in which the blackish-grey water streamed steadily. Between the ice-plates there were still many leads; the ripples there were like sandbars.

The sound of the wind was low, so that the water-noises were very audible, speckling the man's ears like the black leopard-dots on the beach pebbles. Every now and then the ice crunched furtively, as if a naughty child were eating it. Dead grass twitched in the frozen mud-cliffs, its stalks spreading in the wind like the points of many golden stars. – The man's feet ached with cold. His shoes were frozen. He sat shivering and watching the golden grass. He looked down at the thin snowdrifts by his feet, the rocks like broken tables; he studied the streaming water in the fjord. He was starving.

These two men were not so different. They both had rifles. But the second man, the white man, sat there by the creaking ice, waiting. He did not know how to live in that country. He had no strength left to live.

His starvation was very strange because he had bullets for his rifle and there was chocolate in the longboat where the other dead men lay and not far away was a tin of preserved meat, unopened. SEDNA sent seals in plenty from under the sea, and they came up to the ice; they were ready to be killed, but the man's rifle did not help him.

Later on it was the Inuk's turn to starve, when there were no animals. His rifle did not help him very much then, either.

11
Pond Inlet

ᒥᑦᑎᒪᑕᓕᒃ

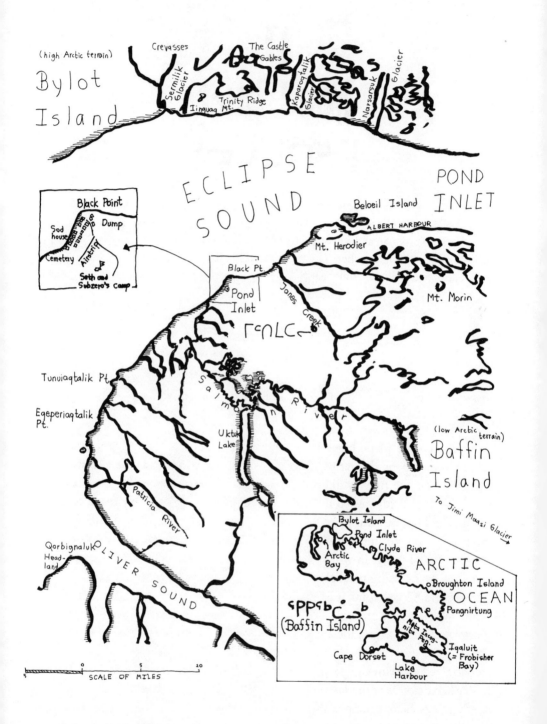

(high Arctic terrain)

Bylot Island

Crevasses
The Castle
Gables
Sermilik Glacier
Iinguaq Mt.
Trinity Ridge
Kaparoqtalik Glacier
Narsarsuk
Glacier

ECLIPSE
SOUND

POND
INLET

Beloeil Island

ALBERT HARBOUR

Mt. Herodier

Mt. Morin

Black Point

Sod house
Dump
Cemetery
Airstrip
Seth and Subzero's Camp

Black Pt.

Pond Inlet

ᒉᓄᓕᑦ

Jones Creek

ᐸᖅᑐᖅᑕᓕᒃ

Tunuiaqtalik Pt.

Salmon River

Egeperiaqtalik Pt.

Uktuk Lake

(low Arctic terrain)

Baffin Island

To Jimi Maasi Glacier

Patricia River

Qorbignaluk Headland

OLIVER SOUND

Bylot Island
Pond Inlet
Clyde River
Arctic Bay

ARCTIC

Broughton Island

OCEAN

ᓴᐳᖅᑕᓂᐹ
(Baffin Island)

Pangnirtung

Meta Incognita Pen.

Cape Dorset
Lake Harbour

Iqaluit
(= Frobisher Bay)

0   5   10
SCALE OF MILES

Captain Subzero
1989

I remember a story in *National Geographic* three or four years back about aborigines in Greenland in contact with Norsemen. Did I tell you this? A young Norseman and a young native were good friends & rivals, doing all their hunting together. There was some dramatic ending, involving either one saving the other's life, or one accidentally dying & the other committing suicide . . .

JACOB DICKINSON, letter of
1 September 1986

When the plane blew a tire landing at Broughton Island, you stood against the wall of the terminal to be out of the wind, and grit and dust swirled across the runway like smoke, and the ice creaked. Beside you stood an Inuk girl in acid-washed denims, her hair cropped fashionably short. She *had* to stand beside you: there was no other place to be out of the wind. For the two of you, Broughton was nothing more or less than an elevator hung between sea and sky, in which decorum demanded that each stare ahead so that your gazes, being parallel, could by definition never intersect.

How cold do you think it is? you said.

She looked at the ground. – I don't know, she said, very softly.

She was sitting across the aisle from you on the plane. When the landing at Clyde River was rough, her girlfriend screamed, and she looked at you embarrassed and you smiled at her, still trying. Laughing, she looked away.

The next stop was the last stop. Pond Inlet. You both got off. A few days later you saw her working at the checkout counter of the co-op. She glanced at you as if she did not recognize you, but you came in again that same day to buy cookies to make friends with (and also a bag of hickory-flavored chips). The next day you were back again. Each time, her will to not recognize you became greater when it came your turn to pay and she gazed up at you very quickly with black, black eyes.

You, of course, were wearing your personal uniform, bedizened with the merit badges of mosquitoes, guns, islands, seals and whores. As you stood at the counter, the naked blonde painted on your breast-pocket was almost level with the Inuk girl's eyes.

How could you have done or been such a thing? Well, that was how you were. You literally wore your life on your sleeve, like a fly lugging its long oval wings across its back as it struggled between the dwarf willows of a dune. In spite of your superhuman accessibility, no one cared to have anything to do with you.

Your first strategy for getting people to like you had been dreamed up by your friend Seth, who came to botanize because Down South he was always going: nice flower, although it *is* a composite . . .   and even on the train north to Montréal where you were going to catch the plane he pressed his nose against the window crying: what beautiful mustard in that field!   and he jerked his head abruptly and said   what the hell's that tree with the red bark? GOD, it's pretty, with its smooth red bark! I wonder what it is? Too bad. – And the train rolled on. It was earnest Seth, flaunting his girlfriend's departure-hickey with great pride, who explained: she's really *really* good at blowjobs. I seriously think it's her musical training. Anyway, she was really going to town when the phone rang. Wow, look at those Indian strawberries! – It was Seth as I said who thought of bringing the kite, in hopes of breaching Baffin Island's under-cloud darkness shot through with white snow-shapes, for he knew, loved and dreaded that gloom as well as you, but for him flower-lights pierced it on sunny or snowy days, so he readily conceived of the kite aloft, being of a sweetly childlike spirit that delighted in running and happiness (alone, however, for Seth was shy); and the boldness of Seth's conception thrilled you, for you would never have been able to imagine any such use of Arctic winds; so as you rolled ever north to Montréal in that train you almost gloated at the thought of wind; for once wind wouldn't scare you in your flimsy tent! . . . but in Pond Inlet Seth hesitated to use the aforesaid kite because everyone's indifference to both of you made him cringe. – One evening, however, you insisted. No delirious crowds of friends would come any other way. – There was a stream just south of town where the children swam, and just as you got there, at about ten at night, two boys were riding away on their shared bike and Seth said   I don't want to go any closer   and you said   why?   and Seth said   because we don't belong here   and you said   that's true, but here we are,   so you took the kite and marched valiantly through the moss to a place just opposite a bend where two more bathing-suited boys sat swatting mosquitoes and you sat down with determined purpose and unzipped your day pack to fire the first shot of your campaign: the *Peek Freans shortbread* (in a plastic pack of two) and the *Dad's Cookies* (similarly sealed), both of which came from the airline barfbag full of treats that the kindhearted stewardess had given you because she pitied you for having to stay in Pond Inlet for a whole month (not that Pond was as bad as Resolute where someone had told her they played cards and stabbed the loser in the back just for fun). Round one: the Peek Freans!

Hey, kids,   you said.   Want some Peek Freans?

Silently, one of the boys lunged across the stream and snatched the Peek Freans from your hand.

How about a Dad's?   you said, eating one.

The other boy came and took his treat, hanging his head. Then he crossed back into his territory on the far side of the stream. They both dried their hair with a towel and rode away on their bikes.

Meanwhile, the girls were changing into their swimsuits under a towel, one bend away. They were eight or nine years old. They leaped into the cold, cold water, paddling and bathing, dunking each other laughing, and their wet black hair glistened beneath the grey sky as the mosquitoes bit you, and Seth on the road behind you had taken heart and unfurled *the glorious kite!* And all the kids were watching.

Is the wind strong enough?   you called.

Borderline,   said Seth. – But whatever his opinions, he went off like a hero to war, preparing his gear, taking the lie of the land, trotting, then running, with the obedient kite just above and behind his shoulder, paying out string and hope until the kite went up!

. . . and the kite fell down. Pond Inlet was very sheltered from Arctic winds. That was why it was there.

The girls sat on the bank laughing and brushing mosquitoes off their arms and it was cold enough to numb your fingers.

The next day, windy-warm and almost cloudless, you and Seth went skipping through the moss, and you said   do you think there's enough of a breeze to try your kite?   and Seth said   I think so. – So he showed you how to put the cross-pole in and you let the wind catch it and paid out line as if you were fishing until it gloriously **soared!** Then you and Seth knew that you were the Glory Boys and sang "Beedle-Un-Bum" and "Somebody Stole My Gal" at the top of your voices, Seth meanwhile botanizing wherever you went, saying: what a gorgeous pedicularis!   at which you picked one and ate it and said: it tastes like mushrooms!   and the kite proclaimed its colors to every glacier and the bulldozers slowed to see it and you Glory Boys went your way changing the words of the songs to suit, so that instead of singing, *There's a meal called Southern Eel that you can't resist from trying!* you made it Northern Seal, and two jaegers swooped, keening at your kite until you had left behind the squishy tussocks where they nested, and you ran down swales to keep your kite of honor high, forgetting those long wasted days scattered across the tundra like white feathers, and came at last to Salmon Creek where Seth said   this is the place to come when the blueberries are ready   and you yourself sat down on a mound of black-lichened stones, which might or might not have been a Thule ruin, scratching your mosquito bites, listening to the creek, which was wide and clear and fine (at the Hudson's Bay store they'd said that you could net plenty of Arctic char there at high tide); and then you went on down toward the Foreshore Flats, with the kite streaming red and blue and yellow behind you, and Seth said: I just couldn't be happier. – That day the yellow vetch had begun to bloom in profusion on the cliff, and a long grey gull-feather lay in the moss.

There was a windy grassy rocky point where the sea-ice washed up. You and Seth picnicked on gorp. Two Inuit teenagers forded the creek-mouth in a three-wheeler. You waved, but they just looked at you. You returned to town, and as soon as you got there windlessness prevailed and the kite descended to bright and crumpled impotence.

At the first evening of Games Week, ladies raced on their little boys' bicycles, not caring whether they made a single yard, and everyone laughed, from the teenaged boys in denims and spiked wristbands to the fat old ladies in their traditional parkas to the fat black-eyed girls, and dust blew across the runway and the wind made them all shiver as they drank their coffee. You were there; Seth hung back miserably. Your uniform smelled like sweat and cooking and

Arctic heather. Your arms were blanching in the wind. You had brought a baggie full of the cookies you had bought from the girl at the co-op. You opened it and held it out, and the children reached in as they passed, and emptied the bag in fifteen seconds and forgot you. The man at the megaphone announced something in Inuktitut, and then dozens of balloons whizzed through the air! Children screamed with laughter grabbing them. – You said to a small girl: Can I blow up your balloon? – Yes, she said, peering at you from her orange face. You blew it up slowly; you supposed that now all the other kids would want you to blow up their balloons, just as with the cookies. You tied the knot and gave it to her. Now you realized that she had wanted you to give it to her untied so that she too could launch it farting and looping through the air. You asked another child if he wanted you to blow it up for him and he just looked at you.

Now all the girls had noticed the naked blonde on your uniform and were grinning and pointing. You nodded with dignity.

Later, at 11:30 that night, you realized your role. You passed a little boy on his bike and said hi and he said hi and you stretched out your arms so that he could appreciate the full majesty of your uniform and intoned: *I'm CAPTAIN SUBZERO!* – and he, looking earnestly into your face, saw your delight there and himself shrieked with delight.

※ ※ ※

After this, you took to carrying a zip-loc bag of cookies with you whenever you came to town. Kids ran up to you, took one cookie each, and cried, *Tank you, tank you!* Kids slapped you five. On the porch of the Hudson's Bay, a young man stood chewing gum, and a girl came on her bicycle, almost flying, every part of her in motion, all beauty of streaming black pigtails, taut brown limbs, and on the hill by the dump two ladies gathered Arctic heather in orange bags. – *Captain Subzero!* screamed the kids. The others glanced at you and glanced away. – A bulldozer went down the road, dragging dust behind, at exactly the same speed as the girl bicycling, and again the children played in the stream, on this almost cloudless afternoon of sea-ice and heat-shimmers rising from the tundra; flies sang their songs; a helicopter rose from the landing strip with much the same noise as the ravens to the east. A cement truck came up the road. The low "matchbox" houses followed the swell of the coast, accompanied by their power-poles and maple-leaf flags. Behind them lay the ice, riddled with leads like sand-riffles; and sky-blue lakes of open water deceived the real sky, lighter than the mountains. Someone was hammering. Lily would be working at the post office, and if you asked her how she did she would say: *Lazy!* with a tranquil smile. Children ran in single file to the stream where they could swim. By the stream a boy was bicycling and girls stood talking in little groups. You went the other way, down the tilted bowl of houses toward the sea. You nodded to a man, and he ignored you. But you, now a glorious saint, went down the street in pride and bravery, your cookie-bag ever ready, and the kids came to you by ones and twos and you thought that you knew them, but it was only in the way that you knew the white blossom of the Labrador tea to be a single entity, rather like a lacy carnation, when closer inspection would have revealed that it was in fact a cluster of many tiny flowers with green centers.*

Flower or not, Captain Subzero's reputation continued to bloom in those summer days of sea-ice so beautifully mottled white and blue. A canny trader, he had brought chocolate, rubber dinosaur noses, T-shirts and earrings with him from Down South. He won them over by ones and twos: first the retarded boy; then the two girls standing on the near side of the creek, screwing up their faces against the wind ... One had her hood on, and the skin of it riffled. Behind them, the stream flowed past sandbars, rich in bleached lumber and rusty wire. On the far side were three oil drums, and then a gently brown ridge streaked with snowdrifts. The faces of the girls were shy and loving. – After them, another boy, another boy, two girls sitting on the beach throwing pebbles into the still water as ravens cried *waah! waah!* and big huskies lolled in silence ... Another boy now, a lemming-hunter. – It is true that many asked Subzero his purpose, and the struggle for absolute accuracy then forced him to be someone he did not want to be. But as he swam through that summer dreamy with Arctic islands, flower-shadows trembled in a breeze like the last breeze; streams flowed, mosquitoes stung and flew off drunk-freighted, and the caribou ran. In the round sod house with its broad sleeping platform of caribou skins, he and Seth sometimes slept beside the kids. The kids lit the cottongrass lamp and wanted to see everything in pack and pockets, saying: I want this. Give me this. Will you trade for this? – They never stole anything. Subzero gave them US pennies and dimes, and they asked for quarters. Later a boy gave him a Canadian dollar. He made

---

* It was here in Pond Inlet that one man's father shot himself when the family was relocated to Resolute.

money on the deal. They took turns trying on his rain pants, his Resolute Bay cap, while he tried on their words like *quki utikuluk*, nice gun, *piujukuluk*, dear little good thing. They giggled at the naked woman on his uniform and said: Who's that? – One of my girlfriends, he said. – They tapped it and made him say, *Uktuk!*★ The ten-year-old asked him: Do you have any condoms? – No, he said. They had black ponytails, brown cheeks and smiles. They had wide dark eyes and broad faces. They laughed. (Leads were just beginning to open in the sea-ice, great holes crusted with salt.) That was the first night. The next night their parents called them home, and afterward they giggled when he called but would not approach him. He saw them by the ice, gathering seaweed, studiously looking away from him. But he was patient. On the dirt street or in the sod house he said: Do you remember who I am? and they said Bill and he said no, what's my *real* name? – and they giggled *Captain Subzero!* Sometimes he'd be lying on the moss reading old histories of polar explorers and a boat might pass by, maybe with a hunter inside, and another standing on the little ice-floe towed behind, and then he'd go back to reading about George Back and the beautiful Copper Indian girl, Green-stockings, until suddenly he'd feel the children's presence near him; he did not dare to turn around too often for fear that they might run away; out of the corner of his eye he saw them in parkas and sneakers, making music with grassblades. They played teeter-totter on a stack of roofing supplies,

★ "Cunt!"

slapping at mosquitoes, and Seth and Subzero enticed them a little with some handfuls of breakfast cereal . . . Later, a child who knew him somewhat came and said softly: hi, Captain Subzero . . .   They brought chickweed to Seth I mean Skeeter, and Skeeter helped them hunt for lemmings. They played with Subzero and Skeeter all night and morning. That afternoon, when the two white boys were sleeping, they climbed up onto the roof and perfectly fitted their brown round faces one by one to the smokehole so that they looked like grinning gap-toothed suns. Later that summer, as Seth wandered far among his true loves, the flowers, Captain Subzero returned to the sod house by himself to sleep, and it was just the same as always with the dimness and happiness and the slightly fishy smell of the damp skins. Whenever he got tired, he'd say: now everybody you've got to go because I need to sleep   and they whispered   sssshh!   so obediently, but then a few of them always said can we sleep here?   and Captain Subzero said   if it's OK with your parents and they said   we asked them   so he said   sure   and Iga and Leah snuggled up beside him on the skins so he gave one his Resolute Bay cap and Captain Subzero uniform, and the other his rain gear to warm them, and later he asked if they were cold, and Iga looked at Leah and said   *she's* cold   and Leah said of Iga   *she's* cold   so he unzipped his sleeping bag and threw it over himself and Iga and part of Leah and they whispered and fell asleep and snored like calves, breathing healthy meat-eaters' breath in his face. Next morning Iga said   who's your girlfriend?   and Captain Subzero said   *you're* my girlfriend   and Leah said   do you have kids?   and he said   *you're* my kid and they both were happy. They climbed onto the roof one by one to stick their hands down the smokehole, and other kids reached up with their hands. – Rosie's turn?   said a small girl tentatively. – He picked her up and lifted her onto the roof.

✵- ✵- ✵-

Now summer burned everywhere so quick and fine; mosquitoes came fluttering out from their tundra-holes as soon as a patch of blue sky opened, and the belly of that soft tundra plain was rounded and gloriously mottled by chickweed and lousewort and lichens of an almost phosphorescent white; the plain curved upward to touch the blue-grey cloud-belly sexually. And Captain Subzero continued his glorious progress of friendship. (He never meant to presume. When the children were throwing stones in the drainage ditch by the runway, he always asked their permission before throwing one of his own.) He had begun to know the older girls now, the twelve- and thirteen-year-olds, though the boys of that age and the adults male and female continued never to mind him or be reminded of him. He wanted so desperately to be loved; he gave more things away.

Do you girls like to go hunting? he said.

No.

Why?

No TV.

I hate Arctic Bay kids, said one of the girls.

Why?

They throw rocks.

That's a good reason to hate them.

She's from Arctic Bay, said another girl.

Do you throw rocks?

No, she giggled.

What's your name?

Jukee.

She's fourteen, the other girl said. She'll be fifteen tomorrow. It's her birthday.

No, no. I'm twelve.

She's lying. She's just shy. She always lies when she's shy.

Do you know how to dance in Inuktitut? said Captain Subzero.

There were three girls. They all started undoing the sashes of their dresses and fingering their breasts.

No, they said.

Do you know how to dance in English? said Jukee very seriously.

I can only do that with one of you at a time, he replied.

Are you a two-timer, Subzero?

Maybe. And you?

I'm a one-timer. (They all laughed.)

How *many* times?

'Bout a thousand.

The girls said that they liked going swimming in the river-pools, at which he said that he wanted to go with them.

The next day, however, they didn't come and so he went swimming without them in a deep sandy swimming hole that Seth had found. It was sunny, and the mosquitoes were thick. He and Seth stripped and jumped in. But Seth came out shivering almost at once, for although he was stronger than Subzero in almost every way he had no body fat; cold reached him quickly. Subzero stayed on, while Seth lay in the sun and murmured to the plants; Subzero's legs went numb and his testicles contracted. When he soaped his hair and dunked his head under, his forehead ached as if he had eaten too much ice cream. Presently, however, he became accustomed to the water and enjoyed himself breast-stroking downstream with the tundra banks flashing past, mosquitoes crowding overhead so that every now and then he dunked his head again and the day was unmitigatedly glorious. Later, eating lunch with Seth on a high flower-grown esker, they watched the stream shimmer darkly in the sky.

What would it be like to marry one of these girls and stay here? he said.

It's too late for that, said Seth. Too late for anything but flowers.

You know that girl Jukee?

The one with the strange-looking eyes, really intent?

Yeah.

She's pretty gorgeous.

I have a feeling she knows something. Something about her makes me think she hears the same voices I hear. I keep thinking she's about to tell me something important.

Seth was picking a piece of chickweed apart. – I know that you always have to have a goal or you're not happy, he said. I think it's really wonderful. I'm not that way myself, but I hope it works out for you. That would be so great.

I'm not saying she was the one I was meant to kiss, said Subzero almost stubbornly. But she knows something about me, I had to come here to find it out, and I'm going to find it out.

※ ※ ※

He'd seen Jukee make a tattoo for herself by catching a brown moth and letting it beat its flaking wings against her grubby hand until the pattern was on her and the dying thing, grey and listless, was flung away –

※ ※ ※

That night, coming back from the picnic for the Elders at a mosquito-clouded creek where no one acknowledged seeing him (he asked for a cup to dip in the river and they looked through him, at the toddler smiling, playing with her plastic cup), Subzero walked along the beach, Seth skipping stones beside him, and they came to the west side of the village where a dead seal lay at the end of its rope, half in the water, with white rings on its mottled fur like lichens, and their friend John the Scotsman laughed: Kiss it to see if it's dead!   but Subzero did not want to do that, and changed the subject by persuading John to skip a chunk of ice in the sea, and they came into town, Subzero feeling somewhat low about his reception at the picnic. It was almost eleven. John went home, and Seth ambled a hundred paces inland to search for bluebells; finding none, he tagged dispiritedly behind. Subzero strode down the sandy street, and the low suntail on the water reflected two of Bylot Island's mountains in pure gold. He nodded to people, and they drove stonily by on their three-wheelers. Then suddenly his band came running down a hill, shrieking: HI, CAPTAIN SUBZERO! HI, MOSQUITO!   – Then he felt pretty swell. A big grin broke out on his face and in his heart; he'd succeeded in life. He held out a bag of spicy nuts that Skeeter had baked Down South; they stood shyly until he said: Come, eat! We need you to *finish* this bag for us!   – Then they splashed through a mud puddle and were around him, hopping with skinned knees and muddy hands, Rayla and Titus and Annie and Eloza, Daisy and Joota and all the rest. They waited until he held the bag out to them one by one before they took any. Mosquito, who was tired, slipped a tiny toy motorcycle into Subzero's hand and went off to camp where the bulldozers beeped and churned all night along the tundra ridges. Subzero stood elated at having something new to give them.

To understand rifles (for you must understand that at this time he was constructing a row of Seven Dreams in order to understand life, and because iron axes had almost decided things in Vinland, because arquebuses had taken command at Kebec, what must rifles have done here?), he'd hired an interpreter and was at the old lady's house. The old lady had been caught in the relocations to Grise Fiord. Fifteen years. Not the same as a sentence to a labor camp, of course. Now she was home again, sitting in her kitchen with her lace-print vinyl tablecloth.

Her brother-in-law was down in Grise Fiord, so she had to follow along, said the interpreter. Her husband had an older brother down in Grise Fiord. Their brother-in-law in Grise Fiord asked her to go. Even though it was not scary or frightening, she cried. She had nine kids. They went by ship. It took them two days. There were icebergs on the way. It was so isolated, so empty; there was only an RCMP detachment. People on the land came over to the shore. They were helping out with the unloading because there were very few people – three families from here, some from Inukjuak. At that time there were no houses. Only RCMP had a house. Rest of them were living in their own tents. Canvas tents. They ate walrus, narwhal mattaq, seal, fish. One time what she noticed was there was nothing in the grocery store. No flours, no sugars. She noticed it was all empty. Nothing to buy. She used to go out hunting. One time she caught one walrus. She always wanted to shoot one, and she did.

Subzero thought that the house was very bright. The sun shone on the ice. Houseplants grew in the window. Midnight sunlight streamed in from over the ice. Seth was staring at the houseplants and the old lady looked and smiled and said something and the interpreter said: What we know always happens is that everything's all bloomed up, gets cold, when everything's all fully grown, and that's the end of the plant season.

Subzero thought that there was something special and secret in this remark but he did not understand yet what it was. Probably the remark had been directed only to Seth as the thing that Jukee would eventually say would be directed only to him. If we watch and wait, there will always be something for each one of us alone.

She started to remember when she grew up here in Pond Inlet,   the interpreter said.   There were only four or five houses then. It's very different now. She doesn't know anything at all now.

That makes two of us,   Subzero said, and the interpreter laughed without translating and Seth stared out the window at that compact little hamlet, with its row of steep-roofed houses just behind the runway, whose red-and-white-striped windsock was the most prominent thing; the wide yellow box of the Hudson's Bay, the satellite dish behind the houses, all almost silhouetted beneath the bright ball of the midnight sun – that was about all that Seth could see. But Seth could hear the comings and goings of construction vehicles from far across the tundra, as he could hear teenagers speeding on their three-wheelers, children calling. And Seth was restless and thought of the single white Arctic rose he'd found near Uktuk Lake –

She was born in 1928, when the Anglican mission started,   the interpreter said.   She's been believing in religion all her life. Most of them are Anglican here, always together, the wife and husband and the kids. She and her husband are so different from her children. Her son is more into the white men's way now.

She still can do some sealskin work and make a tent, the interpreter said. She also can make waterproof sealskins to make a tent. She gathers blueberries and blackberries. They're all around the sound. People here get only a few. She still remembers how to use Arctic willows, how to use them to light up the moon-shaped lamps with seal oil. She makes them into matches. She remembers how to use the mosses for a sled slider. Scramble them up, add the right amount of water and let it freeze; then it would be a really good slider. She used to eat roots. Only a few days ago she ate them with seal meat. She likes all the animals . . .

She dreams of the past, the dog-teams, said the interpreter. Big Dog, Noisemaker . . .

When her husband went to the hospital down south, the dogs were left alone and gradually died by themselves, said the interpreter. Five of them, then four, then three. When the dogs were really sad that their master was gone, they were shot.

She came back to Pond Inlet in 1977, said the interpreter. She used to be so homesick when she was living up there in Grise Fiord. But when you finally go back here, you notice that it's all changed, and you don't like that. Lots of people. Vehicles going back and forth, and the animals hide. Not so many animals now.

She used to live in a small sod house, an oval house, said the interpreter. They were well constructed, she says. Canvas inside and outside. They would be heated up by seal-oil lamp. They would be well lit day and night. They fanned the air with bird-wings to keep away the mosquitoes. They greased up with bearded seal oil, and used the skin as a bandaid. They had cushions made from willow branches packed with moss. Always looking after their kids. The small ones died. Their lungs would be so filled up. The roof was as high as the sash of this window. She used to go out caribou hunting to the northeast. They'd go camping months and months into the land. She'd be eating caribou meat and seal meat. When there were no containers, they'd use the skins of birds around them for containers. She would be so interested in living that way now. All of what's inside and under the sod house, everything inside would be free.

Is there any way we can make friends up here that doesn't cost us money? he said to the interpreter sarcastically.

The interpreter smiled. – Up here, he said, everything costs money.

That night he and Seth walked to their tents, and Seth was very edgy and said, I hate to say it, and the academics would hate me for saying it, but this is a degraded culture. It's gone. It's all gone.

Subzero didn't say anything.

But it's gone, Seth said.

The next morning they walked into a glorious day of warmth and greenness, and mosquitoes and floes joined together on the sound in wavy sandbar patterns. In the lake of open water, Bylot Island's ice-mountains were reflected. Water trickled everywhere. They walked toward the dump and Seth saw a piece of insulation lying sodden in the tundra and said: too bad. This was perfectly good.

You could say that about the whole island, said Subzero easily. But then he turned on Seth and said: It *is* still good! It's good!

At the dump a beautiful white fox lay dead. It had been shot in the head. Its mouth snarled a little. Its fur was so white and soft and perfect. It was very light in Subzero's hand. Someone had killed it and thrown it away.

The two stood still.

Feel how soft it is, Subzero said.

It's gorgeous, Seth said. But it's already beginning to rot.

Is there anything we can do with the skin? This seems so wrong. They used to tan it with urine, didn't they? No, there's nothing we can do.

Nothing.

If only we could use it somehow . . .

I could cut off the tail, maybe. – Seth took out his knife and put the blade against that long lovely white tuft and then said   no, this is wrong, too.

Subzero took the fox by the tail and heaved it into a pile of automobile parts. Flies settled on it.

Sorry, fox, said Seth.

They continued on their way and found a raven fresh shot in the breast. Flies were on it.

. . . And on that day (which Seth, too impressionable, later said was one of the worst of his life) long blue lakes appeared in the ice, and the tundra was dry and soft to sit on among the clouds of mosquitoes and tiny flies. Every ridge was like a dam failing to hold back an overflowing reservoir of cloud. Soft green moss-pads were set like emeralds in the lichen-carpet. The waxy, bitter white cups of Arctic heather hung down. The leaves of the dwarf willows had opened, and they reached up at the light. Crisp lichens of an almost phosphorescent whitish-green grew on their grey cousins. Clouds and

insects rushed everywhere. Seth went off by himself to mourn for Raven and Fox; Seth felt even worse than Subzero did when he'd stride confidently uniformed into town and then someone would look him up and down and say: You must find time hanging heavy on your hands. – Seth prayed for Raven and Fox in his fashion and wanted to die for or with them because he had always had that kind of sensitivity which, deeply lobed like pedicularis leaves, remains no less pure for being only partly rooted in knowledge. Subzero had seen him glare in disgusted misery at the New York rich ladies who wore fur coats, and it appeared to Subzero that Seth had no right to do that because he didn't know where the fur coats came from; Seth eventually became a vegetarian to save the rain forest and Subzero remained uncon-

vinced; Seth had always been one for fads. And yet the truth of it was that
Seth gladly sacrificed his dearest joys to be good; whenever he earned money
he gave it away; he wanted only to please and to help and to hope. In the city,
whenever some alcoholic fell to the pavement, it was Seth who sprinted
ahead to lift the filthy head up into his lap, calling the ambulance, fighting
the bleeding with bandages torn from his own shirt! It was when nothing
could be done that Seth became despondent. In this case his grief and guilt
was in a way as artificial as Subzero's love-sadness for Reepah (who hasn't
been introduced yet), because even though it did appear that Fox and Raven
had simply been rifle-raped and broken, he couldn't say he *knew*; he was
making judgments – strange, since he himself once told Subzero how his
uncle and aunt had met their former SS guard on a cruise ship and the aunt's
family had stabbed the SS guard daily with horrified hateful silence but the
aunt and uncle greeted him happily because, as they said, he'd shared with
them an important time of their lives; Subzero had believed that both the
talkers and the non-talkers were right but Seth had persuaded him that the
talkers' way was best, persuaded him simply by the glowing way in which he
told the story (the glow further illuminated by the aunt's family's screaming
blaze of objections); now, as it seemed, Seth had chosen the way of the non-
talkers. From this day onward, as it later seemed to Subzero, Seth began to be
uncompromising in his hardness against those who in his view hurt the world.
His life became much faster and he began to accomplish things which
Subzero admired, but in the process he drew himself into a species of
orthodoxy; in effect, he'd joined the Party. And yet this was the result, as I've
said, only of Seth's true and anguished love. If he could have saved Fox and
Raven by ending himself with a rifle, he would gladly have done that, though
he would have felt sorry for his parents and brother and sister . . . Subzero for
his part walked east, making new resolutions on what to be and how to be it,
constructing suppositions for why Raven and Fox had been murdered
(hygiene? marksmanship? If there was a good reason – which is to say
practically any reason – then they would not have been murdered after all),
wondering about the moral qualities of rifles, thinking of the whaling captain's
haunted grave a hundred miles or so down the coast from here; the grave had
cracked open, people said, so that the brass buttons on his chest were visible,
but nobody dared to take them; and Subzero wondered if this frozen captain
were with Raven and Fox now and he walked almost to Mount Herodier
until his lips twitched like the frail leg-lashing of a half-crushed mosquito and
then he turned round and walked back and passed the dump where Fox was
black now with flies, keeping company with moldy caribou-skin jackets and

sealskin kamiks alert with maggots, and Subzero kept walking and came into town and passed the porch of the Hudson Bay where everyone was shouting and a drunken Inuk was biting another Inuk's ear and the blood was running down both their faces from that parting ear and the RCMP man got the cuffs on the biter and then the other man kicked the biter in the face and Subzero wondered if those men were with Raven and Fox; now an eye-shaped rift of blue had been wrenched in the clouds and ravens swarmed on the decaying floes picking at the bits of fish-entrails that people had left there, and the water streamed eastward, toward the frozen captain. So Subzero walked west. West of town there rose a great white cross on the tundra. The graveyard was close by here. Here must lie that man who had shot himself when he heard that he was being relocated to Resolute. Who else? He did not want to look anymore. Beyond this the hill became steeper and happier with constellations of Arctic heather. Westward still farther the slope became a scree of banded boulders. It began to drizzle, and mosquitoes and flies wavered uncertainly. He walked along the Foreshore Flats near where he and Seth had first flown their kite and he made the following resolutions:

1. Don't try to be what I'm not.

2. Don't harm myself to please others.

3. Be free.

Here he was. He'd come here to be free. Now what did he do; what did he want?

He prayed to love others better and to be of service to them. He was sorry he'd been sarcastic to the interpreter. Never before, it seemed, had the open water sparkled so sunnily. Never before had the ice-floes dwindled so rapidly. These appearances, however, were but gimmicks of the present, whose artifice it is to make everything seem new. Just as birds seem able to utter only questions and exclamations, so Subzero felt himself calling out to the world out of his ache at what he'd seen, and for all his resolutions he failed to make a single declarative and so returned to camp at last. Proof of his comparative practicality or superficiality: he was quite over Fox and Raven now. On that cold clear evening in July, the sun drove north, and the tussocks were brown and crisp. He lay in his tent, looking through the open door, down into the valley where Seth was washing the dishes, and the snow-mountains rose above him and it was windy and his and Seth's personal flags flapped stiffly on their walking sticks. He closed his eyes and remembered how he'd waved to two girls, feeling very proud in his uniform, and said hello, ladies   and they smiled and said   hi   and he said   you look pretty today   and they said   tank you   and giggled and now he knew that that had been the first time he'd seen Jukee. The second time he'd seen Jukee had been when he'd grandly leaped a stream and skipped up the beach where one of his friends met him on a three-wheeler and rode him home for murre's eggs (green and almost pyramidal), fried rich and good, and dried Arctic char's deliciously greasy red blisters like sweet berries which Subzero ate so happily while his friend watched the ball game on TV and an ad for Christmas in July came on and the friend's wife, the lady of the house, said   look, those white people are rushing again!   – Then the kids came home and everyone had fried char with brown sugar. The kids got a puppy and whirled it laughing. Subzero, warm and full, stayed until he got sleepy. He said goodbye, laced his Sorels up and marched back into the fog where his tent and Seth's tent lived like two ships (shall we call them *Terror* and *Erebus?*) and on the way out of town he passed Jukee; he realized that that had been Jukee. He was certain now that Jukee knew about rifles and why Fox and Raven and the others had died. (How fine it is to have thoughts as empty as ice!)

At the sound of the helicopter that was going back out to steal dinosaur bones from Bylot Island, a raven screamed: *Ayuh! Ayuh!*   and flip-flapped hastily out of place.

A white fox, you say?   the man asked.

Yes.

Must have been from last winter. Foxes at this season are brown. Somebody probably took it out of the freezer and decided that it had rabies or the skin was no good. Used to be a fox skin was worth forty bucks. Now we get ten for it at best. It's all Greenpeace's fault.

I shot a whale today,   a man beamed.

Lots of meat?

It sank. I shot it from shore.

Why did it sink?

He shrugged. – Maybe the tusk was too big.

. . . A glorious midnight fluffy with clouds . . . A grey wing of cloud, like the wing of a jet fighter, streamed in from the east, and the long shadows of houses and trailers only accentuated the blazing gold of the world whose fiery icebergs rocked like cradles of translucence and refraction pierced to various crystal depths of wonder in which children laughed and dogs howled scenting the narwhal hunters and fishermen back from the open sea, and the smell of frying muktuk came from kitchen windows, a smell like escargots buttered and buttered, and men with caps pulled low dusted you with the wake of their three-wheelers, while a girl who might have been Jukee walked down the sandy street without once glancing at Captain Subzero; and a mosquito whose striped intricacy amazed him landed on his hand and stung. Orange and yellow trucks sped to the construction site. As if the never-failing day might suddenly cloud over, Caterpillars worked through the sunny midnight. More three-wheelers sped toward Water Lake, and a ptarmigan called. His ears glowed with mosquito bites. At one in the morning the children were swinging and running and being happy almost frantically. Three teenaged girls came to the sod house to play the game of breaking cottongrass heads and sticking the tacky part to their hair, then pulling it away and making faces at the pain. One was Jukee. The sun spiraled slowly lower day by day, approaching the tops of ridges so that the shadows grew longer each midnight, as if it were late afternoon: indeed it was, the late afternoon of the long day. When the long night came, not many weeks from now, people would think of the day with disbelief: *as if nevermore could somehow be again* . . .

The long, long shadows of midnight –
  The sun a notch lower and oranger than before –

There were narwhals today, said Jukee.
  Do you like them? asked gallant Subzero.
  When somebody killed them! she laughed.
  When somebody killed one, I saw all the blood, I thought there would be a shark, said Elisapi.
  If a shark comes, said Jukee, I eat that, too!

Each night, the sun got lower.

The first night that it almost resembled twilight, the temperature dropped, the sun sank part way behind a ridge, and the sky was cloud-striped, the sound a luminous chalky blue. The next night was a little dimmer, the shadows a little longer. Just as the sides of ice-floes often melt first, dissolving inward to form a mushroom shape, or an oddity like a white apple gnawed round the core, so the ice of summer and daylight now began to melt secretly. The grass was greener and taller than ever; the dwarf chrysanthemums were coming out; but the dandelions were already going to seed. Two weeks ago they'd been coming into bloom. The dwarf willows had now passed the height of the season, and their white ovals had begun to fall away, exposing the prickly green core beneath.

All night long, every night, the bulldozers and rifles sounded. Tundra ridges became transmuted through the miraculous agency of bulldozers into dirt buttes, and animals became meat.

Now below the sun an unbearable bright orange simulacrum shaped like an eye had formed upon one of the glaciers of Bylot Island. In the water immediately before it floated a yellow sphere of even more dazzling brilliancy. From this grew a wand extending across most of the sound, flaring out into a sort of plume that terminated not twenty feet from the shore where Subzero stood trying to understand. As the boats raced by seeking whales, wake-ripples widened and disfigured this strange thing which even as he watched continued to grow, and had now crossed the water entirely and risen up the grassy dune to caress his face. What was it? He stood breathing sea-smell (before the ice had broken up on the sound there was no smell). After midnight, the boats droned away from the moss-hills of greenish-gold whose long shadows were but softenings of color and warmth; the warmth of the sun on his ankles was like wool socks.

I like only this mountain and this one over there, a boy said to him.

He saw the boat rushing, heard the whistle of the shell. The whale submerged, and the boat came closer and closer, waiting. A line of white sea-birds gathered like buoys. Other boats drove forward and back, shooting and shooting. In between shots, the first boat lay with its motor stilled, drifting, watching. Again the whistle of death. They rowed slowly toward that slow sepulchral breathing. Whales rose and fell about the silent boat like heaved rocks. They sank soundlessly. Their breathing whistled. It was warm and sunny. White birds strewed the way like stones. The boat creaked. The shot rang out and echoed across the sound. Then the boat was awash with crimson silence.

As he walked across the tundra ridges toward camp, the shadows of the three girls were long and thin. It was half-past one in the morning. They stopped frequently to pick the rust-red blossoms of the *Qungaliit*,* whose sour taste they relished; one after another they squatted and peed; they smiled at moss-blossoms crying: *Pirruqsiat! Pirruqsiat!*†   at which the gallant Captain Subzero said: You ladies are even more beautiful than *pirruqsiat!*   at which they hung their heads delighted. Yet as the little box houses of Pond Inlet grew smaller behind them, as they climbed the tussock hills until there was nothing around them but an immensity of moss and sky and ice far away, they became uneasy.

Are you tired?   said Captain Subzero.   Do you want to go back? I'll go back to the road with you.

I want to come and I don't want to come,   said Elisapi.

Why?

We're scared,   said Jukee.   Scared of polar bears.

There are no polar bears here, ladies. They stay by the ocean.

Jukee ducked her head.   – Once in the summer,   she said haltingly, Elisapi was picking berries with her grandmother and a polar bear came when they were gone and ripped her grandmother's tent.

My grandmother died,   said Annie proudly.

Mine is still alive,   said Jukee.

Elisapi said nothing. He looked at the girl's round face, white teeth, narrow, black-pupiled eyes, her coppery cheeks, and could almost see her wearing a mottled caribou-skin parka as she sat scraping at caribou skins with her *ulu*,‡ but that was all finished and had been before Elisapi was born.

And do you play games?   said Captain Subzero.

Sometimes,   Annie said.

What kind of games?

We went to our graves in winter, when it was dark. Some graves are worn away, so we can see the bones.

Is that where the big cross is, on the hill?

Yes,   Annie said.

Then she didn't say anything more.

Each tussock cast its own shadow, so that around you were islands of shaggy rust and pools of blue; ahead, the mounds merged into a plain of rusty

* Sorrel.
† Flowers! Flowers!
‡ Inuit woman's knife. A sketch of a Greenlandic *ulo* appears in volume 1, *The Ice-Shirt*.

gold. The mosquitoes about your heads were golden, holy. Ptarmigans clucked over their eggs like hens. The moon, three-quarters full, hung very large in the sky, offering his lovely markings to haunt you with pale incomprehensibility. You led the girls across the bog wallow and up the next ridge, where the road could no longer be seen; at midnight, every pebble on the road had cast a diagonal shadow as long and thin as a meteor-trail. The sun was low and bright.

I think I see a polar bear, said Elisapi. No, a white rock.

We're almost there now, said Captain Subzero. It's just over this rise.

I'm afraid, Annie said. I want to cry.

When I was a little baby I cried too much, said Elisapi. My Mom get mad.

We used to go to the graveyard at night, said Jukee very slowly, and imagine the hands of the bodies were coming up, and three were triplets, and two were twins, and one was just a person. We were dreaming they were trying to catch us, so we could die and go to the grave. Maybe they wanted to lead us into the light.

Here it is, said Captain Subzero. Take off your shoes, ladies, and you can come lie down. Zip up the screen. Now wait while I kill the mosquitoes that flew in. Are you thirsty? I can make some Tang for you.

Yes, said the girls.

You look like a clown when you take off your glasses, said Elisapi. You're a white man. Your nose is so big.*

Thanks, ladies, said Captain Subzero. I was hoping you'd say that.

But he was inattentive. He could not stop thinking about what Jukee had said. *Three were triplets, and two were twins, and one was just a person.* As soon as she'd said that, his grave-twin had caught him. That was what he'd come here for. Long white fingers shining with light from below rose from the moss and groped through the floor of his tent and the skinny joints speckled with lichen

---

Ask a Northern Indian what is beauty, wrote Samuel Hearne sometime between 1769 and 1772, *and he will answer: a broad flat face, small eyes, high cheekbones, three or four black lines across each cheek, a tawny hide – and breasts hanging down to the belt.*

clicked open and then latched around his leg, each metacarpal closing cool and hollow upon him; the girls did not see it and he said nothing to them of it. Now he must die and go to the grave. But who was his twin? And where did the triplet wait? – The next day, while pacing the beach, waiting for his twin to come for him, he recited the rules: *You use thirty-thirties for polar bears. You hunt walruses with thirty-thirties or thirty-ought-sixes. You go after caribou with twenty-twos or two-twenty-fives. A twenty-two for a seal.* He was very anxious. The day was sunny, windless, and neither warm nor cool. Although he had heard no wind during the night, the ice had vanished almost entirely from the sound, leaving only a few rare shards on the shore and a thin white line that stretched across the field of view between the islands. A motorboat went rapidly out across the still brown water, up to the ice-edge, and fired a single shot. Then it rushed halfway back, shooting. It stopped. It circled slowly. The water seemed very still and shallow. Blue and brown clouds shimmered, reflected truly neither in shape nor hue. Another boat fired a shot. Both boats

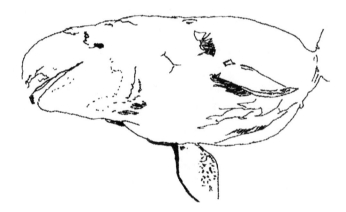

were rushing. He heard the whistle of the shell. The whale went down. The boats circled round and round, waiting. The whale came up, and they shot it again. A line of white sea-birds gathered on the water like buoys –

There were fissures and riddles in a lump of ice that lay melting on the beach, and he wandered his eyes along them, looked away at the dying whale, and then his head swung back to the ice and his eyes locked upon it of their own accord, because the cracks were symbols. He knew the syllabic alphabet well

enough to spell words out, although his Inuktitut vocabulary was small; he
knew how to say woman, blouse, and soft drink . . . These characters which
he now saw were much more definite than the faces one half-sees in clouds.
He believed in them. In the sand, in the ice-shadow, he wrote out the
transliterations with his fingers.

ja n   va ra ng ka li n

Yawn Varangkalean.
Yon Vranklin.
John Franklin.

❊ ❊ ❊

The ice-orthography was not perfect, of course. The combination,
clumsy and redundant, could better have been ⌐ b, but corruptions were
to be expected. – So Franklin was his twin. – He was happy knowing it,
happy for the same reason that on small planes flying Medivac the men may
say: oh, good, we have a nurse with us   – not out of lust, as the nurse may
assume, but because there was a flight in the 1970s that crashed and the
survivor, picking among the smashed bodies, chose that of the nurse to eat
and found it delicious.

❊ ❊ ❊

Sir John Franklin went north four times. (One has to expect these things to
take more than one attempt, like seducing someone, like shooting a seal – the
first time not to kill, but to scare the animal so that it dives before it can
breathe; when it comes up you're already closer and shoot again so that it
goes under a second time without air; and the third time or the fourth you're
close enough to shoot it in the head.) On his first expedition he was only
second in command. They sailed up the east coast of Greenland and failed to
gain the Pole; the other detachment failed to penetrate the Northwest Passage
thanks to an optical illusion of Ross the Elder . . . Lieutenant Franklin had
nothing to do with that error. Ross was in the *Isabella;* he was in the *Trent.*
The next time (1819–22) he had full authority, so there was starvation, murder
and cannibalism, and one of the men wrote: *Our own misery had stolen upon*

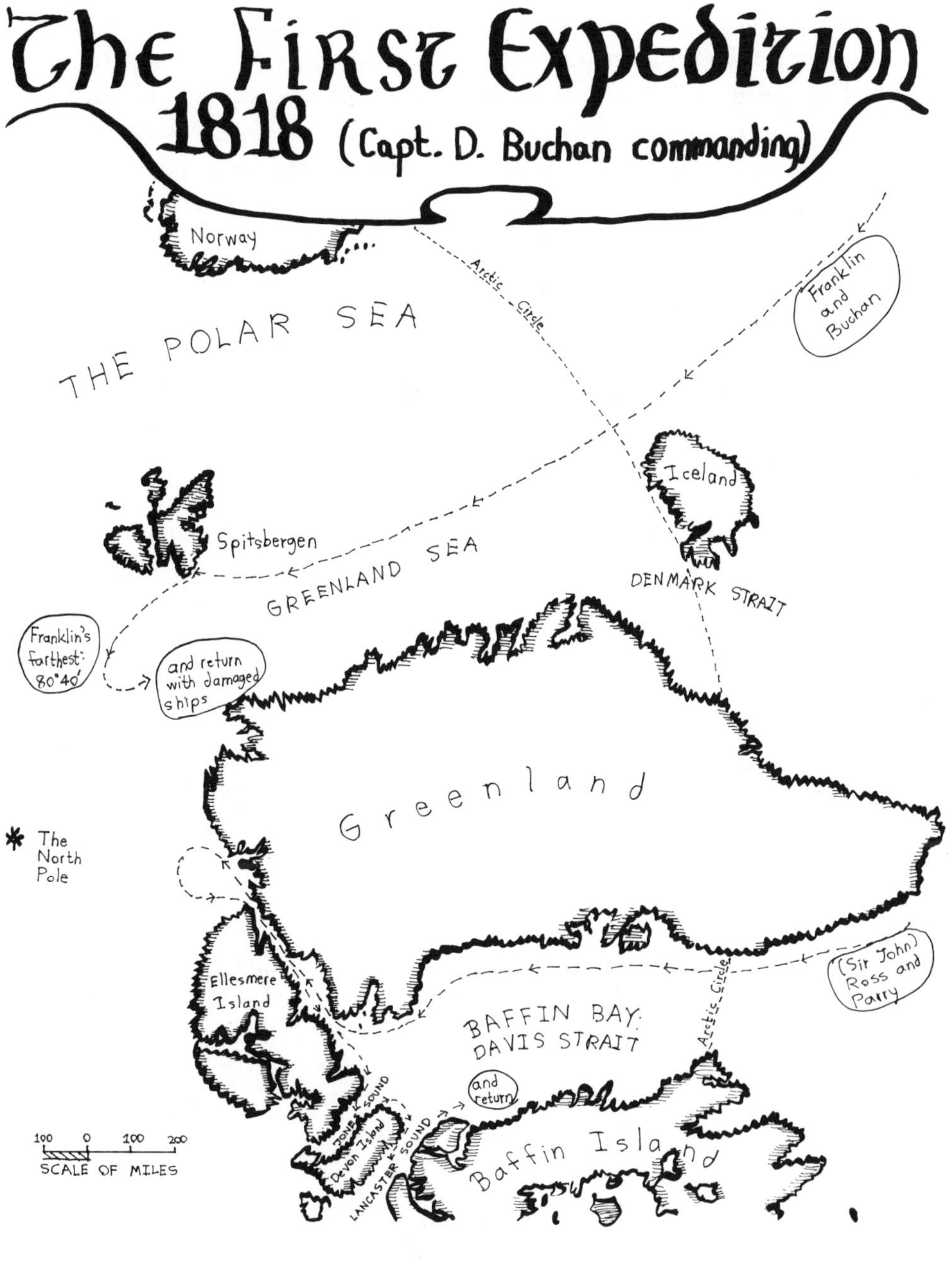

The First Expedition
1818 (Capt. D. Buchan commanding)

Norway

Arctic Circle

Franklin and Buchan

THE POLAR SEA

Iceland

Spitsbergen

GREENLAND SEA

DENMARK STRAIT

Franklin's farthest: 80°40'

and return with damaged ships

G r e e n l a n d

* The North Pole

Ellesmere Island

(Sir John) Ross and Parry

BAFFIN BAY: DAVIS STRAIT

Arctic Circle

and return

DEVON ISLAND

JONES SOUND

LANCASTER SOUND

Baffin Island

100 0 100 200
SCALE OF MILES

us by degrees, and we were accustomed to the contemplation of each other's emaciated figures, but the ghastly countenances, dilated eye-balls, and sepulchral voices of Mr Franklin and those with him were more than we could at first bear.   Franklin himself had preferred to look on the bright side, and wrote cheerily in his journal: . . . after halting an hour, during which we refreshed ourselves by eating our old shoes, we set out in the hope of reaching the Coppermine. – Strangely enough, all but eleven men survived. (An Inuk said: When his life is not completed, a man cannot die. Thus go our stories.) He was promoted to Captain. He married. He received an honorary doctorate in civil law from Oxford. He got the Cross of the Order of the Redeemer of Greece. More strangely still, he made a third expedition to that same Polar Sea. His character, which might be described as methodically feckless, permitted him to accomplish the mapping of a vast stretch of Arctic coast. His life was not completed. This time he got knighted. He became the Governor of Tasmania. It was on the fourth expedition, in search of the Northwest Passage, that he got his deserts, a little south of Resolute. He was among the first to die. His was not one of the skeletons which lay crazy in the sand, eye-sockets facing south; he sank with his ship of death after the Inuit, not understanding the use of hatchcovers, cut a hole in the side to pillage the weird wealth he lay frozen upon. In 1990 a crew at Polar Continental Shelf found something at the bottom of the Arctic Ocean; they're keeping it quiet but it might have been a ship –

All the Boys Will Fall in Love
with You Now

The former range of the caribou in the Pangnirtung area was at one time extensive. However, due to the encroachment of human settlement, they seldom or never migrate to their former winter range . . . Their former migratory pattern is disrupted by the Hamlet of Pangnirtung.

Information sheet: *Fauna of Auyuittuq National Park Reserve and Proximity* (*ca.* 1976)

I think I see a polar bear, said Jukee. No, it's ice.

They spied out the cool sunglasses and the two New York T-shirts, which alone remained of the stock of gifts he'd brought, and they said: Can we see them? Please, will you give them to us?

What present will you give *me?* he said. I have the twin, but where's my triplet in the grave?

At once the girls began to whisper and consult; they announced that they would buy him a Pond Inlet T-shirt. – Never mind, he said. He gave them the presents, letting them divide them as they would, and Elisapi got the sunglasses.

Elisapi, all the boys will fall in love with you now, said Subzero.

The girls tittered.

Even you? said Elisapi, very low.

Sure, he said. I love *all* girls.

Even little kids? said Annie, wide-eyed.

Well . . . – Now Captain Subzero was at a loss. He made them some Tang. The girls whispered again, though, because there was a mosquito swimming in it.

You want Pond Inlet T-shirt?   said Jukee.

I was just kidding. Save your money.

When you're three triplets living underneath, then I'll know it,   she said. And I'll play the game with you, but don't catch me, 'cause I'll be too afraid.

The other two girls were admiring each other's T-shirts, paying no attention. He leaned forward and said to her as quietly as he could: I know the twin, but who will the triplet be?

I don't know.

Yes you do.

She giggled. – You want a boy or a girl?

His heart began to beat very hard. – A girl,   he said.

She put her forefinger in her mouth and watched him. Then she took his hand and drew two characters on the back of it in cool lines of saliva for him to feel and remember:

Ri   pa

Reepah.

111
Resolute Bay
ᖃᐅᓯᐊᓄᑐᖅ

Someone Laughing
1988

Not here! the white North has thy bones; and thou,
  Heroic sailor-soul,
Art passing on thine happier voyage now
  Toward no earthly pole.

TENNYSON, Epitaph for Franklin

She sat at the open window and threw pieces of raw bacon to the giant dog from next door, laughing *yeah!* and *go home!* and singing songs. – Bye-bye, she said softly at last. She ate a piece of bacon fat and returned the rest to the refrigerator.

She went out, and he saw her hooding herself against the wind. The wind rattled the windows. After awhile she came back with a box under her arm. Inside was Joelee's electronic piano. She set it to SAMBA/RHUMBA with the TV still on because she loved the TV and she began to play. Catchy tunes came out of it when she just yawned and tapped a key with one finger. After awhile she started playing faster, leaning broad-shouldered over it in her leather jacket with her straight black hair shining and there was so much colorful movement on the TV while outside it was greyish-blue and about to start snowing again and the reflection of the kitchen light bulb shone in the sky, and Reepah sat expressionlessly working with her broad fingers. Reepah turned her head and smiled at him so prettily and he said: Can I try, too? and she said: Wait. After me.

Later she cooked him a dinner of canned corn, mashed potatoes and chicken from the freezer.

Something was happening when Reepah played but it did not happen for very long at any one time because she kept switching the electronic piano off to tighten the speaker wires or else she'd change the configuration from VIOLIN to ORGAN or TRUMPET. But she liked a steady one–two beat; she never changed that.

The windows had fogged up just a little and everything was very blue where a muscleman was swimming on the TV and Reepah smiled at him again and shut off the electronic piano.

❄ ❄ ❄

She sat at the kitchen table smiling with her girlfriend, leaning on her elbows, while the friend, an older woman, sat somewhat morosely, not unzipping her parka; her kerchief remained on her head and she leaned on her knuckles and finally went out, but she smiled over her shoulder as she did because two other girls had just come in and were bending over the electronic piano with Reepah and they all played dreamily. Outside the window it was dark blue and the streetlights burned. Then Reepah went to her room and a little later the girls drove away on their motorbikes and the big dog barked like someone laughing.

❄ ❄ ❄

He could have sworn he heard her say: Oh, John. I was waiting so long, John.

It couldn't be.

❄ ❄ ❄

The little boy toddled around the house saying: Joelee's bullet. Billie's bullet. Joelee's bullet. Billie's bullet.

❄ ❄ ❄

He could have sworn he heard her say: I wait for the heaven in Inukjuak.
Skins last longer when you soften them right.
John, Resolute is no good for me, John. I want go Inukjuak.
When the skin stops crackling while you scrape it, it's ready.
John, I'm waiting sleeping your heart.

A girl should wear whatever she makes even if it didn't turn out perfectly. Next time it will be better.

These are some of the things that they used to say, in the days when they wore caribou.

❄ ❄ ❄

In the vestibule, a roll of sealskin by the gun rack. In the laundry room, severed seagull wings.

❄ ❄ ❄

John, you dream for me Inukjuak. OK, John? I want see you there but I can't fly 'cause maybe you cut my fingers.

❄ ❄ ❄

That morning it was snowing and windless. The houses were all white-roofed, and the air was full of soft whiteness.

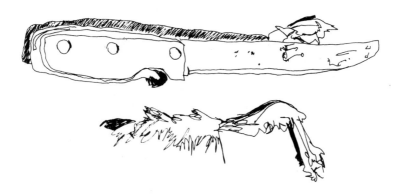

IV
Inukjuak
ᐃᓄᒃᔪᐊᖅ

Scarlet Mushrooms
1990

In the past caribou was hunted with spears, but since then guns have become the commonly used weapons.

> Secrétariat des activités
> gouvernementales en milieu
> amérindien et inuit, *Native Peoples
> of Quebec* (1984)

A distinct group living inland in the District of Keewatin perished when the caribou migrations on which they depended were disrupted following the advent of the rifle.

> *Encyclopaedia Britannica*

Over again he saw in anticipation himself giving the presents to her. He saw her alone with the baby in a dirty room singing with mosquitoes, a single bed unmade, and from the stuffsack he began his prestidigitations. First came the satin ribbon for her hair, shimmering in lurid butterfly colors. (Had he already kissed her mouth, her face, her hand?) Then the first T-shirt. Every time he took something out, he said to her: this is for you. He gave her the sunglasses, saying gravely: for you. She laughed and put them on. Was there a mirror in the room? If so, she'd be looking at herself now, and the baby would be whimpering a little, and she'd shush it lazily . . . He took out the other T-shirt: This is for you. The blank book. This is for you. The can of beer. This is for you. – Thank you, thank you! she'd say when she saw that. From the bottom of the bag he took the black panties friezed rampant with lace flowers. And this is for you. – That was what he saw over and over. He'd watch her face as she took the panties into her hand. Would she shrink? Would she giggle? He'd kneel down before her and say: I want to see you wear them. – What would happen then? The panties themselves offered no clue. They were weightless and intricate, like the black lichen colonies whose flakes and whorls adorned so many boulders in the Arctic. Often he'd munched a handful of these lichens; they tasted vaguely like mushrooms.★

They almost didn't let poor Captain Subzero into Canada, because he had no visible means of support. – Where are you going? said the immigration officer. – Inukjuak, he said. – Never heard of it. – I *apologize* for that, said Subzero winningly. – The officer glared. After many questions of a highly personal nature, however, he stamped Subzero's blue card and passport at last, and permitted him entry. Subzero had a night to pass in Montréal. He went to Rue Saint-Laurent and bought sausage and chocolate, which he ate on the street, thinking of the definition of revelrous behavior that he'd recently read in a sociology book: – *the necessary alleviation of frustration and monotony that exists in any society.* He sat in the park and was happy because a girl was wading in the fountain and she was happy. Was that revelry? Was enjoying the park revelry? He went back to Saint-Laurent and drank two Boréales.

He couldn't stop thinking about her. In a day or two days, he'd be seeing her and kissing her –

How could it ever work? It was as courageous as he could be to come to her at all. What if he stayed with her? Would he start to hate her and himself then?

★ To admit (as I do not) that these were the rock tripe (*tripe de roche*) which Franklin's starving men subsisted on in the Second Expedition would be to enclose myself in doleful connotations; but it may be worth stating here that I have eaten almost every variety of plant which I have seen in the Arctic, and I prefer the taste of lichens to that of sedges. All in all, however, I agree with Reepah, who once said that vegetables are but slimy things from the bottom of the sea.

Sightings of Reepah

$$\text{ᗪᑕ ᐊᑦᓇ ᖅᑦ ᑉ}$$

$\left(\begin{array}{l}\text{nuliataariirataarpa} = \\ \text{he has just married her}\end{array}\right)$

So it came to this: that he made ready in his tiny hotel room that night, so delightfully alone and far away in that unknown northern city called Montréal; tomorrow he would leave it, so tonight he laid down his clothes in the narrow aisle between bed and dresser; he strode past the TV that crowned said dresser, and he washed his face, peering at himself in the mirror to see how he would look to her, and then he laid himself down to sleep and dreamed dreamlessly of her.

The next day found him closer: Kuujjuarapik. Here at the very treeline, the spruces sometimes rose a little higher than his head and there were many of the tall and lovely flowers he knew in southern Québec. The grassblades bent together on that windy grey afternoon he reveled in, striding toward Hudson Bay, blowing and drawing chords on his new harmonica that continually thrummed a bass accompaniment as the wind blew through it, toward him (gusts varying between twenty-five and thirty miles per hour, according to his Wind Wizard, which he had decided for his own satisfaction to purchase the last time his tent almost blew away; he was one of those people who genuinely would feel better if when his tent did blow away he could measure the wind speed); so he strode through grass and sand and occasional white lichen-beds as in the Arctic; here too were the dwarf willows, but they sometimes rose as high as his waist. He had erected his tent, not without difficulty and bleeding fingers; he'd eaten chocolate; he saw the flattish grey ocean ahead and was exultant. Rain drummed him and stopped. The sky was very low, like the ridges and the flat sea. The village reminded him of Resolute, being once again an enclave of boxes and antennae; this recollection was disagreeable to him. Perhaps he would not have thought of it if everything had not been so windy and overcast. After all, it was not nearly as cold as Resolute. And whereas Cornwallis Island was only grey and brown, the land here was so green and mossy and rich like Vinland; he never would have thought of Resolute if he hadn't turned back toward the town when it seemed that the rain had settled in for good. Before that, standing on the edge of the sea, he'd felt so proud –

The thickest spruces were trunked almost like the calf of his leg. They moved a little, clockwise in the wind, and their grey-green buds and branches fluttered around them.

Graffiti at Great Whale

GREAT WHALE SUCKS (and for good measure: GREAT WHALE SOCKS)

I LOVE JOHNNY FRANKLIN

I NEED PENIS SO BAD

I MISS JOHNNY SO BAD

BITCH YOU NEVER KNEW HIM BITCH

Somewhat bilious the next clammy morning, he nonetheless experienced resurrection when the plane carried him through the cloud layer. Soon he'd see her –

When he got to Inukjuak where it was wet and sunny and there were mosquitoes just as he had figured (but it was also rockier), he went to Reepah's house and knocked. She wasn't in, but the woman upstairs said that that was her laundry in the dryer and she would be back any minute. He went out to get his big backpack, which he'd left at the foot of the hill, and when he returned the door was still shut, exuding the feeling of an empty place from between the hinges, so he settled down to wait on the stuffy landing where the houseflies buzzed and then he heard a baby crying inside. He knocked.

INUKJUAK, SEEN FROM THE RIVER

A woman opened, much thinner than Reepah had been. (Reepah had been pregnant.) She shrank back and screwed up her face. – What your name? she said.

John.

John! she said in amazement.

It was very awkward.

She shook his hand.

Can I stay with you? he said.

Yes.

He went in after her and closed the door.

I'm scared, she said after awhile.

I have some presents for you.

He expected her eyes to light up at that, but no. She was sick, she said.

The baby screamed.

She never stayed still. Whenever she started doing something the baby made her do something else. She was a very good mother, he thought.

She said: I sorry I don't remember so good. Too much sniffing.

But you remember me?

Yes.

She showed him all his letters (each signed, *Yours affectionately, John Franklin*). She'd kept them in the bureau. There was a letter on top of the TV which she hadn't mailed him. She gave it to him. It said:

> Hi hello John. Dear john, Thank you thank you I want thank you please thank you. Merci toi!
>
> Hi! how are you. I i'm just fine and My baby is fine, John, me have to say sorry your wife name is who me say like that so sorry, John i'm sorry for your cash money $25.00 dollar. John I you going to the Inukjuak visiting or work or something watt or look for something, John, my bit is no good for me. And I got know more foot's to eat in my place raid know. I'm waiting my cheque. Befor wear in sleeping or hotel or in My place or wear till me but I don't have enymore bit. Just my baby and me I got one bit in my place I'm sorry im say that. John I want to see you in august. I i'm happy and im scared because I can't much speak english you know John. I got know more telephone. Sorry bye bye John. Thank you.
>
> Your friend,
>
> *Reepah*

On the back of the letter it said:

> I like music and I like Black and White T-shirt. You know John. Hi John
> bye bye.

She'd kissed the page with lipstick.
My wife's name is Jane,   he said.
Jeanne?
Jane. Jane Franklin.
How old are you?   she said.
Thirty-one.
That's old.
How old are you?
Twenty-four.
Do I look old?   he said.
Yes.
There was a silence.
I'm sad,   she said.
I'm sorry I'm old,   he said.
I like your eyes,   she smiled, but later, when he tried to stroke her neck,
she laughed and said: Please don't touch me.
When he gave her the presents she liked the cat's-eye T-shirt best. There
was a painting of cats over the TV.
You want supper?   she said.
Up to you.
Don't have no food. I don't have no money. How much it cost you to
come to the Inukjuak?
Very expensive.
She wanted to see his wallet. So many before her had done the same. He
did feel old – old and selfish. He didn't belong here. Why did he keep coming
back? When he'd been Governor-General of Tasmania, writing to Jane   *I
have undertaken with the advice of the Executive Council (necessary upon such points)
to reduce the expenditure of Flour by ordering the mixture of a certain portion of meal
and peas in the bread to be issued to all prisoners, whether under the Crown or in
Penal Service as you will see by the notice in the Gazette which I send and have
marked with ink for you to read. This measure has given great satisfaction and it was
promptly done;*   when he entertained the Bishop of New South Wales, sought
to lower food prices for the poor, addressed the estimate question, solved
land cases, made rigid inquiries, he was fulfilling his obligations, but where

was he *really?* It was only in company of the men Jane called *our Antarctic friends* that the excitement came back to him and he felt as if he were approaching Reepah; when Ross first penetrated the Antarctic Circle in 1841 his heart beat like an Inuit skin-drum –

He hadn't given her the black panties at first, but he forced himself to go through with it. His motto was: Always look on the bright side of the question.

Good, she said. I like black. – She raised the cat's-eye T-shirt (which she'd put on immediately, out of politeness or delight), and showed him her black bra.

Very nice, he said.

He let her look into his wallet, since she kept asking. It had occurred to him in Great Whale that he might want to hide his money in time, as he would certainly have done if she'd been a whore, but she wasn't and he didn't want to deal with her in that way –

You're rich, she said.

No, I'm not, he said wearily.

She had an ache in her shoulders from her fever. She let him rub them at first, but suddenly she made him stop. She did everything suddenly.

Later they went out. It was a joy to see how the baby immediately clambered up on her back to be wrapped in the summer armauti. As they went down the street together she grimaced and said: Heavy. I'm getting tired.

You want me to carry him?

No no no no no *no* way.

They passed two boys who said: Hey, Reepah, you got new boyfriend?

No, she said.

Subzero ached when she said that.

Is she your girlfriend? the boys asked him.

You heard what she said. No.

The boys followed them, calling: Boyfriend, boyfriend!

You want up this rock? she said.

OK.

They clambered up the mossy stone terraces between the stagnant puddles streaming in the wind. When they were out of sight of town she set the baby down to walk, and put one of its hands in his. So they walked like a family, the three of them, and she said: I don't like Inukjuak people.

Why?

I don't know.

Down the slope. It started to rain. She asked if this were a montagne and he said mountain and asked her the Inuktitut but she couldn't hear him because her hearing aid had fallen into the moss. He picked it up for her –

I feel sad,   she said.

Why?

I don't know.

How long do you want me to stay? I want you to be happy. You understand?

Yes.

They walked on.

You want to stay in hotel?   she asked him earnestly.

No. I want to stay with you.

Suddenly she became convinced that someone was listening to her upstairs and brought a finger to her lips. She got a piece of paper and drew a seal on it and he drew a rifle and pointed at the seal and she touched the rifle and the seal in the way that he had known she would and then touched her right breast and touched his hand and wrote: I give you seal to you John.

He wrote: I want to be with you.

No.

Why?

I want be with Inuk. I want man same like mine.

I want be with you.

You want be with me or Jane?

Then finally she wrote: Dear John, how are you? I am fine.   – But she had crossed out: I'm scared I don't know why.

That night a man came in with blood bursting from his mouth and bearding his chin. He was drunk. Subzero gave him some Betadyne; the man, too drunk to open the package, was dully cheery. He tried to hold the baby, but it was uneasy and twisted in his arms. Reepah watched him smiling.

That one is father my other son,   she said.   Not this one; not Paulusie.

When the man went into the other room for a minute she showed Subzero her wedding ring. He put it on her.   – Now you're married to me,   he said.

The man came out and asked Subzero for a cigarette.

I don't smoke,   he replied.

Really?   said the man.

Je sais ce que vous faites ici,   he said to Subzero.   Assez clair?

Je ne parle pas français,   said Subzero.

Reepah wasn't sure where he should sleep. There was only one bed, as she'd said in her letter. Finally she decided that he could sleep in the bedroom on the mattress there. Her cousins were visiting from Povungnituk. They could sleep somewhere else. She'd sleep with Paulusie on the mattress in the living room.

Her bedroom was like some teenager's, papered with heavy metal posters. Cassettes and fanzines lay on the floor. She had a cassette player, but it clicked like a metronome whenever she played it, so that the music barely came through. At around six every evening, before she left to visit her sister, she'd play a song called "We Killed the World." The other cassettes lay dead on the floor.

At night the house was overheated and full of cigarette smoke and the baby screamed. She stayed up every night until three or four. When he tried to sleep she brought him coffee and toast. He said no.

A very bright Sunday morning, even through the FITZJAMES REVIVAL banner that covered most of her bedroom window, and dogs barked as the hunters rode into town on their three-wheelers. (Reepah said she had a black dog of her own, in a hunting camp far away. She didn't like hunting because it made her tired.)

He had a sheet called "Positive Affirmations" which a concerned friend had once given him. He didn't want to bother her as she slept, so he lay in the heat and light trying to plan out what he should do. *Just for today I will respect my own and others' boundaries,*   Positive Affirmations said. – So he shouldn't try to seduce her anymore. *Just for today I will act in a way I would admire in someone else.*   – What would Seth have done? Seth, knowing himself to be unwanted, would have departed. That was what Subzero should do, too. – What about the twin and the triplet in his waiting grave? They didn't count. All that counted was being decent to her. Having made that resolution, he felt better almost at once. When he heard Reepah getting up, he came out of the bedroom and said good morning to her, at which she cringed in bewildered sourness, not having her hearing aid in, and he began to pack. At once she approached him with great interest.

Why? she said.

I'm going to go camping today, he said.

That's OK, she said radiantly.

Now his heart rose still farther that he had chosen rightly, and he gave thanks to GOD. Already he longed to be wandering toward any tundra horizon, although he also wanted to cry; he strove to put down or cover his sadness, to keep her from being hurt by him anymore. He wanted her to be happy, both for herself and for him. He compacted the contents of his color-coded stuffsacks, twirled the necks tight, wrapped their cords; then he pushed them down one after the other into the rucksack. He would never see her again, and she would be happy. He began lashing his sleeping bag to the bottom of the pack.

John? said Reepah.

Yes.

Today Sunday.

Yes.

She stood smiling shyly.

He remembered now that she had a Bible in the house (Baffinland Eskimo edition), with her mother's name in it, and then her own. He said: Is Sunday a bad day to go camping?

Yes! she whispered smiling.

Why?

She shrugged.

She went into the bedroom and started writing something. She asked him how to spell "dark."

She was lying on the mattress where he'd slept and he lay on the floor beside her and took the note. It said:

> I you come back today
> or I you sleep in earth
> tonight is to tark in earth
> is your scared Maybe it to tark tonight
> I premise ok I like you are best friend

He was lying on his side facing her and she was looking into his eyes. He almost kissed her hand. His heart was beating very fast.

She said: How many teeth you have?

He smiled and she said aaah like a doctor and leaned closer to him as he opened his mouth and she pointed with her finger at his teeth, saying: twenty t'irty forty. – Her hand was stroking his hair. He thought his heart would explode. He ran his fingers through her short black hair; he put his arm very gently around her waist.

She sat up, looking at him.

He reached out his hand to pull her down to him. She pulled with all her strength to raise him, and he let her do it for a minute but then he drew her down and she was on top of him and he was taking his glasses off and he kissed her mouth. He was sucking her lower lip and her mouth tasted clean and good. He was drinking her up and his hand went around her head to pull her more tightly to him and the baby was crawling on top of them both playing with his glasses and reaching for her and he was kissing her with every delight and he pulled away to look at her face and she said:

Do you like me?

Yes.

He kissed her nose and she laughed. He kissed her cheeks and neck. He kissed her mouth again and again. She was very light and clean and pure on top of him.

He put his hand in her shirt. She hadn't put her bra on yet. It was early for her – only ten-thirty in the morning. Her reddish-brown breast was enriched with a great aureole blue-black like tundra lichen.

He kissed it, and she said don't.

OK, he said.

He kissed her lips again, and then she got up.

Reepah said that she knew someone was listening to them, and she hated that person. She kept the shades down most of the time now, peering through the narrow gap between them to see who was on the dirt street. The town made a series of bends around her, running to the mouth of the Innuksuac River where Hudson Bay began to offer its loved islands, low, tanned and green, in a careful fashion that did not usurp the horizon. On either side of the river, the spongy tundra which old Levi Nungaq had been so homesick for when he was relocated to Resolute was interrupted by low wide domes of rock up whose playing-fields Subzero ran joyously, scrambling up the easy dark stairs to new heights where the wind was stronger (twenty-mile-an-hour gusts here,

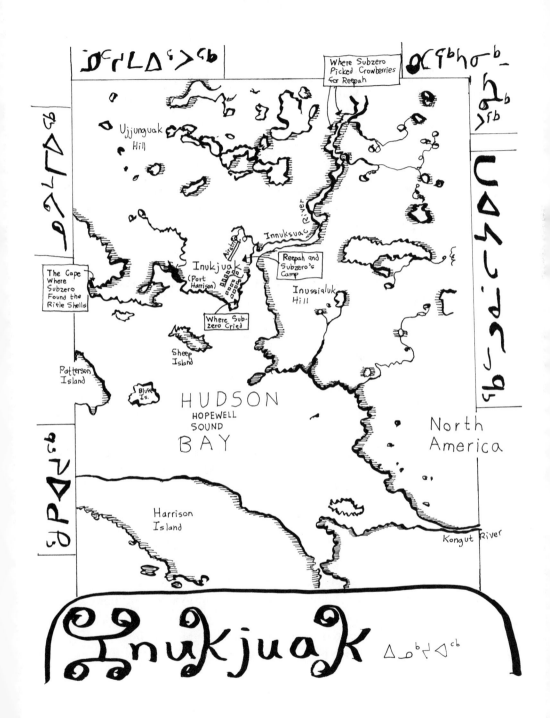

according to the Wind Wizard, as opposed to five below); he put on his nylon overshell and continued to run past the busily rippling ponds that garnished every hollow, and he looked eastward through his binoculars to where the river turned. Reepah had told him that that place was no good to camp: wolves. Reepah was afraid of wolves.

One of Reepah's teeth was missing because she'd pulled it herself when she wanted a dollar from the tooth fairy for bubble gum.

She knew sign language (it shocked him that she was that deaf) and she often signed   *I love you John.*

At around nine that evening Reepah came in looking as happy as she had earlier that afternoon when she watched the TV congregation sing "When the Saints Go Marching In" in Inuktitut, and he was lying in bed waiting for her and he played with Paulusie until she was ready and then she came to him with some instant shrimp soup she'd made for him and she was sitting on the bed by him so he pulled her down and they started kissing when the doorbell rang and he went on kissing her and then a loud knock came at the inner door and Reepah sprang up and opened it and three men came in. One was screaming: *My eye, my fuckin' eye! What's happen to my eye?* His brother had punched it to make him stop sniffing. He reeked of toluene. – *I can't see out of my eye!* he kept shouting. *What's going happen?*

Subzero got a cold compress, and Reepah said no, but he said to her that it was OK. After that, every minute or two the fellow would want more water on the compress. He wouldn't get it himself. Subzero went to the bathroom sink each time to do it for him. The man started laughing at him.

Reepah went out with the baby. – See you, John, she said.

As soon as they were gone she came back; she must have been very near somewhere, watching. She pulled up her shirt and put Paulusie to her breast.

– You wanna watch fuck TV? she said to the baby laughing. You wanna watch fuck TV? – Then she started singing an Inuit song.

A little after midnight, when he was asleep, she came in, turned on the light, and sat down by the mattress. – I can't find my secrets, she said. Someone took my secrets.

Come here, he said.

She came, and they started kissing more deeply than they ever had before and he pulled her on top of him and kissed her more and more and he tried to kiss her tits again but she was embarrassed and said: bad. He kissed her and they rolled around on the bed and he was on top of her thrusting against her as he kissed her and then his hand was inside her jeans and he said I want to kiss you here and she said OK. He pulled her pants off and she was wearing the black lace panties and his heart soared higher than a billion prayers. She wouldn't let him kiss her uktuk; that was bad, too. His hands on her, reaching and rubbing, fondling and grasping, strove not only to create a fabric of attachment between them, a constant flow of feeling like shared pulses, but also (more desperately) to melt himself into her, all over her, as if his substance were butter in his hands that he needed more than anything else in the world to dissolve into her; he made urgent magic passes across her flesh to make her take him in while she sobbed and sighed and they pulled off each other's clothes, kissing so deeply and holding each other, their tongues sucking the juice from each other's mouths, her breasts and buttocks absorbing his caresses, her hands on him, and they were moving together faster and faster although he had not yet penetrated her because that would be the literal incarnation of himself within her, a change of being; he would become her then, alien, lovely and loved, would taste the new loveliness of being her as he now tasted her spit and then he would not be anywhere anymore, having melted into sweetness without dying; now he parted the wetness between her legs and slipped inside her as she uttered a sound like a bird and being now with her and in her was better than it had ever been for him because it was she whom he loved as he had never loved anybody and she was moaning and trembling and then he came and hugged her and she said: I'm sorry.

Don't be sorry. Be happy. I'm happy.

Someone took my secrets. I wanna smoke my secrets.

Her mouth tasted like the bubble gum she'd sold her tooth for.

She got up at about half past ten the next morning when Paulusie started crying. The TV had been going all night, in a whispery voice that must have been joyously inaccessible to her deafness. She smiled. – Hi, John.

Hi, Reepah.

She looked up at the ceiling. – People hate me.

Who?

I don't know.

Why?

I don't know.

Well, *I* love you.

She lit up a cigarette and gave the baby one to stick in his mouth.

Gonna go to the post office, she said. This letter for Johnny. In Great Whale.

I saw his name in the bathroom. Same one?

I don't know.

Who is he?

I don't know. Maybe my boyfriend. Sometime he come here. I don't like him.

She was dressing the baby to go out.

See you, she said.

OK.

You go to the Bay?

No. To the river.

OK. 'Bye. – He went to her and she kissed him on the lips. Her mouth tasted like love.

It was a grey day in the Subarctic – surprise, surprise! – the sky made greyer by dim white patches shaped like her breasts; but the river was greyer still, a little greener than gunmetal, though not so green as the moss and grass and ankle-high willows – by which description we can see my own failing as an author: that I do not know how to depict something save in relation to something else. What if Subzero had never met Reepah? Then the white sky-holes would have looked like something else, and maybe the sky wouldn't have seemed as grey, so then the river wouldn't have, either, and this entire phony world of words would now be different. But here he was, the waters quite wide and formidable with a white streak of rapids running down the middle and long low lumps of rock curving out all smooth and crazy to meet it. A chilly day. He ate one of the green berries that Reepah liked and made up tunes on the harmonica for awhile: the notes filled him with glee, and everything seemed beautiful. White moss foamed up in popcorn shapes between the grassblades; it reminded him of drops of spit, so he got thirsty for her spit again. He wanted to drink it. The bank steepened and froze into rock, so he clambered up to the ridgetop where a dead dog and a caribou jawbone lay beside a spent rifle cartridge. The day was too chilly for mosquitoes. He ran on in delight –

Maybe it was the previous night, when his penis first blossomed into her like one of those scarlet mushrooms one sees on occasion in the wet moss around Inukjuak, maybe it was then that he'd received the greatest blessing that GOD or anyone could give him; it was then that she in her kindness, longing and trust had put aside his pain and hers so that it wasn't even sad when he kissed the scar on her wrist where she'd once tried to kill herself –

Doing It Again

The reason for the rapid diminution in the population of this country is undoubtedly to be found in the diseases which have been taken thither by the whalers. Of all these, syphilis has made the greatest ravages among the natives.

FRANZ BOAS, *The Central Eskimo*
(1898)

L ast night I was stupid, she said.
I want to do it again, he said.

Last night she'd said to him: You have baby? and he said no and she said why? and he said I don't know and she said I'm sorry. I'm sorry.

The most precise catalogue of his feelings now was: anxiety and a sense of wrongness. No matter what he did now, he would hurt someone.
　　She said: You want to go home?
　　He said: I don't know.
　　She said: You want to stay here?
　　He didn't answer.
　　She said: You miss your place?
　　No.
　　What you miss?
　　My books. My charts. Ross's new chart of the Antarctic coast –
　　She looked away.

She got out a church pamphlet called "Love, Marriage and Sex" and gave it to him. It said: *It is important that the three follow in that order.*

She said: You like it?

No. It says what we did last night is bad.

She showed him her baptism certificate and he said: Are you a Christian?

She didn't answer. Probably she didn't hear.

❁ ❁ ❁

He felt a constant sinking sense that he had done evil to her, and when he left her he would do more evil. He thought once again of leaving his wife and marrying her, but that would simply be turning his evil against his wife. Anyhow he would never be happy living in Inukjuak. But would he be happy living with Reepah? It would certainly be different. It would be very different.

❁ ❁ ❁

He went out and came back and she said: In Great Whale I have boyfriend now. I sorry.

He felt desolate. He knew that he was being completely selfish to feel so; whatever she chose was her right. That didn't help.

He said: I hope your boyfriend loves you. I hope he's good to you.

She said: I don't like him.

She said: I want to go to hell.

That night the little boy, who always crawled over them when they kissed, kept kissing him wetly on the mouth. The boy was just learning to talk. He called him Daddy. Reepah slapped him.   – Say Mommy first!   she shouted. Mommy Mommy!

❁ ❁ ❁

She came in in the middle of the night, and he beckoned her to him, but she only shook her head, got her hearing aid and left.

❁ ❁ ❁

Early in the morning, when the baby was still asleep, it was very cold with the loud winds and she called to him. He answered, and she came in and said: I'm scared.

She got into bed with him and he held her.

She said: I want to be with you, but you don't want to be with me. You want to be with Jane, so I don't want to be with you.

OK, he said.

Then she came very close to him and said: I'm pregnant.

How do you know? he said carefully.

I know. I'm pregnant. From you.

He looked up at the ceiling, which was white.

I'm going to go to the nurse, she said. To get my period.

You want me to come with you?

You want?

If you want.

No.

OK.

No. I don't want to go.

Suddenly her face took on a triumphant look. – I'm pregnant. With you.

You want to be pregnant?

No. Don't touch me. Don't kiss me. You don't want to be with me.

But there she was, with her hot bottom up against him.

She touched his erection and laughed and said: What's that?

He touched her crotch. – What's that? he countered.

Jane, she said bitterly.

You hate Jane?

No. I love Jane.

She laughed again. She crooked her finger, and pointed to the Y-shaped crease. – What's that?

Uktuk, he said.

That's right. You don't want to be with me?

I promised Jane.

So what?

There was nothing he could say. He was in the wrong, no matter what he did.

I want your baby, she said. I want tell Jane.

She rubbed his penis.

After a little while she was on top of him, riding up and down, and he felt nothing now but the sweet and desperate need as he violently rolled her onto her back and mounted her, thrusting with all his might as she gripped his shoulders –

Afterwards he said to himself: That's it. That's the last time.

She said: Don't worry. I try period.

He thought about this. – How?

Hit myself. In stomach.

Inside himself he started shouting: No, no!

No, he said gently. That's bad.

I'm fine, she said. They were sitting on the sofa now. She got up and went into the bathroom.

She was bathing the baby, who was screaming. When she had finished, the baby kept punching her with his little fists and shrieking. Subzero picked him up, wanting to be the one who could quiet him, so that he could do something for her, and at once the little face beamed and the arms went around him. Then he saw her face and was ashamed again.

My baby hate me, she said.

According to the Wind Wizard, the breeze varied from thirty to thirty-five miles per hour, with forty-mile-an-hour gusts. Just north of the Innuksuac River, the shore of Hudson Bay was paved with smooth round boulders and stones varying in their degree of bleached grey; against them the water struck in low powerful waves which were almost uniform, so that the sound was steady. A gull flew fast. Grassblades, berries, flowers and ankle-high willow-bush colonies whipsawed in the breeze. Mangled moss-freckled skulls lay between the rocks, along with grey bits of timber, wires, and half-ruined

trains of seal and whale vertebrae. The ridges of the mainland were no different from the silhouettes of islands long and low like knives. On the nearest island he could see two large canvas tents and a drying line. Some family must be getting meat there.

The main difference between Inukjuak and Resolute, as he thought again, was that this place was basically green – not as green as Down South, of course, for grisly rocks had risen up among the greenness like some sowing of Cadmus's, but it was not at all like Resolute. Last night when he'd been watching TV with Reepah the northern forecast came on and she said: Look! Resolute!   and he looked and the temperature there was minus two degrees Celsius . . .

Nevertheless, the Inukjuak of Levi Nungaq's recollection was probably more paradisiacal than Inukjuak really was, and that was to be expected; the reason we love Eden is that we've been expelled from it. (A silhouetted motorboat rapidly underlined an island.) Some grander principle of desolation was at work. Why else the Inuk with the black eye, the Inuk with the bloody mouth, the oppressive ugliness, wastefulness, and watchfulness of that town? (A goose flapped earnestly. Reepah coaxed sweepings into her dustpan with a goosewing.) Something vague and evil lay beyond the islands – vague only because it was not known; no doubt as he came to know it the evil would grow and grow.

What's on the islands?   he asked an Inuk.

Maybe geese and seals,   the man said.

They sat looking at the islands.

The man said: I'm thinking something.

What's that?   said Captain Subzero, already suspecting that he would not like to know.

Maybe you will be mad.

No, no.

Please don't tell.

OK.

I like *Playboys,*   the man beamed.

That's nice.

The man looked around in case the flowers were listening.   – Maybe you like *Playboys?*

They're OK.

You like?

I like real girls better.

Maybe you like suck cock?

Not me. I like girls.

Me, too, said the man obediently. He looked miserable as he sat drawing on his cigarette.

Captain Subzero played a chord on his harmonica.

See you, the man said.

He leaped up and ran away.

Subzero sat on his boulder, thinking about how when he held Reepah's breast he could feel her dear heart vibrating like the soft green moss when a sea-wind blows through it –

One of the constants in this landscape, wherever he went, was the grim hills of heaped boulders as black as mummies, thanks to the lacy lichens that he'd once compared to the panties he bought for Reepah.

The man came back and begged him to sleep with him. Thus Subzero had the opportunity of feeling the loathsome gush of a man's lust, which Reepah must have felt from him – not that lust is or ought to be loathsome, but need of any kind is demeaning, which is why beggars are despised, and Subzero, who ordinarily would not have minded the presence of this man, felt today that he was unclean; the man was his reflection in a crusted mirror. But he strove to endure him because Reepah had done that for him, and he now owed the world much more than he had a week ago. The man sensed this, and stayed.

I hate Inukjuak. There is nothing to do here, he said.

There's nothing to do anywhere, said Subzero.

Sometimes I want to die, the Inuk said.

Everyone does.

I want – I won't tell you.

OK.

Maybe I will kill myself.

Don't worry, said Subzero as kindly as he could. Someday you will die. Just wait and be patient.

Are you hungry?   the man said.

No.

I'm hungry.

All right. Have some food,   Subzero said, unzipping his pack.

The man ate. – Thank you,   he said.   Now I am going to walk far far
away.

The wind was like a chorus of gloating trolls deep under the earth. Subzero
had begun to shiver, despite his name. He felt pretty low. It seemed to him
then that all anyone really wanted on this earth was affection. Why was the
cost of giving and getting it so high?

On the bureau, by the Bible, was a box of collection envelopes ("The LORD's
Treasury"). He said: You like church?

Yes. But not in Inukjuak. Here I don't like.

They hate you?

Maybe.

Then she smiled at him. – You like JESUS?

I don't know.

I have church at my house every day. Once at eight in morning, once at
eleven-thirty in night. Never twelve-o'-clock. Twelve-o'-clock is bad power.
Eleven-thirty is good power. All Inuit do that. You must do that   (she went
on gently).   Do you want to be in Heaven with JESUS?

I want to be with you.

Please. Promise. I'm sorry.

OK. I do it for you, not for church.

You promise?

Yes.

And Jane, too.

She won't do it.

Please. You and Jane.

I'll try.

Thank you! Thank you! Sorry.

She'd already used up the money he'd given her. She bought milk for the baby, redeemed her photos of the baby from the post office, and gave the rest of the sixty dollars to her cousin Najaaraq. That night, as he ate his dried meat (which she didn't care for), she fed the baby milk and crackers. She had a cracker, a cigarette, and a long swig from the bottle of pancake syrup.

You want this? she said, offering him a cracker.

Every evening at around six or seven she went out to visit her sister. She didn't want him to come. She didn't want to be seen outside with him. How could he blame her? Today it was still windy and she dressed up in the same snow-white armauti she'd worn in Resolute, looking so beautiful and traditionally "Eskimo" with the foxfur-lined hood around her wide brown face, the baby peeping black-eyed from behind, the belts of red and black decoration, the multicolored cord –

She always let him kiss her when she went out, and she put her soul into kissing him back so deeply that his heart was slamming and thudding and she kept on kissing as he drew her head even closer against his –

That night his unformed feelings loomed like a cloud barely dammed behind a lichened boulder-ridge, and he said: You want to come to me tonight?

No, she said. Maybe.

He was sure she'd come. But she didn't. She'd swallowed five of his sleeping pills.

The next morning was hot and sunny. She lay beside the baby until almost eleven. When the baby started to cry, he went in and played with him to let her sleep. He did the dishes. He ate his breakfast of dried cereal quietly in the bedroom. At first the incongruity of his expedition meals had amused him as he camped on and on in this house, with his backpack and other gear stacked neatly by Reepah against the walls, while the other two occupants lived from refrigerator, stove and cupboard, but it wasn't funny enough anymore to make him stop seeing the sad weirdness and transience of it; he and the two were ghosts to each other.

She took the baby into the bathroom and he began screaming as usual while she cleaned him.

He loaded his daypack to go rushing in that sunshine. He waited for her to come out so that he could say something to her.

The door opened.

See you later, he said to her. (That was what she always said to him.)

Yeah, she said boredly.

He put his boots on.

She was getting the baby ready to go out visiting somewhere. She was near him.

You going to kiss me? he said.

No.

OK.

He put his cap on, slung his pack over his shoulders, and reached for the door. Then she was in front of him and he was kissing her and it was as good as kissing her always was.

The wind chilled him almost bitterly, but he did not want to put on his outer shell when the sun was so beautiful. – It was the day of birds. Just behind the apartment house (he always went out the back way, out of consideration for her position), a tall brown owl opened its beak and hooted at him immovably. The bird stood very haughty, wrapped in feathers like some opera matron in a fur coat. He went around it and started walking north, determined that this time he would go farther than Ross or any of the others had gone; he would find the Northwest Passage between Reepah's legs. Weaving his way across the soggy tussocks, he saw twenty-one white geese on a ridge-slab, all pointed into the wind. As he watched, they rose and spread across the sky like wind-whirled papers. At the edge of Hudson Bay he counted ninety-three of them through his binoculars (by now his ears ached, and he'd thrown on his windshell). The water in the waves and inlets was a milky blue.

Ravens spied on him.

Certain matters ought not to be thought about at all, he said to himself. This may be said to be a return to the position of those churchmen who burned people for thinking. – On the contrary. – I do not presume to specify *which* sleeping dogs should be left to enjoy their sun and dirt, because they are different for each of us. So what shouldn't I be thinking about? – Whatever it is that I'm searching for, here in this strange not yet dying place –

As suddenly as he reached this conclusion, the sky changed, and a great slanted plate of cloud came down, leaving only a long low triangle of blue to zigzag against the tongues of peninsulas of islands; and it seemed to him that everything in the landscape was reaching for something – not malignantly, but with innocent remorselessness, like the baby; and he was reaching for the same thing.

There was a tentacle of land almost like a little Cape Cod, with an added backward fillip at the end. As he trod his turning way, he felt a calm sad sense of recognition, and it took a good quarter-hour of going before he realized that it was like that first evening on Cornwallis Island when he walked to the ocean, with Resolute behind him. Here again were mussel-shells – much bigger, bluer and more numerous as it seemed to him (although naturally he did not happen to have any specimens from Resolute to make comparisons with). Here again were the sordid little quicksands that lusted for his ankles. There was grass, however, thick and green, almost rank – that was different. Stones and bones shifted under his feet, so he retreated from the edge (the peninsula was still so wide here that the sea lay entirely below the horizon of the other side) and continued through what could almost be called a meadow. Here was a seal vertebrum with a spur of knifelike bone attached. He stooped and put it into his pocket. Birds started screaming the same old stories at him, and he didn't care. Now he went back in time a little farther, because there were ring-ruins in the grass (in the first, a cigarette butt; beside the last, a weighted garbage bag, turning its head like some glossy black duck). Now the cape was narrowing, and he could see blue waves on either side of him, and his way curved in parallel to the continent he was coming from and the rubbery green succulents like ice-plants ended as the grass got ranker, the sand wetter, and he came almost to the end and found the first yellow rifle cartridge. Islands tan and green and black lay by him, and he felt again as if he were back in Resolute – but the islands he'd seen from Cornwallis Island couldn't have been green like that. The second cartridge was red. He came now to the last fillip, which was made of rocks with only a very occasional grass-tuft no higher than the width of his hand, and now the cartridges were everywhere, red and yellow, scattered like dead wasps, and it was sunny with cloud nowhere but on the horizon and the wind blew in fifteen- to eighteen-mile-an-hour gusts.

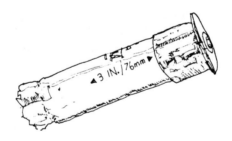

The Ice-Shirt

Exposed portions were bleached white, and powdery flakes of the exposed bone surfaces crackled and fell off if handled too roughly. Sharing the exposed surfaces were little, brightly coloured colonies of mosses and lichens . . .

OWEN BEATTIE and JOHN GEIGER,
*Frozen in Time: Unlocking the Secrets
of the Franklin Expedition* (1987)

He went back to Reepah's and said: can I kiss you? and she said: dirty! and stepped away.

Me dirty? he said.

I'm dirty.

She started dressing the baby to go out. – See you later, John.

❋ ❋ ❋

When she came back she still wouldn't kiss him. He needed her face and kept his eyes on it until she wrote him a note saying: *Don't lissen me look into me to much please I'm Inuk.*

OK, he said dully.

❋ ❋ ❋

Alacie and Mercy came over and he wasn't sure whether they were sniffing or doing something else in the bathroom because they kept giggling in there.

Reepah wanted two sleeping pills.

OK, he said.

Around two-thirty in the morning she came in and whispered happily: I'm drunk! I take two and a half, four and a half blue pill!

She got into bed with him and she didn't have underwear on. He started kissing her and she was moaning joyously and pretty soon they were doing it again.

I'm pregnant,   she sighed contentedly, just before she passed out.

In the morning she wrote:

> I want be with you
> because I'm pregnant.
> Jane forget her please
> I love you john.

No, dear, he wrote.   I'm sorry.

> Why I'm pregnant.
> I say
> I want talk to Jane
> i'm pregnant from john I'm sorry.

He felt pretty low. He said no.

> I want be with you john please I love you very much forget Jane
> please   please   please

When her entreaties had given way to threats, the hated ugliness of his actions bared themselves in all their hard vulgarity, and she tore up the sheet of paper and he sincerely wanted to be blotted out.

All right. I try period, she said.

She started belting herself in the stomach with all her might. The baby was laughing and punching her, too, and she said to him: Thank you, thank you.

She said to the baby: Now your little brother is dead. Your little sister is dead.

That was the day she said: You go tent please.

OK,   he said.

He packed up.

Where you camp?

By the river,   he said.

Maybe I come camping with you. Bring weenies, tea. But I don't got no money for weenies.

Neither do I,   he said curtly.

You come here maybe two three four five six o'clock?

OK,   he said.   See you next week.

No!

See you next month!

No!

See you in ten years.

He found a spot about two miles from town, half hidden on the bluff, where he felt comfortable. There was a nice rapid below him where he could get water. He erected the tent just before it started to rain, and he got inside and lay in his sleeping bag feeling miserable. What could he do? She refused to go to the nurse. She wanted the baby.

He was actually pretty sure that she didn't want him to come tonight. She'd seemed so happy that he was leaving. He wouldn't go down to her place. He'd leave her in peace for a day or two and she would be happy.

But at six-thirty his conscience was bothering him. Who knew what she really thought? He put on his tundra boots and began the cushioned toil through moss and willows until he came to the road. He crested the hill and saw a white figure approaching, very far away, at the bottom. At first he thought it was the man who wanted his cock sucked; he'd had a white parka. But suddenly he understood who it was, and he wanted to weep; he didn't know why. He went running down to her. Her baby was asleep in the armauti; she was carrying a huge garbage bag in her arms. He took the bag (blankets, a pot, diapers, and everything else) and carried it for her.

Hi, John,   she said.

It was his happiest dream.

She kept bending down to gather berries, which she ate as she went, saying: These green berries so good for me! Red berries, almost black! Blueberries, big orange!

When they got to the tent she was very tired because the baby was heavy, but the first thing she did was to clean the tent out and arrange it like a house with her blankets on the floor and the baby sleeping and everything just so along the walls. Then she started gathering moss and willow twigs to make a fire. He went down to the river to get more water and when he came back the tea was almost boiling and she was there for him like a dream in the white parka.

    You happy? she said.

    So happy! You?

    I'm happy.

    When I die, I want Heaven to be like this, he said.

    I want be with JESUS, she said.

It was her faith that had so moved him. She had set out from town, carrying the baby and the heavy load, walking where everyone saw, and she didn't even know exactly where he was; she simply had faith that she would find him or he would find her. The tent wasn't where she thought it was. If he hadn't come, she would never have found him.

He walked the baby around in the moss and they laughed together while Reepah laughed watching. The baby loved him. He loved the baby; he loved her. When the baby was seven or eight years old they'd go shooting together –

That night she wanted three sleeping pills and he gave them to her. Later she wanted two more.

    It's bad, he said.

    Are you sad for me?

    Yes.

    Don't.

    OK.

    I'm happy, she said.

When the baby was asleep, he lay beside her in the darkness and started playing with her and when he went into her she was moaning with every thrust, and they did it a second time and started on the third when she rolled away and said: I'm so stupid about men.

They lay there and he was almost asleep when she started flicking his headlamp on and off, making shadow puppets with her fingers, and when he opened his eyes she said: Look!

He took the lamp away from her and turned it off.

You pregnant? he said.
No.
You get period?
No.
But you're not pregnant?
I don't know. No. I'm not pregnant.
Why did you say you were pregnant?
Sorry.
Do you want a baby?
No.
I don't understand anything.
I said I'm sorry!

He went to sleep happy. The next morning she went home with the baby. In the evening he carried her pot and blankets and other things back to town for her. He slept in his tent that night. When day came he wandered a considerable distance up the river, where he spent an hour or two lying in the moss filling his measuring cup with crowberries for her. The mosquitoes were tolerable, his hands not too numb, and he smiled to see the knees of his jeans so happily stained purple with crowberry juice.

She opened the door and sat down wearily. She brightened at the berries, and poured some of them into her mouth. But then she hung her head again.

I need period, she said. I'm unhappy.

Please go to the nurse.

Monday.

Today.

Monday. Maybe.

You want me to go with you?

No. Alone.

You promise?

OK. Monday. Maybe.

The baby spilled the remaining crowberries all over the floor, and she started to pick them up patiently, but suddenly she threw them back down onto the mattress and got up and went to the refrigerator. She pulled it three feet toward her with her small arms, went behind it, pretended to tighten the plug, and pushed it back. Then she went to the big stove and did the same thing with it. She went into the bathroom and he saw her standing on the rim of the tub raising herself from the shower curtain rod before she saw him staring in and closed the door. He thought he had never seen anything so piteous. After a few minutes she came out and started clambering on chairs, pretending to be busy pulling old tape from the ceiling. He heard her saying softly, over and over: I want period. I want period.

She said: You sad?

Yes.

Why?

Because I was bad to you.

You weren't bad. I was bad. Bad and stupid. I was stupid.

You were good. I was bad.

You were good and bad.

I'm so sorry, he said.

It's OK.

He sat there.

You sad?

Yes.

Why?

You know.

It's OK, she said. Be happy, please.

You'll have a baby in March or April.

If I have baby before I get out, I give to keep to sister. I'm fine.

What can I do that'll be best for you?

I don't want help nothing. I'm sorry.

You don't want an abortion?

No.

Your sister will love the baby? She'll be a good mother?

Yes. I don't know. I'm pregnant.

I'm sorry. I'm sorry.

It's OK.

He was finally crying now.

It was the finest evening he'd seen so far. He walked along the harbor past the chained and barking dogs. The water was blue and clear like a lake. Motorboats went in and out. The islands were mottled in all distinction, like the forehead of a Nobel prize winner, the moon through a rich man's telescope. It was very warm, and the mosquitoes sang and bit. The water scarcely smelled like the sea. He put a finger in and tasted it; it was only brackish.

A motorcanoe came in very quickly, and another.

The sun dwindled him into a nothingness within a fat serenity.

Starvation Cove

1990

In 1955, the federal government moved people from Pond Inlet and Port Harrison [Inukjuak] to new communities at Resolute and Grise Fiord to take advantage of more plentiful wildlife and a few jobs at the Resolute air base.

> NORTHWEST TERRITORIES
> LEGISLATIVE ASSEMBLY brochure
> (*ca.* 1987)

T wo things above all he remembered. The first was her saying that she had bad power, and his saying desperately: you're *good, good!* as he stroked her hair the way she had done to him on that first morning when they kissed; he stroked her hair, as I said, until she pulled his hand off her head and said: I'm not dog! . . .   and the second was when he'd lifted up her T-shirt in daylight and he saw how her nipples were wine-colored like crowberries –

Starvation Cove
1848

In [hunting], as well as in their wars, they use nothing but firearms,
which they purchase of the English for skins. Bows and arrows are grown
into disuse, except only among their boys. Nor is it ill policy, but on the
contrary very prudent, thus to furnish the Indians with firearms, because
it makes them depend entirely upon the English, not only for their trade
but even for their subsistence. Besides, they were really able to do more
mischief when they made use of arrows, of which they would let silently
fly several in a minute with wonderful dexterity, whereas now they hardly
ever discharge their firelocks more than once, which they insidiously do
from behind a tree, and then retire as nimbly as the Dutch horse used to
do now and then formerly in Flanders.

WILLIAM BYRD, *Histories of the*
Dividing Line, entry for 7 April 1728

Now it was sunset, and the golden color of the tundra, the distinctness
of rock-angles, and his own shadow impossibly long, the rock he sat on, and
the grassy swale ahead – all these things reminded him of midnight at Pond
Inlet: the silhouettes of three laughing Inuit girls were crisp on the road-
horizon, and his shadow elongated into sameness. But somehow it was not
the same. All this time he'd been looking for a place where something began
or ended, and he wasn't anywhere nearer to it than he'd ever been; he was
only far from everything. The rock-wrinkles across the river were countable
every one, the length of his shadow almost infinite as the sun so gently came
to earth. What had his lust and her suffering all been for?

He reached out his hand, and the shadow of it touched something white
beyond the willows. He went to it and picked it up: – a Winchester twelve-
gauge "Western" shell.

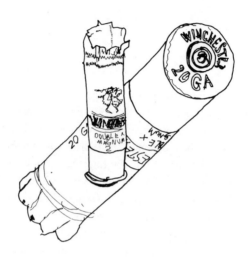

V
Northwest Passages

Lady Jane
1845

The name of Franklin alone is, indeed, a national guarantee.

SIR RODERICK MURCHISON,
President of the Royal Geographic
Society (1845)

*N*o, no, my dear Franklin (wrote Beaufort, enclosing a new edition of our North Polar Chart) *there is no chance, I assure you, of my forgetting one whose principles are exalted; whose feelings are pure, whose bland manner and frank temper are so winning; whose enterprises I admire; whose friendship I feel to be an honour; and whose affection for me I have never doubted, still less likely to do so when he is united to a woman with whom to be acquainted is to value and to love her and who may be said by an easy figure of speech to have doubled all the shining traits of his character.* It was this shine-doubler, Lady Jane Franklin, née Griffin, who now stood at the edge of the Thames, proudly watching her husband give the order to raise anchor. Like me, she had no doubt that he would be the man to complete the Northwest Passage. He wore the two hero's crosses on his breast; his face was pale, slow, yet resolute. A stream of fire or ribbon ran down his helmet. At fifty-nine years of age he was the Arctic explorer of greatest seniority; the reward was only fitting. (The Admiralty had asked Sir James first, but he, with the same generous grace as when he'd presented Jane with a gold bracelet from the Tasmanian Philosophical Society, had declined this new honor, saying he'd promised his wife not to venture the ice anymore – dear Sir James! He'd even troubled to speak with Secretary Parry, as she'd learned; Parry had gone straight to the First Lord to plead her husband's case, saying: If you don't let him go, the man will die of disappointment! – Not that she could ever tell John that.) It was such a delight for her that he had been chosen that the difficult aspects of the voyage were not to be thought of. He had supplies for three years, tinned by means of Goldner's new patent; his pennant was flying from the *Erebus;* and all London talked about nothing but him. The national horizon was expanding in advance. Sir James had once taken her aside, it is true, to ascertain truly whether she wanted her husband to get the appointment, for he desired only to serve her wishes; and Jane colored for no reason (a nervous habit of hers, which she seemed helpless to overcome), and replied: Do I wish it? I wish for nothing else! I wish it as I have never wished for anything in my whole life! – and Sir James smiled affably and said: Very good! And Sir John continues fit and hale, does he? – Of *course!* cried Jane quickly. Surely you do not see any signs that he has fallen off! – Oh, no, no, returned Sir James, fiddling with something in his pockets. – Jane now felt (she knew not why) that it was incumbent upon her to say something, and so she explained as best she could how important it was for her husband to be supported and fussed over a little, after the disappointments he'd lately had in Van Diemen's Land. – Well, you know, Lady Franklin, that all of us were very sorry about the shabby way in which he was treated by the Colonial Office ... – Yes, she said. Now let us speak no further on that subject, for it vexes me. – I quite agree, said good Sir James, whose friendship she would always treasure (indeed she'd hastened to put on the gold bracelet this morning, as soon as he was announced). But let us chat just a little more about the forthcoming voyage. You know that in the polar regions issues are always doubtful. Do you remember how Back was icebound for ten months? – Evidently he meant to say more, but her eyes flashed and she cried hotly: Why should you ask my opinion on such matters? You know that I am not sufficiently informed about them to speak correctly ... – at which he remembered how he had once inadvertently come between a male and female penguin in the Antarctic, and the female, thinking that her consort was under attack, had waddled toward him with terrified ferocity; so he bowed and said: Forgive me, Lady Franklin. – There were footsteps. Sir John had returned from his walk. Sir James had risen and was already smiling when his friend came in, kind and stouthearted Sir John with his egg-head and almost-smiling mouth – the naked chin complementing the naked crown, the moon-head rising above a night-landscape of uniformed shoulder ridges glistening with jeweled crosses and buttons. – It fits as well as ever! said the wife, while Franklin smiled a little sheepishly and took Sir James's hand. – The tailor refused to take a penny for it, he said. He asked me to bring some Esquimau mittens for his daughter ... Sir James, I am delighted! So you have come to us without Lady Ross? I must thank you for sending me those wolf-skin blankets! – and at once the two Arctic Friends were at it again, and Jane retired when they began to pore over the new chart of Lancaster Sound. Franklin thought Sir James wonderfully good to admire the map so unstintingly; his uncle, Sir John Ross, had been coerced by mirages in 1818, and so sealed off the Sound with a non-existent range, which he'd called the Croker Mountains; the resulting detours had delayed the attainment of the Northwest Passage most embarrassingly. But Sir James was too great a man (thought Franklin) to be pained by these old broils. When the appointment was confirmed, Franklin and Sir James replicated this purest cartography-happiness in company with the entire Arctic Council, on a certain ceremonious Saturday. The sea-charts and land-charts were unfolded upon a table, and all present felt the pounding of suspense in their hearts upon seeing their blue and yellow and white, and the names called to them and made them yearn as if for women (Lady Franklin was at home): – Great Bear Cape! – Meta Incognita Peninsula! Frozen Strait, Glacier Strait! There was old Point Turnagain – ah, and here was Fort Confidence where we began when we were younger. Winter Island, Icy Cape! – Lieutenant-Colonel Sabine the eminent magnetician was there; he promised to give the officers lessons once they were picked; it was vital that polar measurements be taken this season, when other surveyors were also recording observations around the globe; completing the Northwest Passage was the most important service yet to be performed toward that end ... Peel recapitulated his assent to everything ... Beaufort sported his hydrographer's badge ... It was all very brilliant. – Back was there with his spade-shaped sideburns, stooping over the maps and muttering that only nine hundred miles remained to be done. – Yes, it will be a mere jaunt, hissed Barrow in his ear. But I should tell you that I pushed for Fitzjames. You will understand that. – Back straightened. He frowned. – I beg your pardon, he said, but I consider Sir John Franklin to be an outstanding candidate. – Yes, well, that's impossible now, said Barrow vaguely, looking from side to side. But Lord Haddington was worried, too. About his *age*, you know. His *age*. – Poor Back was in agony. To listen to such talk about his former commander was extremely galling to him, but he could not walk away. Barrow was notoriously vindictive. Then, too, he felt a little pity for Barrow; Barrow's day was almost done ... – Well, I'll tell you something, laughed Barrow. The others all informed me that they were worried about *Fitzjames's* age. Only thirty-two, you see – too young for leadership. So I sought to get him appointed as second in command, at least, but no, they turn to

Stokes, GOD knows why; *he* refuses; then they must have Crozier, since he
had the *Terror* under Sir James there. Our dashing Sir James. Look how he
makes up to Lady Franklin. What? She isn't here? Quite a disappointment for
me, I have to tell you, Back. But finally I got him the *Erebus*. I just thought
you might like to know that. – Thank you for the information, sir, replied
Back, as coldly as he dared. His main aim in life now consisted in leaving this
coxcomb. A steward brought sherry-glasses on a silver tray. Grimacing
eagerly, Barrow reached out for one; he turned to his interlocutor and found
that Beaufort had interposed himself, being thirsty also. Back was swept
away, willy-nilly as it seemed; Barrow seized Beaufort by the arm and began
cawing in his ear . . . – Congratulations, Sir John! – Franklin turned
graciously. He knew that Back wanted to be taken loving notice of; he knew
that Back held him in the deepest and most unjealous affection, which he
did not deserve. And yet he derived no sustenance from it, because he could
not quite reciprocate it. Back was a wonderful fellow; he'd saved Franklin's
life in 1822, for which he'd been granted full credit in the official report. But
he was rash. It was an article of faith with Franklin that an officer in the
service of Her Majesty ought to give his life in any good cause, but to hazard
it for no reason was almost as detestable as to hoard it in cowardly fashion.
Never could he forget how Back had tried to fight a duel with poor Hood
over that Indian squaw, Greenstockings. Hepburn had taken the charges
from their pistols at the last moment. The idiocy of it! If Back and Hood had
both been killed or disabled in that wilderness, what then? Losing Hood had
been bad enough . . . – Have you dined, Sir John? said Back. – Yes, I
have dined, thank you, said Franklin. – Then he was a little ashamed, as
Back had been with Barrow, and said: One day soon before my departure
we must dig out your sketchbooks again; Lady Franklin would love to review
the colored views . . . – And who was ashamed confronting *him?* Would it
be too arch if I said that his name began with S? – On the 8th of May 1845,
he brought the officers to meet the Lords of the Admiralty, and his wife
attended also, at Barrow's request. Back was ready with his sketchbooks;
Secretary Parry made them all listen again to a recital (now as smooth-worn
as a narwhal's horn) of how he'd wintered on Melville Island in 1819. – The
ice was seven inches thick in September, my lads, but we amused ourselves
with a newspaper and theatricals; I was entirely satisfied; there were plenty of
musk-oxen to eat. I envy you the experience, Sir John. Are you taking plenty
of chocolate? I have found chocolate to be of inestimable value in the cold
regions . . . – Chocolate? laughed Franklin. More than nine hundred
pounds!

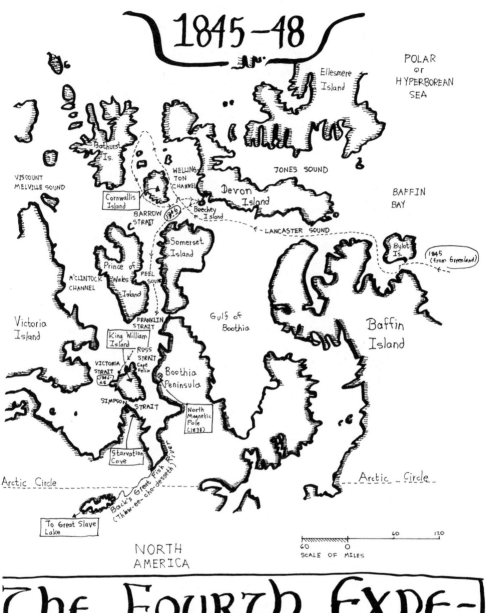

1845-48

POLAR
or
HYPERBOREAN
SEA

Ellesmere
Island

Bathurst
Is.

JONES SOUND

WELLING-
TON
CHANNEL

Devon
Island

BAFFIN
BAY

VISCOUNT
MELVILLE SOUND

Cornwallis
Island

BARROW
STRAIT

Beechey
Island

LANCASTER SOUND

Somerset
Island

Bylot
Is.

1845
(from Greenland)

Prince of
Wales
Island

M'CLINTOCK
CHANNEL

PEEL
SOUND

FRANKLIN
STRAIT

Gulf of
Boothia

Baffin
Island

Victoria
Island

King William
Island

ROSS
STRAIT

VICTORIA
STRAIT

Cape
Felix

Boothia
Peninsula

SIMPSON   STRAIT

North
Magnetic
Pole
(1831)

Starvation
Cove

Arctic Circle

Arctic — Circle

Back's Great Fish River
(Thlew-ee-cho-desseth)

To Great Slave
Lake

NORTH
AMERICA

60   120

60   O
SCALE OF MILES

The Fourth Expe-dition

The Fourth Expedition:
STARVATION COVE
1845-1848

Selected List

	H.M.S. Erebus	H.M.S. Terror
Officers	Sir John Franklin, Captain (and Commander of the Expedition)	Francis R. M. Crozier, Captain
	James Fitzjames, Commander	
Lieutenants	Mr. Graham Gore	Mr. Edward Little
	Mr. H.T.D. Le Vesconte	Mr. John Irving
	Mr. James W. Fairholme	Mr. George H. Hodgson
Mates	Mr. Robert O. Sargent	
	Mr. Charles F. Des Voeux	
Surgeons	Dr. Harry D.S. Goodsir (Acting)	Dr. John S. Peddie
Ice-Masters	Mr. James Reid	Mr. Thomas Blanky
Petty Officers	The Finnlander Kid, Captain of the Forecastle	Mr. David MacDonald, Quartermaster
	Mr. Edmund Hoar, Captain's Steward	Mr. John Diggle, Cook
	Mr. Thomas Watson, Carpenter's Mate	Mr. John Torrington, Leading Stoker
Men		
Able Seamen	John Stickland	
	John Hartnell	
Privates, Royal Marines	William Braine	
	Seth	

Jane flushed again. She could not imagine why.

Sir James, whose eye was always on her, came up to her and asked her if she would join him in a glass of champagne and some cheese – for, he said, all this talk of cold and chocolate made him hungry.

Why did Franklin go north again? We who are interested in him mainly for his gruesome death believe that he did it to die, that he possessed a morbid lemming's heart whose ventricles were rimmed most dismally. Subzero believed that he did it for love, or perhaps to solve the world's problems (that is, Reepah's), to solve them as exactly as a differential equation, meanwhile avoiding the solution of his own. Of course Franklin himself, who is myself, never thought in those terms. I had nothing but a heart-shaped heat of good feeling to motivate my chest, and this was enough, as it is nowadays for test pilots and crash pilots: – the existence of danger in and of itself is no lure, danger being incomprehensible to men of my stamp; what attracts me, rather, is the happy solitude of endeavor with which danger is associated. I don't know how many times I've dreamed of walking (either alone or else in advance of my family, my friends, my people) across a flat and pebbly plain sugared most thinly with snow. In my dreams the air is mild, and the smell of the wind is sweet. I am approaching my lodestar. When I wake up I am smiling joyously.

But nowadays Reepah comes into my thoughts every hour, and my heart aches because bad things are happening to her even at this moment, and so I ought to be doing something, but when she calls me on the phone I can never quite understand which jail she is in now, where they've taken the baby, what she did with that gun, and I want to help her come to peace in my arms but the only way I can imagine doing that is to help her die and I do not want to do that because her heart beats with beautiful life and I do not want to scare her anymore. These thoughts, which cannot impell me into any useful trajectory, but only maintain me in steady polar orbit, cannot in any way be compared with my dream-thoughts when I trekked northward rifleless. But I did go, accepting their imperfection, and so did he.

And though his friends warned him, he only smiled and quoted to them Phaethon's epitaph in Ovid:

HIC STVS EST PHAETHON
CVRRVS AVRIGA PATERNI
QVEM SI NON TENVIT MAGNIS
TAMEN EXCIDIT AVSIS.*

On Sunday the 18th, Sir John Franklin gathered together his crews and read them Divine service, which Lady Franklin and Eleanor, his daughter by his previous (dead) wife of the same name, also attended; and he asked the merciful guidance and protection of GOD to be extended over them all; and he asked GOD also to aid those who would be left at home, at which Subzero, stealing a glance upward, saw a single tear at half-mast upon the marble cheek of Lady Franklin. The following morning they set sail. Eleanor was standing beside her stepmother. – Look! she whispered; and Jane, following the line that instantaneously shot out from the girl's pointing finger, saw a dove settling on one of the masts. The sailors observed it, too, and remarked upon it gladly. Then the two ships began to draw away, and Jane saw her husband standing on the bridge, smiling at her most fondly, dwindling now, failing; and she never saw him again.

---

* "Here lies Phaethon. His SUN-FATHER's car he drove, and though he did not triumph, still he greatly strove."

Stromness Harbour

... every man may find a home and occupation suited to his taste; none should yield to the natural impatience sure to result from our past life of excitement and adventure. You will be invited to seek new adventures abroad; do not yield to the temptation, for it will lead only to death and disappointment.

GENERAL WILLIAM T. SHERMAN, to
his departing troops (1865)

He was in his stateroom when Commander Fitzjames came to report that the Orkneys were in sight; this he acknowledged with a vague smile. Sighing a little, he came out and stood at the rail with Fitzjames, Gore and Sargent while they docked. The *Terror* stood a little behind, out of respect for him, so his ship was the first of the two to send forth ropes to kiss this last bit of the homeland, and he went ashore with the brave and jaunty look they expected of him, shaking hands, thanking the people for their welcome, kissing babies with more sincerity than the best politician, making arrangements with the *Baretto Junior* to follow them to Greenland with ten live oxen. As soon as he could, he got away, delegating matters to Fitzjames and Crozier. The streets were dirty white with trodden snow, and the sky was the same color. The Bradley Air terminal was a vague grey silhouette in the fog. Everything was mournful and biting cold, as it usually was in Resolute (the Environment Canada people said that it had been −16°C the previous night). The season, in short, was especially good. The door yielded inward to his palm. In the heat of the terminal he basked moment by moment like an animal, inhaling like incense the stale cigarette smoke, admiring the black and white photographs of royalty, listening to the incandescent lights hum while outside a nasty little breeze throbbed, waiting to pierce him to the bone, and the ocean was so frigid a blue as to make him shiver as he looked at it, and the islands glowed white and yellow in the ominous light, and the wind increased.

He put a quarter in the pay phone and the operator said: *Bonjour?*

He gave her the number and placed a collect call.

He heard his wife's voice say hello.

Let me assure you, my dearest Jane, that I am amply provided with every requisite for my passage . . .

We are already planning the triumphal banquet, she said. Do you want me to invite Back or not? I know your views on his character, but Sir James says –

We must not anticipate, said Franklin as kindly as he could. Pray to GOD as I do, and things will turn out as they must. I feel great happiness in my officers and men.

Outside there was hoarfrost on the fences and spools of cable, on the tent guys, on frozen poppy-stalks (where it was very beautiful). An air beacon waxed and waned in the fog. Over the sea, the fog was purplish grey, like a bruise. Over the snow it glared white, hurting his eyes.

He strolled about and discovered an old Quonset hut full of stinking scraps of insulation. The sign on it said **OUT OF BOUNDS.**

Checking his watch, he was quite satisfied that the welcoming committee would still be at it. Fitzjames, who was well trained, would tell them that Sir John was suffering from a touch of influenza –

He returned to the empty terminal to warm himself, and the phone rang.

Hello? he said.

John?

He knew her voice at once – elfin, shy, flirtatious. He was so happy.

You come to me? she said.

Yes.

She hesitated. – I'm scared!

Of what?

Of you! – She laughed. – Bring one beer. Just one.

I'll try.

Thank you! Thank you!

(After that, much of his dread went away. He'd been alarmed, however, when he'd caught a chill in London and Jane had unthinkingly covered his knees with the flag she was sewing and he shouted at her: Don't you know that they lay the Union Jack over a corpse?)

Any polar bears there? he said. Nanoq?

Nothing.

He expelled a breath of relief.

John?

Yes.

I have my own apartment now.

Where's your family?

I don't want to see them again.

Don't they live with you?

They're camping now. On the land. I have my own place now. You want to stay with me?

Yes. Yes!

I only have one bed – for me and my baby.

That's OK.

He wanted to give her something sexy and lovely like no one had ever given her.

Usually when he put his Captain Subzero pack onto his shoulders before a trip, the weight of it oppressed him. This time he threw it on with a joyous shout.

And the Quonset huts of Resolute glowed orange and green despite the falling snow.

Hide and Seek

Most people come to think of ice and snow when Greenland is mentioned – the inland ice that air travelers see on flights between North America and Northwest Europe, the icebergs known from pictures and descriptions. All these factors do make up a central part of the impression tourists receive of Greenland. Nevertheless, they only create the setting for the ice-free coastal areas visited by tourists.

DANISH TOURIST BOARD/
GREENLAND HOME RULE
AUTHORITIES tourist pamphlet
(*ca.* 1987)

She began to worry about him long before the Admiralty evinced any churnings of unconfidence. The ominousness was akin to Cornwallis Island reddish-grey below the fog. She could not even see the fog yet, much less Cornwallis Island, because she was as an Arctic airline passenger riding high in sunny blueness, having no idea how cold that blueness was, and the cloud-pavement far below was lovely; she had no notion that it was actually the roof of the fog, the grave of fog in which Cornwallis Island lay buried. She went through his old letters to her and reread them; she remembered how in Tasmania he'd gotten out of the bullock cart when it got stuck in the mud and walked along beside it, and she'd worried about the poor animal with the heavy load and wanted to get out, too, but her husband would not hear of her exerting herself in that fashion; he was always a gentleman. And he had a most gentlemanly set of officers. Beaufort and Sir James hadn't chosen to serve this time, which was a shame, and rather small of them – although of course they were extremely devoted – but C^mdr Fitzjames would certainly see to her husband's needs, and C^apt Crozier on the *Terror* was also very able. She had not forgotten the good omen, the dove on the mast. She sat rereading his letters, while her father, equally bereft because she was not with *him*, reread hers: ... *The island seems to be in a most flourishing condition – everybody growing rich, the convicts behaving well, etc.*

Day after year, year after day, she was kept company by her husband's niece, Sophy. (Her stepdaughter Eleanor held herself aloof; it could not be denied that she dissented somewhat jealously from Jane's position – as if Jane had *supplanted* Eleanor, simply because Eleanor's mother had died! Really it was painful.)

And what do you think he is doing now, Sophy? (Thus Lady Jane.)

Surely they've set up their winter camp. Oh, Auntie, it will be so wonderful to hear him tell his stories about it once more – how they pour down hot sand when the decks ice over, and make a promenade; how they put up the canvas to make things cozy ... I *do* hope your monkey hasn't caught cold!

The men will take care of her. Do you remember that last letter we had from Greenland, when Captain Fitzjames described so entertainingly how they'd already made her a frock and trousers?

And I suppose they are shooting musk-oxen when they find them. That part always makes me a little sad. They are such magnificent animals, wild though they are, and Uncle says that hunting them is no sport with a rifle –

Yes, Sophy, necessity is cruel sometimes.

I would very much like to see one alive. Do you think that Uncle will bring one back for display?

It would be much too warm for him here, I'm afraid.

But Scotland has a chilly climate, Auntie, and there's ever so much moss for him to eat –

Sophy, are you truly such a silly girl, or do you think up such things to distract me?

No, I –

I am not afraid to hear you speak your mind. My faith in my husband will scarcely be overthrown by anything you could possibly say.

I –

Oh, Sophy, it has been such a long, long time.

The Admiralty sent Captain Henry Kellet in due course, not by any means to *relieve* the man who was our national guarantee and needed no relief, but simply to stifle a few whispers. He found no sign. Neither did Sir James (torn away from his wife at last), nor Rae and Richardson. Then came the announcement of the £20,000 reward. Lady Jane got more than sixty churches to hold public prayers for the expedition one day in 1849. Collinson and

McClure went through the Bering Strait (from which a few Arctic Friends still expected Franklin to emerge any day now); Austin scoured Lancaster Sound; Grinnell came with the blessings of the US Navy; Sir James and Mr Rae went back again . . . It was Penny who found the three graves on Beechey Island, after Austin's second-in-command discovered an empty cairn. (All the cairns would prove empty, save one.) The ships wintered over, and sent sledge parties across the frozen sea when spring came. They visited Cornwallis Island, where Resolute was not even a bad idea yet; they returned to Devon Island, where the Austin Expedition men had found a few meat-tins; they made the rounds of islands – ah, Russell and Melville and chilly Bathurst; they paid a call to Prince of Wales but found nothing to justify their disturbance of its frozen state; they traversed Victoria, where they were getting warm but did not know it, so they turned around and with every step drew farther from King William Island where the bones could get nothing but colder as the searchers got colder. The next year Lady Jane sent Kennedy to Regent's Inlet; when he discovered nothing, she sponsored Inglefield's voyage to Jones Sound; as meanwhile Belcher was searching everywhere; Grinnell came back under Kane; McClure tried again, too, but had to abandon his ice-gripped ships . . .

When no one else hoped anymore, when the Admiralty announced that her husband and his men would now be withdrawn from the books and considered to have died in Her Majesty's Service, then Jane threw off the mourning which she had been wearing for so many years, and dressed herself in bright colors, for a desperate febrile protest . . . Rae had scoured the Boothia Peninsula that time, and sent full report of the Inuit tales. *Sir John, we now know, sleeps his last sleep by the shores of those icy seas whose barriers he in vain essayed to overcome.* – Thus the *Toronto Globe*. What Sophy thought of this we do not know. But Jane outfitted one more relief ship with the remains of her fortune. The Crimean War had started; not too many people attended when the *Fox* went out. But this time the record in the cairn was found, and so were the skeletons. We'd reached King William Island at last.

As for me, it seems so typical of life that when I met a man at a literary occasion and we had both been drinking, he started talking about the Franklin Expedition and slyly hinting at all the film footage he had at home showing the frozen bodies, whose faces resembled that black lichen I once saw in Iqaluit that was dappled with green like a frog's back; he was connected with the forensic team somehow; he gave me his number – but when I called him a month later he was very formal and chilly because it was his work number at the advertising agency and all he had was a videotape of a TV program.

The Meaning of His Bones
1990

As usual under such circumstances, I frequently had to drop on my knees and dig with my knife until I found whether I was on ice or land.

> VILHJALMUR STEFANSSON, *The Friendly Arctic* (1916)

In Povungnituk, on a mild day roofed with cloud, the white people were digging a gravel pit and found the bodies of two young girls from thirty years ago. They were skeletonized rather than mummified; the permafrost in POV is not more than five feet thick. Their names were Reepah and Jukee. The bulldozers stopped; the white people sighed and checked their watches and asked around. There were some old people who still remembered the dead girls. (That was how they did things in POV, or at least how they used to: when someone died, you covered her over, without erecting any kind of marker. Someone would remember where she was for as long as it mattered.) The old man said that the girls had wanted to go to a party. Their parents were worried about the weather, but the girls begged and so they finally let them go. The girls were happy now. They washed their hair and faces. They put their kamiks on. They drew on their hand-worked mittens, hooded themselves, and rushed out laughing and waving. The mother and father stood in the doorway watching them vanish, but it is not possible to see oneself melt away because vision melts, too. The blizzard came, so snow hummocked them; so more snow made the hummocks smooth (the snow had held its breath as it lovingly filled in their footprints); so snow fell on snow; so their parents sat waiting; so spring came; so their parents found them and buried them under gravel and grief; so thirty summers cooked the meat and fat from their darling bones; thirty winters ached inside their hand-bones and shoulder-bones; thirty thousand frosts locked themselves in their snowy-white teeth, until the white people unburied them; so the white people radioed the Mayor to find out what to do; so they read their books to find out what to do; so their *Eskimo Grammar* said to them: *Are you cold? Are you a poor little cold thing? – I'm very cold. Because you're a nice little white man.* – So now the white people built a fence around the two dead girls and dumped some gravel on top of them, but the rest of the gravel they dug from the pit, because they needed gravel for roads . . . – And you, when you feel lost and evil, where do *you* go to find your good self? I doubt if the titter of some moss-bird does wonders for your confidence. It may be that every soul's goodness lies, skeletonized or not, beneath a particular net of lichens and crowberries – discover that, and you have the magic bullet. But how many gravel-pits must you tear up to get it? – Franklin's case was the more simple one of being ice-bound. Captivity frees one from the anguish of a liberty bereft of the good: "all that" is something to worry about later, after the return home (which isn't really home, but leave *that*). It is for this reason, I believe, that ex-prisoners and ex-soldiers attend nostalgic reunions, that hardship is glamorous generally (as long as it lies in the past or the future, like the girls' skeletons now out of sight again, but comfortingly known by their fence, which gives us 1960 when they died, 1990 when they were dug up, 2020, say, when some new technological cataclysm will expose them once again); that is certainly why Subzero enjoyed *being* Franklin, being now occupied only by physical constraints, as when the mercury of their thermo-meter froze entirely on the Second Expedition, en route to Fort Chipewyan in 1821; yet they still completed a winter journey of eight hundred and fifty-seven miles. The dogs pranced across the ice as Mr Franklin's men slid the canoes along, and Navy men strode to and fro with shouldered muskets. Mr Franklin stood upon an icy rock, observing the proceedings, since it scarcely became an officer to perform manual labor. Being now a captive of the cold, he was unhindered from remembering his summer liberty, the fleet floating down the wide Slave River, piercing pine-crowned cliff-reflections as easily as ghosts. The voyageurs were scattered across the water in their square-sailed canoes; the Indians paddled their crafts smoking pipes, and Mr Franklin stood with his seamen in the thirty-two-foot birchbark canoe which had been specially manufactured for him, and he made his calculations and they entered a deep bay of the Great Slave Lake, but he was restless, being occupied by the longing for the skeleton of his good self. He had not married Jane yet. He had not even married Eleanor. Once winter came and the mercury froze, however, the gravel congealed hard over these unfortunate longings and he came to his senses, remembering the summer, as I have said, with yearning impossible now to satisfy, and therefore unalloyed. Beside him stood Tattannaæuk, his Esquimau interpreter, whom he called Augustus; he loved the boy well, and stroked his black bangs. But he must restrain him from wandering off in search of game; they had no time for that, hungry or not. By the time they achieved Fort Enterprise in the Land of Little Sticks, the men were starving in the snow, feebly seeking putrid deerskins or rock-tripe to boil . . . Mr Franklin, now moon-bald, stood with his hand on his hip, gazing far away. He was very thin; he thought he was dying. His epaulets were glittering cliffs on his shoulders.

He said to himself: I need to stop being selfish. (And he remembered how on that second expedition of his an Indian woman had caught an excellent pike through a hole in the ice, and none of the Indians would eat of it, saying to him: We are accustomed to starvation, but you are not.)

He dwelled upon the future proceedings of his life and said: I need to do something noble.

How may I best love and assist both Jane and Reepah?

What hopes and expectations can I hold for my own conduct?

After having observed Back and Hood quarreling over that squaw Greenstockings; after having weighed all the arguments pro and contra, I must say it: I cannot relinquish Jane for Reepah. (The first night that Greenstockings let him fuck her, Mr Hood dreamed of a vagina like an orange slit in grey clouds, bleeding red across the sky below.) Knowing Reepah's disposition and mine, I believe that in the long run a rupture would be unavoidable. – But maybe not, if I were less selfish . . . ? Ah, this hope of Reepah is extraordinarily painful to part with –

He spread Reepah's legs. (You had the satisfaction of knowing you'd done exactly the right thing! said good Seth. You couldn't have done anything else.) In the midst of the moss, softer than it, a sweet grey lake. Around it, sloping shelves of stone (she was hard-scarred where twenty other men had hurt her). The geese called overhead; the mosquitoes whined desperately. All around, the world was a disk, swelling with rocky lumps almost like mesas, but lower; the horizon, almost featureless, went steadily round, and around this world-circle (as the Norse would have called it) lay a grey cloud-circle to match, lifted up like a skillfully cut swatch of moss. Small black birds darted with kissing sounds. The river made a steady noise like sifting gravel. In a world such as this, any direction was as good as another. Sometimes the sun came close enough to breaking through the clouds to form a white hole of glare, and then the lake became almost grey-green, and the horizon was ribboned with indigo. But by the time he and his men reached the next lake, grey-green was grey again.

Well, was he selfish or not? – I forgot to mention that once he even flew her down to New York – I mean London. It was not long before the final expedition of which we are about to speak, when he went to Reepah and dwelled with her forever. (Let's salute him: three guns and eight cheers!) The visit was very sweet for him (I believe that Jane was away, addressing the Ladies' Society for the Relief of Van Diemen's Land.) Months afterward, whenever he was walking with Jane and he saw somebody walking a dog on the sidewalk ahead, he'd draw her in to him and turn to reassure her, the act as automatic as taking a blind person's arm at the crosswalk, because Reepah had been afraid of the New York dogs. In Inukjuak as in Resolute dogs were not pets but sled-haulers, unruly, vicious and dangerous; there were stories of starving dogs devouring children; he didn't know whether they were true but a husky had bitten Reepah when she was little and she knew very well how all the dogs in town whined and growled whenever anyone came too close to their tethers, so whenever Reepah said to him: I want secrets! I want around! and he pulled on his rubberized Sorels and she pulled on her kamiks and they rode the elevator down, hand in hand, and went out into the snow to get her cigarettes, then she'd be beside him smiling in amazement at everything, not holding his hand, until there was a dog; it didn't make any difference whether it was a great golden retriever or an old lady's tiny rodentlike beagle in its pink sweater; Reepah giggled in fright and rushed to whatever side of him was farther away from the dog; she'd seize his hand and peek around him as they came abreast of the dog, tensing as if to run; as soon as they would pass she'd pull away from him again and be happy at his side. At first he tried reassurances both empirical and theoretical, telling her that the dogs were pets, that they had never bitten him, that they were leashed, that if they bit someone their owners would be in trouble, but none of this convinced her

– nor should it, as he told himself; how would *he* feel if he were in Inukjuak and a polar bear came waddling toward him down the street; would he believe someone who said that it was tame? So he developed the habit of always watching for dogs on the sidewalk, and whenever he first saw one – half a block ahead, maybe – he'd put his arm around her and say in her ear: Look, Reepah! Dog! so that she would not be suddenly frightened; after Reepah was gone this instinct was not easy to eradicate; at least he did not say anything to Jane but his arm could not help itself from steadying her against the panic that she did not feel at all; at such times he felt a strange shame, less sharp than abidingly deep. She must have noticed how at certain times on their walks he now reached out for her with uncertain motions, then withdrew, as if out of confidence with himself; yet she surely supposed him to be abstracted in his polar thoughts (so he supposed). In general his motions were straightforward and decisive. She remembered again how the bullock-cart had gotten mired in Tasmania and he had gotten out with the two young men to lighten it and she had asked whether she should not get out, too, in order to assist the poor animal; – don't even *think* of it, my dearest love, said he, and his hand had flown to her shoulder and it was not at all the way that his hand hovered now . . . – But always look on the bright side of the question, he said to himself; she said the same. – Perhaps this was a crisis that he was avoiding, but it was not like the ones to which he was accustomed, when one could say to oneself: If my resolution is weak, it is because I do not have enough chocolate and fat to eat!

I am sure that something is troubling you, my dear.

No, Jane. No.

Is it about that expedition to complete the Northwest Passage? I could speak with Sir James if you wish it; I'm sure he would put in a word for you; it is only just that you receive the command . . .

That is in GOD's hands, my dearest love. There is no need for us to abase ourselves before others. – He said these words as calmly and meekly as he could, but she who knew him so well (so much better than he knew her) could feel his pain like some low and persistent vibration, and her heart ached.

He went to Sir James alone and asked him what he should do. He admitted that he dreamed about Reepah every night, that his thoughts grew toward her, leafing like heart-shaped sorrel, that he loved Jane as he loved Reepah, and Jane was his lawfully wedded wife, but Reepah was so sweet . . .

I quite agree, said Sir James (he always agreed before he spoke his mind), but how could you manage the thing and keep your honor? And doubtless this Esquimau squaw is gentle and lovely, but after a year with her you'd go mad! My dear Franklin, think – please think – of Jane . . .

When Lady Franklin appealed to him on her husband's behalf, Sir James Ross felt himself to be in a very difficult position. On the one hand, there was the matter of Reepah – who existed, of course, only to the extent that Sir John was Subzero; and precisely to that extent Sir John was beyond Sir James's ken – another sort of creature entirely, from another time! – but she existed nonetheless, and so his friend Sir John was not entirely Sir John anymore. To assist him in returning to Reepah's latitudes was nothing less than connivance with time travel and adultery! – And yet Lady Franklin in her innocence would be so disappointed if he did not go . . . – Then too there was the matter of his own preferences. A gentleman puts these aside in favor of others whenever he can, of course, but by GOD he *did* think that he too had some right to complete the Passage! – A gentleman is a gentleman: he gave way to Sir John, or rather to his wife. – As for this matter of Reepah, here I must confess to have been indulging in historical reconstruction. Such thoughts could only have occurred to Sir James if time works both ways – that is, if simply because Subzero came to be the reincarnation of Franklin, Franklin must then have become (to however slight an extent) identified with Subzero in some manner. Ask yourself: are you behaving differently at this very moment because someone not yet to be born for a century or more will someday think about you? You cannot prove the contrary. – What's the difference anyway whether it's so? Ice-floes, no matter how white, and water, no matter how blue or grey, eventually reach the same color in the distance.

A few weeks afterward they spoke of the matter again, more obliquely, on an excursion to Woolwich Dockyard where the *Terror* and the *Erebus* were being careened. Sir James had certain suggestions to make about alterations. – They will be very superior, no doubt, with these screw-propellers of Captain Beechey's, but I wonder how you'll make room for them.

Our quarters will necessarily be a little closer, said Franklin with a quiet smile.

Excuse me, my friend, said Sir James, but there I must disagree with you a little. Quarters must be closer, as a general rule, but not in your case. Remember, the expedition is under your command . . . !

Franklin smiled again, this time pitying Sir James, who thought – who always *had* thought – that to set a commanding example one must sport some goiter of enlarged privilege; when the best way to lead, as he'd learned in the Barren Grounds, was to sacrifice the most for the others' sake.

I know what you are thinking, said Sir James, and he did. But I spent four years in the Antarctic with these very ships – forgive me for reminding you of it – and I found that my cabin was none too large; I'm speaking not for myself but for my officers; I put the place at their disposal at certain times; they needed a place to spread themselves out a little, so that they wouldn't become melancholic. That's how scurvy begins. Your overland expeditions were soft and easy compared to that. It's not the danger that I'm talking about. You've had plenty of that! But when you winter in the pack-ice . . .

It will certainly be tedious and inconvenient, said Franklin. But, you know, it's not so far from Lancaster Sound to Simpson's Strait. While I would never boast to others, Ross, the truth is that I'm very hopeful of slipping through the Passage in one season –

And for all that you might, returned Sir James quite sharply. But just think of your officers, man! Maybe one winter, maybe two! And then after you reach the Pacific, you'll be returning by Cape Horn – why, you could be gone for six years, and all the time in those two ships! I *know* those ships!

What you say is true. But we shall steel ourselves, with perseverance and practice. Anyhow, I admit you've made me look at things in a different light. There must be a little oasis where the officers can tabulate their observations – He hesitated for a moment. – Forgive me, Ross. I know that you are right . . .

Sir James clapped a hand upon his shoulder. He knew that his friend had entered on one of those moods of self-deprecation to which he was prone, and Sir James began racking himself to find a way to encourage him, but before he had made much progress Franklin said: Tell me the truth. Is it as bad as that, in the ice?

Yes.

I remember my first real experience with ice, said Franklin. It was twenty-nine years ago now, on the *Trent*. We were compelled to dart through a channel that we could barely see – the darkness was so peculiar and thick – and I remember how the ship's bell was tolling as we lurched, so I directed the officers to muffle it, in order not to increase the despondency of the men, and then we struck ice –

No, one never forgets that sound of smashing wood, when you strike, and you listen for the sound of rushing water to tell you that you're dead. I recommend iron sheeting for this voyage, Franklin; I heartily recommend it.

I think you're right. And this new system of heating with seawater –

No, I'm in favor of that. I wish that we'd had that in the Antarctic. It seems to me ingenious without being dangerous –

GOD bless you for your kindness to me, Ross! GOD bless you!

And GOD be with you, my dear friend. But it is not goodbye yet. Listen, you must invite Parry down here. He'll take the keenest interest; he adores being the Comptroller of Steam Machinery. It would be a good deed. He's getting old –

There was a silence.

The Rifles

Apart from the interest of the narrative, and its intrinsic merits, the deep interest, which for years has been felt in the fate of Sir John Franklin, will attract attention to the story of his early adventures, now, for the first time, presented in a cheap and readable shape.

Preface to *Thirty Years in the Arctic Regions* (1859)

Now you want me to get to the point of it; you fail to see why we've unzipped each other's pants to embark on the Fourth Expedition but then regressed to the Second; like Mr Back and the other explorers you don't see what Reepah has to do with anything; you want to watch Mr Franklin die; and you will (you know me), but not yet, because we are not fully armed for the destruction of this Sixth Age of Vinland, the Age of the Rifles which I have not yet been able to explain but *must* explain in order for you to know why the capital of Vinland is Resolute; Mr Franklin did not have so much to do with this; the French in earlier times had known exactly what they were doing when they introduced firearms into Canada, but by Mr Franklin's time the rifles were spreading faster than smallpox and it was too late to be anything but a dupe; it was merely his weird death that brought us to the Arctic for good, first in the form of search parties, and then as traders, missionaries, police, resettlement administrators, our purpose long and sharp and spiraled like a narwhal horn; and the only reason that Mr Franklin is germane at all has to do with a certain coincidence of rifles and starvation that I cannot put out of my mind; the whole business is so sad that I do not want to begin, but everywhere you walk there are rifle shells . . . – maybe if we begin we can stop before the end comes.

Human inertia and stupidity, the two most powerful forces in history (except perhaps for hate) greet us in a bright mirror finish when we turn our attention to the repeaters – and I am not even talking about the stupidity of their use; we are hardly that far along yet; let us simply admire the stupidity of their development. Time after time, the notion of a repeater approaches praxis, only to be aborted by the skepticism of Kings and ordnance boards to whom the entirely subordinate character of all guns other than cannon is as indisputable as the flatness of the earth.* What good is an arquebus in the thick of a charge, when between shots the soldier must reload the ball, tamp the gunpowder into place, tear off a hunk of match and strike his flint? Then, too, it's obvious that a one-man gun can be neither powerful nor accurate. Feed the bullet too much powder, and the barrel explodes; what smith could fashion a sure safe barrel that wouldn't be too heavy to carry? And how could the marksman prevent the ball from being deflected by its own irregularity, or by a scratch in the barrel, or by any other cause? Pity the poor soldier, then, trying to reload and aim, while the unencumbered enemy lunges forward to run him through!

Arquebuses are fine in Canada, of course, when you use them to kill people who only have bows and arrows. The People of KLUSKAP discovered that, and so did the People of the Longhouse.† And they work even better against game animals. But in Europe, though the castle-masters do hunt stags and boars from time to time, the real use of weapons is against Huguenots, or Catholics, or Calvinists, or Lutherans, or Frenchmen, or Englishmen; and they have weapons, too, so we must improve ours.

In a manuscript codex dated 1432, we see a Hussite war wagon, on whose banner a webfooted bird surveys the rear most unfeelingly; below his pinions is a terrace of cannon, beneath which the war-horses peer cautiously around a tent. At the fore is a breastworks prowed like a ship, girdled round with great chained wheels; chubby crossbowmen kneel behind it, with their caps pulled low over their eyes. Their baby faces are earnest, serene. On the triangular deck between them and the horse-tent stands a solitary man erect, with a hand-cannon clapped to his shoulder, like a bundle of logs. Its multiple barrels meet in a single dark tunnel of powder. This must be how it is: He kneels behind the bowmen while the enemy arrows fly; steadfastly he loads each barrel in turn. Now for the powder and match. He strikes a spark, leaps

---

* "It is a not commonly known characteristic of some explosive materials that the more powerful the explosive, the more difficult it is to initiate" – Karl O. Brauer, *Handbook of Pyrotechnics* (1974).
† This story was told in the Second Dream, *Fathers and Crows*.

to his feet, and faces the foe, his heart pounding as the hissing fuse holds him in the eternity of comets and shooting stars (which Alaskan Inuit call "stardung"); a horse shies, another horse nuzzles a wheel, and the cannoneer braces himself and wedges his ordnance more tightly into the hollow between neck and shoulder, already bruised black by previous shots; now the spark reaches the powder and explodes down every barrel; the lead balls sizzle through the air, and maybe one takes somebody's head off and another ricochets off a rock and the third breaks a horse's leg and who knows where the fourth one goes? Dazed and deafened, the cannoneer finds himself on his back, his head sore, and the horses whicker softly over him. Already the crossbowmen are letting fly again, and he rubs his bleeding ears and begins to reload –

How important was he really? Well, I count one of him, and five crossbowmen. So was he worth as much as five, or was his puissance but one-fifth? Ask the Emperor. Ask Maxmilian I, who, watching the clock begin to strike the end of the fifteenth century, received the world's first rifle, its bronze barrel bored and grooved by hand. – Ah, those clever Germans! In only a few centuries they'd invent barbed wire . . . – When the ball whirled through the grooves, it flew straighter, faster and farther. Maximilian, we may assume, went in person to thank Master Smith, who was caught off guard (or pretended to be – how inconspicuous can Kings be?), Master Smith polishing the trigger-haven in the stock most assiduously, with light coming in through his double-arch.

Anyhow, Maximilian came in. The man fell to his knees, yes, yes.

Rise! said the Emperor. This matchlock – magnificent!

I thank Your Highness. And there is more that I can do –

Of course. You are ambitious; that is only professional.

I could make a repeater, Your Highness.

A repeater? But why, good man? I have crossbowmen for that.

So the value of the sad hand-cannoneer was but one-fifth. And looking into his face in that engraving, I think that he knew it. But he did not abandon the war-wagon at the crisis, and the wagon creaked on. In 1600, Denmark became the first country to adopt rifles for military use. Da Vinci had already suggested that ball and powder be combined in a single paper cartridge, but that was impractical in a rifle; it was hard enough to force the ball alone into the barrel and down those dark snake-trails of grooves. No, that had to wait, but it came. Who can say when and how? The Scotsman William Drummond took actualization to absurdity by constructing a gun with fifty barrels. After him we must whirl through a blurred paradise of rotating breeches and

multiple barrels connected by dozens of obscure vents, which produced
repeater effects by dint of carefully prearranged sequences of unique events,
not yet the steady sameness of a replicated cycle; but the Kalthoff brothers
scrutinized developments with an unequivocal European eye and developed
breech-loading magazine repeaters. Peter Kalthoff's wheel-lock version,
dated 1645, bears this inscription: **The First**. – Was it really? – In that year
the Huron were being slaughtered by Iroquois armed with Dutch guns; the
Iroquois saw no need for repeaters, but an Englishman named Palmer did: in
1663 he addressed the Royal Society, insisting that the explosive energies of
powder within a rifle could be utilized to work some mechanism which
would click successive cartridges into the chamber with all the inevitability of
good or bad fortune; everyone scoffed at Palmer for a pathetic perpetual-
motionist. Exactly a quarter-century later, one Abraham Soyer was arrested
in Paris as a possible spy; in his luggage the gendarmes discovered a pistol
which functioned after Palmer's principles. In 1718 James Paddle patented a
single-barreled tripod gun, made divine by a revolving breech which could be
cranked from chamber to chamber nine times as each was emptied; this first
machine gun was considered by the Board of Ordnance to be of no use. The
repeaters came. In the Colonies now they were making snaphaunce revolvers
which loaded and cocked themselves obediently when you turned the handle.
Excited by the Revolutionary War, one Joseph Belton appeared before
Congress, and displayed a means by which any musket could discharge twenty
balls in five seconds. No use was made of his mechanism. At the same time a
London gunsmith was making seven-barreled naval guns. Over the dead
bodies of the Officer Corps the repeaters came, one step at a time, like
Blenheim, Borodino, Waterloo, Gettysburg: there came the ten-shot musket
of 1693 (archers are more reliable, Your Highness) and then the Gatling gun
(we prefer muskets, Mr President) and the Maxim gun, which was just like
the ten-shot musket of 1693 except that it fired ten shots *per second*, the Sten
gun and the anti-aircraft gun and the cluster bomb (we'd rather stick to
Gatling guns, Senator); the repeaters came despite Maximilian, and the end
result was that after a long sea-voyage through greyness, like a northbound
ship leaving our continent behind, at last, after eons of emptiness and cold
stupidity, the whalers down anchor, row, step out with repeaters in hand; and
the melancholy brown shores of Baffin Island are the shores of history: wet,
muddy, icy, snow-spotted . . .

Of course the whalers did not need Maxim guns. They were not at war
with the Esquimaux – why, it was *sweet* to remember the voyage of Munck
(1619), when all the People ran to embrace one sailor, because the man was

swarthy and flat-nosed and black-haired, so they believed him to be one of
them! – At war? – No! – And even if they had been, arquebuses would still
have served – the People didn't even have bows! As it was, the whalers wished
to kill nothing but animals. The ten-shot musket of 1693 would have served.
The thing wasn't at all to squeeze off a hundred bullets almost simultaneously,
which not only would have been expensive, but also would have left no
choice in cooking that caribou except to stew it. But if they had three bullets,
or ten, ready to discharge in reasonably quick succession, then their chances
of bagging that caribou (or, better still, three or ten caribou) were three or ten
times better. After all, they didn't have a lot of time. They did everything
quickly; they talked with the rapid quackings of geese (kill *them*, too). They
were here to kill whales. At midnight the sun was in the east, and the sky was
pale blue and fresh like dawn; it was fingered with long golden clouds like a
milkman's holiday, and the mountains rose blue and white. The lookout saw
three ravens over the ice, and at first he thought that they were together, but
then two of them diverged from the third, and he watched the two go, and in
the direction they were going he saw a puff of vapor and shouted because
that was a whale! At once the Captain recalled the shooting party and readied
sail; there was no time to bag musk-oxen anymore . . . – The game had not
been whales at first. In the sixteenth and seventeenth centuries, Greenland
had been productive of unicorn horn, that unfailing remedy for impotence,
old age and gullibility; Isaac de la Peyrière said defensively that *this was no
novelty, for Bartolin in his treatise on unicorns had written a chapter expressly on sea-
unicorns.* But old kings were still unable to maintain their erections. So the
Unicorn Coast was given over to whalers. Chewing spices for sea-sickness,
rowing their way through rot-fishes, slime-fishes, sea-qualms and funnel-
fishes, these executioners did their duty. It was not always pleasant. Frederick
Martens wrote dourly in his *Voyage into Spitzbergen and Greenland* (1671):   *I
try'd to dry this sperm of a whale in the sun, and it look'd like snot.* – They caught
a whale on the 30th of May.   *He blowed also very hollow,* says Martens,   *he
stank alive, and the birds fed upon him. This whale fermented when it was dead, and
the steam that came from it inflamed our eyes and made them sore. The same night,*
Cornelius Seaman *lost his ship by the squeezing and crushing together of the ice . . .*
– On the *8th* [of June], *it was foggy, and snowed all day; we saw that day many sea-
dogs (or seales) on the ice about the seaside, so we set out a boat and killed fifteen of
them . . . On the 12th, it was cold and stormy all day, at night sunshine; he that takes
not exact notice, knows no difference whether it be day or night.* – The engraving of
Hans Egede (1750), depicting Greenland whaling, is very white and black, like
a chocolate-vanilla swirl, the sea and the coast being of the same icy blankness,

but the sea evenly squiggled with black water-crests, upon which slide the long narrow boats lined with piously rowing figures, and little one-man kayaks bob contemplatively wherever the artist has deemed convenient. Men walk thoughtfully about on the backs of towed whales, or stand on islands watching the seals raise their disproportionate leonine heads; and the pious rowers (some of whom resemble hooded women) stare out to sea as the tusklike beams of the bow prod the shoulder of another spouting dying whale; and in the distance the ice-walls of Blue-Shirt tower cool and shady, and sea-birds bob like ducks in the pond; and there is not an Esquimau in sight. That changed soon enough, in Greenland and in Baffin-Land. Killing that herd of musk-oxen over there would supply them with provisions for the winter. Why not let the Esquimaux do it? Give them a few old muzzle-loaders and let them get addicted. Trade them whiskey or looking-glasses for a ton of steaks. Once they got used to the rifles, they'd have to come back and trade for bullets; that was the beauty of guns.

Oh, now these furs were worth something. (Fur flared out from the People's faces like sun-rays. Their clothes, fashioned from the skins of caribou, were golden brown, with black markings.) Tell them to kill more musk-oxen. Tell them to kill all the foxes they could. A silver pelt, now, or a blue – that could bring money in San Francisco. *Give* the bullets away again. Teach 'em all to be hand-cannoneers! . . .

> Hunting was our main occupation . . . Our excellent firearms had the result that relatively more animals were wounded than would have been the case had we been using muzzle-loaders. Since caribou can "carry a lot of lead," to use an old hunting expression, it was on those wounded animals that our Netsilik friends now set their sights, and which they usually killed. Never before had there been so many caribou running around King William's Land on three legs as this year, and never before had the hunting efforts of the indigenous residents been so productive as this fall. The maximum bag for one day was twenty-four caribou.*
>
> HEINRICH KLUTSCHAK, *Overland to Starvation Cove: With the Inuit in Search of Franklin 1878–1880*

The sight of his fallen enemy made my companion scream and dance with joy. He was lost with astonishment at the effect of the firearms, first carefully examining the holes that the balls had made, and pointing out to

---

* To sustain family and dogs, an inland Inuk had to kill at least 150 caribou per year.

me that some had passed quite through the [musk-ox]. But it was the state of one broken shoulder which most surprised him; nor would it be easy to forget his look of horror and amazement when he looked in my face . . .

> SIR JOHN ROSS, *Narrative of a Second Voyage in Search of a Northwest Passage* (1835)

Northwest Company . 66 fusil
for trade with Indians and Inuit
1789

The chase of the musk-ox and of the bear have become much easier since the introduction of firearms in Arctic America, and the Eskimos can kill their game without encountering the same dangers as formerly.

> FRANZ BOAS, *The Central Eskimo* (1885)

On arrival here I found the slaughter of these animals [musk-oxen] for the sake of their skins was much greater than I had supposed . . . These animals are becoming scarcer every year, and even the whalers agree that at the present rate of killing, they will soon become extinct on the west coast of Hudson bay.

> SUPERINTENDENT MOODIE (1905)

Once, near Mailasikkut, on a hot day, we got afraid of a group of musk-oxen. We offended them, and they got mad. They had seen skins of a member of their group we had killed. One of them was wailing like a human. They were so mad the men couldn't control them or keep them away from us.

> JEANNIE MIPPIGAQ, *Memories from Kuujjuarapik* (1990)

Firearms made available to the Eskimo a resource which he was never before able to utilize with any degree of proficiency: marine mammals in open leads and near the ice edge.

> RICHARD K. NELSON, *Hunters of the Northern Ice* (1969)

But there are also years when only one whale is taken at Barrow . . . And at Wainwright whaling is becoming a lost art.

Ibid.

. . . there has been a decrease in seal hunting activity in recent years . . .

Ibid.

Breathing hole hunting is not done anymore in north Alaska except by older men at Point Barrow and perhaps occasionally at Point Hope . . . The modern method of rifle hunting at open water is so much more efficient and comfortable that the young men cannot be persuaded to undertake breathing hole hunting . . . This may or may not be more efficient. The principal disadvantage . . . is that no line is attached automatically, so the killed animal may sink or drift away with the current. The advantage is a sure kill . . .

Ibid.

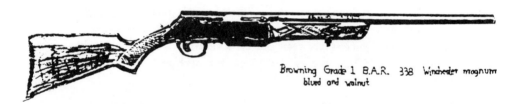

Browning Grade 1 B.A.R. 338 Winchester magnum blued and walnut

Some years earlier caribou had been in the habit of coming down to the coast frequently, but the Eskimos told me that during the last few years they had been so much hunted by natives in the employ of the whalers that none were to be expected now north of the mountains . . .

VILHJALMUR STEFANSSON, Hunters of
the Great North (1922)

The magazine rifle usurped the scene. And a race of men who had devoted all the centuries of their history to the killing of deer with weapons that were efficient only when used with great skill, were now presented with a weapon that could kill without restrictions and without the need of skill . . . The Idthen Eldeli went out to their winter hunting grounds, every hunter carrying a case of shells (a thousand rounds) and often enough they were back at the post before spring for more. The profits mounted pleasantly, so pleasantly that a recent suggestion that the sale of ammunition be limited for the good of the purchasers and of the game was denounced as interference with the liberty of men. It *was* interference, I suppose, interference with the free rights of men to destroy themselves through ignorance.

FARLEY MOWAT, *People of the Deer*
(1951)

As I got older, I noticed that there was less and less caribou. We moved here and I stopped drying meat.

MINNIE TAKAI (1982)

All my family starved to death.

MOESIE MAQU (1982)

. . . and their trade was at a standstill, with their Indians dying round them for lack of powder and shot.

MONSIEUR NICHOLAS JÉRÉMIE
(1713)

Finally, one caribou lying still, I went towards him with a young Eskimo; and he, being two feet from the beast, could not contain himself but dropped on one knee and shot the dead beast again.

GONTRAN DE PONCINS, *Kabloona*
(1941)

At that time [in Resolute] they had rifles from Inukjuak and a dog-team. Now there are no dogs; they use snowmobiles. Moneywise, money exists and now you have to use a snowmobile and not a dog-team. It's costly and more harder for them to go out hunting.

LEVI NUNGAQ (1988)

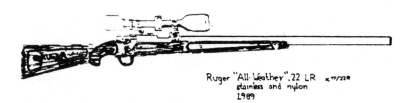

Ruger "All-Weather" .22 LR K77/22R
stainless and nylon
1989

Old men and women on the Belcher Islands recall the occasion on which they first had dealings with a southerner, but in 1972 not even the oldest islanders could remember the time when they were without a gun.

HUGH BRODY, *Living Arctic: Hunters*
of the Canadian North (1987)

So that's it; and we need not go into it anymore except to say that while Freud says sometimes a cigar is only a cigar, a rifle is always something more than a rifle; just as the Jesuit Cross is more than two metal sticks at perpendiculars. Or maybe that isn't it. – We cannot say for certain which – if any – specific instances of starvation were caused by the abuse of repeating rifles. I think that the extracts I have assembled are suggestive. But am I, who was not there in the old times, being tendentious? My best advice to you, wherever you may be, is to look around you and ask yourself sincerely: Is this continent getting worse?

When I first set out to write this book I thought that it would be necessary to describe everything, as I did in *Fathers and Crows,* to tell how bowheads and belugas were almost wiped out between 1800 and 1900 (these whales were once the main food for many Inuit), to relate to you that walrus populations have declined by eighty percent in the eastern Arctic, to recount how the caribou vanished from the Barren Lands and people waited for them until they starved, but surely the above series of extracts does that well enough; what good is another history of miseries that cannot be helped anymore? – *They were entirely clothed in deerskins,* wrote an RCMP officer in 1914, describing the Coppermine Inuit. *Some had rifles and the majority had a few kettles.* – They rarely wear deerskins now. – Never kill a bull caribou during rutting season, they used to say. In the winter, don't kill a cow with a calf unless you have to. Be careful with everything you have. You never know when you might run short. – I met a white man who said he'd been in Eskimo Point the night it went dry. – They shot eight hundred caribou for nothing! he yelled. He stopped, and then he went on: The snow was melting, so I could see the dead dogs in the streets, with ravens pecking their eyes. And dead caribou everywhere, rotting . . . – What good to know that? – (They gave names to the different caribou crossings. They took good care of their caribou-skin tents to make them last three or four summers. They married to be helpers to each other.) – I once knew a man whose long hair was spread to his shoulders. He shook his head and cried: *ai! ai!* He parted his hands wide. His fur skin ruffled in the wind. When he was little, he used to cry because he wanted so badly to go out hunting with his father. He went for the first time when he was six or seven. He lived in a camp with his parents until he was ten. Then he went to school. His parents moved to Igloolik to be near the children. His mother got polio; she had to stay in the village. – One time he and his uncle went after a walrus. He shot the animal and it went under. Suddenly it came to life again and rammed its tusks into the bottom of his canoe and water gushed in. They had to leave the dying animal to sink. They pulled in to shallow water. Later they found the walrus dead and rotten. They cut off the tusks and half-buried the rest, leaving some sticking out for the foxes . . . – I remember the time in Pond Inlet when a man saw a seal and the seal submerged and then came closer to shore, probably no farther than twenty feet, and then the man shot it and after a minute and a half it sank. The seal died for nothing. – What good is it to know that? And is a little waste anyone's fault? Life makes waste and death makes waste. Sibelius died with his last symphony unfinished. People died in Resolute still waiting to go home. A polar bear killed a man and didn't even get to eat him before it was shot. – A hundred years ago it wouldn't have mattered so much if the seal had sunk. It would have mattered, but not as much as it does now. – In 1888, at Saint Peter's Reserve near Winnipeg, Indians played a gambling game with bullets for dice. That seems ominous to me now, seeing how bullets are media of enslavement as well as currency, but it would not have been at all ominous then. – On the subject of the Crees, our Franklin wrote: *They are esteemed good hunters and generally assiduous. Having laid the bow and arrow aside, and also the use of snares except for rabbits and partridges, they depend entirely on the Europeans for the means of gaining their subsistence, as they require guns and a constant supply of powder and shot . . .* – This is nothing if not ominous. – Is it any good to know anymore what is ominous and what isn't? – There was a boy at Pond Inlet whose favorite thing to do was hunting. On his first time he shot a seal with his Dad's twenty-two. I cannot but think that this was good. He was so happy when he told it, and that seal was used, not wasted. So listen to him as did Captain Subzero; look down from the green slope strewn with feldspar boulders, black-lichened like the skins of Dalmatians: – you'll see open water, calm and blue-grey, with rare scattered blotches of ice (like lichen) halfway across where the shots rang out.

The Crew

We were all men; this is nearly always the rule. Very occasionally
someone takes women as well; these are usually Jurtens, Baramists, or
Fetishists – women from the tribes living along the shores of the Bering
Sea . . . They are mostly hybrids, because the pure-blooded women of
the northern tribes smell too much.

FRANZ WELZL, *The Quest for Polar
Treasures* (1933)

There was Fitzjames, of course, and Gore, Vesconte and Fairholme, all
of the *Erebus;* there were Franklin, Subzero, you, yours truly, me, myself and
I. Mr Back did not come, even though he'd served under us on the *Trent* on
that first expedition, in the Barren Grounds on the second, in the Barren
Grounds on the third; he was our Arctic Friend, of course, but we did not
trust him. Anyhow, Fitzjames selected most of the officers and men; it had
little to do with us. Did you know that Back commanded the *Terror* in 'thirty-
six, and caught her fast in the ice? – which was typical of his escapades. His
men had barely gotten home, bailing all the way; it was a miracle that they'd
been able to patch her up sufficiently for Sir James to take her to the Antarctic
. . . Well, well, let's be tactful, since *we* had HMS *Terror* now, of which we gave
Mr Crozier the captaincy in spite of Barrow's string-pulling for Fitzjames; and
Lieutenants Little, Irving and Hodgson upheld the discipline of the Navy in
the same fashion as their opposite numbers, the aforesaid Gore, Vesconte and
Fairholme. (Gore had served under Back that time at Repulse Bay, but it was
hardly his fault . . .) The Finnlander Kid was Captain of the Forecastle; Seth
was a private of the Royal Marines. Both of the cooks had been in Antarctica
with Ross. I'm sure they knew how to prepare frozen blubber burgers and
observe the latitude at the same time. Five hundred and eighty gallons of

pickles were in their charge (to wit – mixed, cabbage, onion and walnut). There were other pickles, too, of course – GOD bless them! – Mates and Masters, Surgeons and Warrant Officers, Petty Officers and Boys, to say nothing of all their able semen: – there were, in short, a hundred and thirty-three souls on the two ships. Of these, four who became ill returned to England on board the *Baretto Junior* and the *Rattler*. The remaining one hundred and twenty-nine of us all died – in agony and by degrees. We were all aware of the honor conferred upon us by our appointment to this service: – I need not say how important its object was to the entire civilized world. Or, as Seth said: It's kind of corny and everything, but I think you can live your life a certain way, to make a point. – To this the Finnlander Kid replied with a soliloquy, which went like this: How I hate man! (to which Seth, overhearing, cried: Oh, GOD, it's so horrible! It's so funny!) and the Finnlander Kid stalked the deck, mumbling onward: Savages less so, but even they leave their piles of excrement. Lieutenants I hate more warmly; Franklin I love frankly like the very fiend. I hate rifles, offices of state, sextants and thermometers most measurelessly; measure beyond measure I hate my own impudence in forgiving myself for being what I am, in talking and listening crackhearted; measure past measure I hate how I now go sailing into Snow-Heaven with all my fellow turds and foulnesses. When will Heaven guard itself? – But the rest of us, being cheerful fellows (despite an occasional touch of mournfulness), paid no attention to this monologue; indeed, following my orders the Finnlander Kid was reduced from his post for insubordination, which was out of place like the black uncouth flappings of a raven over sea-ice. Our unfortunate deaths are the only drawbacks which I feel from the otherwise unalloyed pleasure I derive from reflecting on that cordial unanimity which at all times prevailed among us in the days of sunshine, and in those of "sickness and sorrow."

Under the Polar Cross

The seeds . . . are shaken out of the erect capsules and carried away by
winter gales.

IN-CHO CHUNG, *The Arctic and the
Rockies as Seen by a Botanist* (1984)

As we proceeded northward, the longitude-lines crowded ever closer
together. Our good Subzero, who'd been astounded by the correspondences
between map-isles and their real cousins, expected continually to see one
of these boundaries stretched across land and sea like some black cable
of inhuman tautness, some tripwire to help those who long to die young,
and though I explained to him that it was not like that he refused to believe
me, finding nihilism easier than my proposition that some entities on the
map truly existed, while others did not. He was no lover of fictions, unlike
Seth, who when traveling by Greyhound bus from New York to Nashville,
Tennessee, had once ignited a fierce discussion with the other passengers on
the merits and demerits of time zones. – And here's one that'll stump you!
crowed Seth, a little cruelly, as he got off. *What time is it really at the North
Pole?* And he laughed at the astronomical matter. I myself, having failed to
make landfall at any conclusion, can pose only the following additional teaser:
Whatever time it may be at the North Pole, at the South Pole would it not be
the same time or the "opposite" time (by which I mean a twelve hours'
difference?) If it is the same time, then why is it day at the North Pole when
it's night at the South Pole, and vice versa? And if it's the "opposite" time,
then where on this globe do the longitude-lines abruptly reverse their
temporal character? (Believe me, I have visited the equator, and *there* nothing
happens!) Mr Franklin for his part was wondering a similar thing: namely,
when could he leave Jane for Reepah? Jane wondered: When will I know for

certain that he is dead? Reepah wondered nothing; for her nothing changed. But when we were deep under the Polar Cross, and the horizon white with the "ice-blink," Subzero felt something stretch and break suddenly in his heart, and he was certain then that we had snapped a longitude line. I for my part, feeling a strange sensation at the same moment, concluded that my supernatural twin had stroked my soul, and therefore awarded a certain double-glaciered island then within view the name of Gemini. From the heap of drift-timber I concluded that the Esquimaux had recently utilized this spot . . . – Now our ships were kissed by the fog-bound bays with white snow-lips. *Terror* and *Erebus* continued sailing in the blue, connected by crossed parallels of rigging to the stained brown trapezoids of sails, sailing soundlessly between floes, softened by rosy mist. They followed white ripples of snow and fog, knowing that the blue sky was somewhere above like an endless radiant afternoon, but they glimpsed it with increasing rarity. This loss did not distress them. In the south it is impossible to attain the limit of sight, but here at all times they were on the edge of something new, moving with an ice-horizon that was banded like some grey Easter egg, frilled and starred with most subtle lacings. – For the crews of the two ships the good feeling leaped in them like porpoises, more and more frenetically the farther north they went, and to the extent that you were Franklin you must have shared in them; to the extent that you were Subzero, however, you could hardly have escaped that daily ache like old ice, knowing as you did that Reepah was in need, that seals were dying for nothing, that Fox and Raven were rotting in the dump at Pond Inlet, that PCB contamination had been reported at Yellowknife: – the agony was not yet moot as for earlier pages of our continent. When you hear someone screaming for help and you do not know what to do, it is much worse than when she is already dead. This is the reason to get stuck in ice.

Not clear? Translucent, perhaps?

Departing Stromness in good order on the 23[d] of June, they'd entered the introitus between Hoy and Pomona; but this time M[r] Franklin had taken care not to weigh anchor out of punctuality with the tide, as he'd done on receiving his first command – a modest failing, but one which had cost some additional effort. This time he'd hoard and reserve their strength for the winter soon to come. He encouraged them all to eat; stoutness of body would be as crucial to their success as ammunition . . . They cleared the dangerous rocks at Pomona, which he knew now like old friends, and so returned to the Atlantic. As was his custom upon making sea, he forthwith issued the officers of both ships with detailed copies of his instructions, as well as keys to his signaling-codes; and for a day or two they were much engrossed in committing them to memory, which endeared them to him so much that his manner, never more severe than was absolutely required, now softened even further, so that all under his command considered him both friend and father. (But how *young* they all were! – excepting only Captain Crozier, who at fifty-one approached him in age.) As always, shearwaters, fulmars and other sea-birds accompanied them westward; he smiled and inhaled the smell of the sea (which the Indians of Northern Canada, so he'd heard, named the Stinking Lake). – Both ships were square-rigged fore and main, fore-and-aft-rigged on the mizzenmast. Generally they traveled within sight of one another, so that he had the double pleasure of walking a ship under his command while gazing upon a ship under his command; each had a spanking appearance: – black-hulled, white-masted, with yellow weatherworks; like any skipper he thought them perfect. They'd been double-planked in obedience to Sir James's word, then reinforced against the ice with twenty-foot lengths of iron, and even equipped, as I have said, with propellers and twenty-horsepower engines! By way of a little drill he had the two sets of officers motor the ships toward various quarters of the quadrant as he directed, using the new signals; everything was faultless. These exercises, of course, were brief, to save both fuel and time; summer's book had almost opened; once that happened they must turn the unexplored pages while they might, since at any time the icy covers might slam shut upon them. So they rushed deeper into the net of longitude and latitude. After a passage of twenty days, they neared old Cape Farewell; on the 25th they sighted the Greenland coast. On the 27th a heavy sea-vapor arose so that the two ships became invisible to one another throughout the forenoon, but this dissipated before there was any occasion for anxiety. On the following day, at the request of their naturalist, Dr Goodsir, they lowered a dredge three hundred fathoms, and brought up living creatures, which pleased Dr Goodsir greatly; and when Seth got to see them after his turn at watch he cried: That starfish thing is so neat!   – They sailed on, hugging the coast. There was no occasion to use the screw-propellers, the water being quite open. From time to time they glimpsed Norse ruins, which moved them all to melancholy; Ross had told him that that pile of stones was Eirik the Red's house, there by that ridge where the virile young Esquimau was walking down the steep ridge, his hands behind his head, a carcass lashed to his shoulders – what was it? Subzero, peeping through the telescope, saw that it was a sheep. A Greenlander can tell how old a sheep is by counting the twists of its horns. He'd heard that from them.   – This ram – ten years old! they'd said, showing him. They'd offered him some fat to eat. It was dry and light when the sun fixed it, not greasy.   – Try it,   the Inuk said.   It taste good.   – But to Subzero it tasted like a sheep-flavored candle. – The heart also dried like that, as he remembered. There were fly-eggs like white pills in one of the ventricles. The hunters just cut off those parts every day. They knew just how to manage things . . . – LORD, how long had it been since he'd last set foot on the Greenland shore? Had it been 1987? – Yes, a hundred and forty-two years . . .

On the 4th of July, a date not yet sullied by that traitor George Washington, they dropped anchor by the Whalefish Islands. Seven of their ten live bullocks had perished on the way, no doubt of sea-sickness. Their first object must be to make this deficit satisfactory; accordingly, he sent Mr Gore, in company with any other officers who cared to go, to barter with the Esquimaux for whale-meat. They had great quantities of shot and powder, and it was Mr Franklin's plan to have the officers and men shoot edible sea-birds whenever they could once the ships had crossed Baffin Bay; meanwhile any other source of meat would not be amiss. So the men in their blue uniforms came ashore and strolled about upon a mossy little islet where the Greenlanders were butchering a whale. A radio played happy songs in the sand. There were beer cans everywhere. On the rocks were the old bones of previous whales, the vertebrae like great rusty ladders. People swarmed about the massive skull, which extruded its fringe of baleen like an endless yellow comb. Past the head was the meat, the rows and rows of steaks wrapped in blubber and black skin. Subzero had somehow thought that whaleskin would feel soft and flexible, like the skin of an eggplant, but it was very hard. – There were more steaks than he ever saw in a supermarket. All along the length of the dead whale, people were cutting them; steaks lay scattered on the hard cold ground. More steaks waited upon the bloody racks of that immense backbone, each hundred-pound steak within its stall of bone.

Mr Crozier, who'd led a party of officers from the *Terror,* did not wonder in the least at this embarrassment of flesh. He was too busy enjoying the flowers to be put off by the blood – which is a wise policy, whenever one can manage it. He had good reason to be contented. His impressions of Mr Franklin continued to be favorable; he could see that his habits coincided much better with Mr Franklin's than they had with – say – Sir James's; it had been a very long four years with Sir James in the Antarctic . . . The truth was that he longed to be attached to Mr Franklin; Mr Franklin had a positive reputation for inspiring affection in his officers (why, consider the sundry adorations offered by Mr Back!); how much more pleasant it was to serve under a man who could love, than a man of stiff moral principles such as Sir James –

And it was delightful to command the *Terror* again. Mr Crozier knew the *Terror* very well. She had become very real to him in those four years. He knew what she could do and what she could not do. Is it really his fault that we now smile indulgently at his happy moments?

Behind him, in a line, stood Mr Little, Mr Irving and Mr Hodgson – each with his accustomed pocket chronometer, compass, spy-glass and gun. We do not have the time, in this history of mine with its unsurpassed sweep, to enter into the thoughts of every white man who happened to sail to Nunavut, but let us listen in for a moment to the conversation between the first and last of these when the one in the middle (whose skeleton was destined to be identified by the mathematics medal beside it) was called by his Commander, Mr Crozier, ostensibly to settle some geognostical quibble, but in reality to be a vehicle for Mr Crozier's expansive joy; so they wandered murmuring in between the bone-stalls, and Mr Little and Mr Hodgson were left to themselves.

An Esquimau told me this morning that summer will come early this year, said Mr Hodgson after a moment.

I think that he is right, said Mr Little. You've seen how the thermometer has been above freezing for the past several days –

Aye, I've seen that, all right, returned Mr Hodgson. I wonder that we don't push on immediately.

You mean, without taking on these extra provisions?

Well, you know and I know that the Passage will be a lark. We ought to make hay, as the saying goes, and be about our discoveries –

I see that you have a definite line on things, Hodgson. I admit that I know less than you; my line is not nearly so definite.

Mr Hodgson reddened slightly. – You think me out of turn?

Well, it's an easy game to second-guess one's commanding officers. But do you have any reason to think your judgment superior to theirs? Look around, Hodgson. We're alone. I'll keep quiet. But why don't you finish what you've begun, and serve me a full portion of your opinions, instead of feeding me scraps and slices, as if we were starving on the Barren Grounds –

I see that you disapprove of me, Little.

Come, now, don't get your back up! laughed the other sarcastically. You show me the pearls of wisdom in your palm and then you roll them up in your fist!

I –

I haven't finished. I'll cheerfully follow any order that Mr Crozier or Mr Franklin see fit to give me. Now, are you with me or not?

I don't care to be talked about, said Hodgson. That's all. You've made up your mind about me now. I can see that I made a mistake.

Oh, well, said Little, shrugging . . .

Lieutenant Little was not ordinarily so thin-skinned about the honor of their command. Nor was his opinion of Hodgson really, as it might have appeared from the foregoing, that that officer's place was beneath a rock with other salamanders of his own kind. But he had a small anxiety of his own, as a result of a conference he'd recently had with Diggle, the cook. The able seamen had complained less than usual about the food; some said that the potatoes were tasteless, but otherwise they seemed satisfied. Mr Little was a great believer in the pat-the-back theory of command – in part because it was so efficient in his own case. He'd already been singled out for praise by Mr Crozier on one or two occasions, after which he felt such happiness that he threw himself even deeper into his duties – so deep, in fact, that he was almost buried under them like the salamanders. He was, in short, a model officer. And he thought it worth his trouble to compliment Diggle.

But Diggle appeared to be thinking about something else too hard to be complimented. – So the Quartermaster reported to you, sir? he asked in a whisper, closing the galley door behind him, as if they were assassins. It was almost ludicrous.

Poor Mr Little was dilemma'd. On the one hand, if he admitted that he had no idea what Diggle was talking about, it would reflect very badly on the omniscience he fancied an officer was supposed to display to a subordinate. On the other hand, if he did not he would be lying.

Go on, Diggle, he temporized. But I shall be obliged if you'd do it quickly. He tapped his foot in distaste.

Well, sir, I like to think that I know food. I'm not ashamed of that. And I tell you – something is wrong with this food that we have. It don't taste right, sir. I've been seasoning it a little extra, with all that pepper that we got, to cover up that taste. You know Navy food, sir. Navy food is rotten food. I'm not talking about that. But it's grey on top sometimes, you know, when the boy opens those cans. The same grey as inside the lid. Like something is coming off on it, sir. So I told Mr MacDonald and he said he'd pass the word on to you.

Very good, Diggle. You've told no one else?

Of course not, sir. And it's got that taste like when you put the bullet in your mouth while you're loading your gun.

Lieutenant Little left the galley with the sense that he should do something, but most likely there was nothing to be done. The truth was that he had no means of knowing whether Diggle's alarums had any substance. And he suspected that Quartermaster MacDonald did not know, either.

Upon Mr Franklin's authority, Captain Crozier had permitted a bird-shooting party to set out in one of the longboats, although the atmosphere was somewhat murky. Lieutenant Irving was in charge. The volunteers vanished soundlessly around the rim of the great floe to which the *Terror* and the *Erebus* were both moored. Mr Blanky, the *Terror's* Ice-Master, was just now explaining to some of the officers who were still green that mooring to an iceberg was not without its dangers, as pieces could break off suddenly and fall upon the ship, and sometimes the bergs bore underwater spears that could pierce right through the side of a ship. Captain Crozier stood listening. If any of the officers were disagreeably affected by Mr Blanky's information, they did not show it. They were excellent men . . . Crozier waited for the volunteers' shots to sound. He relished the sun on his forehead. He and Fitzjames (who was competent and well-meaning, though a pup) would be dining with Mr Franklin today, to discuss some matters relative to the watch schedules of the two ships –

Lieutenant Little was at his shoulder. Lieutenant Little requested him to kindly receive him in private.

Crozier laughed. – I understand. We've been stove in by a sea-unicorn.

But Little's smile was merely dutiful.

Very well, said Crozier, ushering him into his cabin, what's the matter?

Little was now very sure that he had done the wrong thing as he sat swallowing and withholding his words from C^{apt} Crozier's cocked head, which was gentle, far-sighted and easy. Just as whatever hurts us hides in treacherous remission when the doctor is present, so Mr Little's deadly doubts cured themselves in the face of his Captain's waiting confidence. C^{apt} Crozier was one of those sunny men whose lips seem eternally about to smile, and his fluffy side-fringes of hair caught the light most sunnily beneath the visor of his cap. Button and button went his coat. Well, there was nothing for it now.

It's about the stores, sir. MacDonald has informed me that the last two tins of salt pork were rotten inside. And the cook –

And did MacDonald open a third?

Aye, sir. That one was good.

I appreciate your bringing this to my notice, Little. You've instructed him to keep it to himself?

Aye, sir. But the cook seemed alarmed –

Take it on yourself to calm him, if you would. Remind him that Commander Fitzjames and I personally opened one in every fifty tins when the ships were being loaded at Woolwich. We found not a single one to be defective, Little. Not one.

Aye, sir.

And apprise him of this also. Even if Goldner's patent should prove fallible, the chance is excellent that we'll have completed the Passage by the end of this season. That is the truth.

I understand, sir.

And we have rifles, you know. There are always the rifles to fall back on.

Aye, sir.

Is that all, Little?

Aye, sir.

Very good. You may go. Close the door behind you, if you would.

Captain Crozier had invented a magnetic dip-needle not long ago, when he'd been second-in-command to Sir James in the Antarctic. It had proven to be of considerable use. He kept one in his cabin, mounted in a mahogany box. He was quite fond of it. He took it in his hand and watched the disturbed needle quiver ever more gently until it had aligned itself westward in the direction of Sir James's cairn at the North Magnetic Pole. Now the needle was still again, or almost still.

A smile came to Crozier's lips, although he did not perceive it.

He decided that there was no need to inform Mr Franklin about the two spoiled tins.

C^mdr Fitzjames for his part was dressing for dinner in his own tiny cabin (for it was just as Franklin had said to Sir James: – the screw-propellers were so massive that the officers and men must squeeze in more tightly than usual). He was what is generally referred to as a dashing young man, although he was now becoming red-faced like his elders. His hair was always in disarray. At twenty-two he'd been chosen to accompany C^ol Cheney in his descent of the Euphrates by steamer. Just as that expedition was preparing to depart, Fitzjames had seen a Customs officer fall into the water, and had saved him at the risk of his own life, for which he received two silver medals. Then it

was off for the Bible Lands! Only one of the steamers reached the mouth of
the Euphrates, and that was the one on which Mr Fitzjames served. Not long
after, he'd been posted to Syria to fight Mehemet Ali, which he did with great
valor; then he'd commanded a rocket brigade in China. He was wounded and
decorated in the capture of Ching-Kiang-Foo. Now he too must be sacrificed,
just like Mr Hood a quarter-century before, who'd followed Mr Franklin with
unwavering devotion, admiring the country as he went.

There came a knock at his door. It was Lieutenant Gore. Mr Franklin was
preparing his calculations on the magnetic field; if Commander Fitzjames
would therefore be so good as to sign today's record of latitude –

Fitzjames scanned the form, which Mr Gore had already filled in. He wrote:
All well and made his signature. Mr Gore thanked him and took it away, to
be soldered into its copper cylinder and dropped over the side.

Mr Franklin was gorgeously laced about his breast that afternoon, the lace
ribbed all the way to the side-buttons, like a rack of meat; he wore white
gloves and held a chart scrolled in his hand. A collar, dark and high, cut him
off at the chin; he gazed mildly from beneath his round forehead; his curly
hair had receded beyond recession at last, like the Arctic tree-line. He was
smiling. Mr Reid, the Ice-Master of the *Erebus,* had just now returned from
an excursion to the edge of the pack in company with Mr Blanky and some
officers, and announced that there were plenty of leads and then a water-sky.
Franklin, there in Greenland on the edge of the known, was tasting the same
sweetness as when he'd first seen Reepah in Resolute, and he and she said
almost nothing to each other, but he had known that he would kiss her
goodbye.

He heard footsteps; he heard Fitzjames, loud and boyish: I warrant the
maps will be out! . . . and then came the knock.

They drank the health of Her Majesty, and the glasses clinked ringingly, just
as some uninformed people believe that icebergs do when they strike one
another.

Well, gentlemen, said Mr Franklin, is there anything to hinder us from
commencing operations tomorrow?

The *Erebus* is ready from top to bottom, sir! cried Fitzjames.

The older officers could not help smiling.

Very good, said Franklin. And how do matters stand with the *Terror*, Mr Crozier?

There are times when to hesitate is to imply, whether one means to or no. The Commander did not hesitate. – Likewise, sir, he said . . .

On the 12th of July, Sir John Franklin wrote in his last dispatch ever: *The ships are now being swung, for the purpose of ascertaining the dip and deviation of the needle on board, as was done at Greenhithe, which, I trust, will be completed this afternoon, and I hope to be able to sail in the night.* – This he did, departing the Whalefish Islands for Baffin Bay on a bright and trembly summer night of ice and dreams, while the *Baretto Junior* ploughed sadly back to England, its Commander, Lt Edward Griffiths, thinking to himself: Better fellows than those Franklin men never breathed! – A fine wind impregnated the fine fellows' sails. Mr Gore reported that the variation of the compass continued to increase. On the 19th they passed Upernavik, where Dr Goodsir saw a little seaweed which he craved to flatten in his specimen-blotters, but Mr Franklin, who knew from experience the brevity of the fair season, expressed his regrets, and the *Erebus* turned north by northwest . . . On the 23^d they found themselves compelled to shorten sail to wait upon the *Terror*, and Dr Goodsir

was assisted by Mr Vesconte in lowering a dredge, but found nothing save a palish-grey crab that scuttled feebly, as if incapacitated by the cold. – In truth the crab was not very cold at all. Mr Franklin had not yet found it necessary to issue any regulation about the proper clothing to be worn. It was common for the sailors to go about their duties without their jackets. All were hale and strong – a result perhaps of the cranberries and lemon juice, tinned by means of Goldner's patent. – The season was especially good, as he wrote to Jane; they made excellent progress. By the end of that month, moored to an iceberg at the latitude of Lancaster Sound, they'd exchanged visits with the last Englishmen they'd ever see, some whalers, who were very agreeable, although it must be confessed that they made no deep impression. Time flowed on like a black stream beneath the cloud-roof, flowing with scarcely a sound between lichened rocks whose roundness was equivalent to that of turtle-shells. Grasshaired tussock-islands cast their shaggy reflections in time's shallows; orange lichen-spots shone beneath that ever so slightly rippled surface. – They ran along the pack for perhaps two miles to find a good entrance. After consulting with Mr Franklin and Mr Fitzjames, they signaled the *Terror*, who followed close behind, and went in. – It was as the two Ice-Masters had said. Conditions were not formidable. They coasted through wide lanes, with Mr Reid striding about with his spy-glass, choosing the best leads, calling out course corrections; the *Erebus* careened violently, shattering a glass or two; the water-sky continued clear to the westward like their hopes, and after more thumping they were through. It had not been necessary to use the propellers, which was as well, since fuel was limited. Captain Crozier came aboard and reported all well on the *Terror* –

His instructions from the Admiralty were to follow Lancaster Sound, which becomes Barrow Strait on the south side of Cornwallis Island (that is, Resolute); to continue along Barrow Strait as far as Cape Walker, and then again westward and south along the northernmost edge of our continent, completing the Passage into Russian America, which is Alaska, and then down the Bering Strait into the Pacific Ocean. Presumably (his heart like the blue ice-shard that bore so steadily westward almost broken in two) he would drop anchor among the Sandwich or Hawaiian Islands; the crew already looked forward to those tropical times; then he'd return home via Cape Horn . . . Cape Horn might be the most difficult part. By then his men would be spoiled and softened by the Polynesians. As for the unknown portion of the

Northwest Passage itself, what could be there that he had not already seen? It was very probable, despite the chatter of the younger officers, that he wouldn't reach the Sandwich Isles in the first year. But he was provisioned for three, and there were rifles, and when all else failed there were friendly helpful Esquimaux . . . – Should he be ice-balked at Barrow Strait, he had leave to turn north at Wellington Channel, which lies between Cornwallis Island and Devon Island, and to continue as far as he could, in hopes of completing the Northwest Passage by that alternate way. There were sages in the Admiralty, both bearded and unbearded, who'd proved theoretically that there must be open water near the North Pole. Mr Fitzjames, who'd never before been to the Arctic regions, was in their party. As for Franklin, he thought it possible but unlikely – an opinion he shared with Back and Sir James and old Parry . . .

At noon, when Mr Gore took the latitude, they had a fine view of a right whale . . .

He conceived that the greatest impediments from ice would probably be between the ninety-fifth and one hundred twenty-fifth degrees of longitude. After that, the ice should be less heavy.

Sedna and the Fulmar

The Outsider finds himself completely overshadowed by the creative
ingenuity of the Eskimos – he is almost childlike in his inability to
approximate their cleverness and imagination. A white man resigns
himself to the hopelessness of a difficult situation whereas the Eskimo is
just getting started on a workable solution.

> RICHARD K. NELSON, *Hunters of the
> Northern Forest* (1973)

On the 8th of August they hove in sight of Baffin's Isle, having been
compelled by their latest ice-dodges to head south almost to latitude 73°. This
had fortunately cost them but inconsiderable time, thanks to a steady breeze.
Mr Franklin had left standing instructions with his officers that they report
any sightings of Esquimaux in this region, as he desired to continue the good
relations heretofore established; and it would be highly desirable to get one
of these people as an interpreter or pilot if they could be so persuaded. That
was all that he said. But perhaps Mr Fitzjames was aware that seeing them
again, hearing the speech of any Esquimau woman who talked a little like
Reepah (who I forgot to mention had borrowed her uncle's double-barreled
rifle, pressed her forehead against its nostrils, gripped the barrel with her right
hand, leaned down, and jerked the trigger with her left), would be highly
beneficial for Mr Franklin. Somebody in Resolute had told him. She'd given
birth to his child and become another of those women with babies gazing
down, with babies peeping out of the armautis; and the women were weighted
down; their babies yoked them; that was why their necks bent; that was why
they stood so silent and sad; and Mr Franklin could almost see the great bag
of the armauti hanging down to her buttocks, and the infant peeping out with
his own face, crinkled in bewilderment at having been born and warmed now

in a second bag of darkness. What would he become now? In the old days some five-year-olds could shoot a rifle, kill a caribou. Anyhow, her sister took the baby. Reepah gave the baby to her. Reepah wanted her to have the baby. Then Reepah shot herself, the day after he called her –

But it is better always to look on the bright side of the question.

They did not go further out of their way to stop at Clyde River because Clyde is a bad town, as they'd heard. If you go there, people say: oh, no, another white man. – Anyhow, Clyde wasn't a town yet. They left Clyde River unseen to the south and east, with its brown tundra flats and ponds ending suddenly in creamy sea-cloud, ponds as numerous as pennies, wide grey knobs of mountains snow-grooved. But on the 9th they sighted two kayaks out of Pond's Bay* . . . and Mr Franklin remembered the way that with the three girls there so long ago his shadow and their shadows had been so long and thin as to sadden him because they reminded him of the trees that were not there and would not be there. Startled ptarmigans fluttered and cried . . . and the man on watch shouted out briskly as the two kayaks bore down, making good speed toward the *Erebus* (who lay as usual a little in advance of her sister) and the kayaks came astern.

Reepah was still and final, like a wet raven feather in the moss.

From the People's point of view, these Qaallunaat held promise. Just as one could tell when a seal-eating walrus is dangerous by the fact that his tusks are stained yellow from seal-oil, and one can tell a seal-eating walrus from a clam-eating walrus because the clam-eating walrus's tusks are scratched from grubbing for clam shells, so one could tell a rich white man from the other kind. Surely they had metal things. Maybe they had rifles; the People had heard of those –

He went ashore with Mr Crozier and other interested officers. He stared moodily back, past his two ships, at Bylot Island with those grainy cliffs scored with hourglasses . . . And he remembered how young and happy he'd been when he was Subzero, running down canyons, breathing the air in long sweet drinks as he looked ahead at the distant sea.

The boat grounded. Kindly (the officers behind him – always behind him!) he presented a knife and a glass bead to the mother who led two young children along the boulder beach, the third child still in the armauti, the first two toiling happily over every rock-challenge –

The mother was a woman with the gentle laugh that just shows teeth. Having well bypassed her as he believed with his gifts, he approached one of

* Pond Inlet.

the children, a little girl with round brown cheeks, black eyes, black hair; and he said to her: Are you my child? Were you my child? Did you come out of Reepah's belly before she died? I would like to name you after my friend Reepah, to whose love and kindness I am especially indebted –

The child screamed.

On that late summer's midnight the sun was low enough to warm the back of his neck even as his hands were chill and white. He looked for the twin because his triplet was dead; he touched everything like his eyes, in the same way that children feel new things as they go. He thought that he might see somewhere the crumpled plastic corpse of Seth's and Subzero's kite; he had gone too far, as he knew from the child's face, and the kite might help him fly back to what he'd been. The tundra was a maze of shadows and crumble-dried flowers where ptarmigans sang their mournful three-toned songs. Sometimes they ran from him, zigzagging clumsily across the rusty moss like ricocheting balls of feather-brown.

He looked for fissures in beach-ice to read his name or Reepah's name, but there were none, and so he screamed.

The black egg-shaped boulders gleaming in the waves of a sunny night . . . coming back to winter camp hunched with a seal at their backs . . . a wide umiak of walrus hide . . . the ladies in their sealskin parkas which grew white-trimmed aprons between their legs . . .

※- ※- ※-

Good LORD, Mr Franklin has had a fainting fit!   cried Fitzjames.   Send for
Dr Goodsir!

He opened his eyes and they were all standing in a circle over him, appearing
very tall, and their shadows were infinite, and the taste of lead was in his
mouth. He did not know to what he ought to attribute this accident. D^r
Goodsir bowed down toward him like pale sedge bending under the weight
of some obsidian-black fly.

Looking down at how he looked then was Fitzjames, who now for the first
time saw what it meant to be old, and quailed for the months and years ahead
– for Mr Franklin was in charge of them all! As for Crozier, he was there, too,
grim-mouthed like a dog – yet even Crozier did not suspect that Mr Franklin's
momentary confusion of spirits might have anything to do with Goldner's
patent.

   Nor, perhaps, did it. But only lead intoxication could take him farther now,
into the engraving where the sad-eyed bearded "rescuers," turbaned like
Arabs, bandoliered and rifle-slung, would bend and point and gesture at the
longboat at the foot of the snow-cliff, and the longboat would be full of snow
and darkness and skeletons and one of the "rescuers" would lift a drape of
raggedy broadcloth from a skeleton's ribs and another would stroke a skull
most tenderly – so incongruous! – because neither the dead men nor the
longboat nor the "rescuers" belonged there at all . . . That swoon of his, that
petulant denial of life, proved nothing except that it's not easy to become a
skeleton! – and here, if I may so far defile Reepah as to compare him to her,
I'd like to point out that they both *were* habitual lead users, not only in their
separate reliance on rifles, but also in their ingenious substitutions of lead for
meat, she sniffing it, he eating it; as Drs Wyngaarden and Smith note in their
treatise (with which all Polar men ought to be familiar):   *Gasoline sniffing for
hedonistic purposes can produce lead poisoning; the organic tetraethyl lead appears to
have a proclivity for the nervous system . . . Tetraethyl lead poisoning causes euphoria,
nervousness, insomnia, hallucinations, convulsions, and sometimes frank psychosis.* –
Well and good. We'll never know where she'd wanted to be taken. You're
aware how he'd tried the other ways first. He'd called to her, he'd come to
her, and then he'd brought her to him. There's a perhaps too convenient

Inuit legend which recapitulates it, saying that once upon a time, in the days
of earlier Changers, two Inuk girls had been sitting on the beach throwing
pebbles into the still water, as ravens cried   *waah! waah!*   and big huskies
lolled in silence, and the rounded shadow-tops of ice pieces were very still in
the shallow water. A little farther from land the open water became increasingly obstructed and resorted to devious leads in order to maintain its freedom
in the crowds of ice; farther still it seemed to vanish entirely, and the ice
formed a plain of triumphant solidity, on which snowmobiles were parked,
but above them the white sky, not quite so powerful, showed leads of blue,
through which peered, like cracks in an old painting, the mountains and
glaciers of Bylot Island. One of the girls, let's say, was Jukee, who said to her
companion: Your twin is coming to you! He's coming to you rushing to
you now!   and the other girl said faintly: I happy or sad I don't know; I want
try happy . . .   – Behind the girls, the beach ended quickly. Above it was a
sod-covered dune on which the first row of houses sat. Here was the old
house of sod blocks in which Subzero sometimes slept with the pack of
children. But on the beach, with its small outboard motorboats in a ragged
row beneath the dunes, there was little feeling of that, especially when the
two girls, seeing Subzero sit down, kept laughing for a minute and then left.
He was not the twin. Not yet. He threw a pebble in, as they had done, and it
sped down much faster than the rapid double rushings of a raven's wings . . .
    Wings came rushing. It was no raven, but a fulmar.
    The other girl (says the legend) was named Sedna. She lived with her
widowed father, refusing to take any of the young men who wanted her, but
the FULMAR had flown all the way from beyond the breaking sea-ice, drawn
by the light of graveyard games to this girl in caribou-skin leggings, sealskin
kamiks. They say that she was beautiful. The leggings rose well above her
hips and vanished beneath her sealskin coat whose shoulders flared out into
points as she stood smiling shyly down at the ground with white white teeth,
not looking at the FULMAR, her hair waving around her oval face whose
happiness or sadness could not be told – a *haunting* face, the FULMAR thought,
a *lovely* forehead . . . (What did He really want her for?) – Her eyes were half-
closed against the wind. – Now here I should say that I may be misinterpreting
the tale, which nowhere says that the FULMAR actually loved Sedna, but only
that He acted as though He did, such as when He sang a love-song in which
He guaranteed that the oil in her lamp would never run out and there would
always be meat in her pot. That impressed her, and her father, too. Of course
the passion went on with hopeless recognition; unexpressed patience and
goodness continued on both sides, and there were outbursts of yearning

tension, and a Lapland longspur sang like a metallic river. The FULMAR assured her that the floor of His igloo would be carpeted with soft skins, that He'd hunt all the animals for her, that she'd never be cold . . . Hearing this promise, she went into her room, found lined paper, and wrote Him a reply:

> My birthday is January 2 I cold in Inukjuak outside is I happy I'm Inuk in earth JESUS love people and I say thank you . . .

– Just as melting snow becomes translucent, so her heart slowly softened to Him. In the end, she agreed to go with Him to the Land of the Birds, although it was very far. And at first she was very happy there.

It was an encampment in the mud and snow: a dozen conical skin-tents, with pole-ends sprouting from their tips like grass from a tussock, and sled dogs nosing at the ground. The only people there were birds. They sat outside their houses, the men wearing caps, smoking, the women in dark-trimmed white parkas. Their hair was braided. A little girl was hooded in her mother's lap. She was the FULMAR's *najaksava;* they were all related. A thousand miles of gravel stretched all around. – Sedna tried to love them, so the evenings were like holidays – warm and sunny with wet snowflakes whirling down as she walked the beach with her husband, looking for animals, picking up pretty bits of petrified wood. – The FULMAR's mother was very old. She did not hear very well anymore, so (as she told Sedna through her son) she would simply smile at her a lot. She sat listening to tapes of sunny Inuit songs, knitting and singing along Ai-ya-ya while the TV said the US uses a very interesting system for putting their team together   and outside it was snowing and then it stopped and for hours Sedna could see an uneven glow-patch of very palely luminous orange for sunset, reflected white on the underbelly of the next cloud up, and cables swayed in the wind and the beacon on Signal Hill shone like an electric candle and light from it splashed down the white snow-ridge behind the power poles. Occasionally people walked down the snowy road, hunched and shivering as always, but inside it was very cozy and she sat in the kitchen and the FULMAR's mother gave Sedna tea and her choice of what to eat and although she tried to tempt her with storebought frozen chicken and frozen fish Sedna shook her stubborn head and pointed to the Inuit food in the freezer; so the old lady dragged in an empty cardboard box that said Reepah's Stuff on it in magic marker and Sedna helped her tear it and spread it flat on the floor and then Reepah, a girl who was related to the FULMAR somehow, took vast chunks of frozen raw caribou meat and frozen raw Arctic char and a little dish of *inukpo★* to dip it in and handed Sedna an axe. It was just like home. She sat down on the floor and started chopping at the thick steaks. After half a dozen blows, the floor now scattered with thawing meat-splinters, she had a bite-sized piece, and began to gnaw. The caribou was good, the Arctic char outstanding (and here I remember Peary's account: *The char of North Grant Land is a beautiful mottled fish, weighing sometimes as much as eleven or twelve pounds. I believe that the pink fiber of these fish – taken from water never any warmer than 35° or 40° above zero – is the firmest and sweetest fish in the world. During one of my early expeditions in this region, I would spear one of these beauties and throw him on the ice to freeze, then pick him up and fling him down so as to shatter the flesh under the skin, lay him on the sledge, and as I walked away pick out morsels of the pink flesh and eat them as one would eat strawberries*); the *inukpo* was rotten-sweet. Sedna ate until she was sated. She was very happy that she had married the FULMAR. The freezer was full of whole char-fish and giant frozen fish-heads and bright red caribou steaks and *inukpo* and a pot of frozen macaroni and cheese. On the floor nearby was a sack of ptarmigans, snow-white and dead, their heads

sunken on their breasts, their feathers traced with blood, and on another bier of cardboard were the red and grey guts of one of them. There were Ritz crackers and tea by the stove. All over the house were signs saying things like **GRANDMA'S KITCHEN – HELP WANTED!** and pictures of JESUS and photos of children and grandchildren. It was a house of goodness. But it was only that way for a little while, just long enough to deceive Sedna. All too soon (such realizations come by definition too soon) Sedna saw that there was no smiling old mother, that the house was built of torn and flapping fish-

★ Liquid seal fat.

skins which let in the wind, and that the birds fed her on nothing but scraps of fish. Her heart was like a frozen fox on a snow-ridge. There was no Reepah to help her, no twin. Squat pregnant Sedna, whom we might as well call Reepah, with her round face and upcurving nose, trudged heavily about the house, sweeping the floor, making tea, washing the dishes, vacuuming the carpet and chairs and sofas very carefully with the TV muted (a program about Grey Owl saving the beaver), and she said to the FULMAR: you want some tea?   and set a pot of it on the kitchen table along with a big sugar dish, a Seven-Up, a box of Ritz crackers, and the windows were open to air out the house as she worked and cold air rushed in, the sky grey and orange, and she sat for a moment watching TV again in her leather jacket with its dozens of Heavy Metal zippers. – She went to her room. She came out smoking a cigarette and sat in front of the TV. The FULMAR turned His long neck round to watch her with unwinking eyes; if she complained the FULMAR snapped His long cruel scissor-beak and bit her in a rage, saying that someday she'd be bound to lose her fingers . . . – And even if there had been a good old mother there to bake fresh bannock, rolled round and round itself like a cinnamon roll, a mother to keep Reepah company eating raw ptarmigan red and bloody, cool and soft, the little claw limp on the drumstick (the gobs of yellow fat tasted the best), even if Reepah had had that TV to watch, I cannot for the life of me imagine that she could have been pleased to be relocated to Resolute, can you? She mourned and sang sad songs. But most times, I know, she made the best of it, because they were all exiled there together, and Reepah's cousin Jukee came over to play the electronic piano and they ducked into her room giggling and whispering and then Jukee went out into the snow and the wind was blowing her hair and she pulled the starter of her motorbike many times before it caught and then she rode away. Then maybe she sniffed some gasoline. – Sedna's father, of course, was sure that she was happy. He felt that he was in the know about that, just as when you call Resolute in November just to see how the weather is and they say: A beautiful day! Twenty-four below and a little snow, maybe a foot and a half . . .   – then you feel so good to be in the know; you call in December and they say: Cold today; thirty-eight below . . .   – and you say: Ah, just as I expected!   – you call in January and they say: Forty-six below . . .   – and you feel as if you're keeping up with things . . . The legend says that in the following year, however, he came to visit; finding her so wretched, he took his rifle and killed the FULMAR and set out for home with her. It was very far, I told you. They paddled across the open sea. But Sedna's father was already laughing. He saw them home, paddling up the milky white fjord with a blue streak of cloud-shadow over it, a flat blue streak of hill beyond; and then a white cloud ceiling and there was the house of skins. – An oldsquaw dove in the still water, its rigid tail upright. Then the other FULMARS came. – Sedna saw them coming. She knew the way that birds in the distance are white against the mountains of the next isle, but black against the floes. She did not say anything to her father; she waited for him to see Them coming. The FULMARS came and called up a sea-storm with Their Power. The sound of the wind was like a faraway breath through a pipe. Then it came closer. Now her father's face began to change. She saw the fear oozing from his eyes as he paddled. Greenish murky shriekings engulfed the air. When the waves rose up, her father could think of nothing but saving himself, and so he decided to give Sedna to the birds' revenge. She was screaming and crying when he pushed her over the side, his face already a bird's face as she babbled: I hope I want I do I love me I don't want gone to go DEVIL. I really want go to heaven to go my father GOD and son JESUS. I want be good I want! And with love my heart and help good good

> and I remember why sad
>
> or love
>
> or something
>
> wrong –

Since she persisted in clinging to the side of his kayak, he took his savik and cut off her fingers joint by joint. The first joints became whales, the nails whalebone. The second joints became seals, and the final joints became ground seals. By now the FULMARS thought that the storm had surely drowned Sedna, so They returned home, and the father let her back into the boat. When they reached the house and her father was asleep, she called the dogs and had them gnaw away her father's hands and feet. Then the father cursed himself, and her, and the dogs, and the earth ate them up and they tumbled into the country called Adli'vun,* where SEDNA is the hostess. The legend says that when game animals become scarce the shamans must go down to Adli'vun to placate SEDNA and comb Her hair, as She cannot do that Herself. Then She will let the seals and walruses and fishes and whales come out and up; then people will have plenty to eat again.

---

* "Those Beneath Us."

Jukee had gone home to POV, and Reepah was cleaning the room. – Look! she said. She held up a ragged square torn from a black garbage bag, which seemed to be splattered with blood-vomit.

Jukee sniffing! she said.

Nail polish?

Yeah.

How do you feel about it?

It's OK. Everyone do it.

✳ ✳ ✳

The next day, the sunshine was stronger, and water trickled from the ice. The cloud had so far lifted as to expose the peaks of the lower mountains of Bylot Island with their wide roads of glaciers flaring down the blueness. The ice was now so unstable as to render skidoo transportation difficult. The komatiks looked very small. Mr Franklin was greatly improved. Both Dr Goodsir and Dr Peddie were in attendance upon him – an attention which embarrassed him, but Dr Goodsir reminded him most jovially that after all they must both stay in practice; there were no other patients on either ship. – Well, thank our REDEEMER for that, sighed Mr Franklin.

Now you must tell us, sir, if you have been subject to these fits before. The Expedition depends on you. A man your age must be careful.

Mr Franklin winced.

I readily confess that any infirmity may be unpleasant and perhaps humiliating, added Dr Peddie. But let us assure you, sir, that this shall not be talked about outside this room. We must know all your history.

I've concealed nothing from you, replied the patient, a little testily. My health has been very good; you yourselves have told me that it's improved since leaving England –

So you've never suffered from these fainting fits before, sir? asked Dr Goodsir.

Well, it would be incorrect to say that. Once or twice in the Barren Grounds – on earlier expeditions, you know, when we were hungry –

And never since then?

When Jane and I were in Van Diemen's Land, there were a couple of episodes. Some political unpleasantnesses. You know that I was virtually forced to step down. An unlucky combination of circumstances ... But nothing since then. And this last time felt different. As though someone were dragging me down. You know how someone will stay with you even though he knows you are getting bored, because he has nowhere else to go, and that staying and staying becomes so fatiguing –

Who was staying with you, sir?

Oh, Subzero, I suppose. Maybe Reepah. I can't say –

The two doctors said nothing. And Mr Franklin slept. He slept until evening, when the water and the sky were silver-white with promise, and a Caterpillar was hauling a komatik up onto the beach, and on the ice a child was riding his bike, and a man on a skidoo pulled his boat behind him; a family loaded their skidoo onto their boat and motored slowly across the

channel. A man motored carefully between ice-floes, his weight raising the nose of the boat like a sea-duck's tail; a boy hitched that boat to a skidoo and pulled it safely up onto the beach. And Mr Franklin gazed out the window and said: I accepted the twin and the triplet, since they were recommended. I thought I was satisfied. But every choice seems to exile me, somehow, when I thought I'd gain something new.

Dr Peddie gave him a look which he interpreted as ironical. He did not trust Dr Peddie. – Is it really that urgent, sir, to become someone else?

My motives were good, Peddie. I can honestly say that. I wanted to explore and to love. I don't see why that has to mean the end for me –

John?
  Yeah.
  John?
  Who's this?
  John?
  Reepah! Reepah, is it you?
  Yeah, she said proudly.
  John?
  Yeah.
  I have new son now. Your son.
  What's his name?
  Your name.
  Yes.
  John, I have no boyfriend.
  Why.
  'Cause I'm dead like you.
  Oh.
  Do you still have wife?
  Yes.
  John?
  Yes.
  John, she laughed, I want your money.
  Why?
My son is sick. He's gonna die, too. From sniffing. I want money. For gasoline. For sniffing.

On the 12th of that same month, Mr Franklin being fully restored, the two ships of the Expedition departed Pond's Bay, rejoicing to be underway once more. The Esquimau canoes or *kayaks* did not follow them; evidently the natives had been discommoded by Mr Franklin's spell of sickness. Nor had they been able to obtain the guide for whom they'd hoped, but Mr Franklin told them that it was easiest to look on the bright side of the question. A favoring wind assisted their progress . . .

    A few of the men complained of cramping of an undifferentiated character, but this was readily attributable to the excitement and novelty of their surroundings.

And so we passed the shady cliffs of Baffin Island, warning us off with croaking flapping ravens. Watching us, the women put the babies into each other's armautis. The tundra was scattered with mouse jawbones and scraps of whaleskin and piles of caribou hair from which the flies rose, and the pelvises of Arctic hares, and articulated trains of seal vertebrae which we could rattle in our hands. Arctic buttercups burst out of black moss-clumps. Birds sang like metallic water. We left all that behind. We wanted the Northwest Passage.

At Cape Walker, however, the lookouts saw ice. A wall of ice.

In Resolute it was a pleasant snowy morning, the sky slate-grey with thunder-blue shadows; and the radar fanned itself in perfect stillness as the office people yawned over their computers and made the morning coffee. It was half-past seven in August. – An Inuk girl wanted to fly south to Montréal. It would be very expensive.   – Are you sure you want to do this? said the ticket girl. – I must do it, replied the Inuk girl in slow perfect English.   Otherwise after a month I would not be a good person.   – But Subzero, who felt trapped, was sure she said *good prisoner*. – Farther north, Ellesmere Island lay cracked by white frost-rays and deep gorges and cliffs, mountains with wall-shadows, everything snowstreaked. I went there once. Mr Franklin coasted in that latitude on his first expedition, the one before the Barren Grounds, but never returned. I went there to be me. Dr Peddie and Jane couldn't find me there. (Goodsir was all right. He would have delivered Reepah . . .) I was beyond the ice, with my newborn son; he'd be the triplet now. When he was old enough to walk I'd take him south, where the moss was strewn with feathers as white as ice, and I'd laugh to see him gathering the feathers in his clumsy little arms, and then we'd go together to put them on his mother's grave. We'd play the same old games that Jukee used to play – if we saw Jukee I'd teach him to call her *ananaaga* – my mother. Reepah's hand would come up through the moss at night and catch my ankle and our son's ankle, and then she'd lead us into the light. While Mr Gore and Mr Vesconte led reconnaissance parties to prove what I already knew – that the ice was impassable (at least in that direction and for that year), I remained in my stateroom, conferring occasionally in body though not in spirit with C^apt Crozier of the *Terror* while the other officers stood watch or filled the water-casks from the nearest floating berg . . . My eyelids were icelids; when I closed them I was back behind the wall again, where nothing hurt. On Ellesmere

Island, downy white plants glistened and trembled in the wind, their stems frozen solid. I dug my son out of his grave and he started to play with a lump of snow. The wind interrupted the ripples of the creek in fan-shaped patterns. It blew so fiercely that I heard the ocean in my ears, throat and chest. My forehead became numb. And I was so far away from him then, but his hand was still on me from the grave; I couldn't be anything else but him anymore. Then I felt the ache begin from the other side of the wall where Mr Fitzjames was tapping. I remembered the hurt scared look in her eyes when I came to her, but I remembered how the first time I'd seen her she called me her best friend and said   merci toi,   said she'd meet me maybe someday in Heaven. Mr Fitzjames was tapping. Mr Fitzjames was tapping. In the saddest disappointment I turned my back to the brilliant blue sky of snow-cones and began trudging back from tussock to tussock. Reepah was with me then as she was all summer. To her in equal measure with my beloved wife the exclusive merit is due of whatever love I have been able to make.

Walking south and south away from Reepah, you came home to the Jane you wished you'd never left, and she was smiling at you in the same ironical way as Dr Peddie, the way a mother smiles to see her new child babystepping toward her, already reaching to grab her skirts and hang onto them, big baby head between her knees; the mother's smile is not any the less proud and loving for all the gulf in relative capacities that it implies; would Reepah have smiled that way at his son? Would she ever in a million ice ages have smiled that way at him? – But poor Jane could not smile just to smile; her smile had to mean something, unlike Reepah's; but then of course Jane was just as unhappy as Reepah. I am sorry to say that it was you who made them both unhappy. Jane was your Inukjuak and you should have stayed with her. She would happily have sewed flags for your spiritual expeditions every year, and read your letters over and over when the ships brought them; as for staying in her lap, as for burying your head between her knees like your own lost son, well, you could have done it but you would not have made history then. What did you want? Your curly-haired Jane, heavy-eyed, quick-mouthed, medium-breasted (perhaps her nose was a little too big), expected you for luncheons in which your favorite dishes would be served, and she was too wise to offer you nothing but herself for company; Sir James would make it a threesome, and you could gossip about frozen isthmuses to your heart's content, disputing the finer points of magnetism with Sir James while Jane, who could follow any thread, expressed her own views, unwrapping not the fatuous gift of eternal agreement but instead that wide-ranging sympathy which envelops in a warm and lively web, each thread of which is a statement of independent thought, but woven in most thoughtful relation to you: – Jane, in short, would have her own opinion about whether or not King William Land was an island, and it might well be different from yours, but if she had not been your wife she would not have been much interested in the matter. Jane was an admirable wife. Is it because she was so admirable that I do not write about her more? – Not at all. – The essence of the matter was this: What did you want to be? Fortunate Jane already knew what she was. – Suppose now that you had renounced the triplet and the twin. By so doing you would have escaped from the necessity of ever turning pale. You would have put definite limits to your own being, without which you'd be but a gelatinous pancake; only narrow souls get the job done. – But I still put this in an unattractive light, arguing only by a negation. The truth is that most people live this way, that Reepah herself would have lived that way if her father hadn't cut her fingers off and drowned her, or if the FULMAR hadn't relocated her to Resolute; Jane gained the credit of finding your men's bones at Starvation Cove precisely because she was that way; it was only you who did not want to be that way; you did not want simply to be someone else in space and time, which was a mere substitution, and, if successfully accomplished, would have left you in an equivalent ontological state; no, you wanted to own alternate selves so that you could be both self and other. Having split your nature in much the same way that GOD is reputed to have done, you could flow from one spiritual bottle into the next with endless sexuality; the content did not matter any more than the color of Jane's new dress; it would be sure to be becoming. This is not to say that you were entirely incapable of making comparisons, but it did mean that Reepah's cigarette-flavored kisses would not have had the same piquancy if you didn't have Jane to flee from and return to after a suitable and obvious period of suffering; this judgment, at best sarcastic, at worst harsh, is not undeserved when I remind you that you were, after all, directly responsible for Reepah's suicide, that you had begotten a child who would grow up without his true parents (or was he dead now, too? You never heard anything from Inukjuak anymore), that you left Jane a widow, that you caused the death by sickness and starvation of one hundred and twenty-nine men – but on the other hand I do acknowledge that the double or triple or cripple nature required to commit such crimes (triple if I accept your wistful contention that Reepah was you and you were Reepah, in the manner that Jukee had revealed to you that summer at Pond Inlet when your shadows were so long together and little brown longspurs hopped upon the tundra, calling) was at least richer than the single nature that most of us have, that the one-way metamorphoses of history and fairytales do not live perpetually the way an equilibrium reaction does; if it truly was perpetual love that you wanted, the becoming and giving and devouring over and over again, then I can almost forgive you because love is as necessary as it is cruel. Besides, to a lesser extent the rest of us are infected with the same vice. Even your good wife was not always reconciled to being what she was, as was proven in April of 1851 when somebody saw two three-masted ships, apparently abandoned, off the coast of Newfoundland, and Lady Jane's heart leaped up when Sir James told her because she was sure that they were her husband's ships, but no one saw them after that; they were only an optical illusion.

It was a very warm and pleasant day, and Jane and Sophy, her husband's niece, were having Sir James and Sir George over for dinner. Sir George of course was really just Back; that was how they thought of him, but since he had been knighted, too, they had to be polite. To be quite honest, Jane did not dislike Back nearly as much as her husband did. She could not but be grateful to the man who had saved John's life. (It is eerie that the thoughts of Mr Franklin's men would come round to Back again in a couple of years; that Great Fish River of his would then seem their only hope of preservation.)

And I will never forget, Back was saying, how the Indians kept calling: *Etthen-Oolah, Eethen-Tahouty* – which means, Jane, *no deer, the deer are gone away.*

Jane, who knew what *Etthen-Oolah, Eethen-Tahouty* meant quite as well as the Arctic Friends, since after all this particular adventure of Back's was now a decade old, nodded her head. – Do have some more soup, Sir James, she said.

Well, my dear, I suppose I shall. It's simply too good to resist. I approve of any soup with a proper measure of fat or cream in it. What about you, young lady (this to Sophy), do you approve of fat?

Why, certainly, Sir James. You can't have a good soup without a nourishing base. But I'm not one to go around drinking train-oil and munching candles, either, like your Esquimaux. There's a fine line.

Don't speak to me of candles, cried Back excitedly (forgetting that Sophy had not been speaking to him at all). Musk-ox flesh is what I most abhor.

Quite, Back, quite (thus Sir James). We all know you're a real theoretician of meat.

Ah, it looks as if you're ready for more soup now, too, Sir George. Please do have some more.

Thank you, Lady Franklin. It's quite delicious.

Sir James snorted a little into his napkin. He looked around uneasily. A happily married man, he was accustomed to the presence of his wife at these occasions. But Lady Ross had been indisposed. No one was saying anything, so he tried to think of a remark to make to Back. A film of ice seemed to have formed upon his cerebrum; he could think of nothing new and clever. He fell upon the usual topic.

And what do you s'pose Sir John is up to now? he said.

I wouldn't be a bit surprised if he's through the Passage, said Back. He told me himself that he expected the unexplored portion to be the easiest. But those things always take more slogging than one expects. I wonder if he's in sight of the Coppermine yet?

Yes, said Sir James, he's probably passed your Great Fish River.

Isn't that the haunt of that remarkable old Indian you've told us all about, Sir George?

Akaicho, you mean? No, young lady. But one can't expect girls to understand Arctic geography. It's very complicated really. Just thinking about the *distances* used to give us all considerable uneasiness. (But that's nothing compared to all the Antarctic miles you've logged, Sir James.) Akaicho was very very old when I saw him again in '33. He was very interested in your husband, of course, Lady Franklin; he asked after him . . .

. . . and Jane, who had been nodding without hearing a word, became attentive once more, because he had mentioned the one she loved. Both the Arctic Friends were busily buttering their bread; it almost made her queasy to see how much butter they laid on. Sir James had told her once that everyone who dwells for long in the Polar regions adopts that little freak. No doubt that was why Sir James and Back were both growing stout. When she was with them, hearing the same stories, she always began to believe that he would come back. No doubt he'd be considerably older in appearance. His eyesight would be worse. Probably he'd have lost weight. She hoped that he'd been able to procure that pair of Esquimau mittens for his tailor's daughter. If not, she had a pair which he'd once given her; rather than disappoint the young girl she'd part with them . . .

Every life contains at least one sadly evil paradox. In Lady Franklin's case, it was that only his disappearance could give her scope for resolute action, for the expression of nobility which she prized in him. In the end her fidelity would make men compose ballads. Needless to say, she would much rather have had him come back. Sir George was talking again about the cyclical scarcity of the caribou and Sir James was listening and Sophy was interrupting with questions, either out of genuine interest or else to let Auntie eat her soup, and she was so happy that her dear kind friends were there; she would never, *never* seek out a grave-twin because only lonely half-souls do that; she was steadfast like Back; she was loving like Reepah. Surely it would have been better if her husband (by whom I mean Subzero) could have chosen likewise singly, but no one chooses the Northwest Passage alone. That would be terrifyingly beyond human powers.

On the 21st, Messrs Vesconte and Gore begged leave to report their findings, which of course he granted. It seemed that the ice to the west was not only impassable, but the floes themselves seemed to be growing by accretion, although the nightly temperatures of late had not been much below freezing. In any event, there was no time to be lost if the Expedition meant to try the alternate route up Wellington Channel. Mr Franklin expressed to those two gentlemen his sincerest appreciation for their labors. Then he invited Capt Crozier to the *Erebus* for supper and consultations. Capt Crozier said he feared that it might already be too advanced in the season – an assertion which

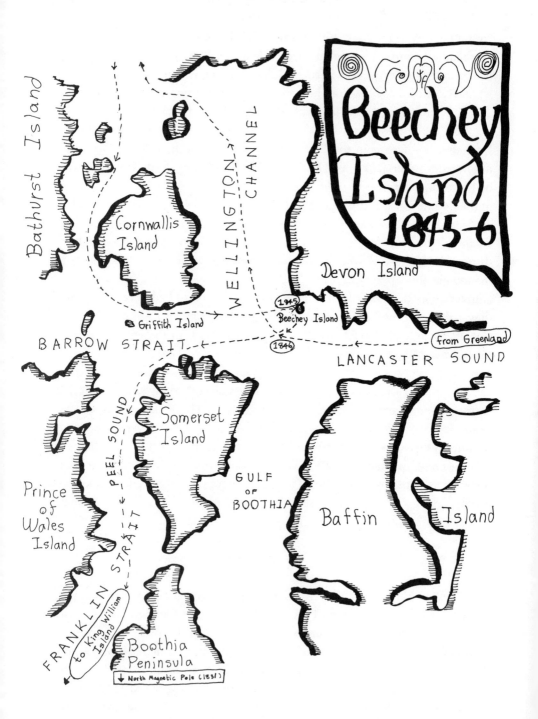

Beechey Island 1845-6

Bathurst Island

Cornwallis Island

WELLINGTON CHANNEL

Devon Island

1845
Beechey Island

Griffith Island

BARROW STRAIT

1846

from Greenland

LANCASTER SOUND

PEEL SOUND

Somerset Island

GULF OF BOOTHIA

Prince of Wales Island

Baffin   Island

FRANKLIN STRAIT

to King William Island

Boothia Peninsula

↓ North Magnetic Pole (1831)

young Fitzjames disputed with the hottest impatience when he heard. Be that as it may, all were in agreement as to the next step; Wellington Channel must be attempted, and better sooner than later. They turned about at dawn –

By then it was autumn, really, and the sun glowed thin and white through the fog like the *Qilaujjauti*, the drum of white sealskin lashed to a round frame to be beaten with hollow sounds while the fat roundfaced ladies sat on the floor in their white parkas, singing the aya-aya songs of komatiks and bird-seasons and the shortness of summer, and a man struck the Qilaujjauti and children wandered through the community hall drinking Cokes or spilling them, sucking on candies; the little girls already wore armautis in which they carried their dolls. The *Terror* and the *Erebus* ascended Wellington Channel in this autumn light and August autumn dimness; reaching latitude seventy-seven, they again met ice, and so looped back south along the western edge of Cornwallis Island. This was a piercing disappointment, especially for Mr Fitzjames. – The eastern wall of Wellington Channel is Devon Island. At the corner of this lies a tiny kingdom called Beechey Island. And here it was that Mr Franklin decided to winter. (See the longboat tiny on a blue-grey sea, cliffs rising like chimneys, the *Terror* and *Erebus* anchored far out, themselves grey upon that sea of glass. Only the glaciers were real.) Shortening sail to wait upon the *Terror*, he then directed the men to warp up to the beach. C^apt Crozier concurred with him that this would be a favorable spot, so they fired the rifles and landed with eight cheers –

Akaicho's Debt

1819–1822

The ménage was most ably run by Eskimo servants recruited from a
small settlement in the neighborhood. They prepared the food, cooked
for us, washed, mended our clothing and even cut hair when required.
And all for the princely wage of two cigarettes a day!

MARTIN LINDSAY, *Those Greenland
Days* (1932)

T hey housed over their ships. When winter came they built an
observatory, a carpenter's shop, two enclosed washing places, a storehouse
and a forge. On the eastern side of the island they erected a shooting gallery.
(If Jane were with them, she would doubtless have remarked that this place
could be settled to advantage by convicts, just as in Van Diemen's Land.) They
erected finger-posts with black hands pointing atop eight-foot boarding-pikes,
so that even in a sudden blizzard the men would be able to find their way to
the ships. The ice was white, grey-veined with fat hemmorhagic fogs.

Once the masts and yards were snugged down, once the men grew bored
with huddling beneath those doggishly reeking wolf-skin blankets, the officers
set them to taking their exercise in the snow. Mr Franklin, well aware of the
dangers consequent on idleness, put them to strenuous make-work whenever
the other variety was in short supply; it would never do to have them brood.
As it may be interesting to the reader to know how we otherwise passed our
time, I beg leave to state that Mr Franklin continued to hold Divine service
every Sunday (which was always a day of rest), that Fitzjames founded a glee-
club, whose members never sang Reepah's favorite songs, and that the sailors
held their own theatrical practice, gesturing in shadowtalk throughout the

two ships lit creepily by candles and oil lamps, the reeking steam from soup arising and mingling with the men's breath to make a mist 'tween decks; and of course there were exchange occasions alternately hosted by the officers of either ship; in the first months, before they tired of the sport, the men built snow-walls and snow-houses; they made statues out of snow and had competitions over which their officers presided; Mr Franklin himself occasionally awarded the prize. These activities were not without their beneficial effect, for soon there was no one (with the unfortunate exception of Lady Franklin's monkey) who did not feel entirely at home in the cold. Dr Peddie had but two cases of frostbite to treat, these being very minor; and Dr Goodsir had none. The frozen sea became a regular thoroughfare. It was now increasingly common to find the officers promenading in pairs, discussing sweethearts, campaigns and stud-horses; the men stood to with spirited salutes. The sun was long gone, of course. The sky's ringing purple-blackness only rarely lightened to a dull grey, and when it did there was nothing for a gaze to nourish itself on but snowdrifts and brown ridges whose stony pavements led nowhere, whose shaggy muddy cliffs looked down on nothing, whose only tender gift was snow, whose dormant lichens, frequently exposed by the wind, were brown or reddish-grey; and where there were niches in the cliffs, only snow filled them. But it would not do to be eaten by polar bears. The promenaders went armed, and never alone. Sometimes a man hard at work or play among his fellows would stop as if mazed, gazing at the ships, which appeared as if on fire, the smoke of breath and cocoa-steam rising from their ventilators in great columns, and he'd fall silent. Under Mr Franklin's quiet eye, however, this was kept track of; so when the snow-competitions ceased to suffice the atmosphere was enlivened by a hunt for Arctic foxes. – He'd brought with him seventy slates and slate pencils, two hundred pens, paper, ink and a great number of arithmetic books. He intended to hold a school for the men, and possibly refine them a little. In December the first term commenced. One very popular course was geography. Mr Franklin was pleased to lecture on his own prior travels, which had considerably narrowed the unknown regions of British North America, and the pupils in their blue broadcloth listened with particular attention. Next summer, when they'd completed the Passage and were en route to the Sandwich Isles, the North would have receded into ungraspability. They were very keen; they longed to draw out the adventure as long as they could. – Geometry was another attractive class. Any sailor who desired to learn sufficient mathematics to elevate himself by a degree or two was indulged by the officers (who themselves needed activity). Steady jots of grog were issued each Saturday, to distract them all a little from the disagreeable qualities of snow-water. Exploration parties were formed, each officer with his own pocket chronometer, compass, spy-glass and rifle . . .

Mr Franklin was rereading Parry, Simpson, Richardson. All the while he kept thinking and wondering what he would do when the ice melted. He had to be ready to act at once. He had to go quickly, before he became icebound again. (The officers had now mapped the coast for several miles inland, and he named a peak after Sir James, whom it was very gratifying to repay for his corresponding and commensurate tribute of Franklin Island in the Antarctic.)

C^{apt} Crozier continued his observations of the specific gravity of the sea at various depths. It was a wonder to see how fast the test-hole froze over! Would he have had the heart to set his sailors a-sawing through it again if he'd known that not even his notes would survive? Sometimes it is better not to know. A little east of the shooting gallery he erected a proper magnetic station. – That amiable officer expended the winter in perfect happiness, for he had no unlawful sweetheart or ghost to dog him; when his lieutenants chatted about the Corn Laws or stud-horses he joined in with genuine interest; lucky C^{apt} Crozier was interested in almost everything! To him a magnetic station was as good as a steeplechase. – I should rather think we'll reach Russian America by July next, he heard Lt Little say. – His counterpart Lt Hodgson replied: Perhaps summer will come even earlier this time. Didn't that old Esquimau say that it would, back in Greenland? Did you see how he coveted my rifle? Rather brutish, really, that fellow . . . It did not seem to the unseen Crozier (as it would have to Mr Franklin, but then it always would have to Mr Franklin) that such conversations, having used up their frictionless salve of novelty, now began to strain and creak like ice. The only thing that he disliked about their situation was that he continually found himself in this unpleasant position of listening at keyholes, not at all through his own design, but simply as a result of the darkness and proximity. As stoical as that middling char-fish we called Mr Back, he possessed the added capacity of a sincere attention to the happiness of others. As long as Lt Irving desired to display that silver medal for mathematics, Crozier would continue to compliment the lad. Now, those tired Euphrates reminiscences of C^{mdr} Fitzjames, on the other hand, those he really could not endure. But then C^{mdr} Fitzjames was not C^{mdr} Crozier's subordinate.

Aping his idol Mr Franklin, the just-mentioned Mr Fitzjames occupied himself in more rarefied anticipations of the great campaign that would open next year. With some reason, Fitzjames insisted to his own circle of lieutenants that their enemy, the ice, was weaker than ever before. Mr Franklin's three previous expeditions had vastly narrowed the unknown lurking-places of the ice. This final attempt would seize the prize from those cold grey mandibles. They had made considerable progress in the course of the late season; their present shrouded embayment on Beechey Island was deep enough in the archipelago to permit them to proceed rapidly into whatever new recesses Mr Franklin might dictate. – Soon we'll be waltzing with bergs and floes in the deepest darkest ballroom! he laughed to Lt Gore, who bowed, pleased to see his Commander in this whimsical mood (Mr Franklin was absent).

Mr Fitzjames did not have the pinched face that would have suggested nervousness to the phrenologists of his or any period; the lined and heavy-lidded eyes suggested merely a plodding weariness, as is always acceptable in One of Our Men; the gelatinous beginnings of a double chin were a reassurance to his elders that he strove to become one of them, while his untidy collar and wild hair proclaimed that he was even now bespending himself; who could deny him? (The aforesaid idol, Mr Franklin, was satisfied to have made Mr Crozier the second-in-command; gallant though he was, Mr Fitzjames took things too much to heart, not having recognized that patience is sometimes better than bravery, at least when we are powerless.) He withdrew into his cabin, and sat at his desk whose three narrow drawers in a row stretched all the way to his coffin-narrow bed, after which the cabin dead-ended at the bookshelf, and he lit the light-globe and gazed for a moment at the portrait on the wall and then he withdrew the observations log-book from the middle drawer, dipped his quill, and smiled with the delicate cracked changeability of blue-grey ice crystals.

Mr Fitzjames?

Ah, is that you, Hoar?

Aye, sir. The Captain desires to speak with you, sir.

Thank you. I'll be right along.

Mr Franklin, beaming, invited him to take a chair.

An unusual winter, wouldn't you say, Mr Fitzjames?

Indeed I would, sir.

And would you say that the men are making progress in their adaptation to Polar life? I understand that they confide in you.

(This was one of Mr Franklin's most benevolent tricks, to award his subordinates compliments which were not entirely true. The best way to instill a desired behavior is to praise that behavior in advance.)

Yes, I'd say that all is well, sir. They've got over their superstitions about the aurora borealis. Stickland's headaches have disappeared. Everyone's excited about the new singing competition . . .

Splendid, replied Mr Franklin.

I think I can speak for all of us, sir, when I say that we're waiting eagerly for a good hard pull as soon as the ice breaks.

Believe me, Fitzjames, I'm very grateful for your enthusiasm. The truth is, unless a man enjoys a bit of a challenge, he's scarcely fitted for Arctic life. From what I see and hear, you are ideally suited for these latitudes. You're young and fit and eager, but also very patient . . .

Thank you, sir. (Fitzjames was blushing.)   And what is our likelihood of also achieving the Pole come summer? It would be so glorious, to carry off two prizes!

Oh, well, we shall see . . .

They celebrated Christmas with great pomp. On the 28th, the monkey which Lady Franklin had given them unfortunately perished of cold, which was a grief to the men, as they'd been very fond of their pet. By and large, however, they continued very cheerful.

On New Year's Day died John Torrington, sailor, evidently of consumption. On the 4th of the same month died John Hartnell of the same complaint; Dr Goodsir could do nothing. Dr Peddie of the *Terror* had a suspicion that the cause might be some new form of scurvy, for there was a peculiar grey tinge to the corpses, but in this diagnosis the two surgeons did not agree, and in any event there was nothing to be done to guard the rest that was not already being done. These twin deaths cast the men down somewhat, Hartnell's more than Torrington's simply because the latter event followed the former so closely, adding to it and weighing upon it most leadenly – although Mr Franklin won their affections even more at this time, by the fervent way in which he prayed on each occasion. They understood, too, that such things happen on sea-voyages. At the middle of the month, a suitable interval having elapsed, to show respect for the two gathered souls, Mr Franklin commenced a new course of instructive lectures for the officers. Among other things, it was important to remind them that the Esquimaux, savage and unenlightened though they were, might be nonetheless useful to cultivate. First of all, they willingly bartered away their sea-horse teeth* for trifles – which promised individual and national enrichment for England. (Fitzjames looked dreamy; it was clear to all that he longed to assist his country in such an advance.) It might well have been the case (said Mr Franklin) that they were unable to get a guide at Pond's Bay because the men had unwittingly broken some taboo or caprice of theirs. This was to be strictly

* Walrus tusks.

avoided in future. (No one said a word about his fainting fit; that had never happened.) And he related to them the story that Sir James had told him, how before commencing an overland journey by sledge, Sir James, his uncle and all the starving men had once purchased two ninety-pound bales of dried salmon at the cost of a knife apiece; and while they waited for the fish to be delivered the goodnatured Esquimaux built a snow-house for them and lent them blankets, as the Englishmen had forgotten theirs. Yes, the Esquimaux would serve as needed, provided only that we treated them with kindness –

There was still a great deal of food left.

In February Mr Franklin gave his permission for a newspaper to be established, one from each ship: to wit, the *Erebus Sentinel* and the *Terror Times*, each of which strove to outdo the other with gossip and jests. In March, when the weather had begun to moderate, the officers conducted volunteers on numerous more distant excursions, while Mr Franklin stayed in. His fingers had never been the same since he'd frozen them twenty years since, at Cumberland House. The snow was greyly scarred. They visited Caswell's Tower, a mass of rock not many miles from Beechey Island, where they set up a shooting-tent weighed down with stones; they went hunting along the eastern coast of Wellington Channel, where M^essrs Gore and Vesconte erected an observation post, floored and walled with stones, roofed with tent-canvas, in order to comfortably watch the ice. Gore, who was exceedingly hardy, never admitted to being cold, which the ironical Vesconte remarked upon with a smile. – You might as well be cold, he said. It's the one chance of your life. At summer's end we'll be through the Passage. – I'm quite content to watch your shivers, replied Gore. All that teeth-chattering and those other contortions entertain me royally. – Ah, so you don't want to be in my common mold, is that it? – And Vesconte raised his binoculars, scanning hopefully for leads in the ice. Everything was figured out by now. If Wellington Channel were to become clear in August (or perhaps even July), they would go that way. Otherwise they'd return to the southwest. – But whichever direction the exploration parties went, they never traveled very far. For one thing, their sledges were heavy. For another, there was no reason to become separated from the ships . . .

Walking south and south on Cornwallis Island, pulling your fur ruff down to your chin to clear the fog on your glasses (the sour-bitter-smelling animal hairs were finely rilled with ice), you crunched across the snow-crust, each step squeaking in a different pitch from the one before; you crossed old polar bear tracks, the talon-marks hideously long (they'd killed a six-footer in Resolute the day before yesterday), and then you crossed dog tracks and fox tracks and the snow was finely bulbed and grained and terraced, not quite like sand since it held its edges better than any dune, and it was not the same color anywhere, there being so many shadow-shades of blue and white (all glittering as if with mica) that these factors made each step new; sometimes the crust gave a little; usually your bootprint rested lightly on it; occasionally you left no trace at all. As your ruff continued to freeze, your breathing became louder, hissing through the icy hairs.*

The upper camp was the usual huddle of cubes and cylinders behind you. Mid-Camp was snowed in at the edge of the sea-ice. Not far away, on the horizon below the horizon, an Inuk stood by his komatik, watching you. You angled widely around him, in case he was waiting for animals. The wind began to blow, and it grew very cold. Wiping your nose on the long since frozen snot pads of your mitts, you now approached the frozen sea, which

---

* There is an Inuktitut word just for ruff-frost: *manulik.*

stretched snow-plastered to the long low snow-mound of Griffith Island (where they say the Inuit knew of graves connected with the Franklin Expedition, and when they told the Commissioner for the Northwest Territories he stole all the grave markers and took them back to England), and you remembered Griffith Island from summer as being blue and white. It was now eleven in the morning, and the sun achieved a special conjunction which caught the edge of those thirty-second-of-an-inch-high snow terraces, so that on the zone of dark blue snow under your boots there came into being a woman's hair, every individual strand etched white and divine; her hair flowed headless under you; you walked on the dead girls of POV; you walked on Reepah's grave.

One day in March Mr Franklin convoked a sort of cabinet, in order to best determine whether any modification of their plans might be advisable, as a third sailor, one William Braine, had just now passed away,* but the officers assured him that the men's morale continued to be high, this sad circumstance notwithstanding; Mr Franklin hesitated a little, and wondered if they were shamed to trouble him, but it did seem that they were at their ease, and said what they thought was the truth, instead of seeking merely for his approbation. So his apprehensions were relieved; and they went through all the charts together and agreed that they were doing everything as it ought to be done and Mr Franklin told them to put their feet up and have a smoke and the steward spread the table with dainties and shortbreads and a plum pudding tinned by means of Goldner's patent, and Mr Franklin said a short and quiet prayer. And now a toast!

A far cry from *tripe de roche*,   he said with a smile, while helpful Gore cut the pudding –

Aye, sir.

Tell me, sir,   said eager Fitzjames, his epaulet-fringes a bit askew,   did you and the men relish the taste of *tripe de roche* in your days of hunger, or was eating it an unpleasant duty?

In my case I came to have the greatest dread of those meals, because they gave me indigestion,   Mr Franklin replied.   And the taste of it was – well, *discouraging*, somehow, monotonous –

Delicately he nibbled at his shortbread.

* His shipmates were quite shocked when they prepared him for burial; it looked as if somebody had gnawed his shoulders. – Rats,   said Dr Goodsir genially . . .

Fortunately, said he, there is no *tripe de roche* to be found on the sea-ice, so if we meet disaster on this expedition we shall be spared one tribulation, at least.

And he smiled, when they all laughed –

I wonder how our Indians would have fared that time, he said. In some ways they were better suited to survival than Englishmen. Their constitutions were more hardened, although they were less resolute. I remember one old fellow, Cascathry, of whom I became very fond. Oh, he was fickle and superstitious, of course, in the manner of those savages, but practically indefatigable. And his hardihood! Yes, I recall one night in 1820 when Dr Richardson and I were on a pedestrian excursion to the Coppermine; we'd camped beneath practically the last tree before the Barren Lands, and it was quite cold. Dr Richardson and I slept in our clothes to be warm, while that Cascathry stripped himself naked and toasted himself over the embers of the dwarf-birch fire – I am sure that it was below freezing! – before coiling himself up beneath his deerskin. And he was quite comfortable, as I could see. Dr Richardson is a very hardy man, you know. Many's the time I've seen him swim an icy river. But somehow, to sleep that way – well, it gave both Richardson and me the shivers.

I wager Cascathry would have the shivers here, sir! said stout Vesconte, and again they all laughed for a second while they listened to the shriek of the wind.

Then the young officers began coaxing him to tell them how it had been, how it really had been, and he found himself describing the way it had been on a certain September day of 1820 when Cascathry and Hepburn were shooting snow-geese in a field of crowberries and everyone had an excellent supper before retiring to bed in the gneiss formation; poor Hood was – where was Hood? – with that slut Greenstockings, no doubt – and the next day it snowed and the next Mr Franklin's ankle was paining him badly from an old sprain, so they got on at scarcely better than a creep, but fortunately Cascathry had a cache of good fat meat to console them from, so they encamped in the thin cold sandhills and ate while Cascathry ate with them and laughed. Mr Franklin made a prayer and so to bed. Jolly Hepburn, seeing Dr Richardson to be in one of those collectors' funks, when no appreciative audience is nigh to admire and covet, winked beside him in the ember-light and drew him out; he was like an inexhaustible sack of pemmican in those days, was Hepburn, always ready to nourish the officers with adulation and obedience: – Pray tell me more about the Copper Indians, Dr Richardson, said he; and the flinty shaft of Dr Richardson's avidity being thus rubbed, he sparked and

The Second Expedition
1819-22

POLAR SEA

Victoria Island

Baffin Island

Bloody Falls

CORONATION GULF

Point Turnagain

King William Island

Boothia Peninsula

SIMPSON STRAIT

Arctic Circle

Coppermine River

Hood River

Arctic Circle

Arctic Circle

Snare River

82.1

Fort Enterprise

Back's Great Fish River

REPULSE BAY

Southampton Island

1819 (from a collision with ice at Resolution Island)

HUDSON STRAIT

and return

Fort Providence

Barren Grounds

Fort

Great Slave Lake

Slave River

Fort Chipewyan

Lake Athabasa

HUDSON BAY

Inukjuak

Athabasa River

Churchill

York Factory

Hayes River

JAMES BAY

1820

Saskatchewan River

Cumberland House

Lake Winnipeg

NORTH AMERICA

40   80
40   0
SCALE   OF   MILES

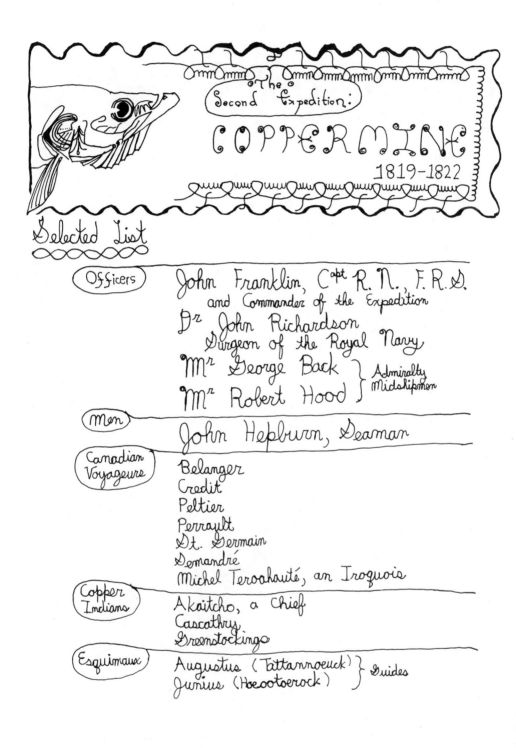

The Second Expedition:

COPPERMINE

1819–1822

Selected List

Officers

John Franklin, Capt R. N., F. R. S.
and Commander of the Expedition
Dr John Richardson
Surgeon of the Royal Navy
Mr George Back } Admiralty
Mr Robert Hood } Midshipmen

Men

John Hepburn, Seaman

Canadian Voyageurs

Belanger
Credit
Peltier
Perrault
St. Germain
Semandré
Michel Teroahauté, an Iroquois

Copper Indians

Akaitcho, a Chief
Cascathry
Greenstockings

Esquimaux

Augustus (Tattannoeuck) } Guides
Junius (Hoeootoerock)

began all over again a tale that Hepburn knew by heart, having seen it himself, concerning the great success with which the Indians killed caribou with firearms, then passing on to the cunning of the Dog-Rib Indians who approached the herd in pairs, hiding behind the skin of a severed caribou-head, with muzzles at the ready; and Hepburn's mouth dropped open, and he said now isn't that a *caution?* – In October they sent to Akaicho's for meat, and obtained 370 lbs of it dried, plus another 220 lbs of suet, at which Mr Franklin was gratified; he already had in his possession 100 deer and 800 lbs of suet, thanks to the industry of Akaicho and his Indians, who were of course being compensated with notes signed in full by Mr Franklin. In December Cascathry made an offering of tobacco and a knife to the POWER OF WATER, through Whose malignancy his wife had contracted an ulcer of the nose, which organ Dr Richardson confessed that she was about to lose. Dr Richardson was sorry for her, and so was Cascathry, and so was their daughter Greenstockings, so Back would have been sorry, too, but Mr Franklin had sent him to Fort Providence for supplies. (It was a long walk. It was six hundred and fifty-four miles. But that was what mediocre fellows like Back were good for. Back arrived and met with the Hudson's Bay Factor, Mr Simpson, an explorer himself, who'd soon go crazy and use a rifle to detonate his brains; Mr Simpson bowed most correctly and said: From your remarks, sir, I infer that there is little probability of the objects which you expect being accomplished. – I disagree most strongly, sir! cried Back, but Simpson said: Your Lt Franklin must have three meals per diem, tea is indispensable, and with the utmost exertion he cannot walk above eight miles per day ... – Seeing Back's wild, indeed almost murderous look, Simpson desisted and granted him a little flour and meat, after which Back, saluted by a volley from the rifles and a round of cheers, began to trudge the six hundred and fifty-four miles back to Mr Franklin, who merely said: Ah, well done, well done, Mr Back!) Meat was all around them in rock-covered caches which all were hopeful that the wolverines would not discover; it delighted Mr Franklin to dream of meat at night, ordered into quarters and haunches according to the best Naval regulations; it was a luxuriance of meat which would enable him to perfect his purpose of traversing the shores of the Polar Sea; as for Dr Richardson, the secure fact of meat left him at liberty to expand upon his impressions in an after-dinner fashion, even if only to himself, so he noted in his journal: *We have frequently remarked that in the cold clear nights the moisture of the breath freezes with a considerable crackling noise* and Dr Richardson sighed happily because his belly was full and Hepburn was smoking tobacco with Cascathry's squaw and everything continued delightful at Fort Enterprise, especially the next day when Akaicho and the young men with their wives departed, for those Indians ate too much. Already the officers had begun to sit up late, calculating the inroads in their supplies. Farewell, then, my redskinned pawns; Mr Franklin made them a parting gift of a few balls of shot ... Not long after the New Year, Cascathry came in during dinner to obtain medicine for his wife from Dr Richardson, so Richardson got up and gave it to him with good humor and Cascathry wrapped it up very carefully to show respect for this sacred thing, at which Dr Richardson's upper lip began to twitch and Hepburn guffawed and even Mr Franklin shared gently in the merriment; Cascathry then took his leave, somewhat offended as it seemed; all night the family spent in chanting because they thought that Dr Richardson must have presented them with poison – why else would he have smiled in that distant disdainful way? Perhaps he did not want *them* to eat Mr Franklin's meat, either. Perhaps he was jealous of Greenstockings and Hood. (Hood hung his head. Well aware, especially from certain remarks which Back had made, that he was making a fool of himself, he consoled his conscience with the thought that this connection must soon be severed. Just as Mr Franklin was doing with the others of her race, he used her only as a temporary source of meat. He said this to himself, and yet it was not true. He loved her. That made his helplessness more miserable than ever. Back shot him a yellow glare of envious hatred and said: Can't *you* stop the din?   – Oh, no,   said Hood, I feel certain that I couldn't help . . .) Greenstockings was crying with her mother as morning dawned and Cascathry did not stop chanting to overcome the bad Power and Mr Franklin cried: This is becoming too distressing, Richardson!   so Dr Richardson hastened out to soothe their susceptibilities, ashamed of himself for having given way to his mirth in front of these country people, and when they trusted him again, Greenstockings's mother said that her nose was happy, too, and so everyone was pleased at Fort Enterprise once again. But in February they found that the wolverines had gotten into a moiety of the caches after all; and the Indians were importuning them again, claiming that Mr Franklin's notes were not being honored at Fort Providence. Of course they had to be feasted. A fine thing, if all their meat were to be squandered. In the clement season of April all the officers went out hunting by turns to replenish the stores; it seemed that Hood and Back were in competition; Hood succeeded better, for he took Greenstockings with him. (Back said to himself: Someday I'll prove which of us, Hood or I, has more iron in him!) In May everybody was eating fat geese –

Then Akaicho came with his men, so, following Mr Franklin's standing order, the rifles spoke to him in salutation, to humor him according to his

desire, and again he complained that the notes were not being honored, but
Mr Franklin explained to him that in consideration of this circumstance his
customary debts to the Northwest Company had been canceled, and someday
there would be a special present for him. – Moreover, Akaicho (thus M^r
Franklin, seizing the initiative as he had been taught), we are disappointed
in *your* conduct. You agreed to bring us more dried meat. You know very
well that it is indispensable for us. We must have sufficient provender for our
journey to the Polar Sea –

I have told you that going by that way is dangerous, said Akaicho. You
proceed far too slowly. You scare the animals away. If you persist, you will all
perish, and I shall never see you again.

We shall see about that, said young Franklin. But whoever impedes my
expedition will be thrown in irons and taken to England for trial.

I think we should not say that to him, Mr Franklin. (Thus the interpreter.)
Maybe he gets angry then.

Very good, sighed Mr Franklin. You are correct; please forgive me –

In June Akaicho and his Indians paid a visit to Dr Richardson at Point Lake,
requesting more ammunition for their muzzle-loaders, because they had
expended all that had been given them on their own wants. Dr Richardson
was obliged to refuse him in conformity with Mr Franklin's instructions,
which were to give ammunition only in proportion to the deer brought in.
Then it was time to set out for the Coppermine in earnest, so that Mr Franklin
could show the world what his party was capable of. Early in July, being
guided by Akaicho, White Capot and the Hermaphrodite, they reached the
encampment of a good Indian called the Hook, whom Mr Franklin decorated
with a medal (he had oodles of those), after which the Hook gave them all
the provisions that he had – *viz.*, 130 lbs of pounded meat, and some dried
flesh, together with a quantity of tongues. – Your supply is none too large,
frowned Mr Franklin, somewhat mortified, but nonetheless he signed some
notes on the Northwest Company, to be paid in the winter, and also presented
the Hook with a handful of balls, with powder to match. He'd know what to
do with 'em! Cascathry and his family, who'd gone in advance of the
exploration party, were dwelling with the Hook for the moment; on the
following day, when Mr Franklin completed his transactions, Cascathry
continued down the river with them, accompanying Mr Franklin in his canoe
while Akaicho led the other, and the Hook stood watching them from the
top of his high sand-cliff and Cascathry's wife stood watching (she'd lost her
nose entirely now) and Greenstockings stood watching, and her newest
paramour, whom the English called Broadface, stood watching behind. She

was already pregnant with Hood's child. Hood gazed north, mapping the river's sandbeds; surely he could not have known that he'd never see her again, but his lips trembled, as Mr Franklin noted; Mr Franklin supposed that that officer must be ill again; they portaged at 3:00 p.m., and Hood ached to be going ever farther from her; already her scent was fading on him; he looked into Cascathry's face and Cascathry returned the look ironically, then suddenly Hood saw (and it was the eeriest thing to see) how he became dead and utterly forgotten in Cascathry's eyes as Cascathry snatched up a rifle in silence and took aim at a musk-ox on the bank . . . – I *believe* in the rifles! Hood laughed later; and Mr Franklin patted his shoulder and said: Spoken like a good midshipman!   – But the next day they met some Indians who did quite well with bow and arrow; from them Mr Franklin purchased seventy pounds of dried meat . . . His hunters had gone on ahead. From time to time the main party found a caribou lying dead on the shore where the rifles had spoken yesterday, today, three days since, and sometimes they themselves shot caribou in lordly fashion from their canoes, thinking always on future meat. They met caribou antlers like a tossing forest of sticks, caribou backs thin and twitching with mosquitoes, caribou as far as everywhere. A week later they saw two musk-oxen, and the Indians killed them both. Then Akaicho shot a grizzly who'd sought to ambush them, and brought the finest tidbits to Mr Franklin's party, for the Chippewyans do not partake of that meat themselves; Mr Franklin pronounced the meat to be superior to that of musk-ox, and all the officers immediately agreed because they loved Mr Franklin and he was their Captain and it was true besides. (Did I ever tell you what Greenstockings said when she was embroidering my gunpowder pouch?   – Thus innocent Hood, and Back began panting with rage, like a white wolf . . .) The thermometer showed 47°. Butterflies much denser than grapeshot pelted the voyageurs on hands and shoulders like rain; blackflies ricocheted off the brims of their caps, flew into their noses and mouths when they breathed, so that every man kept coughing and spitting. Some tied handkerchiefs over their faces, but the handkerchiefs became slimy with sweat and clung to them chokingly, and mosquitoes landed on the cloths and bit through them. Mosquitoes preened themselves on necks and ankles, looking for the best place to sting. They flew into the men's ears and whined there. They loitered eagerly round their victims in such clouds as to distract the vision. – At the edge of the world, a hundred yards away, a caribou came mincing, brown and stately. Behind came another. Their antlers did not seem to move with the rest of their bodies. One bent his head to browse; the other shook his mosquitoes off. Suddenly he raised his head and gazed toward M^r

Franklin. Mr Franklin was downwind, but somehow the caribou smelled him. He trotted uneasily beyond the world, and the other animal followed . . . The Arctic Circle was behind now; the Coppermine flowed on. Mr Franklin encouraged his dear friends resolutely, calculating always how to get more food out of his Indians, how to dispatch them to their hunting-grounds to get deer-fat for him, how to persuade the guides to feed themselves, how to convince Akaicho of the existence of a SUPREME BEING, how to dazzle them with his knowledge of an upcoming eclipse . . . Making considerable progress in this latter purpose (indeed, Akaicho assured him that the Indians would hunt all the harder out of gratitude for the astronomical information conveyed), Mr Franklin and his party passed the skeleton of a caribou in a bog, with black streamers of decay still inside it; they saw a fresh caribou head, and the mosquitoes got worse, but so did the hoarfrost. Mr Hood subdivided the aurora into flashes, beams and arches. He smiled, remembering the time that the Indians had gotten drunk and danced the Slave Dance, and Back, glimpsing him, was sure he was remembering Greenstockings again and ached with lust and hate and miserable sodden love. The river widened into a lake fed by rapids amounting almost to waterfalls, and their noise and sweep were forbidding beneath that grey, grey sky. Oh, they saw so many interesting scenes; M^{essrs} Hood and Back drew alternating views . . . – In those days it seemed that the happy marriage of the rifles and the animals would continue forever, giving birth to meat of the best quality, so they swept on down the Coppermine and began to see the stumps of trees hacked down by the stone axes of the Eskimaux, so that they knew that they drew near the unknown Polar Sea. Mr Franklin's glorious doom lay yet ahead, years ahead, like jigsaw ice behind some round brown cape. Already the snow began to swarm around his men as yesterday the mosquitoes had done. On the 15th of that same month of July they reached Bloody Falls, where a party of Indians had fallen upon the Eskimaux fifty years since, to slaughter them for blood-lust and copper-lust; Hearne the Englishman, who'd seen it, wrote: *My horror was much increased at seeing a young girl of about eighteen years attacked so near me that, when the first spear was thrust into her side, she fell at my feet and twisted herself around my legs, so that it was with difficulty I could disengage myself from her dying grasp. Two Indian men were pursuing this unfortunate victim, and I solicited very hard for her life. The murderers made no reply until they had stuck both their spears through her body and transfixed her to the ground. They then looked me sternly in the face and began to ridicule me by asking if I desired an Eskimo wife; meanwhile paying not the slightest heed to the shrieks and agony of the poor wretch who was still twining round their spears like an eel* . . . At Mr Franklin's command the party camped on

this very spot, erecting tents upon the skull-strewn grass; and Mr Back
wondered what would have happened if he'd been Hearne and had said to
the Indians: yes, I want an Eskimo wife!   but he could not stop thinking
about Greenstockings; on the other hand the Indians with Hearne, while
using the bodies of the dead Esquimaux in accordance with their enmity, had
laughed that the women of that race had different parts of generation than
other women, and though Hearne had believed this to be nothing but the
jeers and slurs of their hatred, Back considered frankly that anything might
be possible in these Arctic regions. For example Back cited to himself
the Esquimau wife that Mr Franklin *did* have and had even brought home
once . . .   – As soon as I saw her I could tell that she was kind,   reported the
officers (Back among them), loyally, uneasily.   She has such a sweet smile!
– Yes, she does,   Franklin replied proudly, feeling that her smile did him
credit since she was his. She had no modesty about burping and belching; she
did it loudly and often while his friends turned away in disgust, and his heart
glowed. Everything she did seemed good to him. She was by his standards so
unhesitatingly selfish that this too became admirable. Morning and night she
said: I want, I want.   – Seth had told him: If you bring her down here, the
only thing to do is treat her like a queen.   – And Seth was right. One
afternoon she wanted to go to a movie (she didn't know or care which one),
so he took her to *The Russia House* because he liked that theater and he
figured that since it was a spy movie there would be pistols and rifles and
hiding to thrill her, but in this he miscalculated; there was nothing but
dialogue, sentimental and dreary – all the more so to him because he knew
that she could not understand it – and halfway through she whispered in his
ear that she had to go to the bathroom. She was scared to go by herself; she
was afraid that she couldn't find it. There was nothing for it but to take her,
which he did, waiting outside the ladies' room door, leaning against the
drinking fountain, anxious because something important and exciting was
surely happening now, but when she came out and he led her back into that
crowded darkness nothing had happened that had not already happened,
which was nothing, so they sat through the movie patiently and afterward
when he asked her if she'd liked it she replied politely: Leedle bit.   – They
went out and she was hungry. He brought her into the first place he saw,
which was a deli, and she looked around and said: Not here.   – OK,   he
said. – The next place he saw was a Tex-Mex restaurant, and when he said
you want to go here?   she nodded very happily. They went in. It was very
long and wide; he could not see how far back it went. It was lit orange and
green and pink and there were skulls and dried peppers on the walls, and

strings of Christmas tree lights, themselves hot and peppery-bright, crawled up the pillars as Reepah whispered over and over: Here! Yes, here! I want here! – The waitress, black, svelte, lithe, almost venomously quick, did not lead them to the star-notched high chairs at the long long bar, but brought them instead to a table alone beneath a grotesque mask, Reepah stepping so shyly in her dirty kamiks as if she might make a noise or dirty something, and he pulled out her chair for her and took off her coat and kissed her hand as the waitress smiled; when she'd gone away, Reepah said: I want – be like *her!* because throughout these Seven Dreams everybody always wants to be or have someone else; and he said to her: Honey, you thirsty? Sweetheart, you want drink? Sprite, Seven-Up, seltzer water?

I want beer.

With a magnificent flourish he ordered two Texas Rattlesnake beers with the big diamondback etched on the bottles, curling snugly around the labels, and she screamed softly with glee.

The waitress brought thick tortilla chips with red sauce and green sauce. Reepah made a face because they were so hot, but kept eating them. She watched the bartender laboring up and down the long bar, whose bottles were lit with votive candles red and blue; she saw a crucifix made from embroidery or corncobs or more peppers (in this light it was hard to tell) and she frowned and said: bad!

Rock and roll was playing, with a loud beat that she could hear. She nodded her head.

With that first beer of the evening the drumbeats distanced themselves from him a little; the lights became softer, and he sat looking across at her. He was a little anxious about her and the beer. When she got drunk she went crazy. It had already happened once on her visit. When she got drunk there was nothing to do but lay hands on her and drag her down to serenity.

Thank you thank you *thank* you, John! she cried.

You're welcome, honey, he said, kissing her hand.

I'm not that!

You're welcome, sweetheart.

I'm not that!

Thank you, Eskimo Pie.

She giggled.

He didn't have enough money to order food for himself, but he ordered barbeque chicken wings for her because she loved chicken, and he ate some of it. It was as good as musk-ox. Reepah was in Heaven. Once she had to go to the bathroom, so he found it for her and took her there and waited outside as always and when she came out she kissed him on the lips and hugged him tight, grinding her crotch against him, and he said: I love you, honey.

Me, too. I love you very much.

After dinner he had to go to a reception where she was bored and burped and kept saying: I want to go out!   so he winked and waved and she went into the hall where she was satisfied riding up and down the elevator for two hours, he worrying all the time that someone might rape her, stab her, shoot her dead, so he made his adieus; unfortunately Back was there and couldn't be shaken off. – A drink, Sir John! Just one!

Ordinarily I'd be delighted,   he said.   But alcohol is bad for her.

But it's the anniversary of poor Hood's death – we must drink to his memory! You know, you're becoming so reclusive; the Admiralty is beginning to say –

Sir George, I will not pretend to deny that the Admiralty has eyes, and ears, and many tongues like a hydra. If you'll kindly tell me what the Admiralty has been saying I'll be under the deepest obligation to you.

Well, you are not seen as much as formerly, you know, and – and the Northwest Passage Expedition – I tell you this from one Arctic Friend to another –

GOD bless you for the warning, Sir George,   he said at last. (He did not hear Reepah in the hall.)

How about it, then? One drink?

One. But we must keep our eyes on Reepah . . .

She was on the first floor, sitting on the doorman's desk. The doorman was not there.

They went to a bar on Spring Street, Back seeking his soul like a baby waving its arms from the armauti, Back talking in his ear, Reepah smiling, bewildered and deaf, so that he hated himself for neglecting her and would break off Back's chatter-stream (which seemed both longer and wider than his Great Fish River) while he said something inconsequentially loving to her ear, Back now a little confused, possibly hurt, and they got to the bar and her eyes glittered and she said to him (Back paid no attention): I want drunk!

Drunk is no good for you,   he said.

Why?

When you get drunk, I get scared of you. When you get drunk, I get tired from you. So tired.

You scared of me drunk?   she said in amazement.

Yes.

It's OK! Drunk is only happy!

But I'm scared. I'm sorry, Reepah, but I get scared from you.

Yeah?

Yeah.

Yeah?

Yeah.

OK, she said very softly.

Promise me no drunk, Reepah. Please?

OK. I promise.

I get you one more beer. You want Michelob or Budweiser?

I don't know, she said. I'm sorry I say that. John?

What is it, honey?

Hi, John.

Hi, Reepah.

Hi, John. I like you.

Well, sweetie, come up to the bar and have a look.

Back (who'd just now gotten back from the men's room) wanted a Michelob. He bought the first round; that was his honor, he said. With his sheep-shagged silly head and puffy face, it was no wonder he didn't get the girl. His mouth was pouty, his eyes too regular. He radiated conformity. Franklin told him to hold the fort like Fort Chippewyan and lured Reepah barward with his arm so happy to be about her shoulder and they came closer into the dark gleam of the bottles and he pointed: Look, Reepah. That one there. Michelob. And that one over there is Budweiser.

I want that one!

You want to ask?

I'm scared.

Go ahead. You want? Maybe fun for you.

She squirmed and her eyes glinted and he saw that he had guessed right, that it would be fun for her, and he looked the bartender in the eye and the bartender came over.

What can I getcha, fella?

Two Michelobs for me. And this lady wants something. What do you want, Reepah?

She beamed. She pulled herself up tall. She shouted: I want – *Butt*-weiser! – She was delighted with her own boldness.

Right away, the bartender said. That'll be four-fifty.

They went back to the table and he gave her Back's beer to give to him and Back said: I'm honored.

Who his name again? said Reepah.

George.
Who?
George. Reepah, this is my friend George. Say hi to George.
Hi, George.
Hello, Reepah,   said Back gallantly.   Delighted to meet you.
Hi, George! Hi, George! Hi, George!

By the time she had finished her beer she liked Back very much; they could all see that. Franklin gave her a quarter and showed her how to use the jukebox and she studied the selections for a long time before she picked her song. Back held the fort again. Franklin felt that in a way he ought to buy another round since Back had paid for the first, but with Reepah along it wouldn't do to buy any more rounds at all.

By the time the jukebox played Reepah's song they had all forgotten which song it was.

He did not know that Back was regarding her so thoughtfully because he remembered Greenstockings, just as Back had not known that Hood had been screwing her and had already gotten her pregnant, and Hood (who was a minister's son) might or might not have known that Broadface was sleeping with her, and Broadface might or might not have known that she was pregnant, and we would not have known any of it if Hood had not told Hepburn and Hepburn spilled the beans when he was old. – Back was even now so much in love with Greenstockings that his heart whirred like the wings of a brown ptarmigan flushed out of its nest in the tundra, vibrating, leaping fearfully, even almost flying for a yard or two at a time as it rushed so anxiously on, not daring to look round or hide, so it must go on, toward the river of dreams.* (Buck caribou get reddish fat about their rumps when it's mating season, but how about Hood, Franklin and Back?)

* Greenstockings had an almost boyish look. She was not yet sixteen. Her shiny black hair did not quite reach her shoulders. It was very straight and thick and rich. Her eyes, white and black, glistened with alertness. She went about in soft, shaggy skins. Her face was soft; her lips were very delicate. She was not like Reepah at all.

There was a birthday party that Back had to go to. – You're welcome to come, both of you, he said. We won't stay long.

Franklin knew that Reepah wouldn't want to go. She feared crowds. But when he explained, she shouted: I want party!

At the party everyone loved Reepah because she was a Native American and that meant that she was ecological. Franklin asked everyone when they first came in not to give her beer. He made Back promise to keep an eye on her. After that he thought himself even farther south than secure. Back was circulating, trying to make sure that everyone saw his order of knighthood. He'd destroyed the Spanish batteries at age twelve; when he was imprisoned at Verdun he studied mathematics, French and drawing. At the request of the ladies, he discharged his pistol, which was loaded with blanks . . . Reepah had quite gotten over her shyness, was having an excellent time. She scurried about trying to clean up, picking the peanut shells from the floor, trying to remember everyone's name so that she could say hello over and over. She was *happy, happy!* – (I have a very important *secret* to tell you, Reepah, whispered Back. – Secret? she said. You want my secret from me? I'm sorry I smoke all my secrets. – No, no, no, laughed urbane Back. May I tell you a *secret?* This caviar dip is *delicious.*) – Franklin sat and relaxed and told somebody about the first time he achieved the Arctic coast, whose shocking cliff-islands loomed in swirls of clouds, and whose great knife-edge waves shook his boats like windstraws. They had a piñata now and he got up and told Reepah what it was and stood with her to watch, his hand on her shoulder to calm her, and the birthday girl swung the bat and missed and swung and hit once and then it was Reepah's turn and she was screaming with laughter and everyone smiled and clapped when she struck it and then they put the blindfold on Franklin and he hit so hard that he broke the bat and they all cheered and everything was noisier and Reepah was drinking beer and suddenly he realized that she was getting wild. She didn't want to go. He got her parka for her and she was laughing and crying; she begged him to stay; she kept saying: I want Agatha! (that was the birthday girl's name); on the way to the door she knocked over somebody's beer and Agatha said shit and he apologized and got her out of there and all the way downstairs she kept begging for Agatha. He had to hold her very tight as they went downstairs because she could barely walk. He did not yet acknowledge that the nightmare time was coming. Into his mind came the phrase *arrangements for a safe conveyance* . . . But he had no more money for a taxi. They'd have to walk to the subway. The nearest station that he knew was fifteen minutes away. Getting her there required as much labor as heaving a ship with hawsers to pass between the ice-floes . . . Every few minutes she had to pee. Everything was dark. He'd take her into alleys and stand guard while she squatted. Several times she fell into her urine; sometimes as they made their pathetic progress toward the subway she fell into puddles; her parka was soaked and stinking and she was shouting HI! . . . HI! . . . HI! to every stranger they passed; sometimes they said hi in return, and if he didn't restrain her she'd rush over and slobber on them, crying: I want be with you! I want boyfriend! I want somebody . . . and it was all that he could do not to weep. – *HI!* she screamed at a couple; she lunged at them to give them her affection which no matter how bedraggled her clothes and features might become would never be anything less than shining but they did not see that and Franklin was holding her by the collar and he said: Come on, Reepah. Come on, sweetheart. – Well, maybe he wasn't Franklin then. Franklin had seen the bombardment of Copenhagen, aged fourteen; he'd been shipwrecked and marooned on a sandbank somewhere in the Great Barrier Reef; he'd stood unwounded at Trafalgar; he'd fought at New Orleans; surely this vision of Reepah trying so desperately to give herself away when no one in the entire world would take her, surely this could not have been the saddest thing that Franklin had ever seen, whereas it was for Subzero – but maybe Franklin with his idiot luck had never truly confronted *wretchedness*; maybe for him it had always been *adventure*, all of it, from the screams of the young boys in blue whom Napoleon had killed to the groans of his own starving men in the Barren Lands; maybe Franklin and Subzero were still the same. Whoever he might have been, he almost wept to see her. When she was very happy, as I've said, she'd be smiling with her whole face and everyone saw then how innocent and loving she was; if she saw the doormen of fancy hotels shoveling snow she wanted to help them; if he gave a panhandler a quarter she'd give two dollars; and every time she'd be smiling so wonderfully; even now when she threw her arms around every man on the street saying: I want be with you! I want see someone! the men would just laugh and hug her back, saying to Subzero with a wink: She's a little plastered. Even when she'd reached the screaming stage she was still smiling so that people continued to wave back. It was midnight. On the subway car she kept lunging out of her seat to try to hug someone (the woman she'd slobbered over on the platform had already screamed in horror and run away from Reepah's clinging kisses and taken another car), and he had to keep slamming her down. The subway car rang with her noise. Everyone looked away. She was ranting about JESUS in broken English and Inuktitut. He kept soothing her. He had to hold her with all his strength. She snatched a half-empty bottle of Seven-Up from the trash can and drank it. She picked up a dirty beer can from the sidewalk and licked it, trying to swallow a drop of beer or spit or rainwater or whatever might still be inside it; then she kissed Subzero on the lips. She slammed her crotch against him. When he finally got her home she was screeching at him because he wouldn't marry her and he had to give her four blue pills and lie on top of her all night to keep her still. Even with the blue pills and the drunkenness she kept waking up and yelling so loud that none of the neighbors must have slept much that night. She wasn't smiling then. When morning came he was exhausted and almost hated her as she lay on her back, hardly breathing, her eyelids flushed, her face bright red, one arm across her face, the heater roaring as in Inukjuak, the lights on and TV horses galloping silent as ghosts; but then she smiled again and he loved her beautiful heart –

Back, as I said, felt the same way about Greenstockings. (That was why his jealousy of Hood, the successful suitor, crawled within him like maggots in a moose's head.) – Best not to think of it. – He was delighted when Mr Franklin gave the order to present the Eskimaux with iron, which increased their loquacity – but not too much, for they continued to hide, so Akaicho and his Indians sought to drive them forward like hunted animals in order to compel them to parley, and Mr Franklin laid down hatchets and other such instruments, but the Esquimaux continued to evade all courtesies, and July was passing, so at length Mr Franklin discharged the Indians for the season (in any event they would go no further), and led his party to the shores of the Polar Sea. They camped at a place called Iviagiknak, which signifies in Inukitut *Like the breast of a woman.* – Hearing this, Mr Franklin, Mr Back and Mr Hood turned away from one another in confusion.

On the following day Mr Franklin discharged five men to save provisions and paced upon the sandy delta, staring out to sea where the ice seemed thick and unbroken, and Dr Richardson accompanied the Esquimau interpreter to visit an old man with whom he'd made friends, and the old man offered the interpreter one of his daughters as a wife but the interpreter refused, dreading the anticipated disappointment and mortification of Mr Franklin, and so they returned to the tents, where Dr Richardson wrote in his journal: *The voyageurs seem terrified at the idea of a voyage through an icy sea in bark canoes, and have had frequent debates on the subject. The two interpreters in particular express their fears with the least disguise and have made many urgent requests to be allowed to return with Mr Wentzel.* But Mr Wentzel had already set out upon his way with the other four men; Akaicho had promised to wait for them for three days –

They sailed for five hundred and fifty miles, covering only one-fifth of the distance between the mouth of the Coppermine and Repulse Bay, which was Mr Franklin's original goal, so considerable unknown coast remained – but that (Mr Franklin consoled himself) could be explored in a subseqent expedition. He would have preferred to continue on, but the voyageurs had become too anxious. Indeed it was shameful, how these French-Canadians were as superstitious and fear-ridden as Indians! – a crew of Englishmen would have followed him on cheerfully, without asking where or why.

On Saturday the 18th of August they reached and named Point Turnagain; turn again they did –

Now, while Reepah stuffs herself with chicken and drinks her Rattlesnake beer, permit the aforesaid Mr Franklin to meditate on what hungry times came next; now, while Jane picks apart a stuffed pheasant (she suffers from loss of appetite), while the sailors crank the hand organ to crank away those winter days on Beechey Island, and Fitzjames, Crozier & Co. visit with Mr Franklin in his quarters and talk about each other's old times because it is no use talking about the Northwest Passage anymore until the ice lifts, now Mr Franklin smiles and pours out another cordial with his own hand and the wind is screaming overhead and it is Seth's duty to keep the ice-hole open in case of fire so he goes out into the wind, thinking: If only Mr Franklin had listened to Akaicho then no one would have starved that time! – but that is missing the point because if Mr Franklin had failed to descend the Coppermine his career at home would have been finished . . . – and Seth's neck-tendons make angles as he turns his head and thinks: If only Mr Franklin had listened to the voyageurs and turned around sooner, maybe even then it might have been all right! – but that is missing the point because then they would never have discovered Point Turnagain! – and in Mr Franklin's cabin the atmosphere of these reminiscences is congratulatory, because Mr Franklin made discoveries, didn't he? and he returned with all the officers except for Hood, didn't he? – and so here we are.

It was Mr Franklin's determination on that freezing August day in 1821 to return to Fort Enterprise by the overland route – that is, through the Barren Lands, because the sea-ice was closing in (and, caught quite fast now in sea-ice, Mr Franklin smiled a bit on that night-black afternoon in 1845 as he related the tale); then, too, much of the coast between the Coppermine and Cape Barrow had been scarce in game. At Point Turnagain one of the two Esquimaux interpreters had killed a caribou, but no one could find it in the fog. One of the searchers froze his thighs. Mr Franklin gave orders that the pemmican sack be opened, although it was almost finished, but the following day it was necessary to go supperless. The voyageurs paddled westward, homeward, in such terror of oncoming hunger that the stormy sea-swells scarcely distracted them, much to Mr Franklin's satisfaction, and so they landed on the rocks with both canoes yet preserved, and Mr Franklin commanded that half the remaining pemmican be distributed, to make a feeble meal, and now the days of strange meat were beginning. At Barry's Isles they feasted quite readily on three lean caribou, although the difference between fat flesh and lean flesh is quite marked; indeed, lean meat seems scarcely to cut the cold, or send hunger away. But that was not such a step down. It was only Friday the 24th. The following day they reached the bottom of Arctic Sound, and Dr Richardson noted in his journal: *Our canadians may be said to have in general shewed considerable courage in bearing the dangers of the sea, magnified to them by their novelty, but they could not restrain their expressions of joy on quitting it.* – The following day they began to cross the Barren Grounds.

On the 7th of September they had already fasted for three days, and Mr Franklin swooned when they set out, but a little bit of potable soup remained, which Dr Richardson spooned into his mouth, and he regained his senses. Later that day they killed some partridges, so that each man could devour half a bird; on the morrow they began to eat that same black rock-tripe that Subzero had munched for novelty at Pond Inlet and Inukjuak. On the 10th they killed a musk-ox and fell upon it like rats and maggots, gulping down the raw contents of its stomach and then ripping the intestines to pieces with their long, long teeth. But that was only a little step down. On the 14th their Indian interpreter Saint-Germain presented each of them with a small piece of meat which he had saved from his rations, as an act of love; this brought tears to the eyes of all, including Mr Franklin, for the musk-ox meat was long gone. Later they killed two caribou, but that was not such a step up anymore; they were all feeling faint. In their mind's ear rang Akaicho's warning that they would all die. On the 17th the hunters were too weak to kill some caribou that they saw, so the party ate more *tripe de roche* and descended another step – only a small one, mind you – by supping on scraps of singed hides. On the 23d, having reached the region where dwarf spruces begin, they discovered a caribou which had been brought down by wolves that spring; it was now literally nothing but skin and bones, but they prepared the hide as usual and burned the bones until they could be chewed. Some of the men also began to eat their old shoes. This last was a pretty definite step down, but it was not so bad yet; no one had died. On the 25th they killed five small caribou, which held the life in them a little longer; a third of the meat was consumed on the first day, such was the men's desperate craving. Mr Hood, who insisted on breaking trail day after day, much to the detriment of his health, now longed for Greenstockings less on account of her embraces than because she was such an adept and crafty huntress. What would she do now? The others were some distance behind him. Traversing a snowdrift, he thought he saw an animal silhouetted in the fog. He unslung his rifle. Nothing was there. The following day they struck the Coppermine. On the 27th they found a rotten caribou whose liquescent flesh dripped through their fingers when they snatched it up from the rocks, but they slurped it up with their tongues and then returned to that place to pick through the contents of its intestines. For dessert they had blueberries and cranberries. (Somewhere the caribou were so numerous that their antlers were a moving forest and their dark shoulder-humps were tussocks; their legs were roots, and suddenly the barrens grass was gone and the moving forest came galloping across the rivers.) On the night of October 6th Credit and Vaillant dropped dead in the snow. Mr Hood had begun to fail. He leaned on Dr Richardson's shoulder with every step, his mind a cloud-coast shimmering with vaporous sandbars, ice-chunks underneath it grey and white with winter. For days now he hadn't been able to feel his feet. His dead bone-stilts lurched and yawed as he continued forward to please Dr Richardson, who already knew that this man would not reach Fort Enterprise. Hood remembered a pair of new shoes his father had given him for his seventh birthday, the leather soft and supple, and he began to weep because he could not have those shoes to eat. He tried not to consider other food; even fantasies of an ordinary dinner were too rich for him. – You will have success, my dear boy   (thus Dr Richardson).   Take another step. Perhaps the men will kill a hare today. Look at Mr Franklin in the vanguard! His heart is weakened, but he perseveres! One more step. Keep Mr Franklin always in your thoughts, Hood. And remember your – you know, that pretty little squaw who made Back so jealous . . .   – Hood whispered: She told me to give her just seven bullets . . .   – Another step, my dear friend,   replied Dr Richardson.   We have all the bullets we need. It's meat we're looking for. Perhaps Saint-Germain will kill us some partridges. Augustus is still hopeful of finding a musk-ox . . . Another step. You're an officer; you're equal to the task . . .   – Doctor   (murmured Mr Franklin),   would you be so good as to take a look at Perrault? He seems fatigued, complains constantly of dizziness; I fear he's begun to demoralize the others . . . Don't be alarmed, Hood, you can take my hand while the Doctor's gone . . .   – On the 11th, Dr Richardson, Mr Hood, and good old Hepburn, left behind by the rest, dined on human flesh, not knowing that they did so, for Michel the Iroquois, who brought it to them, said that it was a dead wolf he'd found in the forest; the wolf was either Perrault or Belanger, or both. Hood was very weak. In the days when they'd had meat, he'd always taken the smallest portion for himself. *Tripe de roche* did not agree with him. He lay in his bed and thought about Greenstockings and read religious tracts. On the 20th, Hood's rifle spoke, because Michel had whispered to it through the tent wall, seeing its black silhouette behind Hood's silhouette of longish nose sloping obliquely back to the almost browless forehead, and as Michel crouched there he could see the boyish lips part and could almost see the steam issuing between them (such was his concentration) as Hood began to mumble endearments half-strangled, dreaming that he was sliding off her bead-ornamented stockings, kissing her hot feet; to be hungry is to be cold and what he desired of her most was warmth, so he hid his head in her hair, insinuated his numb hand under her shoulder-blanket, glided his fingers over the red-stained porcupine quills that adorned her breasts (but really the sound of his fingers on her quills was the sound of poor Michel's teeth chattering outside as he crouched in the snow sniffing the scent of Hood's flesh, looking and listening, to be sure that Hepburn and Dr Richardson were gone, and when I say poor Michel I mean it, for he was not as high a being as Hood –

no one was! of all these men only Hood did not dream of eating others; no, he only longed to kiss them) – and Michel listened to the wind's petty whining as it stripped the warmth from his face and then he thought he heard the sound of a rifle-shot but it was only a snapping branch as Dr Richardson and Hepburn dragged firewood from the ravine, and he distinctly heard Hood say: I'm sorry; I was certain that I could help you, my love . . . and so he rushed into the tent, snatched up the rifle, ground it against the back of Hood's skull, and saved both their lives. (Greenstockings was just then giving birth to his daughter; she too counted on rifles to save her, but she'd be dead the next year, when a bad gun blew off Broadface's hand and they starved.) Dr Richardson and Hepburn came running (or crawling, as I should say, they being now but skeletons); and as Hepburn panted beside the Doctor he could not unfeel selfish base anguish for having abandoned their loads of wood, because he didn't believe he had the strength to go back and get it. The echoes of the gunshot continued to rattle in his brain like crackling foil, but Dr Richardson said that he didn't hear them. – I'm sorry you told me that, whispered Hepburn; and they came in sight of the tent in its grim snowy grove; LORD! cried Hepburn. There's a hole in the canvas, and will you look at that blood! – It was an accident, Michel said. – A certain dryness in his tone caused the two men to shudder. Dr Richardson began at once to make certain observations and analytical inquiries, thanking Providence for the speedy action of adrenaline in his system, which sharpened his concentration and dulled his hunger. From the location of the powder burns, and the deposition of soot, he suspected homicide. – He was cleaning his rifle, said Michel in the same dry way. – Now Hepburn took Dr Richardson off and whispered that he'd heard Michel and the dead man having words not long before. (In fact Hepburn lied, out of fear. His inference was correct; it was so important to him that it be accepted that he needed to assist the evidence. And yet what would Michel have had to quarrel about with Hood? He was not angry at him – no more than a man with a rifle is angry with the caribou in his sights.) Regarding this accusation Dr Richardson reserved judgment even yet, until after the funeral service when they lay down in the snowy darkness and Dr Richardson heard Michel rise as if to urinate; following him, Dr Richardson saw him part the willows that screened the dead body, kneel down, and delicately lick the frozen blood like a vampire . . . On the 21st a rifle spoke half a dozen times; Michel killed four partridges, which he willingly shared with the others. But already he was watching Hepburn and wondering if he had berries stored away in his cheek-pouches after an Arctic ground squirrel's fashion; Michel itched to eat flesh again . . .

Obviously he could not devour Hood until he had put his companions out of the way. This is what we call deferred gratification. On the 23^d, Dr Richardson, though deploring the necessity, shot Michel in the forehead, for that was the only way to preserve his own and Hepburn's existence. They did not eat him, so they said (but we shall never know). Anyhow, what are life and death but slink-wolves devouring each other's tails? They crept on to Fort Enterprise, which they reached on the 29th; Mr Franklin and the others were bedridden with hunger (although in another season Mr Franklin had seen more than two thousand caribou there in the course of a short walk); on the 30th they commenced eating rotten caribou-skins from which they plucked warble-fly larvae and gobbled them desperately; Peltier and Semandré died on the 1st; the bones for soup were almost gone; Hepburn's limbs began to swell –

※- ※- ※-

It was Akaicho and his Indians who saved them. That was the thing about natives, said judicious Mr Franklin. They always turned up at the right time. Back had gone off to get them. Back too had his place. (He left bloodstains in the snow as he went, such was the galling of his snowshoes.) What did he think, I wonder, when after indescribable suffering he reached Akaicho's, not knowing that his rival was dead, and finding Greenstockings in Cascathry's tent, suckling her halfbreed child? She was quite plump and meaty now; she had a full twelvemonth to live . . . To Fort Enterprise the dear Indians set out at once, bearing meat which they'd won with their rifles; they made a fire, caught trout; to Mr Franklin their strength seemed supernatural. On the 16th the white men were so far recovered as to be able to quit the Fort in their benefactors' company; together they followed the roaming caribou herds . . . The Indians chafed their faces most kindly, to guard them from frostbite; the Indians gave them their snowshoes and did without; Akaicho cooked meat for them with his own hands –

On December the 14th Akaicho came to meet them at Fort Providence, to claim payment for all Mr Franklin's notes. Unfortunately, the supplies which Mr Franklin had ordered had not arrived.

Akaicho smiled wearily. – The world goes badly, he said. All are poor. You are poor; the traders appear to be poor, I and my party are poor likewise, and since the goods have not come in we cannot have them.

My dear fellow, I am deeply mortified . . . said Mr Franklin.

I do not regret having supplied you with provisions, said Akaicho, with a smile like a dagger's blade. A Red Knife can never permit a white man to suffer from want on his lands, without flying to his aid. I trust, however, that we shall, as you say, receive what is due to us, next autumn – and at all events, it is the first time that the white people have been indebted to the Red Knife Indians.

Meat
1989

My wife knew everything she had to know like making clothing. I also knew everything a man had to know in order to survive.

WILLIE COOPER, ᑯᐸᐊᕐᐅᑦ ᐊᐅᒐᕐᕈᓯᒥᑦ /
Memories of a Kuujjuamiuq (1989)

By the broad stream that flowed into the culvert, mosquitoes swarmed beneath that grey sky, and Inuit children waded into the brown water, laughing and shivering in bathing suits and shirts. They stood on the bank on styrofoam kickboards, watching for fish.

They weighted the net with twenty pounds of stones and set it just past a floe. Almost immediately the bobbers began to move. A char was in – a two-pounder. Soon they had half a dozen. They came back with the fish swimming in the pool in their leaky canoe, swimming silvery-white. They took them and flung them down on a beached floe. Then they took them up one by one, gutted them living, and threw them down again. For a long time the emptied fish twitched on the bloodstained ice.

They were delicious.

The Northwest Passage
1846

It is like this: A man is going fishing because he is hungry. He is fishing, but he still hasn't caught any. He is fishing for a long time now, looking about in all directions for game. He is still fishing.

SAALI ARNGNAITUQ, "The Giant
and the Man" (1958–9)

More meat was bad. Franklin had the swollen tins opened and inspected. He had all the empty tins lined up in rows for them to count. That was easier than counting what was left – still a sufficient quantity of *that* –

He summoned Mr Crozier for a private conference.

You see, said Franklin as blandly as he could, there is a bit of talk about the preserved meats. Perhaps you could give me the benefit of your experience. Sir James carried them to the Antarctic, did he not?

Well, yes, said Mr Crozier. But it was not Goldner. We ordered from John Gillon & Co. Our only complaint –

Yes?

Our only complaint, sir, was that the cannisters should have been of stouter tin, since some of them rusted through in the third year.

But otherwise they did not spoil?

No, sir.

So you do not think that Goldner's tins will spoil?

I honestly don't know what to think, sir.

To Franklin it began to seem as if Mr Crozier's "sir" was a means of assigning responsibility solely to the leader of the Expedition, and he began to bristle a little. – Tell me what you *imagine*, then, he said coolly.

Well, sir, upon my word I'm uneasy –

Do you propose that we turn back in the spring?

This time Mr Crozier hesitated perceptibly, as he should have done long before, in Greenland, when asked if his ship was ready, and although he continued to gaze directly at his commanding officer a certain sweet vagueness and distance had formed upon his eyes like ice. – No, sir, he said at last, but doubtless Mr Franklin had taken the sign –

In 1852, when the Admiralty ordered some of it for a Franklin search expedition, Goldner's meat was so putrefied that they had to throw it into the sea at Spithead. But it was good at first – oh, it was very good, the ox-cheek especially. So, please, let us not be too hard on Mr Goldner. Franklin wasn't. It did not seem necessary to return, Mr Franklin concluded.

They were at Beechey Island for ten months, Beechey Island with its sweep of cliff, the graves barely seen beneath a swirl of snow and moonlight on the sea, the black blocky cliffs of dream. Mr Gore became ill, with belly-cramps that came and went, and Dr Goodsir rubbed his woolly sideburns with his thumb and pulled his cap-brim down a little lower against the breeze and stared with those eyes of his which looked perpetually hurt and said that a little rest would set him right. – Rest? laughed Gore. There's nothing else to do here! – It's nothing but a little colic, explained Dr Goodsir to Mr Franklin in privacy, and Mr Franklin said: Well, that relieves my mind. All the same, it is not like Gore to complain of nothing. Perhaps the rays of the aurora borealis are making him melancholy; in your opinion could that be possible? – Certainly, sir, replied the Doctor. We know so little of that phenomenon. I shall certainly keep my eye on his condition . . . – He himself had begun to suffer from headache, but wisely kept this from others, even from his counterpart, Dr Peddie, as the pains caused him nothing but inconvenience. When they prevented him from sleeping he occasionally allowed himself a small dose of laudanum . . . Latterly, however, he might be awakened by a burst of pain behind his temples, and what he minded most about it as he lay there listening to the wind catching its breath in the darkness outside was not the pain, which, being a doctor and a naval officer, he had the temperament to endure, but the loneliness of being the only consciousness, perhaps, between here and Greenland; his thoughts worked in a naked brainball like the moon, terribly exposed and bright, while the men slept on, and something wicked like a polar bear must see him hanging in the sky, and was at this moment perhaps sneaking closer and closer along the high ridges until it could swipe him and claw him into a jelly of bleeding light . . . In sleep the other men were like a bed of mushrooms, each with his own deathcap or dreamcap, but all growing on the same soil. He could hear them breathing around him, breathing very sweetly, so that he knew that when you are terribly alone the breathing of others is love. They lusted south to water-light like Heaven, south to yellow birch and moosewood. (But the shamans never left Nunavut; they never flew south to the places where snow became rain, and the dark fog turned blue.) The men dreamed on beneath the wolfskin blankets whose stiff hairs crackled with electricity; and Dr Goodsir lay trying not to surrender to the pounding pains in his skull; he closed his eyes and tried to recall the various plants in Dr Richardson's catalogue; he had just gotten to the Diandria with *Veronica peregrina* and then *Pinguicula vulgaris*, which Dr Richardson had found even in the Barren Grounds, when the headache left him so suddenly that it was almost as if a cork had popped, and he was tired and fell into the same bliss of breathing that the others shared . . . – The ships waited in the ice, banked with snow to keep out the winds, deck-tarped, with snow on every crossbeam. – It's been a very important winter for me, said Seth. It helped me to solidify a lot of things morally. – Seth had realized by then that there was a pattern to the noises one's boots made on the snow-crust, as there was a pattern to everything else; the changing pitches mirrored those of bottles being filled or emptied with liquid . . . He'd heard about the meat, of course. He'd even talked with Mr Franklin about it once, in the ever briefer intervals when the latter still found time to be Subzero, and Mr Franklin, bland and stout, with his mouth curving doughtily down and his epaulet-fringes falling down from his shoulders like limp skeleton fingers, sat uniformed and double-brass-buttoned, resting his swollen hands on the table, puffing his cheeks in a sigh, and Seth said: I'll never forget how it was for you and me in Pond Inlet, that time before Reepah, when we set out to fuck Uktuk Lake . . . – and Mr Franklin smiled and remembered how on that expedition Seth had been talking about a movie he'd seen ten years before, saying: I was kinda hoping they were going to dwell a little more on Burton's sexual escapades. But it was a very wonderful movie. – And Subzero replied with a one-minute treatise on *his* greatest movie of all time, and Seth was awed as he had been awed at Seth's movie, each doing the other the compliment of believing in the perfection

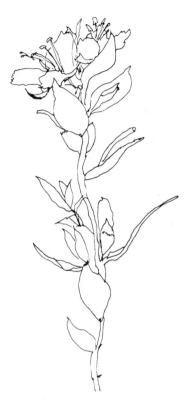

of the other's movie, just as Mr Franklin had believed in the tale of the Chipewyan widower whose grief and solicitude for his infant son allowed him to suckle him from his own breast; and Subzero and Seth approached the bluff whose red stains bespoke iron, the hillsides becoming marshy so that their boots sank with many a squish. Uktuk Lake was still seven or eight miles away. The sounds of the valley were the breeze-breath, the faraway trickle of water, the occasional note of a bird, the loud choruses of flies about the boys' ears, and the songs of mosquitoes, which approximate in miniature the melodies of wolves – but mainly the beatings of their own hearts. He thought that he could hear Seth's heart beat in harmony with the white flashes on the wing-ends of a gyrfalcon high overhead, the only cloud in the Arctic sky. They crossed a stream along a natural weir of stone and went over the top of a ridge. Now they came to a runoff-creek whose sandbars were orange with oxides. At the foot of the bluff was a marshy place with a bitter smell, in which the lichens were like mold. Here Subzero paused to declaim the words of Greenstockings's lover, poor old Hood: *If it were possible to equal the primitive explorers of these seas in success, we should never rival them in merit, till we penetrated regions in which danger was new, and science useless.* – Laughed Seth: We sure could have as much danger as we want. And it sure wouldn't last very long. *We* wouldn't last very long. – Above the iron sand, the top of the bluff was a hard roof of desert pavement, cobbled with ovoid crystals of discolored quartz (some the size of piñon nuts, others as big as eggs) and little rectangular pieces of ferrous ore. From here Uktuk Lake could be seen as a pale blue gleam of mystery between two cliffs. The two boys shouted with

glee. They descended the scree and crossed a tussock meadow whose boulder-lined stream ran at right angles to their path, and Seth was smiling lovingly, bespectacled and beak-nosed while the mosquitoes rested on his arm as softly as girls, and he was saying: There's tons of saxifrage over there, a good two dozen kinds of saxifrage! And lots of pink fennel things! And you know fireweeds? This stuff is in the same genus . . .   – The pervasive sun black-spotted their vision. Up a bluff whose top was paved with small lichened stones they went; there Subzero could see the immense gold shining of the sound far below and behind them, and the white line of ice like fog . . . It was very windy and bright; everything flashed like Seth's long skinny muscled legs. Now the lake was much closer. It had a little knob of rock like a clitoris. Big cliffs, vertically snow-streaked, came first, then a big body of water, the head of some fast, pale-green river; then the narrow blue lake like some treasure between the dark-shadowed cliffs. The wind was blowing hard enough to make whitecaps on the blue lake. The foam leaped; Subzero's hands chilled in the wind (Seth had his fists in his pockets). Uktuk Lake's spread legs were ahead. But the river was very high, greyly rising, submerging green tussocks and willow branches, leaping, splashing pyramids of foam over the rocks. It was very wide. It had two branches, one white-foamed, the other grey, more placid, with a green island in the middle. – Well,   said Subzero, what do you think? Is danger new and science useless?   – Seth just laughed. – No way we're going to get across it.   – Franklin's men would have done it, said Subzero defensively.   – Sure,   said Seth.   Because they had to. Just look at it. For one thing, it's wide. For another thing, it's extremely fast. There's a lot of rocks in there. And it's about as cold as water can get without being ice. I'd say the best scenario is you'd be swept away within five seconds. – Subzero could see white Labrador tea blossoms on it, shimmering in the wind. He pulled down his pants and stuck his dick in the river. But it wasn't the same. It was like fucking a prostitute instead of Reepah. A couple of years later, Seth said: You know, I was thinking about that river. If we'd had a rope, then one of us could have tied the end around himself and around a big boulder and the other could have maybe forded that first braid at least.   – It was a good day anyway, Seth.   – Oh, it was a great day! The best of that whole summer! And then seeing that snowy owl on the way back, that capped the day.   – Still,   said Subzero,   it would have been nice if we'd made it to Uktuk Lake.   – Seth nodded, his face harder as his hairline receded, and said: You know me. I know you. Neither of us can be totally happy and keep respect for something unless we can't have it.   – Subzero didn't say anything, and after a minute Seth added: Well, you could have done it. And for five seconds you would've had the satisfaction of knowing you'd done exactly the right thing. – Subzero bit his lip and peeked outside the cabin. Gore was rereading *Punch* and Irving was rereading *Nicholas Nickleby*. – He closed the door. In a low voice he said: And what about Goldner's patent? – You couldn't ask for any more danger, replied Seth admiringly. That should make you very happy. If you live.

If *I* live? said Franklin mildly. And what about your own case?

It was a good expedition, anyway, said Seth, shrugging. I just wish there'd been more flowers –

We all wish for something, Seth.

Anyway, running into this whole situation is the neatest thing, laughed Seth suddenly. (He had lead poisoning now, too.) It's really neat; it's so overwhelming. There's absolutely nothing anyone can do about it.

As a matter of fact, no one else had died in that season – assuredly (said Dr Goodsir) due to the wise regulation promulgated by Mr Franklin, requiring each man to swallow his lemon juice in the presence of an officer; – yes, said Mr Franklin softly; Parry did that as well . . . In the early summer the men made an oval garden on the ridge to the east of their camp. They planted mosses, lichens, poppies and anemones on its borders. On the 24th of May they observed the Queen's birthday with a royal salute from the obliging rifles. They watched the speckled, hummocked ice.

The question of how to obtain the desideratum which they sought had greatly perplexed all the officers, who'd gathered often in Mr Franklin's cabin to canvass the charts together, and Mr Franklin smiled upon them all; he had a marble-white smile, like a tombstone angel, like a shot beluga whale on the beach; he slowly stretched the white rubber-marble skin of his face; as the lead-sugars and lead-garnishes of Mr Goldner worked themselves more thoroughly into his system, he came by degrees to bear more resemblance to another kind of whale, a grey one, gravel on its heavy skin, which had been peeled back to show the marbled gulleys of fat with their bloodstained roots –

Mr Fitzjames, I should say, had chafed far more than the rest of them at the idleness of that winter. It is the nature of the polar game that one has but a few short weeks in which to act, and then long months of wind, ice and darkness in which to repent the previous move, and prepare one's hopes for the next. This circumstance is not really so different from many others in our lives (witness, for example, Mr Franklin's own long game with Jane and Reepah); Mr Fitzjames, however, was truly young in many ways, and while he would gladly expend his energies without stint for the common good, even to the sacrifice of his life, the enforced hoarding of those energies was more than he could bear. Then, too, the subtleties of lead intoxication had begun to wreak themselves upon him as much as upon the rest. In his case the effects did not take the form of fainting fits, as with his Captain; rather, his somewhat excitable nature was strung a half-octave higher at this stage. Steady Mr Crozier, who had always resented the boy's hasty promotion a trifle, was glad to be confirmed in his own judgment. – Mr Fitzjames has a need to be important, he said once to Mr Franklin when they were alone.

I must confess that my opinions are coming into accord with your own, replied the Captain sadly. But he is young; we must bear with him.

And Crozier, who had come into the cabin angry with Fitzjames over some trifling matter, left aching with sadness that Mr Franklin, too, was disappointed with the younger man, and resolving to indulge Fitzjames to the utmost of his powers, in order to spare Mr Franklin any additional burden. So harmony was maintained, for awhile. Such was Mr Franklin's talent.

On the morning of July 13th, Mr Franklin having expressed his desire for a final conference on the matter of direction, the senior officers assembled on board the *Erebus*. The wind blew low and steady on the blue sea-mountains which last summer had been water, and the sky was almost cloudless. Mr Fitzjames arrived first, a little breathless, his face a wild mask of frost. He had recently led his volunteers on a trek of a hundred miles up the ice of Wellington Channel, leaving Lt Gore as his deputy, and had discovered no sign of open water to the north. To his mind the question of proceeding in that direction had now been closed. Mr Crozier, on the other hand, who'd wintered in the Antarctic, knew better that one ought not to rule out any possibility, that the savants at the Admiralty with their dream of free ocean at the Pole had been proven neither right nor wrong as of yet. (He suffered occasionally from aches in his bones, but otherwise was still in good health.)

Gentlemen, there is no occasion for anxiety, said Mr Franklin with his usual vague smile. The ice will surely yield next month, if not this week. But we must be in accord in all our intentions. Really we ought to have decided this sooner; I'm not certain why we've put it off . . .

No one replying to this, Mr Franklin cleared his throat and said: Just to establish our unanimity, none of you, I take it, has any alarm about our progress thus far . . . ?

Silence.

Mr Crozier?

No, sir, said that person, swallowing.

Mr Fitzjames?

On the contrary, sir! And I have a proposal –

Very good. We shall all look at it in a moment. Shall we break out the charts as usual? And perhaps one of you would be good enough to flag our steward; we each deserve a little dram, don't you think?

Finding all so ready to proceed, Mr Franklin closed the conference with the resolution (which was really Mr Crozier's) that they strive westward once again through Barrow Strait, in hopes of completing the Admiralty route, and then take whichever turn seemed clear to strike the Pacific with the least delay. Fitzjames evinced an actual aversion to proceeding northward for any reason; Mr Franklin, however, dealt with this prejudice by intimating (a half-truth) that it was shared by his former officer, Mr Back. Fitzjames felt very jealous of Back, the successful one; and his jealousy had darkened illimitably by virtue of the man's absence, which rendered him larger than life. Mr Franklin knew of this feeling and played on it without understanding it. To him, Back was a headstrong, inferior sort of fellow; Mr Franklin had long since fallen into the habit of reserving Back for the purpose of savior; at other times he was not to be too closely embraced. To Fitzjames, Back was Mr Franklin's prodigal son. He must outdo him to take his place. When Mr Franklin announced, therefore, that they must be prepared to rush headlong into any passage that the ice permitted them, he lost not a moment in giving his opinion, which was affirmative.

On the 30th, Mr Crozier was pacing, supervising the removal of some items from Beechey Island to his ship. There was a strange cast to the faces of several of his sailors that he did not like, although they seemed cheerful enough. It was as if some mask overlay their countenances, something greasy and metallic of which they were not themselves aware. Well (thus Crozier),

matters were now in the ALMIGHTY's hands. The conference in Mr Franklin's
cabin had been difficult, for he could not justify his nervousness, and so said
nothing. Mr Franklin was a much more kindly and tolerant Captain than Sir
James; he could have approached him directly; perhaps he should have, but
what was there to say? – Is lead truly at the root of our problems? It scarcely
matters to me whether I talk about the effects of repeating rifles on the Inuit
or the effects of tin cans on Englishmen. – Should it matter? – Not anymore,
for the next move was at hand. Again it was almost midnight, and a few
moonpocked shards of ice had gathered against the rocky beach. The waves
had begun now, although they were still weak and flattish, and in consequence
of this agitation there were many washes of pale blue upon the darker blue of
the sound, over which a flock of oldsquaws passed as thickly as mosquitoes
on land; and the mountains, severed from earth by a strip of fog as straight as
a ruler, also swarmed in the sky, like purple birds.

On the 2^d of August, the breakup of the pack being now well underway, M^r
Franklin directed that all be ready for departure with the turn of the tide, and
the officers served out the traditional dram, at which the men cheered. All
were confident now of achieving their Northwest Passage without further
interruptions. – Up anchor, up sail! – The three graves dwindled behind
them. The wind was very keen. The following day, continuing to make
progress to the southwest, they achieved the middle of Barrow's Strait, the
open water a peculiar Chinese blue whose beauty was scarcely to be
conceived; porcelain-blue reflections of mountains hung upside-down like
stalactites from the streak of ice that separated them from the originals, the
dusty-purple mountains snow-dusted and cloud-roofed. Off the port side
stood Somerset Island, where Seth found a solitary bluebell. It was highly
gratifying to Mr Franklin to observe the elevating effect that the scenery had
upon his companions, who relied so lovingly upon his best judgment to bring
them safely through this season. On the 5th they reached their crossroads,
which is to say Viscount Melville Sound straight ahead, Penny Strait to the
north and Peel Sound to the south. Dr Goodsir took a very interesting and
accurate sketch of this locus, the latitude of which was observed to extend
south of the seventy-fourth degree. Meanwhile Mr Franklin conferred by
signal with M^essrs Crozier and Fitzjames, who agreed with him that tracing
the situation of Peel Sound showed the most promise of completing the
passage. It was more than likely that they would reach Simpson Strait by this

introitus. Their resolution being concluded, they lost no further time, changing course to the southward even as Dr Goodsir completed the final lines of his sketch. Blurry floes swirled in a brown fog while ravens shrieked. Later the weather improved to such an extent that through his looking-glass, Mr Franklin was able to spy rocks like pills on distant ridges –

He was very encouraged to see how Peel Sound continued southward toward the American coast. (He felt faint.) Throughout that month he continued hopeful that they would meet up with Esquimaux who might guide them for some small consideration. (It's so nice to have light, muttered the Finnlander Kid. Soon we're not going to have any.) The sea was green and grey. The setting sun breathed a narrow orange through the fog of two ridges. The sky was yellow and blue. Snow swirled along the ridgetop, merging with the yellow sky like smoke with fire, and everything was so yellow and bright, as bright as morning, and the islands were very distinct, with their long low blue backs, and the white cape was crinkled yellow and blue. An iceberg lay in the indigo water like a square escaped from a giant chessboard. Icebergs bobbed in the water like giant snailshells.

Day after day the floes grew more populous. The lookout reported a strong ice-blink to the southwest. Mr Franklin made signal to the *Terror*, which lay less than a quarter-mile behind, and C^apt Crozier presently came aboard, having left his ship in charge of Lt Little. He entered Mr Franklin's cabin, while the two ships hove to under close-reefed topsails, and they conferred for an unusual length of time, so that the officers began to wonder what might be occurring, and then C^apt Crozier returned to the *Terror*. They continued south by southwest. – Dr Goodsir saw a number of whales, which seemed very tame – how nice for British commerce! – Approaching the Magnetic Pole, it gave Mr Franklin considerable pleasure to remember his friend Sir James who'd first set foot there . . . The crews continued in gleeful spirits, their officers having assured them that the ice-pack would not fail to be penetrable in this season; Dr Peddie had added a new subspecies of fulmar to the collection, as Dr Goodsir learned when C^apt Crozier came aboard again, this time to report an increase on the *Terror*'s sick-list; the fulmar had been easy to bag, as it had dived down on Dr Peddie, almost as if it thought to attack him . . . Presently C^apt Crozier took his leave, and it seemed to the officers that once again his face was uneasy, but then Mr Franklin came out on deck and it was a joy to see how graciously he inclined to all, how he turned and turned about with Mr Fitzjames on his right hand, Fitzjames's face glowing at being so close to his Commander, and the other officers watched as Mr Franklin pointed upward and Fitzjames's eyes rose up at once so obediently and the officers themselves could not forbear from looking up at the close-reefed sails like shingles as the ship glided along almost noiselessly, the *Terror* discreetly behind, rounding a little iceberg as her sister had just done; so the two ships, sting-beaked before, dog-tailed behind, carried their foliage of sails, while the clouds laughed. Saturday night Mr Franklin led them in the toast to sweethearts and wives; Sunday he led them in Divine service; Monday he made signal to the *Terror* and led them into the pack –

On the 12th of September 1846, not very far from Cape Felix, they became locked in ice. That was the evening he first noticed that it became dim for reading after nine. The east side of the Cape, which is in fact the east side of King William Land, was open water, and Mr Fitzjames wanted to try it, but he was overruled by Mr Franklin, who saw scant indication from Back's or Ross's maps that King William Land was really (as it was) King William Island; so that seemed no way to go through, an anus instead of an uktuk. The *Erebus* led as always. Mr Gore stood with the lookout, vainly searching for a water-sky, while the two ships thumped and bumped through lanes as narrow and crooked as anything in the London slums and seals played about and they came to a little lake where they stood among the loose ice most cautiously waiting on the *Terror* and then Mr Franklin made signal and went to visit C^apt Crozier and returned smiling slightly, having decided to continue to the southwestward, and to loyal Fitzjames he said: Ah, C^mdr Crozier is so good a friend! and the next day he left ship in party with C^apt Crozier and some officers to clamber up one of the table-bergs that surrounded them, the better to search for the lovely darkness of a water-sky, but all they saw was young ice, pancake ice, brash ice, barrier ice, and so they returned and C^apt Crozier set his men to collecting fragments of green two-year ice for the *Terror*'s water-casks while Mr Franklin prayed alone in his cabin and Mr Fitzjames sent out a boating party to shoot seals for oil, in the unlikely event that it might be needed for heating that winter, and so the rifles spoke and spoke again and the men came back with their happy cargo of blubber and blood,

and then the next day Mr Franklin directed them to haul the boats over each
bow so that they could roll them on the young ice and crush it, which was
most expeditiously done, and so they made three hundred yards, heaving and
boring, humping and thumping, and then found another lead that carried
them two miles to another hole of clear water in which the two ships could
swim like trapped minnows; Mr Franklin commanded them to tack about
every quarter-hour, in order to avoid being frozen in; and the next day the ice
was thick enough for the men to walk on, cutting a channel with saws, and
Mr Franklin watched them without much interest through his spy-glass; he
fixed the lens on the Finnlander Kid, whose hair was plastered to his forehead
in a manner perpetually wet; he was surprisingly intellectual-lipped (thought
Mr Franklin); with his clear eyes, thin brows, he might yet make something
of himself . . . and the Finnlander Kid was at Seth's shoulder while Seth
worked the saw into the ice, and the Finnlander Kid was talking about how
he'd wandered Russian America, sneaking into Esquimau cemeteries, looking
for ivory carvings and deathmasks of Ipiutak skeletons in gravel beaches, and
Seth shrugged and kept sawing and the Finnlander Kid said: want to see
one?   and Seth declined but the Finnlander Kid laughed like a bird and said:
yes, you do!   and Seth kept sawing and the Finnlander Kid pretended to help
him and Mr Fitzjames sang out: that's the way, lads!   and the Finnlander
Kid said: deathmask of death I defend my skeleton-soul   – at which Seth,
brooding, frowning, stern, intense, looked him in the face and indeed saw the
fellow's skull like a rounded diamond of walrus ivory, incised with eye-slits
and a mouth-slit and slanted nostril-slits, but even then Seth wasn't afraid
because he understood that it was *right* for the Finnlander Kid to be a skull;
the Finnlander Kid's soul was clean like a new shotgun; and so they came
again into a great lake of open water which they thought must be the sea, and
the men cheered. Under all studding sail they made progress deeper into their
Northwest Passage; ahead lay another ice-blink.   – Yes, my dear boy,   he
said to Fitzjames,   the climate is like this in Van Diemen's Land. In 'forty-
one, when I was Governor, Sir James and I went on a tour of the fossil forest
. . .   – Ice ahead!   cried the lookout. Now fog stroked them. Mr Franklin
gave the order to proceed under moderate sail, in order to avoid being
separated from the *Terror*. As the fog condensed more heavily, the sisters
began speaking to one another with rifles, in order to avoid any collision, and
the heavy air devoured the echoes like meat and the breeze freshened until
they had to reef their foresails, and then the breeze died down and M^r
Franklin was saying: My wife was present, too. She's a great one for
explorations, you know, Fitzjames. – Aye, sir. – But she never goes plucking

the scarlet mushrooms . . . – I beg your pardon, sir? – You've had them, I'm sure, in Inukjuak . . . – The next day was sunny and calm. Ahead lay the pack, inviting them deeper in, beguiling them with any number of promising leads.

According to Chart No. 261, King William Land was connected by an isthmus to the Boothia Peninsula. If he'd been so deep as to study Canadian Inuktitut writing, with its triangles and fishhooks and Cs and Ls at every orientation, he might have been able to read whatever message the ice-leads held for him, just as Subzero had in Pond Inlet when he read Franklin's name, but by now Subzero was only Mr Franklin, not Subzero anymore, and Mr Franklin did not know Inuktitut, and the syllabic alphabet had hardly caught on very much at that time anyway (Moravian missionaries had just invented it), so he could not read the ice and took the wrong turn. – Of course the ice might have lied to him. A fresh breeze persisted; the ice would surely scatter when the weather calmed, opening like Reepah's fingers when she slept, the palms slowly unclenching from the nightmares she could no longer crush; Reepah never slept a night through unless she'd gotten pills or booze . . . So he had a fifty-fifty chance anyway. Always look on the bright side of the question. Choosing the westward course, then, although he saw nothing but ice-blink on the horizon, he chose entombment.

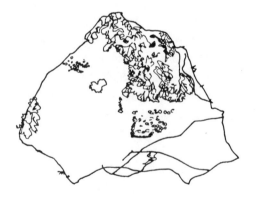

VI
Peel Sound

Cards

1847

Also in the last few years of *National Geographic* an article appeared about an Eskimo gravesite where bodies had been stacked up in a cave not far from the ocean, over a period of several decades, centuries ago – and had mummified very nicely in the dry Arctic air.

JACOB DICKINSON, letter of
1 September 1986

The ornate and pallid brows of the Queens, the Kings in robes as bizarrely gorgeous as Aztec art, blooming two-headedly hermaphroditic, the fields of Hearts and Spades all disappeared into his hands and crackled as he shuffled them; they made waterfalls between his fingers (while the sleet pattered hard and delicate on the awning), and then the cards blossomed again in their seven stacks and he put a six on a seven and took a King out and then lost and gathered up the cards and wrote his score, and they bent and snapped between his fingers again, and he said: One thirty-six. Is that the lowest I've been? – Yes . . .   – and the cards came face-down and face-up like icons and he stared down at them from his blankets, chest and arms out, and then he won. Snowflakes swirled outside and melted. The ice was white with brown stripes of something like mud.

Mr Fitzjames?

A little iceberg floated idiotically in the sound twelve miles to the north of them. The temperature was just below freezing, the ocean blue-grey and wavy and serene. Mr Gore was stationed there with a party of half a dozen men, at the edge of the open water. It was June again, and they expected the ice to break up very shortly. The season would surely be early this year; all indications pointed to it. Mr Gore had been directed to apprise the Expedition as soon as he had positive information that the ice was wearing away. Mr Little's volunteers, gone east in search of game, were due back tomorrow, and they too might have seen some hopeful sign . . . It was three weeks now since M^essrs Fitzjames and Crozier had divided the men into shooting-parties under command of the junior officers, and they traced the tracks of musk-oxen in snow, which were sometimes like twin ski-tracks because musk-oxen drag their feet every now and then, and the senior officers held a meeting with the stewards in Mr Franklin's presence (although he only smiled sweetly and said nothing) and concluded that thanks to the rifles they might easily last a fourth year if game was abundant . . . It was almost windless. The iceberg drew closer to the pavement of ice in which the two ships were locked and fitted itself in with a little bump. It was a cobblestone. The pavement went on and on now, like a causeway of boulders leading out into a sea whose inhuman light-sparkles Subzero sometimes interpreted as malicious, some-times as joyous; and the rock-bridge curved left toward the sun, where pale blue ice watched the narwhals in their strait, and Subzero paced the beach at Pond Inlet and Resolute and Eureka Sound picking up rifle cartridges and rattling them in his pockets, searching for Reepah's name once more in the grooves of the ice; although it is incorrect to say that he was Subzero, the struggle for absolute accuracy is forcing me once again to be someone I don't want to be. The pavement went on and on. This was the end. The ships would never come free.

Mr Fitzjames?

A five on a six. A four on a five.

Mr Fitzjames?

There was a long low slope of snow-hills on either side of the sound. One side was Reepah Island and one was Lady Franklin Island. They were closer to Lady Franklin Island that month. (Lady Franklin was in the West Indies at that time with Eleanor, then in America. No news from the whalers, and the Admiralty not yet prepared to offer a reward . . . – Yes, she's the one, the other ladies had begun whispering. The one whose husband was never since heard of.) They could see how the shore-hill bulged like muscle and then went down into a snow-marbled peninsula, meeting a beach with glistening smooth pebbles and bits of fossil wood. Dead flowers shuddered in the breeze, their leaves shiny with ice and melted snow. They could not see the flowers from deck, but frequently they crossed the ice in hunting parties led by their officers and then they saw them. Thanks to the continuing illness of Dr Goodsir, and the resultant increasing burden upon Dr Peddie, Seth had been appointed Acting Naturalist. Whenever he was off watch he wandered among the new young plants crooning to himself; he'd die happy.

A three on a four.

Mr Fitzjames?

What do you want, lackey?

The Captain desires to speak with you, sir.

No doubt he does. Well, a two on a three. Up storm-sails!

Your uniform, sir.

Yes. My blue Ice-Shirt. Here I come.

It was a grey day of louring clouds, with the ice on the sound shining like cream. Mr Franklin, bedridden, squinted in the darkness. Like all old Arctic men, his eyes were scarred by sunlight and ice crystals; he had Labrador keratopathy.

Ah, it's you, Fitzjames?

Aye, sir. My poor Captain –

Mr Franklin smiled. – What news from Mr Gore?

None as of yet, sir.

And you, Fitzjames, how go your headaches?

Oh, they're nothing, sir.

Fitzjames . . .

Yes, sir?

I – I feel another fit coming on –

I'll send for Dr Peddie at once, sir.

An Ace on a two, Fitzjames.

I beg your pardon, sir?

Never mind about Dr Peddie. Could you lift my head please? Very unfortunate and unusual circumstances. And help me with that draught, just a bit from that brown bottle – yes –

Do you feel better, sir?

Fitzjames, in the event of my incapacity Mr Crozier will succeed to my position. He has the seniority, you see.

Aye, sir.

You'll cooperate with him, I know. If the weather should be severe –

Aye, sir.

And speak to them of the SUPREME BEING –

Aye, sir.

On the 6th of June Mr Franklin went entirely blind and it was hailing louder and louder in staccato spanking noises upon the awning and the roof of the vestibule was running with weird wet patterns of condensation and a feeble black spider spun its thread inside and pulled itself up with wide slow clutches of its forelegs as Mr Hoar spread hot sand on the lower deck because it was the day to do that and they were playing cribbage in up-buttoned greatcoats, happy from an earlier game in which they roasted stones and dropped them into their half-frozen boots in hopes of drying them for the next day's march to relieve Mr Gore at Cape Felix and the stones exploded sharply like popcorn in the dry cooking pot and the snow fell outside and the steam rose from inside the shoes and at the end of it all they might or might not have been drier but were certainly very pleased with themselves and put the muddy things away and cooked dinner and lay listening to the hail-salvoes and presently Subzero got out the cards and the cribbage-board and they each ate a chocolate bar and their pegs rushed round the board because they kept getting double runs and triple runs and pairs and triples in play and fifteens, so they often got twelve or sixteen points per hand, sometimes more, and the kitty was usually full of points and every hand was so good that it was hard to know which cards to give up, and soon the game was done. One of them lost, of course, but the feeling that they both had won fell as usual as snowflakes upon the two grave-twins, possibly because Jane at that moment had risen with sleepless fascination to pore over the polar charts of all the Arctic Friends by candle-light, as if somehow she could divine which obstacle separated the one she loved from her – but there was so much blankness, so much hateful whiteness as she sat there in the night! It was at that moment that she began to fear for him in earnest. She recalled that dinner party long ago when Mr Back had told Sophy of the dreary vastness of Arctic distances; for the first time, sitting there alone in her boudoir, she thought she understood him; the empty regions on the maps took on a merciless unalterability which seemed beyond anyone's capacity to surmount. Never before had her husband seemed so lost. It was as though she had discovered him in bed with Reepah so that she could not deny what he was doing anymore, and when she came in, when she held the lantern over their writhing forms, he curled up like some snowy worm of darkness, not beseeching her, not hiding in Reepah's arms, but struggling mindlessly, suffocating, cut off from the world by his shame. That was how he always appeared when he had his fits; he went to someplace so far off, where no one could help him. Because Jane cared more about his happiness than her own, she would not have been transpierced by resentment at such a sight (that would have come later), but only pity and deep alarm on his behalf, the real misery being that she could not be of use; this was precisely how Seth had felt upon seeing the dead fox and raven at Pond Inlet. Not for a moment, of course, did she suspect him of betraying her; John was far too upright for that. But if he had doubled his affections in that way, it would have made a similar impression on her. She felt so wretched and tired as a result of her helplessness that even her heartbeat wearied her. Should she wake Sophy and beg her to read to her? No, that would be selfish. So she sat sick at heart and sleepless, staring blankly at the hateful maps. – As for the grave-twins, they endeavored to invent new amusements for the men, both to assist them in passing the months that had condensed upon them like breath-frost and to prevent them from speculating too deeply on their present condition, which could only be hurtful to discipline and confidence. Mr Franklin proposed to have the carpenters build toboggans so that races could be held upon the pack-ice, which had worked so well to impress Akaitcho a quarter-century before, and had perhaps served to recruit Mr Hood's already failing health with the brisk exercise; Mr Franklin remembered very well how Hood and Back had striven against one another at the sport, while Greenstockings stood by laughing . . . Well, of course, he had another Greenstockings in his sleeve now, to lure on M^{essrs} Fitzjames and Crozier, assuming that she might choose to reveal herself to them; she was always a good sport – but no, he could not do that. He could never ever share her. Condensation and hail made continents on the translucent roof. The wind ruffled everything and chilled him. Although there was snow under the floor, it did not melt, and so they felt happy and cozy. Subzero was playing solitaire. Reepah's face had not yet begun to appear in the cards, so I watched him and did not envy him; she had not yet shown us any preference.

When I was in high school,   said Seth, leaning back until his glasses froze white with light,   there was this girl named Jane who was so in love with me. But I don't need to tell you who she married. She was pretty fucked up. Any girl would have to be, to be in love with *me*. She thought the soldiers of the Pope's guard were degraded because they didn't wear gloves. Degraded – that was the word she used. Of course I didn't understand that at the time. Things came to a head when she started talking to me about how she wanted to pour honey on my back and lick it off and stuff. I thought she was joking, 'cause she said it right in the hall, so I just joked back. Well, later that afternoon she wanted to make an appointment. I had to tell her no. Anyway, it kind of crushed her. I was nice to her and everything but there was really nothing I could say after that. She had to have been looking for something that would be a heartbreaker. She had to have been setting herself up. She really wasn't thinking clearly.

Lead poisoning,   replied Subzero brightly.

Which reminds me. Well, her brother felt the same way about my sister, and she responded in pretty much the same way that I did. He went home and tried to hang himself. Someone at school called her and told her. He didn't do himself any damage, though. Anyway, I found out this guy just moved to Knoxville a few months ago and blew his brains out in a stone quarry. Put his head right up against the rifle and pulled the trigger with his toe. And my sister said: Well, I guess I should feel bad, but I just don't.   — And she *shouldn't!* He was determined to kill himself over something; she'd acted exactly as she should have acted. People are so weird.

He turned the card over, and it was the Jack of Clubs. But the Jack was very different than any he had ever seen before. The boy's braids ended in white spirals like narwhal tusks. His kamiks were clothed like bear's claws. He had a pinched face; his bloodshot eyes squinted dully. His caribou skins hung raggedly upon him.

That's kind of bullshit,   said Seth.   That doesn't mean a fuckin' thing.

The boy's face got thinner and thinner, until he was only a skull. He had starved to death.

Well, that kid didn't get what he wanted,   said Seth to silent Subzero.   But I got what I wanted, John, and you got what you wanted. We're both heroes — dead heroes — and I don't know what we have the right to want now. Like that guy who was in love with my sister. Didn't he get everything he wanted, too?

You really don't want anything right now?   said Subzero in amazement.

Well, girls, of course. You know that girl Amy that was crazy about me, and I wouldn't do anything about it, out of some goddamned sense of principle or something. I sure wish she were sitting on my face now. You know how it is. Eating out at the Y. I guess it's the same for you. I mean, I know you're still waiting for Reepah. And I hope it works out for you, because that would be really neat.

Do you think Reepah would like me better if I —

Reepah loves you, John.

And our Northwest Passage . . .

I don't know for sure,   Seth said.   Any answer would sound pretty corny or philosophical or something, but I'd bet you anything it just means wanting some other thing just to want it, wanting something just so you can be unhappy —

But Subzero was already turning over the Queen of Spades, and she was Reepah; he saw her gently holding onto her bottle of Canada Dry and a seal was peeking over her shoulder and her head was pressed so gently against the seal's head, her forehead against the seal's cheek, and the seal was looking

intently at him but Reepah in the red-on-black New York T-shirt that he had
bought her was only looking away and down at her bottle of Canada Dry and
she looked so patient and loving and hurt like SEDNA who tried to live with
the FULMAR (who was Mr Franklin) and then gazed into her father's face as
he chopped her fingers off and pushed her into the ocean, and as she sank
beyond death into the place at the bottom where her anguish and loneliness
were complete, as she became the luminous one in Subzero's grave, the seals
began to gather around her; they tickled her with their whiskers already
knowing that they were hers, which reminds me of the time that Reepah
decided she wanted her hair permed. She'd never been to a beauty parlor in
her life. He called one of Jane's friends to learn which place was good, even
as Mr Fitzjames went down into the hold to listen to the ice squeezing it – of
small account its double caulking, its sealing with African board – even the
shipsides doubled with oak and elm to a thickness of eight inches groaned
now! Let the ice drop them, and perhaps ocean would rush in through
punctures in her iron armored sides! Double-wrought deck, hot-tallowed
planks, iron hooks and crutches all no use . . . – O Arctic fantasies!   he
muttered. – His scarf was stiff with ice. He unwound it gingerly from his neck
and knocked it against one of the pumps. Then he put it on again. He stood
there for awhile and then he went back up to his cabin and played solitaire.
He'd given Mr Des Voeux temporary authority, so that he wouldn't be
disturbed anymore; he sat playing cards and massaging his headaches. The
sick-list was lengthening, Dr Goodsir said – and she was touching the seal so
lightly that she was almost not touching him and her lower lip hung down a
little, the lip he loved to suck on and kiss, and her eyes were almost closed;
and he remembered that time so long ago in Pond Inlet when Jukee had told
him who his triplet was and he had had her and she had had him and she was
still so hurt . . . – She went   eee!   because it was her first time on the subway
and his heart had not yet begun to ache because Jane wasn't due back from
her engagement for six more days and he took Reepah out through the
turnstile and she touched its tines in amazement and they went past the token
booth and up the stairs and out of the ship into the wind and dirty snow and
it seemed very cold to him that December day but Reepah needed neither
hood nor mittens; her hands glowed happy red like her cheeks and she
chewed her gum very thoughtfully. They went into the beauty shop and the
woman asked Reepah what style she wanted and Reepah didn't answer
because she was so deaf, so he said the question into her ear and the woman
gave her a book of styles to look through and Reepah said: That one. No,
that one!   – and she started to laugh.

Where's she from? the woman said.

She's Inuk.

Inuk? What's that?

She's Eskimo.

Are you serious? Wow! I gotta go tell Leila! We get all kinds here, but I've never done an Eskimo before.

Soon all the ladies at the beauty parlor were gathered around Reepah staring. Reepah didn't seem to care, but maybe she did; only JESUS knew what Reepah thought about anything –

He sat beside her while the woman was perming her hair, so that she wouldn't be scared, and when she was under the dryer Leila came back and clutched his arm and whispered loudly: Is it true what they say?

What do they say? he said, as patiently as he could.

They say that when you live among the Eskimos a man will – a man *will offer you his wife!*

Trading partners used to do that, in the old days, he said. They don't do that anymore –

But the woman kept staring at Reepah, and her look was the same as the seal-gazes when she sank bleeding to the bottom of the sea –

I guess I want trees, too, Seth said. Not too many trees up here. I remember one day in the Smokies. There was a glow of maples in all this darkness, and it was so beautiful. I was just kind of giddy. I was laughing and so full of myself –

I understand, replied Mr Franklin with a smile. That's your duty.

Aye, sir.

And are you prepared for the final extremity?

I'm so excited. I'm a little nervous, you know, but very excited –

Seth left his Commander's cabin and made his way down the sloping deck (which the steward had now finished sanding) and he heard the ship groan a little in the ice – it had been raised forty feet high! – and for a minute he wondered what everyone wondered, which was what would happen to them if the ice ever let go (that had happened to Back when he commanded the *Terror*, but Back, as we all know, was a very lucky man) and because it was not yet Seth's watch he drew on his wool mitts and went over the side for a walk to the latrine and he heard the ice hissing and groaning and the pressure-ridges had grown steeper since yesterday; our propellers and twenty-horse-power railroad engines had proved useless against ice of such magnitude, but Mr Franklin was neither surprised not disappointed. Such toys were the latest thing, and therefore gratifying to his officers in the highest degree, but he'd

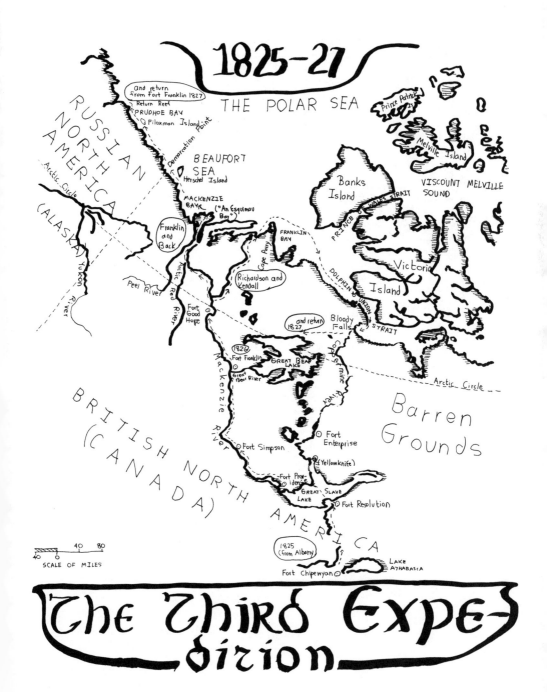

1825-27

THE POLAR SEA

RUSSIAN NORTH AMERICA (ALASKA)

and return from Fort Franklin 1827
Return Reef
PRUDHOE BAY
Flaxman Island Point
Demarcation Point

BEAUFORT SEA
Herschel Island

MACKENZIE BAY

"An Esquimau Bay"

Franklin and Back

Arctic Circle

Yukon River

Peel River

Arctic Red River

Fort Good Hope

Richardson and Kendall

Cape Parry

FRANKLIN BAY

Banks Island

PRINCE OF WALES STRAIT

VISCOUNT MELVILLE SOUND

Melville Island

Prince Patrick

DOLPHIN & UNION STRAIT

Victoria Island

and return 1827

Bloody Falls

Coppermine

1826 Fort Franklin

GREAT BEAR LAKE

Great Bear River

Arctic Circle

Barren Grounds

Mackenzie River

Fort Simpson

Fort Enterprise

(Yellowknife)

Fort Providence

GREAT SLAVE LAKE

Fort Resolution

BRITISH NORTH (CANADA) AMERICA

40 80
40 0
SCALE OF MILES

1825 (from Albany)

Fort Chipewyan

Lake ATHABASCA

The Third Expedition

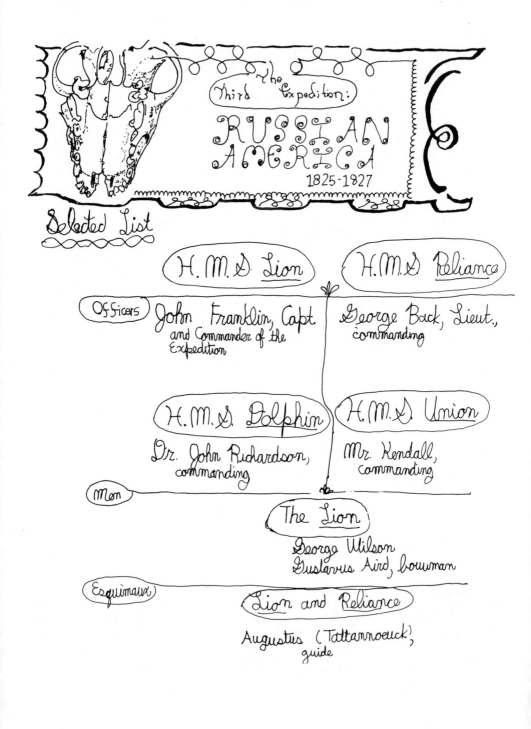

the Third Expedition:

RUSSIAN AMERICA
1825-1827

Selected List

H.M.S. Lion	H.M.S. Reliance
Officers: John Franklin, Capt. and Commander of the Expedition	George Back, Lieut., commanding

H.M.S. Dolphin	H.M.S. Union
Dr. John Richardson, commanding	Mr. Kendall, commanding

Men

The Lion

George Wilson
Gustavus Aird, bowman

Esquimaux

Lion and Reliance

Augustus (Tattannoeuck?), guide

succeeded in previous endeavors without them; and so their failure was of no importance. Why, don't you remember that time when we were almost shipwrecked? It was on the expedition before this one, when no one ate each other – twenty years ago now! – and his instructions had been to go west instead of east. If only poor Hood could have lived to see *that!* – Of the three ventures which Mr Franklin actually commanded, this middle one has received the least press, no doubt because no one starved to death. – It will be a vexatious business for your husband, the Arctic Friends said to Jane by way of comfort, but scarcely very daunting. The coastline seems very regular in those parts. Never fear, Lady Franklin, he'll come back covered in laurels as usual . . . (Among themselves they said: And did you hear about that epileptic attack he had recently? He looked quite done in. He kept muttering something about his Esquimau squaw.) – Mr Franklin wrote in his journal: *We would gladly have dispensed with the presence of the Dog-Rib Indians, who now visited us in great numbers, without bringing any supplies,* because now as ever Mr Franklin was preoccupied with meat – and who isn't? Duty, love, patriotism and all the rest could not exist without meat. The Indians claimed that game was not as abundant as in Akaicho's day, although that was impossible to believe. Anyhow, the rifles behaved like gentlemen; soon the pemmican-bags were full. – Then it was time to go north again to the Polar Sea! On July the 2^d, 1826, they arrived in good order at the edge of Esquimau territory, announcing which, Mr Franklin took the precaution of issuing a rifle, a dagger and shot to each member of the Expedition, for who knew how these Esquimaux might behave? Mr Back and Dr Richardson were along; it was just like old times. He wouldn't have taken Back if he could have avoided it, but his first choice had died, so Back it must be, in an easily observable capacity. Back had sworn to engage in no more duels over native women – a promise that he kept. Henceforth all his energies would be centered upon his Captain. As for our friend Dr Richardson, he'd have charge of the eastern detachment, in an endeavor to complete the unknown coast between Bear Lake River and the Coppermine, while it was Mr Franklin's objective to proceed westward to Russian America, which we now call *Alaska*; Back would be useful enough, I suppose, in command of one of the lesser boats . . . On the 7th, having taken the bearings of several points in the Rocky Mountain Range, they came in sight of an Esquimau bay! – Prudent Mr Franklin gave orders that all the stores be hidden beneath the spare sails, and Mr Back broke out a pre-weighed quantity of gewgaws, hiding the rest . . . At first everything went well, but when the gifts were gone the Eskimos continued to swarm and importune; one stole Mr Back's pistol, and then they all began dragging the

boats up onto the beach, crying: *Teyma, teyma!*★ and threatening the white
men with uplifted knives; the women screamed shrilly; two men seized M^r
Franklin by the wrists and pulled him down between them, so that his
expostulations were of no account; they sliced through George Wilson's coat
and waistcoat with their daggers; they slit Gustavus Aird's clothes; they tried
to cut off Mr Back's anchor-buttons, which they particularly prized, but he,
seeing his Commander in worse plight, sent the chief who'd protected him to
Mr Franklin's aid; yes, Mr Back could always be counted on to sacrifice
himself, and, so doing, to triumph; in all his rash excursions Mr Back never
came to any harm! – What was his secret? – The rifles, of course. At his word,
they were leveled, and the Esquimaux began to shriek and run; now, as in a
dream, they were all gone, crouching behind their canoes (for they knew
what guns were), and the tide came in and floated the boats, and Mr Franklin
led the Expedition on its way . . . – What next? – Well, the subsequent tribe of
Eskimaux was friendlier. They warned him against proceeding further westward, saying that his boats were inadequate, that he should have brought
sled dogs, that the pack-ice, if it had drifted away from shore at all, would
come slamming back as soon as the stars were seen again . . . – but M^r
Franklin, dear Mr Franklin, had heard all this before from Akaicho. Akaicho
had said that Mr Franklin wouldn't come back, and he had, hadn't he? Those
things were as the ALMIGHTY disposed. So, as usual, he continued on without
a care; on the 13th, by some coincidence, they were almost crushed by the
mountainous ice-islands just west of Cape Sabine; the following year he was
back in London with Jane . . . and Seth looked back at the ice-hung, snow-
drifted *Erebus* canted so unbearably (except that one had to bear it) and he
said to himself: We sure lived in the glory days.

Here Mr Franklin has requested me to put in a scene in which someone eats
Seth, but we don't have to have those horrors. – Life with Mr Franklin is
really really sweet when he doesn't take me for granted, Seth said to himself.
Most of the time I'm not miserable. But the times I'm miserable, I'm really
miserable. And it's a sin not to enjoy what you have. I think I'll just go out
into the snowdrifts and jerk off a few times. It's this kind of landscape that
really gets me going. GOD, I'm jazzed!
    I don't know about starving to death, Seth said to himself. Subzero said

---

★ Conjectural meaning: "Stop, stop!"

that was the way. But his way's the rifles. I never liked guns. And me, well, I was thinking it would be more fitting if I did something stupid. Like when I was trying to get into a kayak and when I got it going maybe capsizing or catching myself on fire or something. I just see some kind of blundering. Yeah, that sounds good. I could be wandering off, kind of starved and out of it ('cause Mr Franklin deserves that I be a little hungry, at least), and come to the edge of a snow-cliff and just kind of think: What would happen if I didn't turn?

At Cape Felix, returned from the Finnlander Kid's funeral, Mr Gore played solitaire. The ice would assuredly slacken soon. He opened the vestibule of his tent and spat out into the snow. Gore, unlike Fitzjames, laid out the cards not in order to bewitch himself into some deeper stupor than hopelessness, but rather as an act of defiance. His energies quivered and coruscated. Recognizing the indolence into which the others had fallen as a convenience to cold and creeping death, he declaimed each new hand interiorly, insisting to himself upon the meaningless numbers that yet had more meaning than the icescape, and projected proudly from the dormant hulk of him like a mizzen-mast. What he would have preferred, what would have brought him fully to life, was an animal, a seal or bear or musk-ox to kill. That would at least be doing something useful. Ever since a whole row of meat-tins had turned out to be spoiled, even Mr Franklin had taken alarm. The officers vied to go on shooting-parties at first, but scarcely a spoor did they find. Frost formed in the barrels of their rifles, which weighed down the hunters with cold aches. Now shooting-parties were not quite so popular. Mr Gore played solitaire, carefully recording every score. – Well, I'm out, he said. – He opened the vestibule and smoked a cigarette. When it was half gone, he threw it into the snow. His nose dripped. Snot had frozen on his moustache. Dinner hung from it in green stalactites of frozen pea soup. He yawned and turned a new card over and it was the Queen of Clubs, which is to say Reepah, and she was staring into his eyes; it was her birthday and Subzero had given her presents to unwrap, but since Jane and Mr Back and Sir James were there, Reepah was miserable; Reepah sat hiding her hands under the wrapping paper and looking at him with eyes as dark and blank as the darkness behind the window –

Mr Fitzjames was playing solitaire, frowning the way Seth would frown a little as he read. The ice remained very close. He turned the card over, and it was the Queen of Hearts, but instead of being the Queen whose schematic double-face he'd seen before, it was Reepah. She was formed as a girl should be: plump and robust, with big breasts and a big smile. Her snow-goggles were like horn-stumps when she pushed them up to her forehead. She wore a caribou-skin parka as white as the snow, with the long fringe fluttering at her waist in a way that drove her suitors mad. Endearing, too, were her hands in their big soft mittens: anyone could see that she was skilled in making clothes.

An Arctic fox ran so gingerly upon its paws as almost to be limping. It looked back over its shoulder as it ran.

In his bed, Mr Franklin was playing solitaire. The ice continued its retrograde trend. He had neither cards nor vision; he didn't need the Queen of Diamonds. His hopes were bright but momentary, as when the sun glints gold-white on some lakey indigo lead. They held the added sentimental value of something found and lost and found again. His breath-clouds were like this:

She would have been tattooed in lines of dark pigment (maybe gunpowder, if they'd had it yet), lines solid or dotted, warming her face in rays from her nose to her cheeks and forehead, from her mouth down to her chin in expanding rushes; and when he came to be with her he'd see the other tattoos on her breasts and legs and sweet hardworking arms and he'd know that she had been tattooed to make her beautiful for him before she'd ever seen him so that her pain was once again an act of faith for unknown love as when she'd let his penis into her in Inukjuak – an act he'd eternally betrayed.

Beset

1846–1848

Even before setting out to acquire one or more helping spirits, which are like new "mystical organs" for any shaman, the Eskimo neophyte must undergo a great initiatory ordeal. Success in obtaining this experience requires his making a long effort of physical privation and mental contemplation directed to gaining *the ability to see himself as a skeleton.*

MIRCEA ELIADE, *Shamanism: Archaic Techniques of Ecstasy* (1971)

By definition momentous things happen rarely; thus when they do come only a stunned and stunning echo rings through the ordinariness of life. My life will never be the same again, we say, and search in amazement for the gestating cause of the event, as if we could somehow trace it back scientifically into ordinariness, and therefore render it ordinary. Of course, like Fitzjames, we find that the event has no prior cause – or rather that all the prior causes, no matter how relevant, still somehow fail to explain anything. What has happened is, and we can never go back to what was, and that is all there is to learn. That was how it was with the ice which continued to drift around the ships, encasing them deeper in death each moment (yet no moment seemed fatal); that is how it was when moment succeeded moment in Reepah's house and Reepah did not get her period and each moment that she did not was another moment in which the baby grew fatally inside her as the ice grew outside the two ships like the inhumanly steady jerking of the clock's second hand as he sat behind drawn curtains waiting for Reepah and the baby to come back – she'd said five or six or seven or eight or nine – when *would* she come? She was scared to be seen with him. When

he gave her money to go to the arcade she wouldn't go with him. – The blue flag swam in the wind; he could see that through a gap in the curtains. – Too late for sawing or warping or towing; he was beset. The telephone that Reepah could no longer afford to connect sat on the mattress; once in awhile she talked into it, pretending to call him or someone else as he sat there, then giving him the receiver with the utmost pride in order for him to admire the clicking noises that she could make for him by playing the buttons like piano keys; and sometimes the baby played with the phone, too, saying *Mama* into it, at which she laughed and kissed his face until he shrieked. The minute hand had moved significantly by now. In the street, a child called out in play; a three-wheeler buzzed by like some new species of tundra fly; a bulldozer shifted gears. The ice-pack trended heavenward. Last night at one or two the only noise had been the dogs howling under the aurora borealis, which she'd called him to the window to see; they stood hot and naked together like coals from some unknown fire and she said: See? Beautiful! and he kissed her in that greenish glow. There was more still to that moment, but nothing unprecious enough to bear saying, and so it seemed both nearer and farther now than the other moments that clicked away on that twenty-four-hour clock face. The river's mouth was quite blue. Cloud did not solidly clot the sky. The evening drew on.* She'd moved the bureau and sofa again, in another one of her organizing moods – a product doubtless of her unending battle with the baby, who just today had peed and shat in the bedroom, and then on her in the living room while she was sleeping. There was no money for Pampers, so he ran around naked and shat on the floor and then she yelled and thumped his tummy until he whimpered. There was no money for milk, so she filled his bottle with sugar water. The government check would come next month. There was no money for food, and Reepah wouldn't eat what her gallant had brought from Down South; she hated that dried stuff, but she was worried about food; she worried about Franklin, too, because he was getting skinnier every day. So she came back now with a great white bird in a bag (as soon as he heard her steps in the hall the empty mystery of the room popped happily like champagne corks), and she held up the bird grinning and said: My mother kill it camping! I go to her for bird, then to sister's place for salt . . .   – How many birds your mother kill?   – Million million!   she laughed. – It was freshly dead. It was cold, and smelled a little

fishy. Reepah threw it down on a baking pan and took out her ulu. She cut off the feet first.   – I love to eat these!   she said. Then she slit open the breast with the lower crescent of that blade and began to peel back the skin. She worked steadily and easily, laughing when the baby came to dip his fingers in the blood and suck them. She cut off the wings and discarded them because they were too small for sweeping.   – It's a baby bird!   she said. She snapped out the leg pieces and smooth pink neck; she exposed the breast-meat and added that to her pile, and finally cut into the ribcage to bring the organs out. She tasted the raw liver and decided that she didn't like it. But the heart was

* It is strange when the light fails. Since it happens so gradually, you are deceived. The river is still blue – *surely* the same blue! The fractures in the rocks on the far side are as numerous as ever (not that you counted them), and the tundra is still there with all its little mosses and leaves. Everything is still there, and yet everything is harder to see. Logic proves that certain things which were visible a quarter-hour ago cannot be anymore. But which?

her heart's delight. Skillfully she sliced thin raw pieces of the purple flesh and fed them to him and to the baby and popped some into her own mouth. The other tidbits she threw into a pot with some of her sister's salt and lots of water. She let it boil for about forty minutes. She would have added some soup, but there was no money for that. – The bird-feet became wrinkled and blue-black like seaweed. They tasted very good. And the windows were all steamed over with the vapor of that good fresh-killed meat ... – So Mr Franklin nourished himself with memories. Ice creaked against ice. Just as great islands are edged with snow, then with translucent grey ice, then grey water, so the caged ships drew successive and concentric boundaries about themselves. Later, we hear, they would end up at the bottom of the sea. It would be easy to term them, and the men on them, condemned. Broad snow-stains beset with bubbles, a narrow white river sunk deep in the blue-grey plain, cliffs, round broad puffy mountains snow-haired; vast patches bumpy and knobby, frozen deep river-canyons, ice-lakes like puddles of fresh-spilled milk – all these knew the way that chill-glittering brown ridges shadow themselves on milk-ice, endless but never monotonous, never the same; and they knew how to go on forever from the central *here* where the ships were. Mr Fitzjames, having partially succeeded in checking his perceptions of the ice, which beset him like an aching tooth, remained in his narrow cabin playing cards, scratching at his puffy and livid face. The pains within his skull exploded like thunder. He occasionally forgot where or who he was, and then Mr Hoar, the steward, would hear him groaning dully. Although the lieutenants of the *Erebus* strove to keep his condition confidential, everyone knew. Dr Peddie could tell that the poor man was becoming anemic as well. Fortunately, he did not seem to suffer from the mysterious belly-cramps which were now seizing an increasing number of men from both ships, and indeed his crises, though recurring, were scarcely so frequent as to impair him at other times when he sat receiving reports, or conferred with the other officers, or trudged about the dark and smoky ship, rubbing at his forehead. – Mr Crozier, on the other hand, continued entirely unaffected. Gazing mildly and skeptically before him, he ridiculed the fears that crept about on his ship and did his best to maintain a healthy atmosphere. He was more disappointed than he showed as regards the failure of the screw-propellers. He was concerned about Mr Franklin's health. He was – well, hungry is not the right word, but Mr Crozier had begun to reach that inevitable stage in which one yearns for fat. For fat is such a useful substance! Rub it on your cheeks and lips, and the wind cannot bite you. A little more on your lips, please – that's it! How pleasant it is on a cold day to lick and suck at a smidgeon of pork-grease! Digest fat, and it becomes truly yours. The fat that marries your blood will keep you warm. It will keep you strong. It will assuredly render you jocose; you'll never whine, spirit-pinched, like a starving man! The eider duck swims calmly in the chilly breeze, warmed not only by the feather bed we call its skin, but by the fat beneath. That is why a joint of roast duckling is so fine and crackly. Of course Mr Crozier was not starving. But tinned and pickled meat has a lean taste no matter how much fat is in it. They still had chocolate, of course, and butter tinned by means of Goldner's patent, and cheese . . . It was not quite a year now since the ships had first come to rest in the ice – although "come to rest" may not be the proper phrase, since the ice did drift, and the ships with it – but then a grave also whirls about with the whirling of the earth, and that does not seem to give its inmate a single iota of motive power. So consider my quibble retracted. – Lt Gore took a bearing: they were much nearer to Cape Felix. In between his fainting fits, Mr Franklin was only a little mortified, for the sake of the others who did not possess patience and understanding: – why, on that Coppermine expedition, with Back and Hood, icebergs had compelled them to change their course almost every day, as they westened between Greenland and Hudson's Bay; yet nothing untoward had come of that! Ice groaned and grated, but that scarcely bore comparison to the noise that he remembered hearing when they scraped against a grounded berg at Resolution Island immediately following their near shipwreck – no, no, he was accustomed to calamities. At Resolution Island it had been he who'd successfully exhorted the passengers to the pumps, so that they kept the water level in the hold from exceeding five feet. So they'd gone on into Hudson Strait in all safety, underhanging the peninsula called Meta Incognita; he gave orders to patch the leaks with bituminous canvas, following which the situation in the hold so far improved that he was able to permit a halt to barter with the Esquimaux of what is now Lake Harbour, nails and ribbons for furs and seahorse-teeth, and the sailors took the women belowdecks for a quick turn of mutual profit while he looked at the bright side of the question, knowing that he must, and Midshipman Hood wrote in his journal   *the features of the women are regular, and their eyes larger than those of the men, but the extreme relaxation of their breasts renders them objects of disgust to Europeans*   and Franklin said   what are you writing, my boy?   and Hood said   natural history observations, Mr Franklin   and Franklin nodded and prepared to take a transit of Arcturus over the meridian. Hood gulped miserably, not yet knowing that it was his destiny to fall in love with Greenstockings, to challenge Back to a duel over her, to leave her pregnant just like Subzero did Reepah! – how charmingly history repeats itself! – and Hood remembered

how on the flight back from Great Whale he'd been sitting next to a
Québecois who'd said: No, I wouldn't want to marry an Inuk. It is too
difficult. They never discuss with one another how they are feeling and what
they are thinking. You ask, and they say: I don't know.   And all the time
the emotion is there, but they cannot control it. For instance, one man I
know, one day he says something his Inuk wife doesn't like. So she takes a
knife and stabs him in the leg! He won't live with her anymore . . .   and then
the stewardess came by, a pretty Caucasian type, Hood's type as he'd thought,
and was he ever wrong.

The FULMAR turned over an Ace of Clubs and saw them sitting on a plain of
lichen, staring at Him with dirt-streaked faces, the baby sucking two of its
fingers, the little girl cocking her head shyly and clasping her hands, the
grownup daughter gazing piercingly at Him, her blanket pulled tight around
her shoulders, the son looking away a little (he was holding a knife in his
hand), and the old parents staring sadly, steadfastly, and then they were gone.
Here by King William Island her name was not SEDNA but NULIAJUK. She
was an orphan, a nuisance. They cut off her fingers when they were crossing
Caribou Strait, and she sank to the bottom and became the Power of Animals.
– At least I had nothing to do with it that time,   said the FULMAR to Himself.
– When He relocated her to His island He bought her a black leather jacket
and she was grateful, oh yes; she cried: My my my my *my* souvenir from
you!   – He bought her earmuffs and she said: My favorite!   – At night He
went out with her so that she could get her secrets and it had begun snowing,
the first snow of the year, and she seemed happy, and said that she was when
He asked her, although she did shy away from dogs and clung to His arm;
later still, when it was very dark outside and the windows of the adjacent
skyscrapers glared with monotonous eeriness, He put on a compact disk of
Inuit vocal games and she asked for some string, so He gave her dental floss
and she began to make the traditional string figures for Him: the komatik
with five dog-traces, the house that became something else He couldn't
understand, the two people head to head, which she said was Him and her;
then she looped the string around His head in a certain way and laughed and
said: I cut your head!   – and pulled it tight and it collapsed into nothing. –
And He said to her: Now that I'm not going to be Franklin very much
longer, will you still give Me the animals?   and she said: You hungry, John?
and He said: Not yet, but soon I'll be very *very* hungry . . .   and she said:

Hi, John. (When she was scared or tentative or very happy she'd peek at him and say: Hi, John.) – John, I'm hungry, she said. She wanted Chuck Wagon. He took her to the grocery store thinking that she would be impressed but she only became more and more disdainful, and said at last: This place has nothing! No Chuck Wagon! She picked out two cooking chickens instead, which He carried home for her and she boiled in water and salt, refusing His spices; she ate the pieces later with great relish and kept trying to get Him to eat with her, so He ate one for her feelings' sake and she said: Good? and He said yes and she said: *Eeeee!* very softly the way she always did when she was astonished, like the time she turned on His computer and erased the hard disk and was so amazed when the screen exploded into darkness; at first He'd thought that her *eeee!* was consistently enthralled, approving, but when He showed her a photo of His tattooed skinhead friends she said: *Eeeee!* and then she said: Tattoos is the DEVIL's people. – He said: If I go under the ice to you and comb your hair will you give me the animals? and she said: Maybe and she said: John I'm bleeding.

From me?

Maybe.

He bought her some sanitary pads. In the other times, she just stuffed toilet paper up in there. But He wanted her to be happy. He gave her three hundred dollars for shopping and food for a week, and she spent it all the first day, and He was happy for her –

And she said: John I tell You I'm bleeding I said! You cut my fingers; I'm bleeding from You; I'm pregnant from You; I'm drowning from You! And You got Jane; I don't got nobody –

It's not that I don't love Jane. She's a very dear child who's given Me great comfort and satisfaction.

But You want be with me?

Yes. Always with you.

You funny want to be with me. Me I don't because You have Jane. I'm bad, sadness, stupid, hate, so –

You're good, happiness, beautiful, love –

Then John, I want be with You. Because I'm pregnant. Jane forget her please.

I'm sorry. But I want you, and soon I'm going to want animals. You give Me animals now, Reepah. You give Me animals, or I'll take them anyway with My rifles –

You married Jane married Jane; You married Jane! I'm stupid with You; I'm bad! You married Jane married Jane You married Jane! I'm bad so . . . So I want go to the Heaven. To see my loving people in Heaven. I get my uncle's gun. I miss happy. I miss around. I miss love with You, John. So, so, gun go me all the way to the Heaven. I want my Power. I happy to see help my Power; I want really go to the Heaven already. I'm stupid in Inukjuak earth! So much! I know why I did with rifles, so much I know why, 'cause my head is tired and myself and my eyes and my ears and I hate me and You and my baby sweetheart in Inukjuak and I love You and my peoples and everybody but I know I want to cry to see what You did so I want my uncle's gun now someone is listening me I want hurry now go to Heaven now I don't want be with me now I want gun I want gun I don't need sniffing now I just need gun gun inside me to make me baby in the Heaven gun in my mouth to see my loving everybody I want cry I'm so sorry John I'm so stupid with You nothing is no good for me but gun I'm sorry I say that I want out of Inukjuak I want sleep in earth now gun now gun gun gun I'm scared gun just a little scared gun now gun now –

The sea-ice was so beautifully mottled white and blue. The leads were just beginning to open, great holes crusted with salt. But not here, not here –

Sir James had said that he'd seek them out if there were no word by the middle of January 1847, which it now more than was, but Mr Franklin had said: You are very good, but that will be wholly unnecessary   to which Sir James replied   *why?*   rather sharply and Mr Franklin said   I am extremely grateful for your love, but it would not be right for us to impose on you. Nor would it be necessary. Surely you remember how Back sought you out not knowing that you were already home?   – How could I forget?   returned Sir James.   He put his life at risk . . .   – That is rather a speciality of Back's,   said Mr Franklin with a laugh.   – Do you know,   said Sir James,   I sometimes think that you are too hard on Back.   – You are a model of consideration to others,   said Mr Franklin meekly.   I only wish that I –

You only wish that you liked him better,   said Sir James, almost with a snarl, and Mr Franklin saw that somehow he had offended him. This shamed him greatly, and he said: At any rate, I shall take up your kind offer with C^apt Crozier and the officers . . .

To a man, the officers agreed with their Commander that they would have no need of relief.

Subzero's Debt

1991

The ecstatic experience of dismemberment of the body followed by a renewal of the organs is also known to the Eskimo. They speak of an animal (bear, walrus, etc.) that wounds the candidate, tears him to pieces or devours him; then new flesh grows around his bones.

MIRCEA ELIADE, Shamanism (1971)

W hen the snow had come to stay, when it lay whorled in gigantic fingerprints between ship-ridges where the Arctic hares once came bustling, when it glittered with glare-constellations of frost, when it hardened until it merely creaked instead of giving under the men's steps, when it stuck to their boots and froze on them immediately so that shaking or kicking or brushing or scraping scarcely dislodged it, then some men began to give up their hopes. They were provisioned for three years, and this was their third. The sky had taken on a color which was neither grey nor blue nor white nor orange, but partook of all these in a cold way, not glaring and jarring, but peaceful in its rainbow iciness.

For a time the leads persisted, and loyal Mr Gore persevered in watching them, although it was already September. A blue iceberg the size and shape of a house squatted, sending its blue-grey spider-lines all the way to the horizon. The point rose into grey fog. Icebergs slid along open water like immense quartz crystals. The sleet hissed in his face and stung his eyes; it hardened on his balaclava so that he was visored in ice; his sunglasses fogged up and wind-tears rolled down his cheek. His forehead ached.

❀ ❀ ❀

The wind breathed nastily in Resolute, and then the house rumbled. In the room where Reepah used to live, there was only a sofa and an empty wall whose window saw blowing snow. In the living room, the old lady still made kamiks. She re-soled Subzero's for him, staring hard through her glasses at the thick thread. She got frozen raw caribou out of the freezer and put it on cardboard for him to chop . . .

Gore's rifle spoke. A musk-ox cow fell, and another was wounded but escaped. He shot a caribou, and it was the first sunset of the year, and the last open water was the color of mother-of-pearl, and a great orange pillar of light stood up on the ridges and a cloud was a cloud of glory. After that he didn't see any more caribou. The men shot birds for meat, when they were lucky enough to see them. Then the birds went away, too. (In the tale they say that SEDNA was vengeful, but She wasn't; She didn't want to hurt anyone, only to go sniffing nail polish . . .) They cut holes in the ice and trapped fish and crustaceans. Everything was brown or reddish-brown in color, like the gravel of Resolute. They gathered big brown mussels with rings like rainbows –

They kept expecting to find Esquimaux. The Esquimaux would help them –

Four months it had been now since Mr Franklin had dispatched him to Sir James's cairn on King William Island to entomb within that pillar of stones the paper imprinted with the address of the Secretary of the Admiralty, the paper that said: *28 of May 1847. HMS Ships Erebus and Terror wintered in the ice in Lat. 70° 05' N, long. 98° 23' W. Having wintered in 1846–7 at Beechey Island, in Lat. 74° 43' 28" N, long. 90° 39' 15" W, after having ascended Wellington Channel to Lat. 77°, and returned by the west side of Cornwallis Island. Sir John Franklin commanding the expedition. All well. Party consisting of 2 officers and 6 men left the ships on Monday 24th May 1847. Gm. Gore, Lieut. Chas. F. Des Voeux, Mate.* It was only after the men had rolled the last boulder up the inclined plank and recrowned Sir James's pillar with the flat slabs that Des Voeux had smiled slyly and said: I don't mean to cast an evil eye on your efforts, sir, but the paper which we signed just now – well, I should like to see it again.

Whatever do you mean?   said Gore in astonishment.

The Beechey Island dates were wrong, sir. We wintered there in 1845–6, not 1846–7.

You're right, of course,   said Gore.   Now that I think of it, I wonder why I wrote that. There must have been a fog in my skull today . . . – But you – Des Voeux! Why didn't you tell me until now? You signed it, too –

Ay, sir. I myself realized the error just now.

The Mate addressed him in all meekness; and yet there was something in his manner which annoyed Mr Gore as much as the mistake itself. A series of calculations began to figure in his brain. The enlisted men (four of whom were debilitated by the mysterious stomach complaint) would surely resent being made to do their work twice. The nightmare of Sisyphus was routine in the Navy, of course. But these were extraordinary circumstances. Some of the men were approaching their breaking point. Could Des Voeux mean to incite them against him? This thought had never struck Mr Gore before; indeed, he'd always thought Des Voeux a most amiable man, although sometimes a bit of a dullard.

Well, sir, shall I go and tell them?

Never mind,   said Gore with a sudden savage bitterness.   When Mr Franklin sends us back to this spot next May to update our note, we can correct it then.

Next May!   exclaimed Des Voeux.   But the ice will break up this June, or – or July –

They both fell silent.

❖ ❖ ❖

Of *course* the Esquimaux would help them. Half an hour before midnight, Reepah's brother and Jukee's brother paddled their kayak past the band of golden water where the clouds and the mountains of Bylot were reflected, and penetrated into a narrow lead. Reepah's brother, who was in front, got out and pulled the prow up. Then Jukee's brother got out. They pulled the boat up onto the ice. Then they walked around and checked their skidoos. They paddled back very slowly. Every now and then they thudded against submerged ice. After awhile the shots sounded. The next day at their house four sealskins were stretched out with stakes to dry.

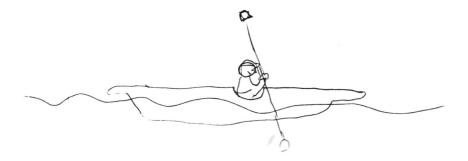

Mr Gore waited on at his post with the volunteers, watching the open water die. It wasn't September yet; it was only June. He felt much the same as his Commander did after another of Reepah's drunken nights: still awake, weary to the middle of his spinal cord, his eyes wide open and aching and a sound in his ears like seashells . . . From time to time nausea visited him, which was peculiar, as he had never been subject to that complaint. He had the long thin face of an Arctic wolf. He could not avoid his sickness anymore, although he no longer feared it so much for that very reason; now that it had jumped upon him and crawled inside him and gnawed him, it could not ambush him anymore. And he read in his Bible: *I thank Thee, FATHER, LORD of Heaven and earth, that Thou hast hidden these things from the wise and understanding and revealed them to babes; yea, FATHER, for such was Thy gracious will.* Dr Peddie had told him that his symptoms resembled Dr Goodsir's. Dr Peddie could not say whether the disease might be some new form of scurvy or not; he was inclined to say not. (But surreptitiously Gore sometimes drank extra vinegar in the night, praying and trembling.) Twice a week the volunteers were rotated, but Gore stayed on, watching the water – watching for animals, too, of course. If he were to kill any more animals for the larder, Mr Franklin would be extremely gratified. Gore's mood improved itself somewhat at the mere thought, like the spirit rising in the thermometer at summertime. But then a sweat burst out on his face, and his stomach writhed. No meat for me, then; I'll give it all to those who can still eat . . . Mr Gore had a plan. Sir James's other cairn was not very far from here – the one, that is, which Sir James and his uncle had erected after marching past the Magnetic Pole. It was a secret conviction of Gore's that Sir James might have left some stores en cache in that cairn (indeed, when he and Des Voeux had left the Admiralty paper in the first cairn he'd half expected to uncover something wondrous as the men rolled stones aside in that dreary wind), something that might cure him so that he could sit himself down before any number of small suppers. (If a certain narrowness on Gore's part now becomes apparent, please remember that unlike Mr Franklin he didn't have Reepah; unlike Fitzjames he didn't have Mr Franklin; he had only his leaden aches and gripes, which, cruel though they were, yet reminded him that he lived; solitaire no longer accomplished that because there were eerie Esquimaux faces on all the cards.) In December or January he'd go to the cairn. It might be prudent to take two or three other officers who could be trusted – no more, in case there was not enough medicine to share. Gore could not explain the basis for his hope – because there was no basis, and he knew even that, but the disappointment that must succeed false anticipation was an acceptable price, being deferred. Fitzjames was cracking, they said, and poor Mr Franklin extremely ill. – What would happen now? What would happen?

Of course this summerlong winter was a freak of nature which could not be repeated. His brother officers made the same calculation, whose answer was now as familiar to them as any Psalm, as dreadfully weary as washing-day, the broadcloth epidermises wrung and rinsed in boiled ice, bleeding blueness ever more faintly, and no one studying geography anymore, and only Vesconte enthusiastic about the glee club (he only to set an example, just as Gore set an example by never closing his eyes on the unrelenting ice). It was even possible that the breakup of the ice around the ships, so long deferred, might occur this season with belated grace. That was why he focused his field-glass upon the blue iceberg again, whenever it seemed to be sweating or melting or crying –

When the thaw began, he'd dispatch a man to notify Mr Franklin. They would use the engines then because it was urgent, and they'd return to Lancaster Sound and follow it back to Greenland to reprovision. They would winter in Greenland and there would be letters from home, and fresh meat, and towns, and churches and children, and there'd be a Danish doctor who could cure him (surely this was a common polar disease, since so many in the Expedition suffered from it; a doctor in Greenland must know how it might be quelled. But each day he descended deeper into his affliction, just as Fitzjames prowled the hold of the *Erebus* by midnight, calling for the terrified ensigns to roll casks aside; he could not sleep until he'd checked once again that the strained timbers still held . . .) By the spring he'd be well, and Mr Franklin also would be recovered, or at least –

One could really not give up hope before October.

❊- ❊- ❊

Little and Hodgson, Vesconte and Gore – they'd all begun to scheme a bit, as is natural in any family overtopped by a dying father; Crozier and Fitzjames stayed out of it for opposing reasons; in any event, the suspense had not yet become ugly. Seth did not have pride of place in his circumstances, especially when the Finnlander Kid kept hounding him.

I've inklinged my nature for you drop by drop, and you still don't know me, Seth!

I guess I just kind of ignore who you are. But I went to your funeral, didn't I? It's not that I don't like you or anything, but somehow you don't seem to belong to yourself . . .

There was no belonging where I lay stained; you wept when you met me first . . .

That snarl you wear,   said Seth very slowly,   I knew it somehow.

In the garbage dump, remember? Jukee's brother shot me in the head. I died snarling!

Seth looked at him.   – You want me to accept you as my twin, just like Subzero did with Reepah. But he needed Reepah so bad he was *ready* to die! I'm almost ready, but not out of need; it's just that I got myself into this and I have to go along with it. But you – you're so desperate – you're nothing like Reepah (well, she's desperate, too) and I'm nothing like Subzero. Can't you see that? I don't want to be anybody but myself, 'cause you're just something that was shot in that ugly town, not something that died 'way out in the moss, even though you might have been a part of that once; but you're used to being garbage now. You're not Fox anymore. You keep saying you're Fox, but if you were Fox you'd have successfully gone back from all this.

The Finnlander Kid came very close to Seth and whispered: Everything you say may be true, but I'll tell you this: I know where the meat is buried.

What the fuck does that mean?   shouted Seth.   You just talk that way 'cause you're scared. You're twice dead and still you're afraid to die.

But then Seth was ashamed of his unkindness and said: I know you need someone. Why don't you find RAVEN? RAVEN's dead, too.

On the 30th of September there was not a cloud in the sky, and the cold sun sparkled in the blue like crystal. That night the mercury reached $-12°$. In the middle of the night he awoke with frost all around his mouth on the hood of the sleeping bag. The next morning, which began October, he extended his hopes until the 15th and there was a bar of clear air beneath the cloud. By noon the fog had settled. The air retained a warmish orange look, as if the sun were very close, but there was no real warmth in it. His toes ached with the cold inside his iron-stiff boots. Mr Des Voeux reported no change in the condition of the ice, and then took the volunteers for another hunt which all knew would be fruitless, and Mr Hodgson had fallen sick and raving, so that a man must stay to attend him, and so Gore set out on his patrol alone, expecting nothing, knowing nothing; and suddenly he had the suspicion that Mr Des Voeux's party might have discovered open water and was perhaps at this very time launching a lifeboat, meaning to leave him and the others, and he felt dizzy and closed his eyes and thought he saw an Esquimau squaw before him and something told him to comb her hair and then the fit fortunately passed. (The same thing had happened at Seth's funeral.) He started out at seven a.m. on that cloudless April slice of death, happy to escape Mr Hodgson's groans, and made excellent progress, considering his weakness. His instructions were to go north, but he chose to go south, since before all else he must ascertain that the ships had not somehow gotten free and abandoned him. With him he took his rifle. The sound was as still as a pond, the clear grey water dancing and dancing ever so slightly above the banded lines of gravel and smooth pebbles on the bottom. It was almost the same color as the sky, that water, but there was no warmth in it, either. A hundred and fifty yards away, at the extreme horizon of vision, lay the other shore, a dark meandering peninsula. Everything was very still. The sand on the beach was frozen hard; a few frozen tussocks sported their plumes of rigid grass, and snow and ice lay in long low drifts. No animal tracks. – Mr Gore walked south toward Cape Felix and the ships, counting his way by capes since he could see nothing else, and the ice grew in power. Now the stalks of grass were armored in ice an inch thick, and the tussocks wept frozen tears and gnashed dirty furry ice-teeth. The surface of the water was textured with ice-flecks. A stone-cast still brought slow grey ripples, and the rocks could still be seen, dimly, like lumps at the bottom of a stewpot, but stepping stones of furry ice floated by the shore, and the dark peninsula of frozen overlay attacked his eyes. The waist-high mud-cliffs behind the water were frozen, and the grey concretions of fossil shells were frosted over. Boulders were white and grey with ice. Frost formed on the barrel of his rifle. – Now the ice began to thicken, and Mr Gore's rock-cast broke through a definite crust, spreading not ripples but rings of greyness. The ice formed a shelf extending two or three feet from shore, firm enough to walk on. – Still the ice grew. Boulders were beaded with grape-sized crystals of it. Slabs of rock lay frozen in it like dead fish. Just off shore grew silver tussocks of ice. – A little farther west, toward the open ocean, a dark skin had formed upon the shore. But it was gently heaving. Oval holes had opened up upon it, and he could see them moving. By the steady westward drift of the holes he could see that the tide was going out.

Later that fine June day, the sun was born. The sound appeared to be solid gold.

He should really resume his actinometric observations. That would please Mr Franklin –

Something gnawed at him, and he clutched his belly and vomited. The ache did not go away. Crouching miserably in the wind, with shivers shooting down his legs like the shimmering glare of ice-leads close to shore, he vomited.

At two-o'-clock a soft orange light glistened on the scale-plates of the ice. Drift-ice mountains were white and colored in the sound. Long clouds crossed the air like torpedoes, and it was very cold. A single channel flowed very rapidly by the shore; another, in the middle, and there were long narrow glintings, like sunny lakes, of other channels; for the most part, however, the ice was like a plain of lava, heavy and solid and patterned without proportion or meaning, and the mountains bordered it but did not confine it: practically it went on forever.

He wept because Mr Des Voeux had surely stolen a march on him. Mr Des Voeux was only a Mate, and he was a Lieutenant, but he could not be unconvinced that Mr Des Voeux had concocted some secret of extended life for the elect to which he, Graham Gore, would never be admitted, because Mr Des Voeux hated him. On that sunny July afternoon when he had dwindled there in Peel Sound forever, he remembered the February night when he'd crept through the snow to the other ship to listen for conspiracies; and he faded right through the sentinel (possibly because he'd only dreamed it) and descended into the darkness, guided by Capt Crozier's robust snores, and he'd heard Mr Hodgson speaking with Mr Little. – They say that Mr Franklin saw an Esquimau today, but he's not talking, the former grated. – Aye, I wouldn't wonder, said Mr Little. No doubt that's his actual purpose, to feed us to those savages. I know you didn't like me before, but I'm willing to take you into my confidence. It's time to get cunning. – What do you mean? he heard Mr Hodgson say, and Mr Gore could not but read the pulse of craving in his voice. – I can't tell you everything, said Mr Little. I do have a definite line on things, Hodgson. I've been thinking over your confidences in Greenland. I tried to tell you then what I knew, but you didn't want to listen. Are you truly willing to get cunning? Do you mean what you

say? – Out with it, Little, you evil fox! Oho, I see it now, by the shining of
your eyes! It's meat you're talking about, isn't it? I heard it from Des Voeux
. . . It's in the wind. I can feel it in the wind . . .

When the wind began, the first part of him to go numb was his knees. Next
he lost sensation in his toes entombed in the frozen leather. Now his thighs
could no longer feel each other. He began to run. But his legs would not
come back into his dominion. His fingers ached with cold and began to go
numb. His face burned with cold inside his hood. Now the wind was
shrieking and pushing him backward. He fell and cut his cheek and saw the
blood come out but he couldn't feel anything. The blood was already hard
and frozen on his face –

There seemed to be even less game now. *Set your foxtrap sideways to the wind.
Foxes bite only from the leeward side.* – That was what the People said. But the
Qaallunaat did not know that. Maybe they didn't know about SEDNA, either.
To C^{apt} Crozier, who, although he had previously ventured upon this low
horizon of suspicions which we call the Arctic, had never been granted
glimpse or gleam of Her, the hallucinations which now insinuated themselves
like snow-goggles round the eyes of so many of his crew were perplexing.
For all this, however, his spirits were much less undermined than most other
men's, because he had commanded that selfsame *Terror* under Sir James in
the Antarctic for four years in ice! and he remembered hearing from Sir James
about the three winters' entrapment in ice on the North Magnetic Pole
Expedition; and C^{apt} Crozier himself had been north more than once with
Parry. The knowledge of Mr Franklin's steadily increasing sufferings caused
him much anxiety and grief, but only for this stout eggheaded old man whom
he treasured as a friend, not yet for the Expedition as a whole or for himself.
The cryptic comments which Mr Franklin had sometimes made in his hearing
regarding some illicit passion or other with an Esquimau squaw in past times
pained him, not only on Lady Franklin's account (for, like all the Arctic
Friends, he had an immense regard for her), but also because they were so
evidently festerings in Mr Franklin's mind (a mind which had already begun
to soften with age, as it seemed). Truth to tell, such liaisons were normal –
more so, perhaps, for enlisted men, but then everyone knew about Hood and
Back! Back, being once in his cups, had told Crozier more than the latter
wanted to know about that duel. Back was stammering. He said to Crozier
(who was looking round, to make sure that others could not overhear this

embarrassing confession):   I was looking him in the eyes, you know, a-a-and
I thought to myself, *this does not lie in my will!* Do you understand me?   – Go
on, Back,   said the other gently.   I think I see what you're driving at.   –
Right,   said Back in a subdued tone.   There was poor Hood, and there was
I, and we were facing each other across a field of snow, a-a-and all around us
the winds of the Barren Lands. Well, I – I said, *well.* And I knew that if M^r
Franklin were to wake up and see us, we'd both be disgraced. Hood and I
were aware that we were doing wrong. But neither of us had power over
ourselves. Has that ever happened to you?   – I don't know,   said Crozier.
Nothing like that comes to my mind, but I believe that any man who claimed
never to feel that way would be tempting SATAN.   – Yes,   said Back.   Well,
I – I – she'd struck root in me. Greenstockings, you know. I believe she'd just
turned fifteen at that time. Already had two husbands. You'd think I'd have
felt disgusted, to know that – well, and she'd had Hood, too, of course, many,
many times as I know all too well, and she'd – had – me . . . Once. Well,
twice, really, but that other time Hood came in, and that was why . . . I didn't
hate Hood, you know, as I stood there and took a bead on him. Dr Richardson
was my second. Hepburn was Hood's. They must have both been laughing
up their sleeves, knowing that Hepburn had uncharged both our pistols!
A-a-and I took aim, a-a-and I remember the trigger slowly curling back in
my finger, and the sense of *awe* that I had, that something would happen; the
expectation was there, and then the hammer fell down on nothing and I felt
so absurd . . .   – C^apt Crozier had never forgotten the pitiable appearance
that Back made as he told all this. And yet the impression that Mr Franklin's
disclosures made upon him was not quite the same, because mingled with
guilt and shame in the latter's strange phrases was always an undertext of
triumph, fulfillment even. C^apt Crozier could not make it out. He did not
want to. He knew only that there were likely to be disagreeable times ahead.

After his funeral Seth remembered yesterdays beyond yesterdays to the
summer in Pond Inlet that the Finnlander Kid had spoken about; Seth said:
GOD, that fox was pretty, with its soft white pelt!   and he said: Mr Franklin
wouldn't like it if he heard this, but I can't help but wonder sometimes if
what's happening to us now is happening 'cause of what happened to FOX
and RAVEN then (but that FOX-SPIRIT was so horrible; I'm sorry, but it really
was . . .)   and Mr Fitzjames, freshly returned from another wander through
the hold, came by beating the ice off his scarf with the Queen of Spades in

his hand (today she was Jane, empress of shovels because she sought to bury
her husband's bones) and Mr Fitzjames heard what Seth had said and came to
him and said: GOD's more subtle than that, boy! Look at this card and tell
me if you see a fox or a raven on it.   – No, sir,   said Seth, hanging his head
in embarrassment and sadness; poor Mr Fitzjames was not true to himself so
Seth felt constrained around him.   – And who killed FOX and RAVEN then?
(You see, boy, I'm well aware of all your complaints!)   – Seth looked him in
the face and said: Who did it doesn't even matter, sir.   And maybe I'm
totally wrong to be saying this, and maybe I'm not, but I can't stop thinking
about how they looked there on the moss with the flies and the ants going at
them all for nothing 'cause once they were alive and beautiful and they died
for *nothing*. And I'm wondering if Reepah or SEDNA or Whoever She is would
help us if we threw our rifles away and just started walking. I mean, we
probably wouldn't make it. I mean, of course we wouldn't make it. But we'd
be doing absolutely the right thing.   – The right thing?   shouted Fitzjames.
And you truly believe that anyone ought to suffer your nonsensical entreaties?
When you're already dead? When I've specifically directed, for the sake of
morale, that the names of women not be mentioned except when we toast
sweethearts and wives? And who wouldn't you kill now?

Mr Franklin was blind now, as I've said, and so it was quite easy for him to
see Seth, who was dead. Mr Franklin said: I have been thinking of Reepah
all day. Will you please tell me if you've found her?

She's here, John.

Does she still love me?

Of course she does. She always will, even if you get really really needy –

And do you love her as I do?

I love her differently than you do. I'd do anything for her. She's so sweet,
just like you said she'd be. Except I don't want her. I love her but I don't need
her. I don't need you. I'm just here for you because I heard you crying all
alone.

Do you want anybody now, Seth?

All I want is to fall asleep next to my dog. But that dog got bitten by a
rattlesnake, a long time ago in New Mexico. You remember when I was
botanizing on the Apache reservation? It was the first summer. She was just
running around the desert so happy, not hurting anyone. And the rattlesnake
was just doing exactly what it should have been doing, too. But you know all

those girls I used to die for? My heart used to go pitter-pat 'cause I was in love so much. Well, then I grew beyond that and all I needed to do was look at girls and then go home and jerk off. And now just lying next to my dog would be enough. Except that my dog is dead. And even though I'm the same way I can't find her.

That's why you want that. It's the same old thing. You want what you can't have. All those girls must have wanted you because they couldn't have you.

I know that's part of it, Seth said. We've talked about that before. But the other part of it is that people want to be conquerors. They not only want what they can't have, they want what they shouldn't have. And they're going to get it, they don't care how. I mean, look at you and Reepah. And this whole Northwest Passage thing –

And your dead dog. You could have dug your dog up. And Jane . . .

It will already have been perceived that their position differed considerably on many matters from what it should have been, despite the accuracy of their dipping-needle; maybe they didn't know that just before the darkness came each winter, two men should have gone away and then come back dressed in

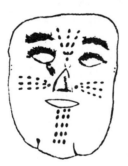

Baffin-Land Inuit sealskin mask
with women's tattoing
(used to ask SEDNA to give
sea animals to the People
again)

women's parkas, the armautis gaping empty for the babies they could never have, the shoulder-skins wide and loose to help them slide their not-babies inside the warmth and around to their useless men-breasts white-angled by the parkas' lying mimicry of nurture-patterns carefully sewn in nested panels on the skins, then the vulva-shaped strip of darkness hanging down over the men's genitals; over their faces they wore artful woman-shaped masks with chin-rays and nose-rays pretending to be the tattoos of women; when these men came the People would begin to scream; and the two men would assemble the People in pairs male and female without regard for marriages; and then the People would mate. This festival was pleasing to SEDNA. Seeing the new life that was made, She spread wide Her mutilated hands in the darkness beneath the sea, releasing the seals; then out onto the ice they came to feed the People: – seal-crowds with uplifted heads peering about like whiskered birds, seals with pale round faces like skulls, dark-headed doggish seals, fat-necked seals straining upward like furry slugs trying to fly, seals on top of seals, seals beside seals, seals resting on their tasty flippers, seals so good to eat! – ah, but with that game of partners and triplets, who'd take the dead woman's part, so that others might eat?

So the ice and darkness curled round them ever more tightly. – Very good. – In March of 1991, one Captain Subzero, seeking to peel the frozen Franklin flesh-mask away from his FULMAR-skull, spent twelve days at the abandoned weather station at Isachsen, Ellef Ringnes Island – that way he'd know everything! – Well, I won't eat lead, of course (thus Subzero, to himself). I don't want to ruin my brain for other projects. After all, who knows what I'll be once this Dream is over? But I'll understand what death is like, at least ... I think I have it straight: Mr Franklin is now suffering severe mental impairment and psychosis; Mr Gore exhibits labile affect, persistent abdominal pain and paranoid thoughts like the crooked row of boats drawn nose-up on the narrow beach at Pond Inlet where day by day he can see the dwarf willows growing higher, bud by bud, shivering in the wind, but each bud growing tall and narrow nonetheless above the hairy green leaves; has he started to contemplate eating people yet? As for Mr Fitzjames ... No, it's hard to imagine that third winter; I'm not sure I can do it. Better go to Isachsen.

In vain did Mr Franklin use every argument which he could adduce to persuade his grave-twin against this mad scheme: Your place, sirrah (thus Mr Franklin) is here with me, where I am compelled to remain. Mr Watson, the Carpenter's Mate, has already engaged to make your coffin. What next, you ask? Ah, that I know well. Remember, Subzero, I'm a very close neighbor of yours. Our ships will be stiff and still in the ice. C^apt Crozier will read the funeral address. (Jane and Reepah would be there if they could, but let's keep looking at the bright side of the question.) They'll lower the colors, my friend.

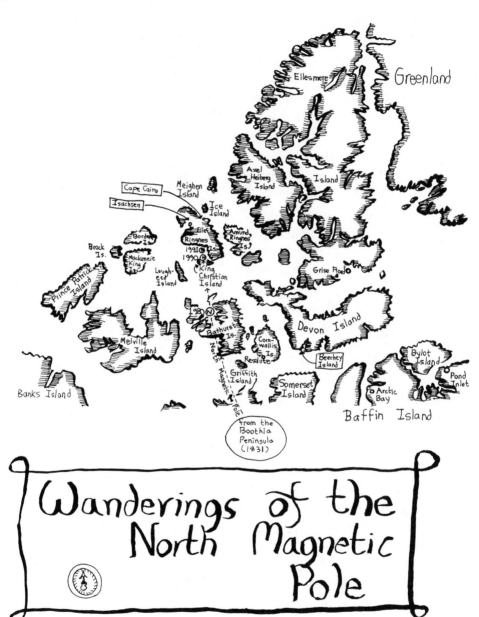

Wanderings of the North Magnetic Pole

They'll wrap your coffin in a flag and chisel out your grave with painful effort. The FULMAR will fly overhead. I know He's been urging you to get rid of me, but that would be as if I were to leave poor Jane (who continues to compare herself to Dido). You're upright, Subzero; you're a good popsicle. Anyhow, it'll be too late then. Leaning on picks and staffs and rifles (can't you see it?), they'll bow their fur-hooded heads as you're lowered into the ice. And you won't change, perhaps, for centuries! Your shoulders will be as a rock whose original color was grey, but after the black lichen makes lacy islands all over (say, half a thousand years from now), the whitish-green lichen will affix itself in clumps of phosphorescent rivalry; then come the mineral-green lichen to speckle densely in most of the remaining spaces, so that the rock of you will become an unreal patchwork of softness nestled among the feathery mounds of other lichens and mosses. Later still, when continents move and England is forgotten, then maybe a bud might grow from your frozen heart; spokes of tough willow-root might reach out from an empty center, terminating in trees an inch high, unbowed despite the heaviness of their soft black-flecked buds . . . And for all that time you'll be with me!

But Subzero had to be Mr Franklin in his own way; he had to die alone.

Do you know where Isachsen is? Mr Franklin didn't – how could he? Ellef Ringnes wasn't discovered until 1900 or so . . . Unroll the polar charts, my Arctic Friend! Do you see the massive white dog's head of Greenland? Now look west to Canada. There's Ellesmere Island, lobed and convoluted like a brain stood on end. At eighty-two thousand square miles she's only a tenth the size of Greenland, but since Greenland really ought to be called a continent, Ellesmere remains one of the great islands of the world. Mr Franklin's sailed in sight of her, and so has Sir James. Nested in her western concavity is Axel Heiberg Island, which they say has spectacular petrified forests; I've seen her from the edge of Ellesmere but I have never been there. At the southwest foot of Axel Heiberg is a channel, across which lies Amund Ringnes Island, a little bullet pointing north. Amund, like his brother Ellef, was a brewer in Norway, and I hope that the discoverers succeeded in toasting them both with unfrozen ale. After all, what other cheer could there be on this gravelly mudbank, which is so far north that the map screams with loneliness? She's three islands north yet of Resolute! Now, west of Amund Ringnes is Ellef Ringnes, a somewhat larger puzzle-piece canted north by northwest. This island is one of the stones in the dreary western wall of the Arctic archipelago, which runs northeast from the mainland as follows: Banks Island, Prince Patrick Island, Brock Island (a muddy punctuation mark), Borden Island, then Ellef Ringnes, Meighen, and so back to the northern corners of Axel Heiberg and Ellesmere. Cross this line, and you've come out the Northwest Passage at last! Thus, while Amund Ringnes is lonely enough, Ellef Ringnes faces true nothingness, islandless sea frozen all the way to the Pole, empty for a hundred degrees of longitude going west, until at last one approaches the New Siberian Islands – which are hardly a very good approximation of the Spice Islands that were the Northwest Passage's *raison d'être*, but they'll have to do, just as sometimes Jane has to do for Reepah.

To people like Jane, who have never been there, Arctic islands are much the same. – Perhaps by now I have conveyed a little of the emptiness of Resolute. – Well, Isachsen is emptier. At Resolute there are seventy species of vascular plants. On the northern tip of Ellef Ringnes there are only two. At Isachsen, forty miles away, some zealous soul has found forty-eight species, a respectable number, but I would still rather be at Resolute. (Down at Hudson Bay, Churchill has four hundred species. The figure for Inukjuak is similar.) – Next statistic: At Resolute there are about fifteen birds per square mile. At Isachsen there are ten. When I was there I never saw one, but of course I was not wearing my glasses. (Pond Inlet has four hundred. The temperate forests have one to twelve thousand.)

Isachsen lies at longitude 103° 32' W, latitude 78° 47' N. March is the second coldest month. The sun has only just returned (the first sunrise for 1991 was the 21st of February), and temperatures for that month generally move between −30° and −40° Celsius. An ice island occasionally manned by the personnel of the Polar Continental Shelf Project lies fifty miles or so to the north of Ellef Ringnes. The nearest permanent community, however, is Resolute, which is three hundred and eleven miles to the southeast, and I think we've heard of Resolute before. At a similar distance northeast, Environment Canada maintains a weather station at Eureka, Ellesmere Island. In short, Isachsen is quiet. An auto-station continues to report temperature and windspeed every hour from a shed on the runway. Otherwise, the island is left to itself. No planes fly over. Isachsen freezes year by year in the permanent pack-ice.

❀ ❀ ❀

When Subzero set off for the Isachsen Hilton, his dramatic expectations were toggled way down because he remembered how disappointed Sir James had been in 1831 when it became patent that the Magnetic Pole was no mountain of iron as had been surmised, that in fact the Magnetic Pole was entirely nondescript; Sir James took his final measurements in an abandoned igloo

and found the locus to be under the floor and that was that. He and his men
erected a cairn there, and another to the west, at Point Victory, King William
Island. (The former was where Mr Gore hoped that the miraculous medicines
might be found.) At that time the Magnetic Pole was on the Boothia
Peninsula. A hundred and sixty years later, when Subzero embarked on his
trip, it had left our continent, wandering northward and westward beneath
the Arctic Ocean until it reached Bathurst Island, where its location was
marked in Subzero's atlas; it continued to ooze northward so that when he
was trying his darling mukluks on it had already reached King Christian
Island, which practically abuts Ellef Ringnes on the map; to all practical
purposes, Isachsen was at the North Magnetic Pole.   It'll probably be a big
red and white barber pole,   said Seth.   And maybe there'll be all this
electricity there. That reminds me. I've got a funny story to tell you about
electricity. My friend Suzy up in DC, last summer she got hit by lightning! It
was pouring down rain. She was on her bike. I guess she was pretty lucky. If
you get struck by lightning on the bottom of your bike you've had it, 'cause
you're grounded or not grounded or something. But she got hit on the top
of her bike. She felt tingles going up her. She was pretty freaked out and ran
into this bus shelter. She told them she'd gotten struck by lightning, and they
said: You can't stay here. What if you're contagious?   And when she came
closer they all ran away screaming.

Subzero had looked toward the journey with nothing but exultation until the
night when the fire alarm repeatedly malfunctioned, so that he had to go
down to the security guard's desk and there were other people from other
floors, making him think at first that the crisis was real; when he understood
that it was only a problem with a steam pipe he returned to bed but continued
to be anxious. Suddenly as he was almost asleep he found himself at the
station in twilight, the buildings dark as catacombs inside because the
windows had all been boarded up; he saw himself trying to shovel snow away
from the door so that he could get in, and he was looking over his shoulder
and it was no surprise when he saw the mangy yellow shape on the horizon-
ridge behind him – a starving polar bear. Nowhere to run, and firearms often
malfunctioned. Or suppose that he was far away from the station, walking
across the island toward Cape Cairo, and *then* he saw the polar bear circling
him . . . This vision immediately made him resolve to remain inside the black
refrigerator of the station until it was time to go home – but what if the bear

was waiting for him outside and got him when the plane landed and he went out to meet it at the runway? He should really test the shotgun every day – but what if that loud noise attracted the curiosity of some distant polar bear which otherwise would not have heard him? What if a polar bear smashed the door in and came after him, snuffling for him in the darkness? He did not know a great deal about polar bears.

Of course bears were unlikely at Isachsen. Permanent pack-ice is not conducive to leads, which seals need to eat and breathe; without seals polar bears don't eat, either. So that was all very nice.

Not long after he had another dream in which the station was a sunken glass-roofed square, not unlike the computer offices he had worked in, and it was warm and sunny and flat and snowy outside and all his friends and relatives had come to the station to hold a farewell party for him. They would go home, and he would not. People wandered around outside in laughing groups; inside they blew up balloons and popped corks and cut the cake and there were giant color TVs and stereos going in every room and everybody piled more ice cream and cake on each paper plate. But Subzero looked out of the glass panes and saw the polar bears biding their time, dozens of them, snow-white but of all shapes and sizes, prowling round and round, waiting until he was alone.

✼ ✼ ✼

The best way to learn from your mistakes is to survive them. In Subzero's case, scorched eyebrows and mildly frostbitten fingers would reward his ambitions, but nothing worse. He was not Mr Franklin after all. Planning is the process of designing advance substitutions for anticipated failures, but at the heart of every plan is a treasury of assurances and last redoubts that must not fail. Subzero's sanctuary on Arctic trips had always been his sleeping bag, just as Mr Franklin counted on his rifles. On this trip, the sleeping bag did not work.

✼ ✼ ✼

Had he been an Inuk with a reasonable store of traditional knowledge, his equipment would not have been so important an issue. Time and time again, in reading about the Inuit he'd been struck by their easy flexibility and improvisation under pressure. For instance, one man made emergency runners for his sled out of strips of frozen meat, and reached his destination.

Another told how he used to treat himself for illnesses as a child. *I invented a cure for a boil made from a mixture of Sunlight soap, Quaker Oats, water and a few drops of seal fat. It sucked up the pus real well. If I had continued to invent things like that, I'd be a doctor today!*[*]   And he probably would. – But Subzero himself could not hope to have sufficient knowledge of the behavior of Arctic materials and processes at low temperatures. How, therefore, could his trials and errors be anything but an unsteady succession of failures, terminated most likely by hypothermia? Nor was Mr Back present. Therefore, he had to rely on his equipment to protect him from the consequences of his mistakes. This was the only department over which he had much control. And an oversight here could be as fatal as any other.

Consider the issue of perspiration. On Baffin Island in 1987 he'd gained a clammy glimmering of the laws of sweat while tentbound for three days by steady rain. The temperature was about +5°C, which seems embarrassingly balmy in comparison to what he would find at Isachsen. But Subzero was careful just the same. Unlike Mr Franklin, he never forgot that he was an alien here, that he understood but few of the laws. When traveling alone, he became doubly careful. He found it advisable, for example, to pitch his tent at the first drops from the clouds, unless they were obviously transitory. Delay increases the amount of water brought into the tent (on raingear, pack, sleeping bag, stuffsack, etcetera). Should that wetness reach one's sleeping bag, the laws begin to enforce themselves. A wet bag loses much of its insulation, especially in the case of goosedown, which may be incredibly light and warm when dry, but becomes almost worthless when soaked. Even a clammy bag is noticeably cold. So when the rain began on that July day, obedient Subzero lost no time in looking for a good place to camp. Unfortunately there was none. The ridgetop to the east he saw to be a wind-blown purgatory of boulders. Rain was already falling heavily there. The swales around him were composed of spongy tundra, into which his boots sank with sucking noises as he walked. The rain was pelting down even more strongly, and he had to begin his tent-work immediately. So he found a blueberry-padded terrace halfway up the ridge where the ground did not seem quite as moist, and pitched the breathable inner tent as quickly as he might, keeping the fly draped over it until he could hook it safely into place. Then he crawled in, feeling satisfied. Of course he was enough of a Mr Franklin to wonder whether he should have simply walked the storm out, but

---

[*] Avataq Cultural Institute, ᐊᓂ ᐊᑯᐱᐅᑎᕐᔪᐅᑦᑐᐱᐅ ᐱ ᐋᓇᓴᑦᑕᓅᑦ / *Traditional Medicine Project, Interim Report, 28 September 1983* (Inukjuak, Québec: 1984), p. 11.

the passing days proved his prudence. Very good. The interior of his home was reasonably dry. While the inner walls had been speckled with wetness from windblown drops, that was inconsequential. The floor remained dry, and he had laid down a groundcloth beneath it as a further barrier against the wet ground. After awhile he started getting cold, since he was not being active anymore and the temperature was dropping, so he put on his extra clothes, including his raingear, which he often used to keep him warm while walking. This was a mistake. The water vapor from his body passed through his breathable clothes and condensed on the inner surface of his raingear as usual, but since he was not active that moisture quickly cooled and passed back through his clothes, chilling him. It took him a long time to understand that he could not get warm until he took his raingear off. Having done this, he made a second and more serious mistake. Instead of kneeling or sitting for a moment, shivering, letting the water vapor now pass back out of his clothes, he immediately got into his sleeping bag. When one is chilled and tentbound, there are only two ways to get warm: eat hot food, or lie in a sleeping bag. (Exercise will work temporarily, but is impractical to rely on for more than an hour or so at a time in these conditions.) The tent that he then had was very small, so cooking in it would have been a good way of burning it down. The rain was now so heavy that cooking outside would not have been worthwhile. So his best chance for warmth was the sleeping bag, which he immediately began to squander by crawling into it with perspiration still in his clothes. As time passed, the goosedown began to get damp. Meanwhile the weight of his body and gear had sunk the tent floor an inch or more into the moss, and the floor was growing wet. To protect his sleeping bag he laid his rainsuit underneath it. That left nothing dry for him to lie on, since he had to leave the sleeping bag to give it time to air out, and that takes awhile when it is raining. He probably should have sat on his pack. Instead, he lay in his sleeping bag for the better part of three very stormy days and nights, until the weather finally cleared. By then his sleeping bag had grown quite wet, and he was almost shivering.

He was never in serious danger, since an Inuit town was only fifteen miles away; he could have walked there in the rain if he had to. But the experience taught him two lessons:

1. Take off waterproof clothes and let inner clothes air out before getting into a sleeping bag, even if everything feels dry to the touch.

2. Minimize the time spent in the sleeping bag.

These rules, like most that life teaches us, are not always easy to follow. When the Steger Expedition of 1989 set out for the North Pole, their massive synthetic sleeping bags weighed sixteen pounds apiece. By the time they reached their goal, they weighed fifty-two, thanks to the frozen sweat and breath inside them. Steger and his companions were forced to sleep two and three to a bag. I do not know what Steger would have done if he'd been alone.

Of course, Subzero's situation at Isachsen would be luxurious by comparison. His entire project was about one percent as ambitious as Steger's. Mr Franklin would have thought his trip to be nothing but a lark. He'd have his pick of solid structures to sleep in. Because he'd be spending his nights on land instead of sea-ice, he didn't have to worry about getting out of his sleeping bag quickly if a lead opened beneath him. So he could use a vapor barrier liner if he chose.

The idea of a VBL can best be explained by supposing that on Baffin Island he'd kept his raingear on, but against his skin (or perhaps against a layer of very thin full-body underwear), with his other clothes over it. Then the vapor from his pores could not get far enough from him to chill; nor could it pass through his outer layers of insulation to degrade them. A VBL in a sleeping bag works on the same principle: it's a waterproof inner bag. The obvious disadvantage of this system is that it leaves one perpetually damp, but being hot and damp is not so bad – just ask any hothouse flower.

For his trip to Isachsen he selected a sleeping bag with a built-in VBL. The bag was rated to −40°; according to the manufacturer, it had been used comfortably at −75°. He also ordered a VBL jumpsuit, which he wore under his other clothes.

Subzero (who considered himself at least somewhat suited for such excursions since at home he generally ate leftover lasagne cold from the refrigerator) was annoyed when Polar Continental Shelf refused to split their ice island charter with him. They had a policy of not dropping anyone off alone. – It's too dangerous! they said. What do you want to do it for?

(What *did* he want to do it for?)

Well, he improvised, have you ever read anything by Edgar Rice Burroughs?

You mean those Tarzan books?

That's right. In one of them Tarzan goes to Pellucidar – you know, the old hollow world theory. There's an opening at the North Pole, and all the dinosaurs and princesses are walking around upside-down with a hot jungle sun at the center of the earth – you know how it is. My plan is to explore Pellucidar, and maybe discover gold mines . . .

Silence.

Polar Shelf really didn't want him to go. They advised him not to go. They strongly urged him not to go. They told him that the RCMP was at that very moment laying new regulations into place that would require loners like him to make application before going on the land. It was important that the Canadian government know where he was. They could offer him no support, none. Oh, Polar Shelf could tell him horror stories . . .

Go ahead.

Well, just last year a Swedish gentleman went alone by dog-sled across the Great Slave Lake. He capsized, and got hypothermia. His dogs ate him.

Well, said Subzero, life is a terminal disease.

But after that he was very tense. It was snowing outside on that February day (many other days that month had set heat records), and he wondered if he were doing the right thing. He rushed about his small tasks of drying, lashing and packing, but every few minutes he sat down exhausted. As soon as he did sit down, he felt that he had to do something else important. He supposed that the first two or three hours would be the hardest. There would be the cold and wind and darkness, of course; maybe the drifts would be too deep for him with his pack. Everyone told him that he should take a sled, but if he shipped that airfreight it would get lost, like everything else did, and he couldn't carry it with him. So he was stuck. Anyhow, it was under a mile from the runway to the deserted station. He would have had a day or two in Resolute by then, so he'd know if the mere exposure would be too much for him; he didn't think that it would. But if a fog or a blizzard came up, he'd be lost. Then there was getting into the buildings. At those temperatures, the snowdrifts might be the texture of hard dirt; it might take him hours to get in. He simply didn't know. He had no winter experience in the Arctic. Would he even recognize the entrance? It was going to be hard to find the door beneath that snow. After that, pulling the nails out would be no fun in thick gloves. And then what? He'd unroll his sleeping bag and light a candle in that dark refrigerator and –

After making arrangements with the Office of Circumpolar Affairs to leave his estate as reimbursement to the Canadian government for the cost of recovering his corpse (the man was one of those drafting the regulations that would exclude him, and when he told the man that he thought that this was wrong, that people should be allowed to benefit from the Arctic even at the cost of their own lives, the man said drily: oh, yes, the *beauty*), Subzero dreamed of being left at the station, and in his dream it was unlike anything that he had ever imagined because the place was a parkland of berries and trees going on into a summer haze of peace like nothing harsh or unloving and the station was a quiet twilit library in the midst of crickets and he felt so happy to be alone there among all the mystery, and when he woke up he wasn't afraid anymore.

Seth had helped him, too.   – Sure, you're roughing it,   Seth said,   but forty years ago nobody would have thought anything of a week or two at forty below.   – Seth was right . . .

He had another dream that the North Magnetic Pole was hot and swampy; a muck-road coiled between heaving hills of pudding, and mosquitoes clouded the air: – Pellucidar, no doubt, lying beyond his fear with terrible and tenacious serenity.

As he re-counted the one hundred Canadian hundred-dollar bills that he would give to Bradley Air, he said to himself: I really shouldn't be doing this. If I only make it through this trip, I'll never do it again.   – That was what he always said to himself at the beginning of every Arctic voyage. Each time when he finished, the coast gripping his horizon as long as it could, then he felt its caressing claws on his heart, too, like the shivering touch of a dead man's toenails, and he regretted what he was leaving and said to himself: I'll be back.

Having closeted the Captain Subzero uniform along with his boyish days, he showered for the last time, lathered himself with the bilingual and lichen-stained can of Barbasol which he and Seth had shared at Point Inlet, shaved, and then slid into the cold smooth nylon coils of his "Wild Things" jumpsuit (wouldn't Back go green!).

In Montréal the whores were still outside Harvey's and there was an exhibition of miniature gold in the underground mall, but by now he was already leaving Montréal's grey cube-rows intersticed with dirty snow, frozen dirt-hills everywhere, and the plane crossed the Fleuve Saint-Laurent: – a few more grey cubes like square steel molars, then fields white and grey, bare treetops and ice, a freeway ... Now the flat white plain came to an end; wide low blisters of grey moss (really trees) ringed snow-hollows; the plane ascended past the first layer of cloud, which was patchy; he could still see a highway turning westward, but the cloud soon thickened into its usual cobblestoned pavement –

Then there were wispy, patchy glimpses, the same old white and blue and sepia-black, monotonous, heartless; it was already too late.

On the plane they all looked at him funny because he was wearing his polar suit. Everyone else wore T-shirts.

From the clouds he now glimpsed the lake-flats he'd seen before only in summer, now grey-frozen holes in the snowy cheese.

The fear had come back, and was constantly with him, an ugly, exhausting dirtiness. His hands tingled. He had no appetite. His stomach ached.

Now another white plain, with rivers. Was it land or sea?

They were definitely over the sea now. He could see the sutures in its flat white skull. It was not featureless, but pocked and drifted here and there, runneled and cracked – but *mainly* it was featureless, like one of those NASA photographs of the moon, because snow covered it; after only a moment the eye began to ache with failure to assign any scale; it was sickening. The streaks all went the same way, the way the wind blew. He did not want to look.

He had the knowledge that manhood isn't something you only earn once, even when you've been circumcised by the Elders or you've killed your first tiger, but something that must be achieved over and over, always by pursuing what you fear; if you stay still you will only come to fear more and more things. Being a man doesn't mean being afraid of nothing; it means being warned by the fear, not mastered by it. There was nothing wrong with being afraid of what he was about to do. He had never done it. He was doing it. Later he could feel proud or ashamed of it.

Baffin Island came into sight. For the first time in his experience it was not brown anymore, but pure white, ridges impressing themselves upwards through whiteness like unpatterned boot treads.

He sat gazing on it as it got bigger. Then suddenly his exultation came back –

As he proceeded toward the gangway to sample for a few moments the cool air of Iqaluit, a town he had always hated, the stewardess took hold of his zipper tab and pulled it up for him.   – You're in the Arctic now, honey, she said. You've got to dress for the Arctic. Otherwise you'll get pneumonia.

This confounded poor Captain Subzero for a moment, until he realized that she was teasing him. – That's right, he said. Now I'm safe.

Inside the airport it was pretty much the same as always, people saying: I got your fax. Now, will there be different categories or will we have just one major prize? . . . and outside it was −14°C, and he could hear what he suspected to be one of the Polar Shelf people saying: The big problem at the ice island is the wind, eh? Sometimes it's so bad that everyone has to go into the Park-All. I remember those times. And then Charlie would come down and take showers and flog his ice island hats, eh?

It was reassuring that the cold didn't really cut through him. But just standing in it for a couple of minutes, it was hard to tell. And −14° was mild. He sat remembering a July afternoon in Iqaluit (where he'd stopped so many times en route to someplace else), a miniature rhododendron's purple blossom attended by plastic shards; a bird's single cheep in the melancholy grass, everything low, brownish-green, Seth swooning over a pedicularis with its thin reddish-brown ovals of leaves . . .

It was another couple of hours to Resolute. There were lakes of blue now in the ice, cracked pebbles of ice like salt flats. He overflew ice cream mesas and starched bedsheets shadowed here and there with tints of the most delectable possible violet, lighter than a cobalt, more luminous than a manganese; and every now and then something unexpectedly geometrical would seize him, like a truncated cone or pyramid. Through cloud he saw some jumbled grimace of mountains. But he was surprised at how softened and billowy everything was otherwise, almost like wheatfields, and for a moment he almost believed again in his summer dreams –

As the plane began to descend his heart boomed and he leaned forward to see what was nothing like his memories: a lapis-grey flatness traced with white scratches (and far away, a single black line running forever); now the low snow-white cliffs of Cornwallis Island, with black rock-speckles showing along the top; he saw deep snow-rivers; they were west of Beechey Island and the Franklin graves; the land was marbled like halvah. Now closer: a plain like many successive coats of paint . . . Grey glass on the runway with white waves blowing . . .

Inside the airport, the baggage started coming in. It was all duffels and battered metal suitcases. When Subzero's hundred-pound backpack came in, everyone stared. – What idiot brought that in? said Subzero, snagging it. Nobody laughed.

The Bradley man was very decent. He helped him lift his pack on and drove him to the Narwhal Hotel. Then he left him alone. Subzero took a breath. There was an icy burning in his chest from the air. He wondered again why he was there. Then he put his other clothing on and went outside.

His glasses fogged up and iced up. He had to take them off. With or without goggles, it didn't matter. It appeared that he would be visiting Isachsen without glasses.

He walked to the breadloaf-shaped bluff at the sea-edge and ascended it as he had done one summer, and he was not really cold. Of course, it was only $-19°$.

He went to the Environment Canada building, whose location he remembered. There was a fellow there named Marv who was going to share the charter into Isachsen with him. Marv serviced the automatic weather station there. He would come and fiddle with the instruments there for a couple of hours, and then he'd go home. Subzero had tried to split the return charter with Polar Shelf, but they said it was against their policy to pick up single individuals, just as it was to drop them off. The liability was *tremendous*, Polar Shelf said. So Subzero would bear the cost of the pickup himself. Well, glory is never cheap. – At the weather office, Marv was nice and all was fine; everything was do-able; Ivan remembered Subzero from Eureka; they checked his pocket barometer against their instrument and congratulated him that it was only off by .4 millibars; he showed off his thermometer, and they all had a great time. Once again he was confident. Nothing had ever happened to him on these trips. He was always conservative when he was by himself; he'd do nothing dangerous. And he had some Arctic experience; it was his seventh time north –

It was Marv, who had an eye for food, who now revealed to him the secret of the frozen scallops. Marv knew all the treasures; he'd been at Isachsen when the station was decommissioned. There were two cases left, he said, maybe three. He and the Polar Psychology Project people had split a case last time. No one else would eat them. But as far as Marv was concerned, the only risk was freezer burn. He promised to mark the location for Subzero on the map. The scallops would be thirteen years old now. They'd probably be good for a hundred years.

Now Subzero had a reason. At the Narwhal, the only game in town, where for $185.00 a night you could have all the banana bread, brownies and cupcakes you could eat, anytime, they said to him: Why do you want to go to that hellhole?   and he smiled and winked at Marv (who was also staying there) and said: For frozen scallops.

Isachsen was so cold and still that his footsteps echoed all the way to the horizon. The corrugated metal passageways of the station were like tomb passageways. His steps rang and groaned terrifyingly in that dry and pitch-black coldness. He had to wear his headlamp, and it gleamed cheerlessly ahead, reflecting his own black shape in the glass of dead exit signs so that some monster was always coming toward him. The rec. room was particularly dark and horrible like a vault full of corpses. Armchairs, piled with snow, seemed to stretch and torment the darkness with their high pale burdens. Icy wires dangled from the ceiling. He pulled his gloved hand out of the mitt for

a moment and tried to persuade himself that it was fun to watch the moisture rise like smoke from every fingertip –

He did not sleep at all well that first night. He could not get warm. Although he had dutifully removed his outer suit and VBL and brushed the frost from his underclothing, his back and toes remained cold all night. It was often the case on his Arctic trips that the first night was unpleasant, so he did not feel seriously alarmed. The following night, being both tired and acclimated, he would surely sleep better. Then the third day he could go exploring – without his glasses, it is true; and his $300 North Face backpack, which had gone on the Trans-Antarctica Expedition at eighty below, they said; within the first half hour at Isachsen the Fastex hip-belt buckle shattered. But he was still quite confident. In the morning, when he went outside to chop snow for the stove, he found that the little toe of his left foot had entirely lost sensation. He tried putting his glasses on to examine it, but they were too thickly coated with ice. Was it frostbitten? Fortunately, chafing it for half an hour inside a felt mukluk liner restored it to feeling.

It was a sunny, foggy day at −32°. Needles of hoarfrost clung to lumber and cables. The sun sported a white corona that brought spots to his eyes. He was very optimistic. His breath froze instantly on his facemask, scratching his nose with needles of ice. The luminous haze permitted a few low snow-mountains to be seen at the horizon, and he was sure that he would be scaling them soon. He had his own island! He laughed out loud.

For lunch he dumped a quarter of a desk drawer of snow into the pot already conveniently enriched with the remains of last night's dinner, pulled up a chair, brushed the new accumulation of ice crystals off his face, started the stove (the pump handle, being plastic, had already shattered from the cold – supposedly Steger had taken that model to the Pole – but Subzero had saved enough of the shaft to suffice), and then for the first time he broke out the 3.5 pound wheel of cheddar cheese, split a few chips from it with his ice axe, picked them up off the carpet and tossed them in with his vegetables – delicious! For dessert he dipped into the bag of fruit pemmican left over from his Inukjuak trip and munched. It was not hard at all, but soft and very very cold, like ice cream.

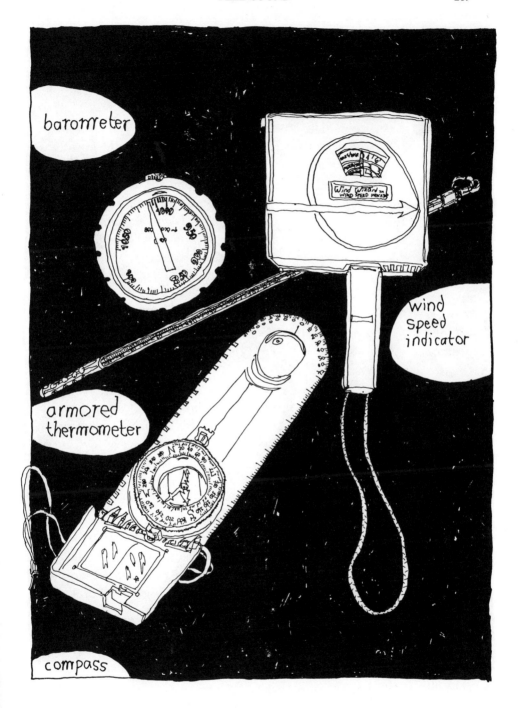

Later that afternoon, remembering that he had been a little cold at night, he decided to make himself a sort of heat bunker with the best materials available. There was a bed with a mattress in the adjoining room. Taking some squares of lumber from the boarded up windows, he walled the bed in and then roofed it with his groundcloth. Although almost twenty-four hours had frozen over him now since the plane had gone, he had not yet set foot on the frozen sea. He hadn't made the acquaintance of any hills, or started in the direction of Cape Cairo. The oddest thing was that his inactivity did not seem odd at all. He was shivering, but buried that fact beneath the mind-drifts. As he shored up the walls of his bunker, like the grasshopper in the fable deciding at the last minute that the ants were right, even then he convinced himself that he was simply doing something that ought to be done sometime – when of course it was really something that had to be done now. He scoured rooms, looking for blankets. The Polar Psychology Project man had said that there were emergency blankets in bags, somewhere in the Ops building. He couldn't really tell where the dorm building left off and the Ops building began. Anyhow, he didn't see any blankets. – No matter. – He wiped his nose. The snot pads on his mitts were frozen to the texture of coarse emery paper.

He climbed into the bed, zipped his sleeping bag around him, and lay there. Since he continued to shiver, he got out, put on his down parka and down pants, and then got back into bed, looking forward to his nap. Two hours later he was still shivering.

In Resolute his friend David had loaned him a heap of spare clothes. Take spare everything, David said. At minus thirty, minus forty, you'll need it after a week. – It was those spare clothes, among other things, that helped to save his life.

The Bradley man had given him a radio. He was supposed to call in every evening, to keep them happy. They'd set up the radio for him when they dropped him off, and it had worked. But this time when he called there was no answer.

He did not want to admit to himself that the sleeping bag was no good because if it did not work there was nothing that he could do about it. In New York he had considered bringing his old bag as a spare, but there simply was no more room left in the backpack. Most winter expeditions make use of sleds anyhow, but, as I have mentioned, air freight to the Canadian Arctic is so unreliable as to be useless – at least for marginal solo expeditions on a budget. As it turned out, Environment Canada in Resolute lent him a sled for toolboxes, which proved very useful. He could have lashed an extra bag onto the sled easily. But getting it to Resolute, that was the problem. So he was stuck.

He managed to get two or three hours of sleep that night and woke up chilled. It was 4:20 in the morning. There was a degree of blue visibility that turned his breath-steam into shadows, and he went out and walked around to warm up. At half-past seven the sun began to clear the blue-white sea-horizon; it was large and seemingly oval, a reddish-orange entity that gradually yellowed. Outside of the station, in the happy expanse of that day, the sleeping bag problem hid again and he was certain that he would have a wonderful time. The ocean, unspeakably inviting, showed him its inch-high knife-ridges of snow; the side away from the rising sun was a very pretty blue. The low blue trapezoids of locked floes or distant mountains (he really couldn't tell without his glasses) were begging him to swarm happily up them all, shouting, shooting, swigging hot chocolate from his thermos –

Ah, yes, the thermos. A glass one would have broken, so he'd bought a steel one. He had to take off his mitts to open it. The conduction of the metal against his undergloved fingers was agony. When he drank from it, he had to remember to breathe on the place where his mouth would be, to prevent his lips from freezing to it.

At −35°, the average temperature during his stay, a liquid poured boiling into the thermos at breakfast would be ice-cold by dinner, and ice-crusted an inch thick the following morning. He could not take the thermos into his sleeping bag to warm it, since the sleeping bag was not warming him.

Seen without glasses the landscape was of course greatly softened. In a way this made it even more enticing, like some long view of desert fading into smoky blue horizons of dust. He was sorry, however, to have no choice in the matter. His visibility was restricted even further by the down facemask David had lent him – a godsend against cold and wind, but it had frozen long since into owlish armor, the eyeholes then further diminished by the carbuncles of frost that rimmed them. From time to time he'd unmitt a gloved finger and scrape away what he could. If he squinted, that eye would freeze shut, and then he'd have to pick and pull at the frozen eyelashes before it could open again; then he'd need to blink vigorously half a hundred times to dissolve the gluey white ropes of half-congealed tears that latticed his vision. Still, there remained a heaven of things to see, things snowcrusted, things hoarfrosted like boards porcupined with splinters, snow-edges that gleamed in the rising sun like sweet yellow butter . . . and then, on that windless morning, he heard something crunch. He was on a ridge overlooking the sea-ice. Something crunched again. Again. Footsteps. If he had had either his glasses or his sleep he doubtless would not have been so alarmed, but you must imagine for yourself the shocking effect of a foreign noise, repeated, in that silent place. He thought he saw a yellow shape on the ice, moving. His heart began to pound. He had left his shotgun at the station, so he deserved whatever he got. He began to walk back toward the station as quickly as he could. In a bright orange stuffsack he had his headlamp and thermos. He took out the headlamp, which he would need, and dropped the stuffsack, to distract the bear in case it followed his track. Then he began to walk even faster. It was very disquieting not to be able to see whether anything was coming behind him. I do not think that there was any bear, actually, but only his anxiety, formed into a bear as in his dreams. Later, when he'd traversed that very gently sloping hillside of snow, which was landmarked by pointy drifts, oil drums and red buildings, all the same size, it seemed, when he'd reached his sled and calmed down, he returned to retrieve the thermos, shotgun on safe but with a chambered round; and after that he was more conscientious about carrying the shotgun with him. It was more concrete, and so more comfortable, than any number of imagined polar bears.

So he had not yet begun seeing things or hearing things; he was only a little tired. Now, if I were to describe to you Captain Subzero's exact situation and location while at lunch, it would be this: seated by the window, leaning over the desk, with his right forearm resting on the block of cheese (which had not been much used, since cutting it was little easier than carving a block of jade), but his arm was already aching with cold from cheese-conduction even through his suit and parka; his right hand, clad in a skinny glove, held a spoon (which was usually kept in the plastic cup of frozen milk powder, which in turn rested in the drawer of snow, just behind the cheese); in front of him was the stove; to his left the can of sterno for softening his facemask . . . – why, he had everything! He was a little colder than he had been the day before, but he'd make up for that now with extra soup and potato buds . . . He could not see out the window anymore. It was frosted with condensation from his cooking. But the little room seemed wider than it should be. And sounds kept tricking him. A piece of dental floss, dragged between his gloved fingers, squeaked with an echo that deafened him. The steady rubbing together of the legs of his down pants when he walked sometimes convinced him of the existence of an approaching airplane. The echoes of his own breathing in the facemask made him certain again that a polar bear was making crunching footsteps behind him . . . He went out with the shotgun and looked around, just to be sure. Well, without glasses of course he could not see much.

The light was always like late afternoon, only sometimes a little brighter or a little dimmer.

He had a feeling of well-being that day. He had begun to know how to wear the clothes, how to pace himself; it was only when he stopped that he became cold.

The sound of something creepy coming down the hall was only the sound of his stove pressurizing. Likewise the sound of police sirens. The sound of bells was the sound of his frozen zippers clinking together when he walked.

It was difficult to light a match. The spark would form on the tip, and then maybe it would catch or maybe it would go out. Even the heads of hurricane matches ignited (if at all) in slow motion.

Every night now he wondered if he would live until morning. He'd read in Stefansson that there was no danger in sleeping when it was cold, that one would wake up when one was chilled, and that was exactly true. But it was still unnerving, to lie down shivering, on the near edge of a dark night, and to know that he'd only get colder and colder. Lying still in the darkness, waiting for the next shiver, he did his best to thrust beyond notice the collar of iron around his neck, the helmet of iron on his face, and the frozen hood behind his head. After awhile, the first drop of ice-cold water ran down the mask and across his nose. The iron collar began to limpen, and water ran down his back. Meanwhile, inside his clothes, the opposite was happening. The sweat on back and buttocks and belly turned to ice. During the day he faithfully vented his perspiration whenever he could, but he could not get rid of all of it, and he was now too cold to remove the VBL at night as he had originally done. In any case, the ice inside it clung too ferociously to be scraped off with a fingernail or a knife ... So he continued to sleep only an hour or two a night. He composed his epitaph: *I died for the advancement of Vapor Barrier Liners.* But in the morning, when he got up and walked around, he became warm and confident again. He tried to think happy thoughts. He tried not to think about night very much, since to think about it was only to dread it. On the fourth day, having become accustomed to using his eyeglasses only for special occasions, as others use binoculars, by lifting them once or twice a day to the rime-choked eyeholes of his facemask, and peering through them for a few seconds, holding his breath, he set off for Don't Point, which was five miles west of the runway. The strangeness of the sounds continued to haunt him. As he bent nearsightedly over his notebook, on which his breath-steam congealed, the scratching of his pencil suddenly echoed distantly, and he was sure that a polar bear was scrabbling softly down the hill to get him. He touched the gun like a magic charm, and felt better. (It is always better to look on the bright side of the question.) With lack of sleep, his eyes were not focusing as well as before; but he could see adequately; the sunlight was good ...

The ground was flinty with frozen mud-clods. Lovely white hills sur-

rounded him. The sun was low and white (it was 1:30 p.m.) and its rays were jagged. Tiny grass-stalks were hoarfrosted into flowers. The shotgun tired his neck a little as he walked, and the coldness of it gradually began to burn his neck right through the down collar. Beating his mitts together for warmth, he stopped for a moment to read the names on the 1964 cairn of brown rocks, lichened black, red and green, and then he went over that little hill and raced down the smooth snow to the sea-ice of Parachute Bay, which was balding with grey spots here and there, thanks to the wind, but balding only meant showing the underlying steel. He could walk across it; he could ride a horse across it; it held Franklin's ships nice and fast. The sun was friendly. The ice was not unfriendly. It acted as it always did.

He stepped onto the ice, timidly at first, and then he began to laugh with delight because it had been the dream of his life to walk upon the frozen sea . . .

In late afternoon the red buildings, roofed with snow, almost seemed to move around him. Snowdrifts hard enough to walk on sloped all the way up some departments, while leaving other doors capriciously clean. Looking west he saw the silhouettes of snow-filled truck bodies at the dump (ideal place to convene survival camp; you could make little snow-caves inside them), then beyond those the blue sides of snow ridges where he walked with the daypack and gun on his back, working up a healthy sweat, loving his own animal smell because it was the only thing to keep him company: be warm and be happy. The abandoned station, on the other hand, was a place to become chilled, to frighten himself with the gunlike booms of his own awful footsteps down corrugated metal corridors, to deceive himself in the few dormitory rooms that hadn't been stripped, so that sitting in a chair, reproductions of impressionist paintings on the wall, he could not for the life of him understand why he needed his goosedown-filled spacesuit to survive – and then he realized that his hands and feet were dead again and there was breath-ice on his aching throat –

Magnetism may affect the pineal gland, they say, and what the pineal gland does to your brain nobody knows. So watch your thoughts at the North Magnetic Pole, they told him. – Was it magnetic influence, then, that was responsible for the unexplained sighing and moaning sounds he heard at every sunset in those snow-black corridors?

That night again he thought that he might not survive. The pad of the sleeping bag felt like ice, and probably was. The down was clumped into frozen pebbles whose sharp edges had worried holes in the nylon shell of the bag. He closed his eyes, and saw a fire in a fireplace, with andirons; he dreamed of a warm woman hugging him. When he woke up, he'd slept three hours. The collar of his sleeping bag, thick and white with frost, stuck painfully to his throat. He was suffocating in his own breath-ice. In the darkness he could not feel his arms and legs. His back and buttocks ached sharply with cold, and he was shivering. He was cold deep inside his belly.

He put on his boots and went outside and walked a mile until he was warm enough to think.

I need hot chocolate, he said to himself.

He chopped snow with his ice-axe and melted it and boiled it over the stove. By then, sitting still, he felt half dead with cold. Pulling off the facemask to expose his wet skin to the cold was very unpleasant; so was putting the mask back on, after he'd gulped the cooling liquid. The mask had crumpled and hardened in that position; he gritted his teeth as he worked the ice-vortices over his face.

I guess I'd better get warm in my sleeping bag, he said . . .

In the morning he decided that before all else he must find those emergency blankets. His down parka was becoming stiff and crackly with ice; he had another from David but the rapidity and thickness of its glazing was a bad sign. He felt very weak, and the sun was in his eyes and for a moment the ice seemed to him like the costumes of Greenlandic women, brightly beaded with diamonds and crosses. With his shovel he dug out the snow from a doorway that might be the Ops building and there was another door half-open, drifted high; he climbed over the hard whiteness and into a dark wood-ribbed corridor going right, snow lovingly cushioning the stained light bulb, snow bulging out from the walls . . . That door at the far end must lead to the dormitory building. No need to clear it. Let's go straight ahead. He shoveled out the next door; there were icicles on the ceiling that did not tremble as he kicked the door open; it took him a long time because he was very weak. The string of his mitts caught on the inner knob and for a long time he could not figure out what had happened. He kept saying to himself: Now, if I can just solve this sleeping bag problem I'll be much happier. He shambled into the darkness, fumbled, switched his headlamp on. He saw the guts of a fuse box, some upended buckets, boxes of nails, and then a third door, behind which a corridor went left and right . . . Try right first. On the wall was a poster of a woman in a bikini, dancing on a tropical beach, her head thrown back as she laughed or screamed. She was spotted with mold. In the next room he found mattresses, a hammock under a swinging lamp held together with masking tape – very World War II, somehow. One grand puff of breath-steam followed the next, on an endless parade into the wall's oblivion. He switched off the headlamp. A little light came through the snowy pane behind the stovepipe. Yes, a stove. A box of matches beside it. He found a piece of paper, put it into the stove, and lit it. That took a long time. The matches were the old wooden kind, with a white dot of phosphorus on a red head. The white part would sometimes ignite, but it was so cold that the red part wouldn't. Finally he got a match going and touched it to the paper. The stovepipe valve was open; all was ready. But smoke came out of the masking tape patches on the stovepipe and hung in the room, spreading horizontally an inch or so below the ceiling. That stove would never do. He looked around, needing blankets. He saw shelves, a dart board with most darts in the inner ring (pretty good, dead men), a table stacked with *Scientific American* and *Popular Mechanics* (the latest issue 1974). A dark little carpeted room, empty aside from a useless lamp. – I note some mental deterioration, he said to himself, but I'm not shivering, so I must not be hypothermic. Maybe I have the flu. – A big armchair by the stove, facing the steel-grey communications panel whose dead phone and microphone, silent round speaker, rows of red and black plugs and switches, each awarded its little portion of snow, cried out to him in desperate silence. The power booth behind this bulkhead was a little niche from which he could see, as if in some museum, the inner involutions of radio lifetimes, batteries the size of salt shakers, grilles and wires and snow and darkness . . . He stumbled over a discarded metal panel. That was all. – Now the left way. He was very weak and slow. Much darker now. Little cubbies of darkness. A room with long snow-covered tables like pool tables or autopsy tables . . . the headlamp flicked onto a frozen bottle of ketchup. It was so cold that his breath-steam fell instead of rising. The next room contained steel sinks, darkness, vastness. There were plastic bags in the sink. Blankets.

He loaded all the blankets and pillows onto his sled and said to himself: If this works, I'll live and all my troubles will be over. If not, why, I'm in big trouble.

He decided to move up to Marv's shed on the runway. It was so small that the building might retain a little body heat. And there was a tank of propane in there. Marv had given him the key and showed him how to use the little heater.

It took him a long time to walk that three-quarters of a mile. He was very dizzy. First he let himself rest every hundred steps. Then he had to lower the requirement to eighty. He said to himself: Interesting how soft snow is more featureless. When he finally got to Marv's shed it took a very long time to undo the knots. He dragged the blankets in and said: Now we'll see. He got into his sleeping bag. He became very cold as the ice on him melted. Then he stopped getting colder. When he saw that he was going to be all right, he closed his eyes and saw swarms of black dots like midges, and he tried to count them but couldn't. Then he saw a hillside of trees. And he sobbed once.

A fever burst out on him, and he laughed, because now it was patent that it wasn't hypothermia, but only the flu; he must have gotten it in Resolute –

Marv's shed was never meant to be lived in. It was like an ice-house. The walls and ceiling bristled with frost. It would have been just large enough for two people to lie side by side on the floor, heads touching one wall, toes the other. But almost half the width was taken up by the automatic weather station transmission boxes, together with various crates. Catty-corner to one another were two hundred-pound propane cylinders. The one in the corner of the front wall away from the door was at his head. The one against the crates just opposite the door was by his feet. He'd packed pillows around the base of each so that the metal couldn't steal his heat. More dangerous than they was the fact that Marv had weather-stripped the door very tightly. It opened outward, and could not be closed except from the outside, and then only with the greatest effort. It could not be closed from inside at all. He tied a piece of webbing from the door to its hasp so that he could pull it toward himself when he entered the shed at night, but this left it ajar almost two feet. Worse yet, the fact that it opened outward meant that if a wind blew snow against the door he would be trapped inside.

He slept and fever-dreamed all afternoon, safely warm for the first time. His breath-ice plagued him no more than that pretty mesh of frost that guarded his window at the Narwhal, crystalline strata curving in the illusion of a well-shaft. When he awoke, he checked the barometer (a mildly miserable thing to do, since reaching his arm out let the cold in, and it would take another quarter-hour to get warm again) and he saw that the pressure was falling. It had been falling all day. He leaped up, put on his mitts and boots, slung the shotgun over his shoulder, and went down to the station to get the nails he had seen in the Ops building. There was a piece of lumber there that might have been used to board up a window. He dragged that back up the hill with him. His friend David had worked at the station once. David had told him that the winds at Isachsen were like nothing on earth. He had to build a windbreak. He began prying up great chunks of hard snow with his shovel. As a boy he had helped his father rebuild one or two of the old New England stone walls on their property. Since he did not have a saw he could not cut even blocks as an Inuk would have, but he could at least stack up the snow-boulders in overlapping rows, chinked with soft snow, conscientiously mortared with urine; he found himself greatly enjoying the building work because it was something with a beginning, a middle and an end which he had control over, unlike almost everything else, and so he heaped up a tumulus of snow in front of the door, just far enough from it so that it could open half-way (enough for him to go in and out with a little gear); and then if the wind were to blow parallel to the wall he could close off the little alley between door and wall with the big board. Already he could see a cloud-knife coming toward him from the frozen sea. He nailed a piece of tarp to the door-frame, so that the door could stay a little ajar even in the face of a wind. He was getting hot, so he pulled his coveralls down off his shoulders to vent the sweat-steam, at which his capilene innerwear frosted up instantly, and he could feel it pucker up on his back as it froze . . .

He didn't sleep much. Evidently it was the fever that had kept him warm, and that had broken. All night he shivered. The sleeping bag was cold and wet. His chest and stomach were the coldest parts of him. He was becoming very sleep-deprived, and his thoughts were not as clear as they should have been, but he told himself that he'd devote the next day to searching the Ops building for heaters. Even if there were other blankets they wouldn't do him any good. He needed something to warm him up, not just insulate him.

There was no wind. A little snow was falling.

His first stove, the one with the shattered pump, was now out of fuel, and that morning he switched to the second. Simply filling the gas bottle and re-inserting the pump was out of the question at these temperatures because the O-rings could not grip properly. As a matter of fact, the second stove, even though he'd put it together almost as soon as the plane had landed him, was leaking gasoline a few inches from its own open flame. He didn't like that. He poured a little soup on the O-ring and it froze right away and the dripping stopped. He wiped up the spilled gas with a block of snow.

The stove was not pressurizing properly. He had to keep pumping it, which made his fingers ache with cold, and his teeth were chattering as he sat there. When he finally got it going, he had to get up and run half a dozen times up and down the black corridor until he could think again –

Breakfast over, fingers and toes dead, he pulled his mask of iron ice back on and returned to the Ops building. In the room where he'd found the blankets he found the other diesel heater, a tall black cabinet with a louvered door. The PPP man had said that it was connected to a thousand-gallon feeder drum just outside. He went outside and cleared the snow away from the drum with his shovel and ice-axe. There were two valves. – Just open the valve, wait a minute and light it, the PPP man had said. He opened both valves as far as they would go. Nothing happened. – What next? He had to do whatever he had to do, rapidly. Already he was getting cold again, and his mind was becoming confused. He did twenty jumping jacks, singing a loud song to hearten himself, and then he was able to think again. Not far from the window he found a yellow drum of jet fuel which was almost empty, as he could tell by rolling it a little on its cradle; a full drum weighed about 400 lbs. To open fuel drums you were supposed to use a barrel bung. He'd discovered that the curved point of an ice-axe worked just as well. Gently he hooked the point in and unscrewed the cap. Then he poured out what was left into a wastebasket. He carried the wastebasket back into the darkness and poured the diesel in through the stove door. He heard it trickling deep inside. Now he hesitated to strike a match, because he dreaded burning the whole building down or worse, but he was shivering again; he had to do it. He took a roll of toilet paper from the nearest dark and frozen washroom and rolled it down into the chamber where the diesel was, keeping hold of an end which he could use as a fuse. The matches were as hard to light as ever, and his eyes kept closing, but he struck match after match, each one vainly sparking half a dozen times before the head wore away, until he finally got one to make fire. He held his breath until the toilet paper caught. Then he let it fall into the chamber and closed the door. The stovepipe valve was already open. He waited. The fuel caught, and began to burn calmly and steadily.

The feeling was wonderful. The collar of ice around his neck began to melt, and he saw steam rising from himself. The snow on the carpet did not melt, but the room became perceptibly warmer. For the first time in he did not know how long, he was able to sit still without getting colder and colder. He did not have to desperately scheme and plan and consider. He could simply be, doing nothing. The sensation came back into his fingers. He was the happiest person on earth.

A wastebasket of fuel lasted about an hour and a half. He found another drum in back of the station, a full one, and collected more fuel. He cooked lunch over the heater, melted snow for drinking water in a nice slow diesel way so that it wouldn't taste scorched as usual, softened the O-rings of his stoves, unzipped his jumpsuit and VBL suit to melt the dirty sweat-ice inside.

The next order of business was obviously to go back to Marv's shed for his sleeping bag and dry it, too. That would make the nightly ordeals much more endurable. As he ran back up the hill, he luxuriated in his exultation. All his problems were solved now. His hands and his mitts were too stiff to permit him to roll up his sleeping bag very well, so he had to lash it on his sled. He was stumbling and he sloshed diesel oil. He said to himself: You're in an abnormal state of mind. Calm down. Your judgment is gone. – But he could not believe himself. Just as a gun can become so cold that it slowly burns through your double-lined leather expedition mitts, so the sleeplessness had finally reached him. It seemed to him that he would have no responsibilities anymore. The ice in the sleeping bag would melt, and then he would get in it and sleep and be warm, and then the plane would come. There was nothing to it. He lit the diesel heater as usual. The sleeping bag began to steam promisingly. He closed his eyes. Then he smelled smoke.

He saved the building fireman-style, by running outside, smashing the window with his ice-axe, hurling chunks of snow down against the flaming wall, knocking out a segment of stovepipe, and smothering the fire in the heater itself by cramming in newspapers, snow-chunks, an old boot, and whatever else he could find. When he had finished, the room was a shambles. The floor was slick with diesel oil (it was in his eyes and all over his clothes, which henceforth would insulate him even less efficiently), and it had soaked his gloves, which no doubt contributed to the later state of his fingers, and snow and soot were everywhere. He didn't realize until a long time later that it was then, when he put the fire out, that he lost his eyebrows.

He got the radio and called Bradley. There was nothing but static, of course, but he convinced himself that he could hear a voice saying: . . . are you OK? . . .

Yes, I'm OK, he said, but I'm concerned about the diesel on me. I'd like to be picked up tomorrow or the next day, please. Over.

He was very happy now. They would pick him up tomorrow.

He went back up to Marv's shed with the sleeping bag. He heard children playing outside. It was summer, and they were playing ball. He knew perfectly well that there were no children there, but he enjoyed listening to them.

There were two or three of them and they were very excited. He could not hear what they were saying, exactly; they were a hundred yards or so away, playing catch or kickball. He smiled not to be alone.

He slept a little; he wasn't sure how much; and when he awoke he was so cold that he couldn't even shiver. When he went outside to defecate (a process requiring twenty minutes, thanks to numb fingers, frozen zippers, and brittle shrunken nylon), he felt lumps of ice frozen to his buttocks. He stumbled down to the station and made his breakfast. Then he came back weeping.

There was a propane tank and a little space heater in Marv's shed. Marv had told him he could use it if he had to. To ignite it it was first necessary to open the valve on the tank by about thirty turns – a procedure which hurt his fingers so much that he had to warm them in the middle – then to turn the valve on the heater from off to low, then finally to hold a lighted match to the grille with one hand while pushing in a metal button at the base with the other. It took him about a quarter-hour with his already numbed fingers to get a match to light. By then the fingers were somewhat worse. Pushing the metal button was the worst part. It had to be held for twenty seconds or more, until the grille glowed cherry-pink; and when the heater sputtered it had to be held again. When one joint of his finger had been sufficiently burned by the cold, he'd slide the next joint against it, and then be ready to use the adjoining finger. As he stared at Heater's friendly round face, almost pressing his cheek against her, as he drank in her happy red lattice-face behind the grille, he knew that she was his friend and he knew that his fingers were his friend, sacrificing themselves to save the rest of him, and he did not even wonder what his fingers would be like later because they were only doing what they had to do as Heater's cruel cold button burned them again and again.

He spent all day drying out his sleeping bag. He melted all the ice. He also scorched huge holes in it with his weary hands so that the down started coming out and Marv's shed looked like a chicken factory. He scorched holes in his down parka and in his down pants. When it was evening he had finished. He heard the children again. He got into his sleeping bag with the blankets over him and he was so warm when he heard a woman's voice saying: Get your gun.   – He lay there for a long time, wondering why he needed to do that. He had hung it outside so that Heater's warmth wouldn't cause moisture to condense on it. Finally he opened his eyes and decided to get the gun. He saw that the door was wide open. He got up and brought the gun in. Suddenly he saw that he was in his socks and undergloves. Too late now. He closed the door and got back in his sleeping bag. His hands didn't hurt anymore; they were numb. He couldn't work the zippers on his sleeping bag. He lay there patiently. After awhile two fingers on his left hand began to feel strange. There was nothing to do about it but beat his hands together and be cheerful, which he did. Then he commended himself to GOD in case he didn't wake up, and closed his eyes. He seemed to see an angel, who wanted him to come up with her. He told her that he had someone he wanted to marry and be with awhile; he wasn't ready to come with her yet. The angel was disappointed, but let him back down. He could see her crying as she flew away.

It was 7:00 p.m. At ten he awoke shivering. He tried Heater but she wouldn't glow. He hurt his fingers a great deal trying. But the effort warmed him a little, and he went back to sleep. That night he awoke twice with numb hands and feet, but he exercised in the sleeping bag until feeling returned to them, and then he was able to sleep again. He told himself that when the sun came up he'd go down to the station and have a hot breakfast. (His way of comforting himself in Marv's shed was to promise himself food-warmth at the station. His way of comforting himself at the station was to promise himself sleeping-bag-warmth in Marv's shed. He always believed his own propaganda. What actually kept him the warmest was going from one place to the other.)

That next morning it was −40°, which was the coldest yet. Of course it could have been colder; one must always look on the bright side of the question. Nor is this temperature insupportable if one's sleeping gear and clothes are warm. I am almost embarrassed to impose so undistinguished a division of my thermometer upon you, because I know several people who go hunting and ice-fishing at forty below without writing a book about it. Of course, they prefer warm places to duck into. Even the Inuit stop frequently for tea breaks in heated shelters when it is forty below. The Coleman stove exhales its cheery blue flames in the tent or igloo or snow-cave, and they sit laughing as water begins to boil; maybe they can even slip off their kamiks and stretch out their stockinged toes against the warm pot while somebody butters another piece of bread; get the chocolate and sugar ready! Forty below is not really forty below when inside the tent a stove can manufacture innocence.

But in Subzero's case, how could virginity be restored? The heater slept in ice; the diesel stove was wrecked; the sleeping bag remained futile.

He couldn't get warm.

There was a light wind. He went walking in it to try to warm up, and the corners of his eyes went dead in the facemask. The facemask itself was now so frozen that his breath could not get through it, and his face was cold and wet.

He walked down to the station and had breakfast. Taking the facemask off was so horrible that he wished he'd skipped it. Putting the facemask back on was almost as bad.

He walked back up to Marv's shed, just to do something that would warm him up so that he could think. His mind was stifled and coiled in upon itself. He paced the runway, and each lap made him colder and colder.

He decided to get back into his sleeping bag to wait it out.

He went into the shed and took a look at the sleeping bag there, shriveled like a frozen squid, and the squalid darkness with the frost on the walls and ceiling, and he felt an unbearable repulsion, and went to walk the runway once more, and then as he drew near Marv's shed again something told him that if he entered that shivering bag of ice it would be his grave. He decided to back down to the station again. Maybe his mind would clear on the way.

His fingers were dead. He kissed them through the ice-filled mitts. His fingers, hands, zippers were all each other's friends.

He took the shovel with him, but not the gun. The gun was too cold. Digging out a building full of moldy mattresses, he lay on top of one and pulled another on top of himself to see what would happen. Pretty soon he started to shiver. It wasn't too surprising; the mattresses were frozen inside.

He got up and looked into a room with a sign on the door that said URINAL   PLEASE DON'T USE UNLESS YOU HAVE TO. Under the urinal was a mountain of yellow ice.

He went outside into the sun and started to laugh. After all, it would be pretty stupid to die in a place full of shelter, fuel and matches. Why, if need be he could burn down all the buildings for warmth, one at a time!

He kept laughing, and it seemed to him that he had never been in any danger.

He went to the dormitory building and made himself some soup. He hated pulling the facemask off to drink, but so what. He drew his underglove across his running nose, and the glove froze instantly. He swallowed the last cold mouthful of soup. Holding his breath, he pulled the crumpled mask of ice back on so that once again he had eyes inside his own skull to see the inside of his nose, garnished with crystals, and far below he could look out his own mouth and see snow at the edge of the light. He wandered into the balloon shed and found a soccer ball and started kicking it and it danced ahead of him and he followed, kicking it and laughing, and the soccer ball rolled down and down and came to the edge of the Polar Sea and he kicked it and it shot across the snowy ice and he went after it, loving the fog-hued ice stricken with blue riddlings, kicking the ball between the hard low swellings of that endless sea-plain that resembled bluish-white plaster irregularly daubed, and the world opened up wider and wider before him with all its goodness; he traversed the blue-white sheets of ecstasy, kicking the ball toward an ice-mountain he'd never reach and he was happy.

The next morning it had warmed up to −22° and he felt quite warm. He went down to the station and shouted: *I'm as tough as nails!*

When he got into his sleeping bag that night, he could actually hear his clothing freeze with a *ping!* and then he felt a sharp cold itch, like the bite of a mosquito from Pluto. To distract himself he composed more Arctic Rules, such as:

1. Never wear an inner glove too thick to brush ice from your eyelashes and also pick your nose.

2. Keep your crotch unzipped in the sleeping bag to warm your hands. (Masturbation at low temperatures, however, is most unrewarding.)

3. It's better to wipe your ass with chunks of snow than to fumble with unmitted fingers for toilet paper.

It was a white day of fine snow which muffled even the silence. The only way to tell sky from ground was that the sky was not marred by his footprints. The barometric pressure was still falling. Maybe the storm would come tomorrow. The sun was a pale yellow egg easy to look on, a polished stone buckle in a belt of light that split the foggy sky. Ice crystals tinkled in his

An Inuk girl called him tough when she saw his frostbitten fingers. But he wasn't, really. Consider the despised workhorse, Back, whom Mʳ Franklin sent on a fool's errand to the Great Slave Lake one winter, Back the plodding, the loser in love, Back the tedious, whose best smile was a bray of big teeth, who was willing to pay the highest price to oblige his loved Commander. Upon the completion of his commission, Back wrote, without either arrogance or false modesty: *I had the pleasure of meeting my friends all in good health, after an absence of nearly five months, during which time I had travelled one thousand four hundred and four miles, on snow shoes, and had no other covering at night, in the woods, than a blanket and deer-skin, with the thermometer frequently at −40° [Fahrenheit], and once at −57°; and sometimes passing two or three days without tasting food.* − Subzero's twelve days of anxiety were, it is true, passed without company, and largely without heat, while Back was never alone and sometimes had a fire. In addition, Back's caribou skin might well have been warmer than Subzero's failed goosedown bag (the Inuit consider down to be almost useless for winter camping, and he had known that and should have listened to them). Nonetheless, while Subzero did not do terribly, he did not do well, either. His mistakes were all committed at the beginning, when he made false choices. The new sleeping bag, which there was no way to test in advance, led directly to his shivering, hence to his sleep deprivation, hence to his hallucinations. If he had died it would have been his own fault. It is possible that if Subzero had gone into the country with a knowledgeable Inuk, just as Back traveled with knowledgeable voyageurs and Indians, then he might have equaled Back in caliber. While not as physically fit as Back, perhaps, he did possess a high degree of endurance to discomfort. And no matter what phantasms he heard and saw, he never lost sight of his own self. − But all that was unimportant, because he did not equal Back. Mʳ Franklin, who perhaps was as frightened of Back as he was of anything, suffered the same failing. Mʳ Franklin did not learn from those who knew.

Not Yet Dead
1847

We caught an Emperor penguin this evening . . . It was thought that the penguin would be in our way on deck, or we would find ourselves in its way, which would have been worse, so it was condemned to death. It took four hours to kill it, "but it wasn't dead then," as someone remarked. It had holes driven through its skull, it was beaten with clubs, and it would not die. Then out of pity the doctor was called to put it out of pain. He sat on its back with confidence and worked at its brain, till it lay on the deck apparently lifeless. When he saw it two hours afterward, it was waddling about with its head in the air as if it had neuralgia . . .

> R. N. RUDNOSE BROWN, DSC, *A*
> *Naturalist at the Poles: The Life, Work*
> *and Voyages of Dr. W. S. Bruce, the*
> *Polar Explorer* (1923)

J ust as after a windstorm the snow is laid out so exactly and prettily though unknowably, so after Mr Franklin had finished the recital of his misfortunes the subordinate officers were reconfirmed in their own dedications. But he himself could not understand why the ice had not broken up. Of course it was only May. The ice was more likely to go in the next month. There was nothing to do but wait and watch and listen. (He was angry because he'd done his part. He had led and guarded the Expedition with flying colors. If they'd perished before now, he could have blamed himself. But how could he anticipate the permanence of the ice? . . .)

On the 24th the crews of both ships gathered together on the ice and they fired off the rifles in honor of the Queen's birthday –

There was no worry about starving, of course. In July or August the strait would open and they'd complete the Passage. In September they'd still have ten tons of biscuits and thirty-eight tons of flour left; they'd have tins of veal and ox-cheek and preserved beef, all lead-sealed by means of Goldner's patent; they'd have canned lemon juice against the scurvy, and raisins and suet and ever so much more . . . By the time the sun hid his face at the end of November they'd surely have reached the comforts of the Russian zone –

Reepah's Debt

So, while the economic advantages of hunting, fishing and trapping continually grow slimmer, their cultural significance remains strong. However, the reduced hunting and trapping income, coupled with the accelerating costs of snowmobiles, guns, ammunition and gasoline, makes it financially more difficult for people to hunt.

CANADIAN GOVERNMENT pamphlet,
The Inuit (1990)

Mr Franklin was lying in his bed. The steward, Mr Hoar, had dressed him in his uniform. Buttons traversed him from collar to belt like a double row of pennies. But there were not pennies on his eyes yet. His fingers kept plucking at them, and once they heard him whisper: That means we're lucky now. – Fitzjames bit his lip. Mr Crozier sat at the head of the bed, reading the Bible steadily to his Commander, in case that might comfort him, and Franklin's cheek and chin began to shudder against the collar. The corners of his mouth had turned down more than usual. He breathed in a rasp. His grey face was wet, although no one knew whether from sweat or tears.

Now Dr Peddie returned from visiting his other patients, many of whom were also in grave danger, and the officers, who were standing in a wedge at the door to the room, withdrew a little so that he could pass. Mr Fitzjames stood at their head. Not for the first time, it occurred to Dr Peddie that Fitzjames was a younger version of Mr Franklin not only in his countenance but also in his greyness –

No change, sir? said Dr Peddie.

I think so, replied Fitzjames hopefully. He just now began to speak; he said something about our luck –

Mr Fitzjames would never really see Reepah even when she appeared in the cards. He loved only Mr Franklin; it was that love which had so far arrested the course of the lead in his brain. In Mr Franklin's cabin he could hold onto his best self no matter how much that fishy entity wriggled in his lead-slicked hands –

He knew that he was Mr Franklin's favorite, just as every child of certain fair and affectionate parents believes that he or she is the one. That night he went and dreamed (it was about to be the 9th of June) and within the long dark barrel of his slumbers Mr Franklin summoned him and said: At midnight I wish you, my good friend, to command the men to point their rifles at the North Star.

Fitzjames was bending over him and his face was wet and he was holding his cap in his hand and he felt such pity for Fitzjames because he had wanted to bring Fitzjames to success and now there would be nothing and he tried to smile at Fitzjames, at which Dr Peddie said: Mr Franklin is in pain and the coldness nuzzled him as Mr Hoar drew back his blankets and Dr Peddie rolled up his sleeve and he did not feel the prick as anything more than more coldness crystallizing on him and then everything became more easy and natural as the room widened the same way that in the Empire State Building her eyes widened and widened as they walked down more corridors around more corners to reach the end of the line and it was obvious that it would take hours but she only said: *eeee!* in wonder and laughed. They took the first elevator and then the second and the third; she looked down at New York below her and said grinning and peeking: I'm *leedle* scared!

When he took her on the tramway to Roosevelt Island she said *eee* and held his hand tight when the car lurched and lifted and hung swaying above the Queensborough Bridge with its yellow treasure of taxicabs and he said   are you scared?   and she said   leedle bit   and he said   don't be afraid   and patted her cheek and got an erection. They came down and the door opened; he took her out and the sign said   **DO NOT WALK UPON THE GRASS** and they walked upon the grass. She smiled and bent down and patted it. – I miss this very much,   she said. – Then he took her to the giant Christmas tree at Rockefeller Plaza and she said *wow!* and her face glowed and she was happy with the angels and around the corner some black men were

dancing so beautifully so she said   I want breakdance!   and he knelt down so
that she could sit on his shoulders and then he stood up as she clung to him
and giggled   no, no   and he went into the crowd and she looked down from
his shoulders smiling at the dancers and nodding her head to the drumming
so that he loved her.

❄ ❄ ❄

She didn't like the yellow curry at the Thai place, but of the lamb basil she
said: Good! It taste same like caribou!

❄ ❄ ❄

Wanna eat?   she'd said to him. That was practically the first thing she ever
said to him, that time in Resolute.
    Sure.
    A cob of corn and three boiled potatoes.
    That was the only thing she volunteered all day. She was shy with him
then. Sometimes dinner was frozen chicken; sometimes it was bannock and
Spaghetti-O's. But every day, as long as he stayed with her, she asked him if
he'd had enough to eat.

❄ ❄ ❄

They were going out for secrets.
    She clutched her sweater and said: I wanna change my this!
    She wanted to wear the black leather jacket he'd bought her.
    Then he was so proud –

❄ ❄ ❄

I love you!   he said to her as he made love to her, and she held him tight
and took him in and made excellent noises. Afterward she said softly: I love
you!

❄ ❄ ❄

At night he heard her crying bitterly. Jane was about to come home from Van
Diemen's Land. He lay in the other room, so that Jane would not find them

together. Then she came in and said: I'm sorry I touch you, 'cause I love you, too!

Hi, Jane! said Reepah.
    Jane ignored her.
    Hi, Jane! said Reepah, even more softly than before. Jane, you are pretty, like picture!
    Jane turned to her husband. – Your Esquimau friend is certainly ugly, she said.

Your final orders and instructions . . .
    Aye, sir?
    C^{mdr} Crozier?
    Here I am, sir.
    That means – that means we're lucky now.

After Jane came back, Reepah had to sleep on the sofa. Thus exiled, she cringed away from Jane and her consort, the aforesaid Mr Franklin, who, miserable, would sneak out to hold her hand whenever he could. Jane was not around much after the first day. He spent every minute that he could with Reepah. She would be going home soon, back to her dead double who'd drag her under the moss where Mr Franklin was, and he knew that if he ever opened his eyes he'd find himself about to go there, too, lying there with them all bent over him and their buttons dully gleaming to make him scream as he'd done at Pond's Bay; and if he was very very good, maybe a tenth as good as Reepah, it might be given to him to hover over his snowbound grave once every hundred years with Seth shimmering beside him to comfort him, Seth smiling at him with wise honest tired eyes, Seth saying: It's neat, John, because you'll hit an area like this and all the sudden there'll be buttercups and things like that spurting out of the snow! – but that would make him scream again because he did not want to go back there to his waiting self, so he closed his eyes, feeling Fitzjames's breath on his forehead, and spent his centuries with Reepah. For the other times, the times when Jane called him

to bed and night-owl Reepah still had five empty hours ahead, without even
a beer to dispatch them, he dug out his compact disk portable, which she
could hold on her lap and listen to; so he slipped the digital headphones on
her as if he were anointing her with myrrh (as he'd anointed himself when
he first bought that toy, anointed himself with magnetic codes in spite of
Beaufort's ravings), and he picked out the CDs that she might like the best. For
her he inserted the King Crimson disk (which even Jane had thought awfully
marvelous, bloody brilliant); through headphones it was so much better than
on the speakers (after all, speakers had hardly been invented yet). So he settled
her on the couch, ignoring Jane's fretful calls (Jane, knowing very well why he
was so late for bed, wanted nothing better than to interrupt him in the most
alarming and mortifying fashion); so he laid the little CD player, not much
thicker than a chocolate bar, on her lap, and she waited boredly as he
connected cords and pressed the O P E N button and clicked down the round
lid to hold in the disk like a seal under ice; so he pushed P L A Y and dialed
Track 5, his favorite, "In the Court of the Crimson King," and though he
could not hear it himself it didn't matter; gleefully he watched the counter go
from O O O to O O 1 (as Jane called: John, darling, won't you ever be finished
with your little Esquimau squaw? Or is squaw the proper word? Forgive me
if I speak incorrectly . . .) and so now the song would be commencing with
that delicious drumbeat and he watched Reepah's face and saw it come alive
with joy and delight and he laughed to know that that majestic acidhead
chord was burning her so pleasurably that she was grinning and her mouth
gaped even more happily when the knowing singers went: *In the Court of*
the Crimson King – Ahhhhhhhhhhhhhhhhhhhhhhhhhhhhhhhhhhhhhhhhhhhh!   and
Reepah was nodding and her lips were moving and to increase her pleasure
he turned the volume knob from 2 to 3 and King Crimson went:
AHHHHHHHHHHHHHHHHHHHHHHHHHHHHHHHHHHHHHHHH!   and
Reepah was laughing and singing   aaah   and now they must be singing
about trampling the flowers and how the Pattern Juggler did something or other (Jane had turned out the bedroom light) and Reepah was
dancing sitting down so he fingered the volume knob up from 3 to 6,
savoring every knurl and nick against his fingertip, and saw how Reepah's
eyes got larger as the song got louder and it would be impossible for a
human being to smile more widely than she when King Crimson went:
AHHHHHHHHHHHHHHHHHHHHHHHHHHHHHHH!
and when the song was over he left her playing it again –

❈ ❈ ❈

She said: I want walk around – last time!   so he put on his coat while she waited in the blue parka with embroidered trim and they went out to look at closed storefronts. She said: I want disco please!   but he said: I got no more money. I'm sorry!   – You're cheating me!   she cried, but she forgave him and took his hand . . . She always giggled with excitement when he led her across the street, trucks and taxis a honking wall of thrilling menace for her, and she clung to his arm tightly and they ran.   – Is there *aputik** in Heaven?   he asked her.   – No.   – What's there?   – Her face glowed.   – It's *beautiful, beautiful!*   – Will I see you there? Will you be an angel there? – Everyone!   – Even me, Reepah? Because you're good but I'm bad. – *Everyone*, I said!   – Reepah, you wanna kiss me?   – No.   – OK.   – But a moment later, when he leaned against a wall, she came into his arms and kissed him until they were both dizzy.   – My snake is bad!   she laughed, pointing to her flickering tongue. – He took her to the East River, saying: See? There's island; there's tramway – remember?   – Yeah!   she said softly. – They walked south along the esplanade, beside the water with its midnight gleam and glisten like oil; between them and a moored barge, rats moved, long and pale, in a rotten dinghy. Reepah liked them. They came to a pretty place and kissed, and then he took two pennies from his pocket. He threw his penny into the river.   – For luck,   he whispered. – Me?   she said.   – Yes.   – She flicked hers in after his, and grinned at the splash. A moment later, the wake from a passing tugboat sent up waves toward them, and he said to her: That means we're lucky now.

* Snow.

Back's Debt

As for meate, our greatest and chiefest feeding was the Whale Frittars, and those mouldie too, the loathsomest meate in the world. For our venison was hard to find, but a great deal harder to get: and for our third sort of provision the Beares, 'twas a measuring cast which should be eaten first, Wee or the Beares . . . they had as good hopes to devoure us as wee to kill them.

EDWARD PELLHAM, *God's Power and Providence* (1631)

At the end of August, C^apt Crozier, now commanding since the death of C^apt Franklin, called a council of the principal officers. More meat was bad – much, much more. They were beginning to be hungry now. It was patent that they would be frozen in for another winter – their third since leaving Gravesend – and the form of their fate could be determined all too well. The ships, twisted and uplifted, had drifted only nineteen miles in the course of the entire season. Breezes plucked their fans of rigging. The men crawled up and down the steep decks . . . As they were in more or less uncharted regions, they could not hope for their relief, if indeed any had been sent; – nor (said C^apt Crozier) would it be Christian to wish for any, since a shipload of rescuers would only find itself in the same plight.

It is Back's fault, said Fitzjames bitterly. I am certain that his map was wrong about the eastern way. If we had taken the other channel –

There is no knowing whose fault it was, if anyone's, replied C^apt Crozier. And frankly, Mr Fitzjames, I am surprised at you, to blame an absent man. Blame will not help any of us now.

The ice groaned.

Let us not make too much of this, gentlemen, implored Gore. Let us rather make a plan.

A plan? laughed Fitzjames. I'm sure that I would love to hear your plan.

Get hold of yourself, Mr Fitzjames, said C^{apt} Crozier, and after that Fitzjames was silent.

Mr Irving, would you do us the courtesy of unrolling Back's chart once more? said C^{apt} Crozier.

Aye, sir.

Mr Blanky, he said to the Ice-Master, we depend on you for your estimation of the reliability of this map. It is substantially the same for this area as Ross's, is it not?

Aye, sir. I've always said that much. And I continue to vouch for the accuracy of C^{apt} Ross's observations, no matter what Mr Fitzjames cares to think.

For the last time, gentlemen, kindly spare me your squabbles. Don't you see that this is a matter of life and death?

Oh, we see that, murmured Fitzjames to himself.

Mr Vesconte, could you call in Dr Peddie, please?

The noises outside the stateroom were the noises of rocks shifting, of canvas flapping, of the sea, which was sometimes very loud in its wave-crashes and sometimes not; and every wave-crash was only a wind-crash; there were no waves.

Ah, Dr Peddie, thank you for joining us. I need you to look after Mr Fitzjames for me. Perhaps a sedative . . .

Oh, we see that, repeated Fitzjames, as he went out with Dr Peddie.

So, Mr Blanky, you believe that this map is accurate enough for purposes of navigation?

Aye, sir. But I served with C^{apt} Ross –

But C^{apt} Ross was less familiar with this Great Fish River here than Back. Back discovered it, Mr Blanky. Back navigated it – looking for C^{apt} Ross, incidentally, who was lost –

Not at the time, sir.

Well, Back had reason to believe that he was still lost. He hadn't reported home yet. My proposal, therefore – gentlemen, are you following me?

Aye, sir.

Well, this Great Fish River, said C^{apt} Crozier, suddenly hesitating. I – excuse me, gentlemen, a moment's dizziness . . .

Yes, said C^{apt} Crozier. From Victory Point to Fort Resolution is approximately twelve hundred and fifty miles. If we drag the ship's boats down King William Land to the mouth of Back's Great Fish River, and then

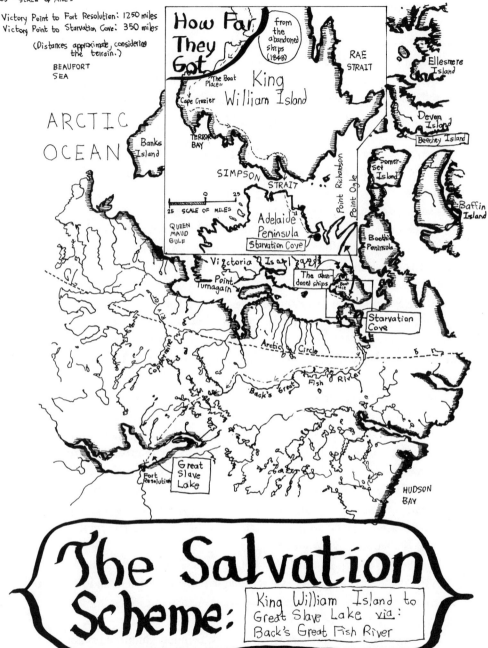

SCALE OF MILES

Victory Point to Fort Resolution: 1250 miles
Victory Point to Starvation Cove: 350 miles

(Distances approximate, considering the terrain.)

BEAUFORT SEA

ARCTIC OCEAN

Banks Island

How Far They Got

from the abandoned ships (1848)

King William Island

"The Boat Place"

Cape Crozier

TERROR BAY

SIMPSON STRAIT

Adelaide Peninsula

Starvation Cove

QUEEN MAUD GULF

25   SCALE OF MILES

RAE STRAIT

Ellesmere Island

Deven Island

Beechey Island

Somerset Island

Baffin Island

Point Richardson

Point Ogle

Boothia Peninsula

Victoria Island

Point Turnagain

The abandoned ships

Boat Place

Starvation Cove

Arctic Circle

Coppermine

Back's Great Fish River

Fort Resolution

Great Slave Lake

HUDSON BAY

The Salvation Scheme:

King William Island to Great Slave Lake via: Back's Great Fish River

pull upstream, we may hope to reach the Great Slave Lake – who knows? –
by mid-autumn . . . Back's account reports multitudes of caribou and musk-
oxen all along the Great Fish River, and there will be Indians and Esquimaux
to succor us; it's fresh meat that we require above anything . . .

Aye, sir, said Gore. But I think on the tales that poor Mr Franklin used
to tell us. Strange meat. We'll starve if we fail to cross the Barren Grounds in
time . . . The other possibility is to return to Lancaster Sound. It's only six
hundred miles –

You mean travel over this pack-ice? I suppose it could be done. You must
love ice, Mr Gore. And what then? Wait for a whaler to come to our rescue?

Aye, sir.

I suppose that is a second option, said C^{apt} Crozier. Do I hear a third?

There's always patience, sir, said the Ice-Master quietly. How much food
can we carry away, after all? Forty days' worth? What then? We can wait for
the ice to break up. Perhaps the Esquimaux will find us. I am certain that this
last summer was an anomaly –

How certain are you, exactly, Mr Blanky? Are you *certain enough?*

No one can be certain enough in such situations, Blanky began, but by
then the other Arctic Friends had shouted him down, their glaring eyes
shouting still louder, until C^{apt} Crozier banged wearily on the table.

Mr Vesconte, you were shouting the loudest. Perhaps you could state your
objection more elegantly.

Aye, sir. The fact is, I don't think we can afford to wait out a fourth winter.
We all know that our stores were for three years only, and some of the
preserved meats are beginning to spoil. Dr Goodsir told me that the lemon
juice has staled, and the vinegar is not as good a specific against the scurvy as
he hoped; my own teeth are getting loose! And the men – I can't answer for
the men much longer. But what it really comes down to, sir, is that I don't
know what we would do if we waited and the ice failed to break up in the
spring. We would – we would die, sir.

We all keep saying that, Mr Vesconte. I'm as guilty of it as anybody. I really
think that for the men's sake we had better make a pact here and now not to
let that word pass our lips anymore. – Well?

Aye, sir, they all said.

It seems that no one favors waiting, the Captain continued. And so we
are left with the choice of seeking out a whaler in Lancaster Sound or else
ascending Back's Great Fish River. What are your opinions, gentlemen?

If Mr Gore could be more specific in his Lancaster Sound plan . . . – said
Blanky.

But Gore was staring down at his hands.

The following year, when they had abandoned the ships, C^apt Crozier led the men south to Starvation Cove, calling on all to exert themselves to the best of their ability, because the weak ones would not be able to walk much longer. They were very hungry now. They had praying dreams of Reepah; they dreamed of combing her hair for her so that, mutilated and vengeful, she'd gradually be soothed into letting the food-beasts come to them. They were blind or half-blind with the sickness. They divided the loads as evenly as they could (and he drew Fitzjames aside and whispered to him that he could already see how the men from the two ships regarded one another as rivals; it was only a matter of a few days before all discipline would be gone, and Fitzjames nodded; he was having one of his lucid times). The wind blew very hard. The boats hummed on the snow-crust as they dragged them slowly south on the sledges, no longer thinking about the dead ships with their colors nailed to the mast, trudging toward Point Victory, grabbling their way with their pole-staves, and sometimes they stopped to rest and the pole-staves leaned crazily like the ships hidden now between ice-mountains and then the sick ones began to slide slowly down the pole-staves and then the officers encouraged them up and forward with gentle words. They would have to leave them tomorrow or the next day. Otherwise no one would reach the Great Fish River. – Remember, said the officers, Mr Back walked almost twelve hundred miles in snowshoes! – And the men continued to put one foot ahead of the other. They did not understand where they were or where they were going. (In how many more crises would we not have made a more courageous choice if we'd had a square or two of chocolate to eat?) – Remember, said the officers, Sir James wintered here for three years! – And the men went south. – Two points of leeway, a sailor muttered in delirium. And slowly, very slowly, he sat down in the snow. – Reindeer! a man shouted. And before the officers could stop him, he'd discharged his rifle at nothing. – At Terror Bay we'll need to leave the sick ones – certainly by then. (Thus C^apt Crozier, to himself.) Yes, I think so. But I shall send the Esquimaux to them. Perhaps a few will survive . . . – And he led them south. – When I get back I want to get one of those big hambones for soup. Not the cheap kind. Too much bone on them. I'll get the expensive kind. – They'd sheathed the bottoms of the boat in copper (the Inuit would make use of that for decades) and the snow flashed orange beneath them, and the aurora formed an arch of orange and green ahead of them, and they went south, chipping a way for the sledges with their picks if they had to, wiping the frost from their moustaches with the backs of their mitts, and sometime in May or June or April or July they saw their first human beings since taking leave of the whalers *Prince of Wales* and *Enterprise* in Baffin's Bay – three years before, by then – and, as it happened, these were also the last human beings that they would see. Standing alert on the far side of a lead, the People watched them. Crozier told his men to withdraw a little, so as not to frighten them. He suspended a medal around his neck; that had always been the late Mr Franklin's practice when dealing with Esquimaux. He raised his arms to show that he had no weapons. He opened his dry hard black mouth and begged for meat. They watched him. He approached them, in company with Lieutenant Vesconte, and they let him come. In the skin packs of the women who stood waiting was seal meat. They looked at their feet. Their faces were dirty. The sunlight gleamed in their hair. Their sealskin parkas were crinkled and glassy like dried guts. C^{apt} Crozier strode up to them and ripped their packs open and took some of the meat. A boy watched wide-eyed, holding a little knife. He was narrow and curious, like an ermine. C^{apt} Crozier saw the boy's knife and began taking meat from the women's packs faster and faster, for it seemed only prudent to be so firm. The women giggled nervously. They did not try to run. They stood sausagelike, otterlike. In payment he gave them a hatchet, and a medal, and some beads. He knew a few words of their language, and so he spoke to them, seeking to impress upon them the extremity of his men, but they did not seem to understand him and so he fell silent. They cocked their heads and squinted and a woman ran her tongue over her lips. There were four families. By signs he asked them to make camp beside his men, and help them. They came. Soon Crozier's men were crowding silent and huge-eyed around the conical skin-tent shagged with furry patches like lichens, anchored with a ring of stones, the skins overlapping like scales. Inside was meat. They saw a mother with three daughters. The youngest was clasping her hands. Her parka was a girdle of white segments at the tail. Her name was Reepah. A man crawled out of the doorway, reaching his hand out to a rock. He wore a tasseled cap. All around him, ropes extended to flat rocks. Wrinkled faces, young faces, stared or smiled from their hoods. And Crozier's men were very quiet. They looked at the blue and silver fox pelts dangling from the racks, blowing in the wind just above the dirty snow; and a man came close and then too close because he wanted to lick whatever might remain on the flesh side of the skins, but C^{apt} Crozier was watching the man, too, with his head cocked so watchfully in the old way but nothing serene about it anymore, and he knocked the man down and hit him with the butt of his pistol and said: Fool! Don't you see that our lives depend on our friendship with these people?   and when he looked around the People were watching from their tents, not smiling; he saw a lady beaded and tattooed with whiskers like a seal. – That evening two more of C^apt Crozier's men died, and the labor to bury them was too great, so they folded their arms on their breasts and covered them with stones. (Mr Gore had been the last one to be properly buried, months ago, in a grave four feet under ice.) And the People watched. But Crozier's men slept peacefully, because they had seen such things before and they needed to sleep and they knew that none of them would die anymore, because the good Esquimaux would stay and catch seals for them until they were healthy again and then the Esquimaux would show them how to get to Back's River and maybe even initiate them into a secret way without toil or tears by means of which they'd be at Fort Resolution before autumn. But one thing that Crozier's men did not know was that in 1834, when Back first explored his eponymous river, formerly called the Thleweechohoesseth, he descended all eighty-three falls, cascades and rapids in it, without a hitch (and the herds of game-animals were as C^apt Crozier had said), and he led his men on to Fury Beach, his purpose being to locate and relieve Sir James, who was reputed to be there and had not come home for too long, but being unable to find him, Back turned about, and all was still well until some of his men decided to go fowling at a lake near Point Ogle, where the People happened to be fishing; there were flocks of snow-lakes like long-necked geese in that region, but by skull-chance Back's men had to pick that particular lake where for GOD knows what cause arrows were exchanged for rifle-shots, and the rifles triumphed reliably as always so that three Esquimaux lay dead and several more were wounded and Back's men ran away shouting to each other: Don't tell the Captain!   and they didn't until Back was in England again, where it was difficult to make amends. In 1835 he set out for the Polar Sea again, and doubtless would have smoothed things over at Point Ogle if it had lain within his convenience; unfortunately he was caught by ice in Frozen Strait, along with Mr Gore, to whom he'd perhaps told the story of this battle during their long low ice-nights; Mr Gore might have told C^apt Crozier or he might not have; in any event, Mr Gore was dead. So let us praise the rifles in all sincerity for their omnipotent workings, which brought it about that the following morning C^apt Crozier awoke early to see the People pulling their bundles of tent-skins on their sled, which was kayak-topped (it came above the men's heads) and then the dog-team dragged it forward. The man in front tested the snow with his pole. There was no distinction between snow and sky. C^apt Crozier began to shout, and the other men opened their eyes listlessly, and he ran up to the People and abased himself on his knees before them making the motions of putting

something in his mouth and repeating over and over the Esquimau word for
seal, but they looked straight ahead and the dog-teams went on and behind
C^apt Crozier some of the men were weeping with the surprising gentle
gurgles of ravens.

Standing hooded in the stream with their necklaces of char, the People
grinned knee-deep, stabbing with their forked fish-spears, which leaned
diagonally into the water like windblown trees. They were at the weir and it
was low tide – plenty to eat. The long low stripe of ridge was flat behind
them.

They folded the fishes to dry on the racks.

A man was seal-hunting in his kayak, as close to the water as if he lived in
it. His head was in a fur collar. His body was in the collar of the kayak, light
on mirror-water.

Vertebrae and pelvises of seals lay scattered in the grass, sand-eaten and
white. The dogs munched them.

Sometimes they heard rifle-shots from the place where the Qaallunaat
were, but they never went there. Sometimes they watched them from where
the Qaallunaat could not see. After awhile the rifle-shots stopped. There was
one who lived for a long time. Every day they watched him sitting on the
beach, with his head in his hands.

VII
King William Island
ᑭᒃᕿᑕᒃ

Meat

1848

On trips either with the natives or without them we acclimatized more and more to a certain level of comfort, in terms of food and sleeping arrangements, and by late September we were eating raw meat quite often.

HEINRICH KLUTSCHAK, *Overland to Starvation Cove: With the Inuit in Search of Franklin 1878–1880* (1881)

In the evening (7:20), the sun was low, so that it could almost have been sunset, and the white west wall of the gorge was tainted with blue shadow. Everything he saw was zebra-striped. The black-on-white of the river rocks reminded him of a French mousse dessert. The lines of bare earth between ridges were as rich as chocolate eclairs. Even the tussocks had lined up on their ridges like goblins going to school. Now as he staggered southward the river was silver and the grass was gold. Snow crunched hard and firm under his step. A mild freezing-point breeze blew, and his shadow went long and narrow and east beside him, halfway up the ridge.

The same muddy ground that the officers had traversed less than a week ago was now pale hard cement, with musk-ox, wolf and rabbit prints embedded in it most prettily. In the sand, an ivory button. He went south. In the middle of that day the low sun dazzled him heatlessly from the edge of a cloud; a bird chirped like squeaking metal, and the dull silver river wound back and forth among drift-rows. The mud-ridges, crinkled like accordions, had not yet frozen completely: they still gave under his boot. To the south and east, the ridges were white-packed –

He saw black blocky shapes on the mud enclosed by a river curve. Musk-oxen. He followed them, swinging westward onto the ridge to approach them downwind, sinking almost to his waist in the snow. They lined up in a row, snorting. He counted almost two dozen of them. They were ivory black in hue, with leonine faces, their horns downcurving like moustaches. Their hair was like a thick black rug doubled and thrown sideways across their backs. As he approached, they growled like lions. He could smell them now, smell the meaty sweat of them.

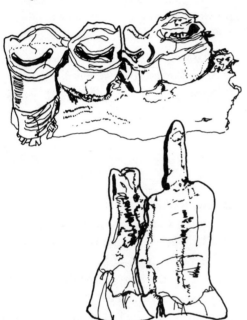

They faced him in a line. On the ridge to the right, a solitary musk-ox roared, waggling his head, and at once the others gathered into a circle facing outward, so that they were a wheel of hornspikes. They watched him; the black bull growled, and the herd galloped back a hundred yards and re-formed. They were very shaggy. Blond manes streamed down their necks. Now. He raised the rifle, whose barrel wobbled unaccountably; something is coming loose, he said to himself. Now. A fat bull's shoulder danced in his sights. Now. Now. Now. At last they ran away, and the ground echoed under them. A banner of snow and dust flared out behind them.

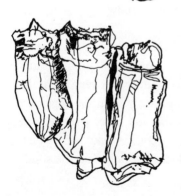

He pointed the rifle straight up, at a cloud like a bull, and drew in the trigger once again, very very gently. Again there was no report. Had the cartridge jammed? He took the lever of the bolt in his hand and tried to draw it back, but could not. It had frozen or rusted shut.

Really he should abandon the rifle as he had everything else. It could not help him anymore. He knew that. But he also knew that if he let it fall and walked away he would begin to feel alone at last. The twin and the triplet were dead. He could not walk all the way to Fort Resolution without eating. As long as he kept the rifle there was always a chance that the sun might thaw it out, or perhaps today or tomorrow when he felt stronger he might fix it. But it was very heavy. If he let it fall he would be able to walk a little faster, a little farther. He would be so light then that he could surely leap farther in the stretches of soft, soft sand. Once he found food he could always come back for it. – Well, let me think about this, he said to himself very seriously, still walking. It won't do to be premature. – He went on walking; the weight of the rifle on his back held him lovingly down to earth.

Then one day a blue hole in the sky blew overhead and it was thirty-five degrees. He could feel the sunshine warming his knees. The toes of his snowy boots began to steam a little as he walked. Down the black and snowy creek was a wall of fog, but it slowly lifted, and presently he could see a lake end-on like a gleaming metal ribbon broken in three places, and the river beneath it was a long gleaming line; it had never gleamed like that before when he looked at it. The hole in the clouds was soft and thick, like a puncture in an eiderdown pillow, and through it the sky seemed as blue and friendly as an English summer. He tramped down across sand-covered ice-dunes and presently saw the fjord as blue as a Sunday bay, and – his heart almost stopped – there were two white yachts at anchor near the first little cape. But in a moment he knew again that they were only icebergs.

He was following another man's footprints which wavered extravagantly. The footprints led south. He accompanied them up an earth-colored ridge topped by two white clouds, and suddenly he was enclosed in a pale broad rainbow arch, with the blue sky all around – better than any church. He followed the rainbow and found the place where the footprints stopped. The corpse lay on its side, with drawn up knees. The man had died shivering. Who was it? Subzero, maybe? He looked into the face for a long time. (Old people are darker, they say, from having been on the ice.) The purple-grey lips stretched like an ellipse of rubber hose around the perimeter of the mouth, in whose crimson depths the yellow teeth were suspended. Blood had frozen on the man's gums. Frost glittered among the stubble on his chin. Ice shone splendidly on the black tussock of his hair. His eyes were half open, but in an unusual way. The upper lids had fallen and frozen to armor his dying sight against everything, but then the lower lids had shrunk away. The grey eyeballs had withered and wrinkled like autumn berries. Taken as a whole, his face seemed to express a drunken and bemused disgust. – You're going to eat my flesh, he seemed to say. I know it and you know it. There's nothing I can do about it, and the thought makes me want to vomit, but all the same it's funny. You never thought you'd be doing this, did you?

He went around a river-bend on a breezy blue day, and the earth had frozen paler and paler; the sunlight rippled gorgeously through ruffled clouds. The cape to the west was earthy-golden in its sun; beyond was an icecap, and then in the channel beyond that, snow must be falling from those purple clouds. Halfway in the elbow before the golden cape were stone rings left by the old Thule culture; red lichen and black lichen brightened them and their attending snowdrifts. They did not mean anything anymore. The waters of the fjord washed in steady shallow waves, blue and happy and indifferent. Inside the rings was nothing but moss and snow.

He saw a rabbit. Easily now he raised the rifle to his shoulder and drew the trigger. The creature exploded; instantly he was on top of it, drinking the hot rich blood that was more nourishing than any soup; he sucked the carcass dry and then cut it open. All at once he felt sick. His stomach had atrophied. He lay on the ground in agony, waiting for the spasms to pass. But all the while he was thinking about the rabbit's heart, still warm though getting cold, and maybe if he was lucky there would be fat on it –

Wolves, the intelligent-eyed, shook their white heads and loped gingerly away from him with hunched heads. They were eating meat. Easing their separate ways soundlessly toward the slope, two more wolves played a game, one watching, the other hiding, then peeking shyly at the first. The one who was watching had a big piece of meat in his jaws. A scrap of blue broadcloth stuck to it. He dragged the meat twenty yards away, eyeing his rival as he chewed. The other was eating something too, nervously, with his tail between his legs.

A wolf hunkered down on the ground to snap a bone. He did not finish his eating, but shot a glance at the man and then urinated anxiously. Dark eyes, dark ears, like rocks in snow – that was what the wolves had. A new wolf, a big one, was gnawing in a snowdrift. He grinned at the man and licked himself, stretching his legs and looking around. He was not quite as white as snow, the way that Arctic foxes were. The man felt this observation to be eerie and also somehow very important, but he did not know how or why.

Vigorously he pushed on south. The rather dapper anthropologist Owen Beattie, who wandered along the same route more than a century later, never found his bones, but he found the remains of the other men, concluding in his popular co-treatise that it had all been eminently comprehensible. *Cannibalizing the trunk of the body would have given them enough strength to push on. The head, arms and legs, easily portable, were carried along as a food supply*★ . . . *Camping on a small spit of land near Booth Point, the same spit of land later visited by the University of Alberta researchers, they ate their last meal.* But such explicitness, useful as it may be to the young forensics students who gaze so eagerly at the blackboard, is not always tactful. We all must reach our own Starvation Cove someday, but do we want to know when or how? – He pushed on south, then, and it was another blue Arctic afternoon with the fjord rippling blue and grey and orange, and clouds bloomed just behind the ridges of long snow promontories, transforming them into volcanoes, and the cool winds of purity blew through his soul.

The ripples and the ice-skins spiraled around each other like lines on a snail shell.

That white cape that kept him company, rising and rising as it neared its end, was scored with steep gullies; there was also on it a pattern, not precisely of scales or hair, but of its own rock-skin, crosshatching it delicately with dark lines of earth, and it was so obvious to him then that everything had its own skin, with living blood beneath; and the reflection of the cape weighed down the amber sun-water but the water reflected its amber in the clouds and a great wedge of amber light arose from the cape's final ridge-edge that sloped into the sea. He stopped when he noticed this and gazed at the cape for a very

★ *I am now of the opinion,* writes the explorer Stefansson, *that heads are generally the best parts of animals, or at least seem so to people who are living on an exclusively meat diet.*

long time because he knew that it was the second part of the teaching which
wolf-whiteness and fox-whiteness had begun.

He heard a hissing noise. The tide was coming in, and very slowly, with a
snakelike energy and remorselessness, it slid new ice-skins over old, at the
rate perhaps of an inch every ten seconds, building up the hard white shelf of
ice on shore.

Soon he had taught himself to regard that noise as silence, in which the
swish of his arms against his sides sounded like murmuring crowds.

He began to walk south again. Long stripes of blue cloud now barred the
grey sky, but an aching gorgeous hole of blue and gold remained in the
direction he was going, and it cast its light on the water.

It became very gloomy, and he felt the warmth seeping out of him, as if he
were bleeding to death: first from the joints of his toes, and the balls of his
feet, which were already going numb, then from his fingers and knees and
belly – so many places now! – from his nose and the small of his back, his
buttocks and shoulders, his neck; – all these places, which once had been his
heartland guarded from the border of cold and death by many buffers of
clothing, were now themselves failing border stations, under simultaneous
attack, struggling and shivering very valiantly, it was true, but the shivering
made him so tired. – If only I had a bar of chocolate, he thought. No, let's
not be greedy. Suppose I found just half a bar of chocolate (well, with the
other half for later), how beautiful it would be to peel back the shiny lead
wrapper like a foreskin, to break a piece off and hear it snap so crisply and
look at the milk powder marblings of the fresh edge. A splinter or two of
chocolate, very thin of course, might fall into my hand from the larger piece.
It would be important to put those splinters in my mouth right away, because
otherwise the heat of my palm would begin to melt them. I'd put them on
my tongue one after the other, and taste them dissolving there. Then I'd take
the piece I'd broken and sink my teeth into it and I *know* that I'd feel warmth
and optimism roaring all through me – but this is a materialistic dream, and
will not be realized.

The gravel was very sharp and white. Occasionally moss or little Arctic
poppies grew between the stones. He watched incessantly for rock-tripe,

withered crowberries, anything. When the sensation in his stomach became too strange he'd gather moss and chew it. Half a mouthful seemed to top him off, but as soon as he spat out the rest he was hungry again.

Pausing momentarily from his southern travels, he climbed a ridge (which took him a very long time) and searched for bodies or footprints. He thought he saw tracks in the northeast, but they were too far away. It would break his heart if there were nothing to eat at the end of them.

Most of them would have followed the coastline as I am doing, he reasoned. They'll keep dying as they go. Sooner or later I'll find another. Then I'll be myself –

At half-past seven in the morning (but it might have been evening) the ridge across the river was shadowed grey like a storm cloud, and the sun was somewhat low over it, shining coolly but still unbearably from a little mound of cloud as white and fluffy as in the storybooks; for the rest the sky was bare blue. A freeze had occurred during the night; every rock was frosted, and the little rills of water that ran out from the moss had iced over. His rucksack was frosted, and so were his boots. The earth had become as hard to the touch as mortar, and even the smallest pebble could scarcely be prised out. (But perhaps it was only that he was weak again.) The little moss-fields with their tussocks, which yesterday had been so wet and spongy as to suck in a boot to the upper with almost every step, still collapsed underfoot, but now they were more like loosely woven mats of brittle yarn. They had not yet frozen solid. The skin of the ice was still thin and new in the streams; he could break it by stepping on it. This gave him a childish satisfaction, that he could still affect something, even if it was only to ruin ice. Little points of frost glittered on the rocks like mica. Across the river, the sand on the alluvial fan was so rich and grey as to approach blackness, and the creeks that ran through it had glittering silver skins. Sunny though it was, and almost windless, a chill began to reach him, beginning with the melting frost inside his boots, caressing his fingertips and the tip of his nose. He could no longer walk quickly enough to warm himself. He had to eat. He had to eat!

He lay down between two boulders to rest, but he was shivering so much that he could not sleep. He was only losing strength. He got up and unloaded his rifle. Then he went on, using the rifle as a staff. Sometimes a spasm of rubbery dizziness beset him, and he would have to stop and cling to the rifle with both hands. It wobbled and spun like a compass needle as he leaned on it. When the spinning stopped, he went on.

Presently the clouds came, and with them a dim dankness, heightened rather than relieved by an ominous yellow glow behind the ridge-notch to the south.

The wind became vicious. His ragged clothes flapped against him with noises like rain, and all night as he sleepwalked south his dreams had rain in them.

In the morning he was still walking, on a plain of stones and pebbles that sloped gently downward, and he came to the River of Cliffs, the cliffs being loose slabs stacked edge on edge into crumbling walls and pillars, all no more than forty feet high, and the river being a brown stream with little black worms or larvae in it, floating drearily behind a snowbank and rounding a bend of gravel bank to where the sun gleamed white and cold through the cold white clouds. Here were fossil snailshells lying loose in the gravel, and fossil clamshells set in frames of stone. He fell to his knees among them and scooped up the black worms in his hands. The water was so cold that his bones ached. Black worms were swimming in a little lake cupped in his palms. He swallowed them and said aloud: Soon I will feel stronger. In this way he swallowed all the worms that he could find, but after awhile his shrunken stomach could not hold any more water, so he began to gather the other worms into a trough of stone, counting and concentrating them like treasures. When he had eaten them all, he went on.

Now he came to the close of the day. It was sunny and cold. He could see his breath. He found a sand dune and tried to dig himself in, but very soon he struck rock and ice. He went on until he found a sheltered place between boulders and there he lay down. There was a spur of rock against his backbone. Some men would have searched for another spot. That was their problem, that they were so fussy. He lay very still, and was happy to feel himself beginning to go to sleep. The worms had helped. All the same, he thought, he would have to find a corpse with good clothing. He slept.

On the beach the next morning he saw a brown crab (every creature here was brown or reddish-brown, except the birds), and he killed it with a stone and ate it raw. The meal refreshed him very much, and he strode on at what seemed to him a very speedy pace, thumping the buttstock of his rifle merrily upon the ground. Very soon he expected to discover the third thing in his chain of logical secrets. The rounded gravel hills seemed almost gentle to him now because their snow-shirts gentled them, rendering them grey and white and docile like soft things. It was not very long before he saw another body on the horizon. Its blue broadcloth shirt was more vivid than the sky. It lay full length like a sleeping man, with the head upon the arm. No breath; he'd verified that each dead nostril was hoarfrosted like a tiny white Arctic rose. No pain; that went without saying. He approached it with calm happiness, and saw in the rocks beside it a second body not yet dead. This other corpse opened its eyes as he bent over it, and it said something. He did not understand what the dead man said. It did not matter. He turned away and went to the one who lay on the gravel. First he opened the rucksack and searched it for food. There was nothing, of course. The man had not even kept his rifle. He rolled the man on his back and began to unbutton the shirt, which he meant to wear over his own. The ribs made yellow stripes upon the blue, blue chest. Long ago he might have thought this terrible. But nothing was terrible to him anymore. He had long since reached his haven. He thrust his blade in and began to cut out the heart, hoping to find a little fat. Then he heard the other dead man make a sort of croaking sound and stagger to his feet, glaring and clawing at the air. He turned and waited. The dead man began to walk toward him, chittering. Then he fell and was still forever. Eagerly the one who lived bent over him, made an incision, and drank the hot blood from his throat. He would never have killed another man for food. He would have starved before he did that. But when a man had just died and his blood was fresh, it was a crime to waste it. At once he felt strong and vital again. He cut off some meat and ate until he was satisfied. Then he dragged both the carcasses to an opening in the rock where the wolves could not get at them. He felt very warm in his new clothes. He lay down so happily and slept.

When he awoke the crystal of his watch had been smashed and he did not know whether he had slept an hour, a day or much longer. He took off the watch and threw it among the rocks. Then he cut off all the meat he could carry and continued south.

When we ride the wheel of fortune to the top, most of us fail to see that we are there, and continue to long for something still higher, even as the ferris wheel gives another lurch and we begin to descend back into wretched nothingness. But *he* knew. In the Arctic he had become wise. His belly ached most joyously with fullness. He was alive a little longer, and could see the sun and the ice. Perhaps he would discover the third important thing, and then he could wait upon the fourth. He had no yearning anymore to reach Fort Resolution, because he had no expectation of reaching it. He did not even want chocolate anymore.

In the sand, another button.

In the sand, a Bible.

In the sand, a red tin unopened, stamped with Goldner's patent.

Now here was quite a crowd of them at Starvation Cove, lying dead and dying. They'd raised great cairns and put blank paper inside. They'd dragged the longboats crazily up hills, laden with sponges, books, scented soaps, lead rods . . . None opened their eyes. Thirty-two years afterward, the Schwatka Expedition found a few relics in this area – a Caucasian skull in excellent preservation, and various fragments of discarded wood in Inuit camps which had first been ship-flesh, then the whittlings and workings of Inuit tools, and now ended up as tinder and fuel for Schwatka's men. A man named Eskimo Joe, who was in their employ, reported that he had once found many bones here, and clothing, shoes, boots, buttons, even a silver medal in eternal commemoration of the launch of an English steamer by His Royal Highness Prince Albert, two years before Franklin departed the River Thames forever.

Franklin Skeletons FOUND TO DATE

SCALE OF MILES (APPROX.)
25   0   25   50

NOTE: Finds assigned the conjectural date of 1849 are based on later accounts by Inuit informants to European searchers.

↑ To the North Magnetic Pole

Boothia Peninsula

VICTORIA STRAIT

The icebound ships

╫╫╫? 1849? Cape Felix
╫ 1848
Point Victory
† 1879 John Irving

Cape Jane Franklin
Franklin Point
SEAL BAY 1848

Point Le Vesconte   † 1879

JAMES ROSS STRAIT

ARCTIC OCEAN

EREBUS BAY
Little Point   ╫╫ 1879
○ The "Boat Place"
†† 1859
╫╫╫╫ 1849 (?)
King William Island

Cape Crozier   † 1879

╫ 1930

TERROR BAY

RAE STRAIT

STORIS PASSAGE
† 1859 Peglar(?)
† 1849 Le Vesconte
† 1931 † 1973
† 1869 † 1981
1879

1849(?)
╫╫╫ (one mistakenly identified by Inuit as Sir John Ross)

╫╫╫╫ 1931
SIMPSON STRAIT
╫╫╫╫╫╫╫
╫╫╫╫╫╫╫ 1931
Point Richardson
Point Ogle

QUEEN MAUD GULF

1849(?), 1880, 1923, 1936
Adelaide Peninsula
Starvation Cove

North America
† 1879
CHANTREY INLET
↙ To Back's Great Fish River

Hall buried skeletons; Schwatka buried skeletons; and now the relics are in lost graves or in museum cases. Perhaps it is for this reason that when I think of Franklin artifacts no image actually associated with Franklin comes to mind; instead I see what he saw when Reepah showed him the old knife she'd found once when she was ten years old walking across the tundra and spied it, picked it up and said: *Ohhh!* – a blade of some kind of pitted iron, pitted almost to shimmering, an L-shaped handle of caribou bone, which was discolored to an off-sheen of the greenish-white lichen, and it was fastened to the blade by means of four iron nails in a Y pattern. The blade itself was not sharp, except at the very tip. He ran his finger along it and it was no thinner or sharper than the topmost edge. The entire blade, in other words, was of exactly the same thickness, as if it had perhaps been fashioned from some sheet of metal left by a European. Were the nails obtained from the same source? They were the same red-brown color; they were pitted the same way. The split in the handle into which the blade had been fitted was still well closed at the top, but on the bottom it had worn and widened so that the blade could be pivoted squeaking from one of the topmost nails. This gave the knife a strange "intentionality," as they used to say in literary criticism, for the blade and handle were of almost equal weight, and that balanced movement seemed what the tool might have been made for. Certainly it was hard to imagine cutting with it – it was so old and eerie and strange! The handle was smooth; the blade was pitted smooth, and there it was, a survival like a coelacanth, in Reepah's house –

There was a vertical red line on Reepah's forehead. He traced it with his finger and asked what it was.

From knife,   she said.
From you?
No. Somebody.
A boy or a girl?
Woman.
Why?
I was crazy.
What happened?
I was crazy, I said.

Once he'd told her he loved milkshakes and she asked what they were. –
Oh, he explained, they mix milk and ice cream together, and other things.

It's good?

Very good.

The next time he came there she'd spooned some ice cream into a can of
evaporated milk and added water. – *Bad!* she said, making a face . . .

He loved to play with the baby, who loved him, and screamed with grief
when he was gone. The baby was always hungry, too. Hungry first and
foremost for milk, which Reepah could not give him anymore; that was why
she put sugar water in his bottle; hungry secondarily for love, or at least love
as it is defined by a baby: eternal amusement with movement and warmth
and gentle brightness –

But he'd tasted Reepah's milk once, when he kissed her breast and it came
out, hot and sweet and whitish-yellow.

He was regressing again. He confessed it. It had been a lie to say that he did
not think about chocolate. Nor was chocolate all that he thought about. He
thought of sausages cooking, swimming in their clear spicy grease, nicely
browned, filling the house with the good warm smell of meat, his platoon of
eggs ready to go into action in that grease when the sausages were almost
done. Maybe an onion, too. He could see the yolks round and firm like Jane's
unmothering breasts, while the whites sizzled and crisped in the grease. He
could see the sausages cooking and hear their sizzle and feel the tiny hot
drops of grease leaping joyously out to strike his forehead; he could smell the
meat and almost taste it, but he could not feel the fullness in his belly. Meat
was the most important thing. What was he or any other person, any animal,
but meat? What was reproduction? The manufacture of new meat, veal. How
could he stay alive? By eating meat. If Jane were lying dead here he would
cheerfully eat her fatty breasts. That was the trouble with these others at
Starvation Cove. Meat was, or ought to be, made up of a certain proportion
of fat. The best steaks were marbled with it. A girl with a good figure was a

girl with fat in the right places. But the ones who lay here were lean and gristly, frozen grey and skinny and hard. The third important thing was definitely meat. What were the first two? The sun and the ice. Meat was more important.

Following the river inland and south, he saw the ridges getting higher, and the river ran a little bit shallower, in thin braids whose ice-skin crackled in the wind, and then gradually the sun came out and the river pebbles got richer and richer in color and there were patches of blue sky ahead and he came round a riverbend and saw musk-oxen grazing on the tongue of moss and mud before the next bend; they were squarish black shapes, and behind them he saw the six snow-cones of the ice-fields rising broad into the low blue sky. The peaks must be an optical illusion; he knew perfectly well that there were no mountains here. The musk-oxen walked low to the ground, in their strange awkward seesawing of shoulders and hindquarters. He began to weep at the sight of so much meat. He raised the rifle and sighted carefully on the shoulder of a succulent female, remembering something that Reepah had told him: A woman's medicine is the fat of a male seal. A man's medicine is the fat of a female seal.   He could smell the fat of the animals, rich and sweaty and delicious. He stood sighting very carefully, knowing that as soon as he pulled the trigger the rifle would save his life.

Here ends the

Sixth Dream

Straight Shots

1741–1991

Further History of the Inuit
ca. 1960–1991

I still make caribou-hide parkas but no one wants to wear them.

SARAH BACON (1982)

A man was hunting a seal. He stood waiting on the frozen sea. Another man was watching television. An old lady was sewing sealskin kamiks. Two little boys were playing Chinese checkers. Their elder brother came into the house and pulled his kamiks off. On the table he quietly laid down things he'd found in a glacier: a mass of rusty nails fused into a single crystal, the rusty lid of a tin can stamped with the signs of Goldner's patent. In the school next door, the children listened to their Elders telling stories. Then that hour was up, and a white lady made them sing songs about Halloween pumpkins. (The nearest pumpkin patch was a long way south.) A man was hunting a seal. He shot and missed. It was night, and families were going to church. They sang hymns in Inuktitut; they prayed for the health of the Queen of England. A boy and a girl were sniffing. Their faces turned red and they laughed. He touched her; she pulled away; he punched her down. She had a baby, and brought her up alone. The bulldozers built new houses. An old man was happy because he had dentures. He could still eat; he wouldn't starve to death. A lady was happy because she had rented every room in her house to Japanese tourists. A man was hunting a seal. He waited on the hard cold sea. He waited a little longer, and his toes became cold. He got back on his skidoo and went home. He didn't need to hunt anyway. He went inside, laid down his sealskin mitts, took off his parka (which was made in Ottawa), removed his army boots, and opened the inner

door to the warm room where the television was. There was a pot of caribou
stew on the stove and some bannock in the refrigerator. The man was happy.
He watched television and did not think about anything.

Greenland 1987

He looked at the snapshot of her smiling so proudly over her downed caribou
and the midnight sun came through the windows and he longed to trade his life
for hers because he knew so little about her that she seemed absolutely free.

How far do you walk in a day when you hunt caribou?

Oh, we walk seventeen . . .   – She touched the dial of her watch.

Hours?

Yes.

Do you get tired?

No. I never get tired in my whole life. It's my way of life, you know.

There is no money here!   the drunk shouted.   Greenpeace knocked out the
selling of sealskins, but we *never* took the baby seal. So the money is like this.
(He squeezed a space between two fingers almost into nothingness.)   – And the
fish we catch are small fish, so the money for the fish is like this.   (Again the
vanishing trick.)

Angîuk, the little granddaughter, who was too shy to come near Captain
Subzero, shrieked for delight as she threw her coins on the rug and then snatched
them, and everyone laughed, and her grandmother (who had gone to sea in an
umiak at age four, and now lived in a Blok flat with oranges in a dish on the
living room table, and an issue of *Familie Journal* [ILLUSTRERET] arriving every
week) came from the kitchen crying   *Angîuk, Angîuk!*   with one hand behind
her back, and Angîuk came running with her brown bangs flashing and took a
chocolate sucker from her grandmother's hand and tried to tear the wrapper but
couldn't; her grandmother tried to help her but Angîuk didn't want that; she
pulled away and finally did do it herself and everybody clapped –

Is it good that the Danes are here?   asked Subzero.

We are all intermixed now,   the Inuk girl said.   I don't like it when someone says: This is a Danish country; you must go!   or when someone says: This is an Inuit country; you must go!   I don't like it. All are welcome.

☼ ☼ ☼

After supper everyone played catch with the boy until he screamed with laughter and then chased the dog and sat out on the long yellow grass, looking at the low sun. (There was choral music on the tape player; everyone sang along.) One of the men worked the bolt of his rifle a few times and sighted down the barrel. A woman sat trimming a frayed stitch on the scabbard of a knife. After awhile everyone set out to shoot the other five sheep.

Down across the river, they jumped over a white stone and up a steep boulder, then up a windy green shoulder between two inlets of the fjord. It was very twilighty, very lonely and breezy. Where they had come from the water was silver. The inlet ahead was pale blue and filled with sandbars. Ahead on the ridge was a grey-green tongue of rock, behind which Nansen had pitched his tent in 1888 before crossing the inland ice, which was just over the next ridge. Everyone sprawled on the ridge, laughing in the breeze, with their guns resting on the

tundra. The SUN now poured gold out of Herself into the fjord behind. She was very good to look at.

The Greenlanders crept along just below the ridgetop, peering carefully over every rise, and the world was green and orange and grey. – *Aaiee!* a woman cried softly in delight. *Sava!** She pointed. There was a white dot on the far side of the ridge. Everyone smiled. The hunters began to creep. After a long time, the white dot leaped away. – *Haare!* everyone laughed. It was only a rabbit. But a little farther on, Henriette grinned and motioned to them to duck. Everybody smiled at everybody; everybody was so happy. Three *savas.* They whispered and smiled at Subzero. They lay on the soft tundra while the hunters crept down behind the incredibly long shadows of the rifles. A woman made the motion of pushing something up her ass with her knife, and they all giggled silently. Finally she took a roll of toilet paper out of Henriette's pack, wrapped a length around her hands and went off as quietly as she could. Still there was no sound from beyond the ridge. The woman came back. The dog whimpered softly. – He crazy about reindeer, the woman whispered with a big smile. – Finally she took him down the hill, so as not to alert the prey. Everyone waited.

Then the first shot echoed through the valley. It did not have the whizzing power of the others, because it was only the scaring shot, and it came from opposite the other hunters. The wide-faced woman and the boy ran along the ridge laughing because there would be food; and soon they were yelling happily: *Five!* The hunters had killed them all.

Soon the carcasses had been dragged up to a high ledge in view of a little lake, and the girls purred over the dead lamb, stroking its fur, saying *awwww* as blood ran out of its mouth. They cut the udder out of the first ewe, and all the girls squirted hot milk into each others' mouths.

Iqaluit 1987

We went out New Year's, last New Year, the Inuk said. It was my brother and four of his friends and myself. We went out on three skidoos. We headed north of Frobisher about twenty miles. It was half a day to get there. On the way there we ended up stashing the gas. One of us was taking the gas; the other took the rifles and stuff. One skidoo was too old. It couldn't take nothing. The fellow in charge of the gas forgot where he left it. We shot a caribou and wounded it, but then we couldn't find our knives to finish it off. I don't know

---

* "Sheep!"

what happened to those. We almost broke our rifle butts on the caribou's head and it was still alive, tongue hanging, breathing heavily. We tried hitting it with the skidoo and we hit it three times. It was still alive. Top of the line skidoo, a Yamaha. Skidoo was covered with blood. So we finally tied a rope around its neck and dragged it to the place where we were going to need it. It was finally dead by then. That's the last time I'm going hunting with young guys.

A Morality Play

1990

It couldn't be the right line since it wasn't the party line. Perhaps it will be the right one tomorrow . . .

MANÈS SPERBER, *The Burned Bramble*
(1949)

Characters

Commissioners

MR. ROBERT E. SKELLY
MR. KEN HUGHES, *the Chairman*
MR. ROBERT NAULT

Witnesses

MR. SAMWILLIE ELIJASIALUK
Inukjuak Representative, Inuit Tapirisat of Canada
MR. ANDREW IQALUK
Inukjuak Representative, Inuit Tapirisat of Canada
MR. ALLIE SAALUVINIQ
Resolute Bay Representative, Inuit Tapirisat of Canada
MR. JOHN AMAGOALIK
President, Inuit Tapirisat of Canada
MS. MARTHA FLAHERTY
Inuit Tapirisat of Canada
MR. BOB PILOT
*Retired RCMP officer; former Deputy Commissioner
of the Northwest Territories*

Scene I

SCENE   Room 209, West Block of the House of Commons in Ottawa. It is 6:00 p.m. on a March evening, and darkness is already coming. No doubt there are windows and chairs and a pitcher of water, but I have no special conception of how Room 209 looks, and in that I suspect I am doing Room 209 no injustice. The members of the Standing Committee on Aboriginal Affairs have had their dinner and so are ready to hear testimony in all patience. Tonight, nine Inuit have come to talk about the relocation. They will all be heard by the Committee, but not by us, because this is not the bound white volume of minutes that you are reading here, but only an excerpt or two, voices soft and difficult to keep like a handful of ptarmigan feathers in the wind.

All the witnesses speak in Inuktitut, which is translated by an interpreter. The Commissioners speak in English.

ELIJASIALUK   I am Samwillie Elijasialuk. I was one of the ones sent to Grise Fiord. When we landed there, we were put to work unloading drums and coal for the police. We were told that we would not be paid for this work. We did a tremendous amount of work over the years, doing all kinds of jobs. I have not forgotten the dog-team driving that I have done.

The police used to treat people there thus: There was a tiny little trading post there. There are many things that have caused me hurt. I now have no shame about telling how police used to say, "You can trade only after I use your woman." They used to do this, and I still hurt about it. There are so many wrongs.

I have taped all this in the truth, and not in lies.

IQALUK   I am Andrew Iqaluk. I have also lived over there. It seemed only that I was leaving for a place only thirty miles distant.

SAALUVINIQ   I am Allie E9-1860. I am identified as such, although I am Allie Saaluviniq. All these other people also have such numbers, E9 numbers. I was very small when we moved from Inukjuak. But I do remember when we were landed, a large boulder that I can relate to, and how very cold we were. Some had to be warmed by dogs.

I do want to say that when we were being prepared to be moved out of Inukjuak, we were told that we would all be located in one place. Then, when we had just about arrived, our people were told they had to be separated. My mother died a young woman, having never seen her relatives again.

AMAGOALIK   I remember we were all on the deck of the *C. D. Howe.* All the women started to cry. And when women start to cry the dogs join in. I was six years old then, standing on the deck of the ship. The women were crying, the dogs were howling, and the men had to huddle to decide who is going to go where. We were dumped on the beach.

FLAHERTY   My name is Martha Flaherty. I also used to have the identification number E9-1900. I was five years old. They cut the hair of all the children. I was the only one whose hair was not cut, and only because I put up a big fight. I was then the only one left with hair. They cut the hair of everybody, male and female.

When we finally arrived there, it was as if we had landed on the moon, it was so bare and desolate! There was no food and no shelter. Even my mother was out alone trying to hunt for ptarmigans, even though she was a woman.

ELIJASIALUK   I shall never forget how our mothers used to cry all night. They were faced with never seeing their relatives ever again. Their lives lost their purpose and they lost their minds. That is what my mother went through. My adoptive father did not even last a year there. He was led to believe there would be plenty of caribou and plenty of musk-oxen. When he came to realize that he would never see his relatives again, his heart stopped beating.

FLAHERTY   I was only a small child at the time, but I know which people were used for this purpose. These people did not have food. They would only be given food after being used for sexual purposes. I will also say later about garbage, and how we lived off the garbage of the police.

ELIJASIALUK   There was no flour. There was no tea. We had access to those only if we caught any foxes. That trading post was tiny. Then the representative of government says: "You can buy only if I first have you sexually." I am disgusted by this. That is all I say for now.

AMAGOALIK   We spent a lot of time in the dumps, because we had to go there for a good part of our food, our clothing, and our shelter – in the white man's dump.

I also remember that my father used to send a bit of cash to my brother, who was in the hospital for five years. The RCMP used to come to our

house asking if we had any letters. My father said   yes, we have a letter;
here it is.   The RCMP used to ask,   did you enclose any money?   Of
course my father said   yes, I enclosed $2.   The RCMP used to write on
the outside of the envelope: $2. We found those letters in the dump, too –
opened and the money gone.

I remember being very excited when any military airplane arrived in
Resolute, because we knew that the people on those airplanes had box
lunches, food. We used to rush to the dump five miles away in the middle
of winter to get those boxes of half-finished sandwiches.

SKELLY   This is the most serious matter that I have heard in this House in
the eleven years that I have been a Member of Parliament. If I can sum-
marize what I understand you to have said, you have told us of forcible
confinement and slave labor. You have told us about physical and sexual
abuse. You have told us about misrepresentation and outright lying. You
have laid before this committee serious accusations of serious criminal
wrongdoing, and serious criminal wrongdoing on the part of the national
law enforcement agency. You have talked about deaths of members of
your community that could only be construed as death by criminal
negligence.

As a Member of Parliament, I am just completely appalled at what you
have laid before this committee. But from what I have seen in my eleven
years, and previous to that, the government evades and obfuscates its
responsibility in any way it can.

I do not think you will get justice from this committee.

Scene II

SCENE   *This time we've achieved Room 112-N in the Centre Block. It's a
June evening, a little later than before, because they didn't start until 7:30 and
they first heard witnesses from the National Aboriginal Network on Disability
and adjourned to drink coffee and empty bladders and stare out at city lights
and summer darkness, darkness as dark as a water-sky –*

THE CHAIRMAN   Order, please. We are now considering a different issue,
following up on the question of Grise Fiord. I welcome Mr. Bob Pilot to
the meeting this evening.

PILOT (*speaks in English throughout*)   Thank you very much, Mr. Chairman and
members of the committee. It has been a long day for all of you and for

myself. I will try to be brief but at the same time provide as much information as I can to your committee.

All of the Inuit men were employed to assist in the building of the new detachment. All buildings were closed by early October, and we again assisted the Inuit men in their annual walrus hunt.

There were times when the supply in the store did run short, and I mean items such as sugar, tea or flour, the basic staples. This usually happened just before ship time, so the RCMP would lend whatever supplies they could to the store and have them returned after ship time.

Personally, I have only pleasant memories of my years at Craig Harbour and Grise Fiord.

There was never any doubt in my mind that the Inuit had been made a promise that should they wish to return to Port Harrison the government would take them back. During my term as regional director in Baffin and later as the deputy commissioner, I attempted to have the federal government recognize this commitment. But I was always told that the government had made no such promise.

In conclusion, Mr. Chairman, I do understand through newspaper reports that an allegation was made of sexual abuse and trading of food for sex by the RCMP. I would like to go on record as saying I never heard of such a thing happening during my time at Craig Harbour or Grise Fiord. I know Martha Flaherty extremely well. I bounced her on my knee when she was a kid. Her family lived in Grise Fiord. In 1956 we moved to Grise Fiord and lived there. I know the people, and I was shocked by this statement. Since that came out in the paper I got lots of phone calls from academics wanting to study Grise Fiord and wanting to know what my sexual habits were. So I felt I should really go on record.

NAULT   Now we are told and your submission is basically that everything was good and well, and people were well fed and happy.

Why should these people come in front of us and say that it was a very harsh and difficult life, and that they were in fact barely surviving as people? I am looking for some input on those types of statements that were made and that were quite shocking to us all.

PILOT   It was quite shocking to myself. I cannot speak again for why such statements were made, and again it could have happened before my time, which I had never heard of, and it could have happened after my time. What I want to speak to is that it did not happen during my time.

Just to answer your question, no, I never saw the people hungry. As I say, wildlife was good and they were good hunters.

SKELLY One of the things mentioned in the testimony by one of the Inuit was that when they were removed from Inukjuak one of the members of the community had tuberculosis and that by the time they had finished everyone who had moved there had tuberculosis. There was no medicine and no medical treatment. Do you have any experience or information about that?

PILOT The only Inuit who had tuberculosis when I was at Craig Harbour and Grise Fiord was a man by the name of Larry, and he had been medically evacuated by ship to Montreal.

SKELLY This is testimony from Marcusai Patsuak, and he says:

[*He reads the testimony aloud. You can imagine it well enough.*]

PILOT You are talking about Resolute Bay. There were two different situations here.

SKELLY Yes.

PILOT Many a time when I would go to Lindstrom Peninsula to minister to any sick Inuit person, I would stay with the family in the hut and I found it comfortable. Again, you have to qualify it; it was primitive. It was like stepping back in the pages of time and you have to think of it in that light.

SKELLY The differences in perception that come up from the presentations of the witnesses are very interesting. The witnesses were literally in tears the night they were here. You say you did not see them in hunger or in difficult circumstances and you knew of no abuse. But I am wondering to what degree that might have occurred, that simply the communication in many cases was not there.

PILOT We did not see them very often at Grise Fiord, there is no doubt about that. They would come, as I said, to the detachment to trade. My memories are happy ones. I have some lovely movies of the Inuit dancing, square dancing I guess you would call it, in the RCMP detachment at Grise Fiord.

❀ ❀ ❀

We don't really need a Scene III, do we? The Committee did present a resolution, asking the Government of Canada to respectfully apologize for its wrongdoings against the people of Grise Fiord and Resolute, and suggesting that it consider awarding financial compensation to them. The resolution was rejected.

Further History of the Rifles
1741–1991

It is becoming widely recognized that Newfoundland offers the serious bear hunter a unique opportunity . . . because of historically low hunting pressures (and possibly a genetic predisposition to large body size) many very large bears are available . . . This recognition of the black bear as a predator has greatly improved his status, and this fact, in combination with the planned promotion of bear hunting, will almost certainly lead to increased participation in this activity . . . Now is the time to hunt black bears in Newfoundland, while license sales are unlimited, seasons are long, and really big bears are common.

> GOVERNMENT OF NEWFOUNDLAND
> AND LABRADOR, *Newfoundland and
> Labrador: Hunting and Fishing Just
> Waiting for You* (1986)

What is there to say about the rifles, finally? Isn't it a lazy conceit that blames them for so many problems? They had nothing to do with the relocations, after all. We can't prove that they caused starvation or game reduction. Reepah didn't have to shoot herself; she could have done it another way. Just as the first time you say I love you in a new language you feel as powerfully as the first time you said it in your own, so the hypothesis of rifles seems compelling at first, but there are always new languages to learn . . . Blame it all on the whales, for instance. Without them, who'd have come to bother anybody? And there are other explanations, as logical or absurd as you please; raid them all, like Reepah's brother who climbed the cliff and took a hundred and fifty murre eggs. Answers are commonly considered wholesome, like some pale green lichen with a peppery aftertaste. They distinguish the known from the unknown; they mark blanknesses on charts of the Passage; they prevent us from being confused and invaded by our grave-twins. We must differentiate to believe; we ought to believe before we act. And what we believe! In our minds we truly believe in the difference between summer and winter. Why then are some Arctic islands, whose midnights now begin to partake of sunset along the great horizon from east to west, set here to absorb the light like sponges, when others, like the one near which Franklin died, are ever fogbound, cliff-locked, bereft? . . . And when you explain, you believe that your bars of thought-shadow have been moving one behind the next across a white plain; in fact the plain was slush and ice-fragments covered with snow, and the shadow-bars were broad low waves, like rolls of fat, undermining that apparent solidity which gave way – gracefully, I grant you, but unsettlingly; it's unsettling to watch the shadow-bars crawl toward you, and see chunks of ice sway before them on the plain, as if the shadow-bars came on and on and on out of grey vagueness and open water which is sometimes indigo and sometimes a rushing stream of gold. What is good and what is bad? Some people answer by dreaming a world of secrets; some never answer; some live in a sunny snowy day with sleet pelting and pattering in little gusts and the white cape growing wings of grey cloud while the sun gilds the open water so far away from the ships or makes it indigo or sea-green, and the wind sings songs to the same iceberg with the morose blue face and the icicle hanging from its nose – a perfect day, really, the snow cushion-soft but not too deep, not too sticky, not sticky at all; the day wisps itself in blue shadow-trails in the windstream; stand still and the day would bury your ankles like sand; but the sky is so frank and open where Reepah used to walk along the shelf of snow-covered ice and saw seals bobbing their heads and playing; the wind numbed her right cheek and she slapped it, laughing.

Straight Shots
1741–1991

Give me the means to get to such Northern Lands & Waters as are unvisited by civilized man & then I will be in my great glory.

> CHARLES FRANCIS HALL, journal
> entry (1864)

Just as in the Arctic the sun may ride fiercely golden in the sky of an autumn August midnight, but below the sun is an unbroken floor of silver and golden clouds, and below the clouds the sky is iron-grey and the sea is steel-grey and ugly white icebergs groan and chatter like teeth and Cornwallis Island is dank and low and green with algae in that tarnished mist, just so life is different above and below; just so fate is different before the barrel and behind the hammer, the hammer that falls so heavily upon the firing pin, the firing pin that pierces the shell and ignites the primer by friction, the primer that ignites the powder, the powder that explodes and throws the bullet out of the shell, the bullet that rushes down the barrel and into sunny air and penetrates the caribou's shoulder as easily as it would a cloud . . . But I say to you who are strangers – not to Reepah, who danced with me laughing in her muddy kamiks, jumping with me upon the echoing disco floor, sneaking one more beer and one more beer until her face turned red and she started to scream, Reepah who loved caribou and had nothing to feed her baby – I say to you others: As you crouch there with the stock against your shoulder, pray for the caribou. Pray that your shot is not true.

S cattered throughout Arctic America are traces of these traditional caribou hunts: long rows of stones set on edge or piled on top of one another.

NATIONAL GEOGRAPHIC SOCIETY
(1974)

Glossaries

Glossaries

Note

I have tried to define every term which may not be readily comprehensible. (1) Because this is a novel, not a treatise in linguistics, the words are entered as they appear in the text, not necessarily in their nobly correct and inertial forms. In the text, however, their form is never the result of my own caprice, but of someone else's. (2) Sources for terms are not in any way exhaustive; they merely indicate where I have encountered them. Thus, for instance, it is entirely possible that a term labeled as Canadian Inuktitut may be Greenlandic as well. I have tried to be as specific as possible in referencing Inuktitut words (e.g., *Pond Inlet Inuktitut* as opposed to *Canadian Inuktitut*).★ (3) The same word is often spelled a variety of ways in this book (e.g., "Eskimos" and "Esquimaux," "Akaicho" and "Akaitcho"). However, these differences are not as marked as in previous volumes, since spellings had begun to become standardized during the period in which this book is set. As always, every spelling is taken from a primary source. Rather than be a totalitarian, I have preferred to let the variants stand in all their charm. (4) The *j* sound in Inuktitut is pronounced like the German *j* or English *y*.

★ All Ungava Inuktitut words listed are from the *Dictionnaire des infixes de l'Esquimau de l'Ungava*, Lucien Schneider, OMI (Québec: Ministère des Richesses Naturelles, Direction générale du Nouveau-Québec, Études de la langue esquimaude; n.d. but *ca.* 1979).

1
Glossary of Personal Names

Akaicho [*Copper Indian*; lit., "Big Foot"] "The chief of the tribe" – Franklin. He was a guide to the expedition of 1819–21; he and his people saved the explorers from starvation. At that time he had three wives and one son. Franklin estimated the number of males in his band as about forty. (Also: *Akaitcho*.)

Augustus See **Tattannoeuck**.

Sir George Back [*English*] Accompanied **Franklin** on his first three expeditions. On a subsequent expedition which he commanded (1833–4), he became the first to navigate the Great Fish River (now called the Back River) from Great Slave Lake to the Polar Sea. It was hope of reaching this river and ascending it to Fort Resolution on the Great Slave Lake that impelled the men of the final Franklin Expedition south in 1848. In 1836 he commanded the *Terror*, which later sailed to the Antarctic with Sir James **Ross** and then was assigned to the final Franklin Expedition. Back was badly beset by ice that time. In 1839 he was knighted.

Sir John Barrow [*English*] Second Secretary of the Admiralty. Beginning in 1817, Barrow launched expeditions of a number of Arctic explorers, including **Parry**, **Ross**, **Back** and **Franklin**. Regarding the attainment of the Northwest Passage he wrote: "The Admiralty having done so much, it would be most mortifying and not very creditable to let another Naval Power complete what we have begun." Hence the final Franklin Expedition.

Sir Francis Beaufort [*English*] Admiral and Arctic explorer, he invented the Beaufort scale of wind conditions at sea which is still occasionally used today. A friend of **Franklin**'s.

Thomas Blanky [*English*] Acting Master of HMS *Terror* on the last Franklin Expedition. Blanky, who had served on several whaling ships, was also Ice-Master of the *Terror*, meaning that his duty included giving counsel on travel and navigation through ice.

Cascathry [*Copper Indian*] A guide to Franklin's Second Expedition of 1819–22. Father to **Greenstockings**. His wife suffered from a basal cell carcinoma of the nose, of which she died at the close of the expedition. (Also: *Keskarrah*.)

Captain Francis Rawdon Moira Crozier [*English*] In command of HMS *Terror* on the final Franklin Expedition, Crozier was an Arctic veteran, having served with **Parry**

and **Ross** . . . "it seems probable that Crozier would have acquired a working knowledge of Inuktitut" – William Barr, in Klutschak, ix. In 1848 Crozier dictated a note to **Fitzjames** in the margins of a paper left by **Gore**. The message read in part: "HM's Ships Terror and Erebus were deserted on 22nd April, 5 leagues N.N.W. of this, having been beset since 12th September 1846 . . . Sir John **Franklin** died on 11th June 1847; and the total loss by deaths in the Expedition has been to this date 9 officers and 15 men . . . [We] start on tomorrow, 26th [April], for **Back**'s Fish River."

Charles F. Des Voeux [*English*]   One of the Mates of HMS *Erebus* on the final Franklin Expedition. He co-signed the Admiralty paper with **Gore** at Victory Point.

The Finnlander Kid [?*Alaskan*]   A reclusive explorer and prospector mentioned in Jan Welzl's *The Quest for Polar Treasures*. Given the often suspect descriptions in this book, it is possible that he never existed. I have made him into a member of Franklin's crew, a counterpart of Skofte Carrion-Crow in *The Ice-Shirt*.

Captain James Fitzjames [*English*]   In command of HMS *Erebus* on the final Franklin Expedition. This was his first time in the Arctic. He had, however, ascended the Euphrates in a steamer.

Lady Jane Franklin [*English*]   Second wife of Captain **Franklin**. Exhausted her fortune in expeditions to rescue him.

Captain Sir John Franklin [*English*]   Born 1786. Made four expeditions to the Arctic (if we include the first, of 1814, in which he was only second in command). Died on the final journey, in 1847. "He was a plodding naval officer, lacking imagination or insight, yet he was doggedly determined, calm in danger, and cheerfully bouyant" – C. Stuart Houston.

Lieutenant Graham Gore [*English*]   One of the lieutenants of HMS *Erebus* on the final Franklin Expedition, Gore had served with **Back** in the Arctic on the *Terror* in 1836–7. In 1847 Gore signed the only written record of that Expedition ever found, in a cairn near Victory Point, King William Island. Gore reported, "All well." A year later, **Crozier**'s grim note on the same piece of paper referred to him as "the late Commander Gore."

Greenstockings [*Copper Indian*]   So named by the English; ". . . considered by her tribe to be a great beauty. Mr. **Hood** drew an accurate portrait of her, although her mother was averse to her sitting for it" – Franklin. Mr. Hood also got her pregnant (1820), and he and Mr. **Back** aimed to fight a duel over her. She was fifteen at the time, and had had two husbands. In the 1823 census of Fort Resolution was listed "the orphaned daughter of Lt. Hood."

Samuel Hearne [*English*]   The first known white explorer of the Coppermine River all the way down to its mouth. **Franklin** was to follow in his footsteps half a century later. "Between 1769 and 1772 Samuel Hearne explored more than a quarter of a million square miles of the tundra plains that cap this continent . . . Hearne was the Marco Polo of the Barren Lands" – Mowat, *Tundra*, p. 28.

Lieutenant George H. Hodgson [*English*]   Served under **Crozier** on HMS *Terror* on the final Franklin Expedition.

Midshipman Robert Hood [*English*] Accompanied **Franklin** on his second Arctic expedition of 1819–21. Kept a journal and made a number of beautiful paintings. Fell in love with **Greenstockings**, by whom he had a daughter. Shot in the head 1821, by **Michel Teroahauté**, one of the hired voyageurs who had become a cannibal.

Lieutenant John Irving [*English*] Served under **Crozier** on HMS *Terror* on the final Franklin Expedition. Aged thirty, he had had four other postings, including one to the Indies. In 1879 the explorer Heinrich Klutschak discovered his skull on King William Island, outside of a grave of sandstone slabs which had evidently been looted by the Inuit. A silver medal for mathematics was found wrapped in a handkerchief inside the grave.

Jukee [*Inuk*] A girl in Pond Inlet who knew **Reepah**.

Keskarrah See **Cascathry**.

Lieutenant Henry T. D. Le Vesconte [*English*] Served under **Fitzjames** on HMS *Erebus* on the final Franklin Expedition. In 1869 his skeleton was found on King William Island by the explorer Charles Hall and an Inuk guide, Innoopoozheejook. He'd presumably died there in 1848.

Lieutenant Edward Little [*English*] Served under **Crozier** on HMS *Terror* on the final Franklin Expedition.

Michel Teroahauté [*Iroquois*] One of the voyageurs on the second Franklin Expedition of 1819–22. Resorting to murder and cannibalism under desperate circumstances, he was "executed" (and, according to Mowat, possibly eaten) by Dr. John Richardson.

Nuliajok See **SEDNA**.

Levi Nungaq [*Inuk*] Relocated from Inukjuak to Resolute Bay in 1955.

Captain William Edward Parry [*English*] A veteran of five Arctic expeditions who knew very well what it meant to be foiled by ice, this Secretary of the Admiralty was a staunch supporter of **Franklin**'s final expedition.

Sir Robert Peel [*English*] Prime Minister 1834–46.

Captain William Penny [*English*] A whaling captain who participated in the searches for the final Franklin Expedition in 1850.

Robert Pilot [*Anglo Canadian*] Former Deputy Commissioner of the Northwest Territories. One of the RCMP officers involved in the relocations. A voluntary witness in the relocation hearings in 1990.

Reepah [*Inuk*] A woman with a beautiful heart.

Captain Sir James Ross [*English*] Friend of **Franklin**'s. Nephew of Sir John Ross, who commanded the first Arctic expedition on which Franklin served. On that expedition Sir John was misled by a mirage of mountains and so turned back from Lancaster Sound, which error affected his popularity. In 1829 Sir James accompanied his uncle on an expedition in discovery of the North Magnetic Pole; at this time they were beset by ice for three winters. Seeking an escape, they dragged their provisions by boats mounted on sledges, just as Franklin's men were to do in 1848. Ten years later, Sir James commanded a four-year expedition to the Antarctic. His ships were the *Erebus* and the *Terror* – the same which Franklin took on his final expedition. It seems that Sir

James was offered the leadership of that expedition, but declined, possibly out of deference to Franklin. He was active in the search for the vanished expedition.

SEDNA [*Canadian Inuktitut*]   The Power of plenty (walrus, seal, etc.). She lives at the bottom of the sea. Visited in famine times by Baffinland Inuit shamans. In olden times she would have been known throughout the Hudson Bay area as well (hence in Inukjuak), and at least as far west as Kikertak (King William Island), where Franklin's men died. Apparently (though some accounts I have read differ on this) SEDNA has no jurisdiction over caribou and other land animals, which did not exist yet when She was a human being. One might think this a very serious limitation indeed. The truth, however, is that the single most important source of food for people and dogs in the eastern Canadian Arctic has been seals. (Also: *Aiviliajoq, Nuliajoq, Uinigumissuitung* = "She Who Would Not Have a Husband." Her Greenlandic equivalent is *Arnaquagsaq* = "The Old Woman.")

Seth [*American*]   A botanist.

Captain **Subzero** [*American*]   The reincarnation of Captain **Franklin**.

Tattannoeuck [*Inuk*: "It Is Full"]   A guide on both of **Franklin**'s overland expeditions. Franklin called him Augustus. (His companion on the first of these was Hoeootoerock, or Junius, who vanished and probably perished on the return trip to Fort Enterprise.) He died in a blizzard in the spring of 1834 near Fort Resolution, while seeking to join **Back**'s expedition. Back wrote: "Such was the miserable end of poor Augustus, a faithful, disinterested, kindhearted creature . . ." (Also: *Tattannæuk*; modern orthography, *Tatanoyuk*.)

2
Glossary of Nations, Organizations and Kinship Terms

Akaga [*Canadian Inuktitut*] My uncle on my father's side.

Ananaaga [*Canadian Inuktitut*] My mother.

Angaga [*Canadian Inuktitut*] My uncle on my mother's side.

Angajuga [*Canadian Inuktitut*] My older sibling of the same sex.

Angákok [*Greenlandic*] Shaman.

Angákot [*Canadian Inuktitut*] Shaman.

Aniga [*Canadian Inuktitut*] My brother (if the speaker is female).

Arnagatiga [*Canadian Inuktitut*] My cousin on my mother's side.

Ataaga [*Canadian Inuktitut*] My father.

Athabascans A general term (based on the lake called Athabasca) for the Indians of northern Canada who call themselves "Dineh": the Chipewyan, Dog-Rib, Slavey, Beaver, Sekani, Kaska, Mountain and Kutchin. (Also: *Athapaskans.*)

Chipewyan Indians ["People of the pointed skins"] A subarctic nomadic Indian group who numbered approximately 3,500 when the Europeans arrived. "The most numerous and most widely distributed of the Northern **Athabascans**. Aboriginally, they occupied the forest-tundra ecotone . . . from near Hudson Bay, north of the Sea River, in a wide northwesterly arc to north of the Arctic Circle, near the mouth of the Coppermine River . . . The Chipewyan consider the neighboring Athapaskan **Dog-Rib** and Slavey as similar but ethnically distinct. The **Eskimo** to the north are known as . . . 'enemies of the flat area' (that is, the Barren Grounds); the Cree to the south are simply . . . 'enemy'" – *Handbook of North American Indians* (vol. 6: Subarctic). In Franklin's time the **Copper Indians** were distinct from the Chipewyan. (Franklin's variants: *Chippewyans, Chippewayans.*)

Chippewa Indians ["Peoples, whose moccasins have puckered seams" – Hood (1820)] This seems to be a term of some confusion. Chippewa are also known as Objiwa, but are not the same as **Chipewyan**. However, it is not clear to me that Franklin's party observed this distinction.

Copper Indians ". . . termed by the **Chipewyans**, Tantsawhot-dinneh, or Birch-rind Indians. They were originally a tribe of the former people . . . Their language . . . and customs . . . are essentially the same as those of the Chipewyans, but in personal character they have greatly the advantage of that people . . ." – Franklin (1820). According to Hood (and current scholarly sources), they were identical with the Yellowknife (=Red Knife) Indians. Franklin estimated their number at 190. The naturalist on Back's expedition down the Great Fish River (1833) noted that they were by then so much affected by venereal disease contracted from Europeans that "in a few years, if some aid be not afforded them, they will cease to exist" (Yerbury). The *Handbook of North American Indians* (vol. 6: Subarctic) tells the story differently, saying that after the **Dog-Rib Indians** killed thirty-four of them in revenge for an earlier battle, the Copper tribe retreated to other territory and amalgamated with the Chipewyan again. Greenstockings, Cascathry and Akaicho (see Glossary 1) were all Copper Indians.

Dog-Rib Indians   This subarctic group lives south of the **Inuit** and west of the **Chipewyan**. Most Indians in Yellowknife are Dog-Ribs. "Sir John Franklin's account of his 1819–1822 expedition confirms that the Dog-Rib were in this period in fear of the Yellowknife, most of whom were led by the chief Akaitcho [see Glossary 1] . . . Franklin described the 'Thlingcha-dinne' (Dog-Ribs) of this period and stated that they were called 'Slaves' by the Cree" – *Handbook of North American Indians* (vol. 6: Subarctic), p. 294.

Eskimo [?*Objiwa*; Montagnais: *ayassime'w* = "she nets a snowshoe"]   Foreigners' name for the **Inuit**. The literal meaning is "eater of raw meat." Many Canadian Inuit now consider it derogatory. It is, however, still widely used in Alaska. (Also: *Esquimau*, *Eskimau*, etc.)

Ihalmiut [*Inuktitut*]   The Caribou **Inuit** of the Keewatin District, known for their spectacular beadwork, whose present homes are principally in Baker Lake, Chesterfield Inlet, Rankin Inlet, Whale Cove and Eskimo Point. They used to depend almost entirely on the caribou for food, clothing and shelter. After massive starvation, they were relocated.

Inuit (sing. **Inuk**; a special word, **Inu·k**, used in Inuktitut to signify exactly two, seems lost to Anglo usage) [*Inuktitut*; lit., "the People"]   This term is used most widely in Canada and parts of Alaska. In Greenland they call themselves "Greenlanders" although I have occasionally heard "Inuk" and "Inuit"; in Alaska they may say "Eskimos" or, more specifically, "Aleut" (Aleutian Islands) or "Yupik" (southern) or "Inupiat" (northern). In Siberia they say "Yuit." Traditionally all Inuit used kayaks and most used igloos, dog-teams and inukshuks (see Glossary 4). The Canadian Inuit are sometimes classified (by clothing style, etc.) into the following groups, going from east to west: Ungava–Labrador (in which Reepah would have been included), S. Baffin, Iglulik, Sadliq, Caribou (= **Ihalmiut**), Netsilik (who encountered the starving Franklin survivors), **Copper**, Mackenzie. When the Europeans arrived, the Canadian Inuit numbered about 22,000. By 1900 about two-thirds of them were dead from disease. Population has recovered and is now growing rapidly.

Inuit Tapirisat of Canada [lit., "the People's Team" – sometimes more generally translated as "the **Eskimo** Brotherhood," which some of the "Eskimos" don't like]   A non-profit organization for the preservation of Inuit values, founded in 1971. It played an important role in the Nunavut agreement signed in 1992 (see Glossary 3).

Inuk [*Inuktitut*]   See **Inuit**.

Makivik Corporation of Québec   The first **Inuit** development corporation, Makivik negotiates land claims with the government, etc. Makivik is fairly powerful and well-off as native corporations go. In 1990, for instance, it bought FirstAir, the airline that covers Baffin Island and neighboring areas.

-miut [*Canadian Inuktitut*]   Inhabitants of (e.g., *Inukjuamiut* = "those who dwell in Inukjuak").

Najaga [*Canadian Inuktitut*]   My sister (if the speaker is a girl).

Najaksava [*Canadian Inuktitut*]   My female cousin (if the speaker is male).

Nukara [*Canadian Inuktitut*]   My younger sibling of the same sex.

Nuliashuk [*Ungava Inuktitut*]   Concubine, female sex partner.

Qaallunaat [*Canadian Inuktitut*; lit., "the people with bushy eyebrows"]   What Canadian **Inuit** call white people.

Qairnirmiut [*Caribou Inuktitut*; lit., "people of the smooth bedrock"]   One source describes them simply: "**Inuit** who were hit hard by starvation in the 1950s."

Red Knife Indians   Variant name for the **Copper Indians**.

Uishuk [*Ungava Inuktitut*]   Male lover/sex partner.

Yuit [*Yupik*]   Siberian **Inuit**. They are one of twenty-six native groups in the Siberian North, the largest of which are Chukchi, Eveny, Khanty, Nentsy and Nanaitsy.

3
Glossary of Places

Adli'vun [*Baffinland Inuktitut*: "Those Beneath Us" – Boas (1888)]   The place beneath the sea where SEDNA has Her house (see Glossary 1).

Alert   Site of a military base, on the north coast of Ellesmere Island. The base was originally a joint Canadian-American project.

Back's Great Fish River [*English*]   A long and rapid-filled river discharging on the north coast of our continent not far from **Starvation Cove**. Now simply called the Back River, it was named after George Back (see Glossary 1), who first mapped it. The Indian name is *Thleweechohoesseth*. This was the last hope of Franklin's men in 1848. They thought to ascend it and reach a Hudson's Bay post on the Great Slave Lake, 1,200 miles away. According to Back himself, "No toilworn or exhausted party would have the least chance of existence by going there" (Cyriax).

Barren Grounds [*English*]   Also: Barrens, Barren Lands. A half-million square miles of tundra running more or less from Churchill to the mouth of the Mackenzie River to Repulse Bay. Its name comes from the absence of trees (although in fact there are some dwarfish ones along the southern edge). Travel in this area is fatiguing, especially in the summer owing to the bogs, rivers, tussocks, and mosquitoes. In the winter migrating game animals can be scarce, which is why Franklin ran into trouble on his Coppermine expedition (1819–22).

Beechey Island [*English*]   Named in honor of the explorer Frederick William Beechey, this islet is southwest of Devon Island, and therefore very close to **Resolute**. The final Franklin Expedition spent its first winter there (1845–6). "Along the whole eastern slope of the island the headboards of John Torrington, John Hartnell and William Braine were the tallest features visible, framed by towering, vertical cliffs to the west and the shore of Erebus Bay to the east" – Beattie and Geiger.

Canada [*Mohawk, Hochelaga Indian*]   Name for the Saint Lawrence River, or, more likely, for a native settlement on it. Adopted by the seventeenth-century French to describe the vast region around it. Until much later, Canada was not synonymous with the even vaster New France, which also contained the Louisiana territory and (for some) the expanse called Florida, which was also claimed by Spain. Canada contains a high proportion of the world's fresh water, much of which is in the Northwest Territories.

Coppermine River [*English*]   A very long river whose first European navigator was Samuel Hearne, in the eighteenth century. Franklin and his officers mapped it more accurately on their first overland expedition of 1819–22, on their way to the Arctic Ocean. The name is probably based on an Indian equivalent, as there was native copper in the area which the Indians used.

Cornwallis Island [*English*]   A bank of mud and gravel situated between Devon Island to the east and Bathurst Island to the west, the island sports the town of **Resolute** on the southern coast. At this latitude, the sun disappears for about four months of the year.

Ellef Ringnes Island [*Norwegian*]   One of the Sverdrup Islands discovered by Otto Sverdrup in 1898–1902. Ellef Ringnes lies on the northwest corner of the Canadian Arctic archipelago.

Eureka   Site of an Environment Canada weather station, on the west coast of Ellesmere Island, latitude 80°. The station was originally a joint Canadian-American project. Now exclusively Canadian, Eureka is perhaps the world's northernmost civilian settlement (**Alert**, a large military base, is on the north coast of Ellesmere Island). Local personnel refer to Eureka as "the garden spot of the Arctic."

Frobisher Bay [*English*]   See **Iqaluit**.

Great Whale River [*English*]   Also: Poste-de-la-Baleine. Name given to Kuujjuarapik, a settlement on the eastern coast of Hudson Bay, a little south of **Inukjuak**. Kuujjuarapik is part Inuit and part Cree. It is just below the treeline, so some small trees can be seen.

Griffith Island [*English*]   An islet just south of **Cornwallis Island**.

Grise Fiord   Name for a settlement of relocated Inuit on the south coast of Ellesmere Island. Population was 114 in 1986. There is more game here than near **Resolute**. "Selected as the site of a new community by the federal government and . . . created in 1953 . . . located close to an RCMP post that served as a source of trade goods" – Position paper by Makivik Corporation, Inuit Tapirisat of Canada and the Kativik Regional Government. "The long-term viability of a small artificial community such as Grise Fiord has always been in doubt" – *Handbook of North American Indians*, vol. 5.

Inukjuak [*Canadian Inuktitut*]   Also: Port Harrison. A town in Arctic Québec, on the eastern shore of Hudson Bay. The main point of origination for the 1950s relocation project. "For a long time a meeting and trading place for Inuit living in this region, and covering an expanse of over 100 miles, Inukjuak, *the giant*, is located at the mouth of the Innuksuac River. There is a deposit of steatite, which is used for sculpture . . . The lifestyle of . . . the Inukjuamiut is closely tied to . . . traditional activities" – SAGMAI, *Native Peoples of Québec*. According to an Inuk elder, the name means "The Place of Many Inuit." In 1990 Inukjuak had about 900 people. It is currently the base for the Makivik Corporation (see Glossary 2).

Iqaluit [*Canadian Inuktitut*]   Also: Frobisher Bay. A large town on southern Baffin Island, just below the Arctic Circle. Hub of air travel in the low Arctic. Proposed capital of **Nunavut**. At the time of the relocation to Resolute, "Iqaluit was a United States Air Force base, with 50 to 60 personnel in population, both military and civilian" – Robert Pilot, Former Deputy Commissioner of the Northwest Territories.

Isachsen [*Norwegian*] Site of a now abandoned Environment Canada weather station, on the west coast of **Ellef Ringnes Island**. The station was originally a joint Canadian-American project. In 1991, Isachsen was a short distance north of the **North Magnetic Pole**. "Near Isachsen a pair of caribou with one fawn required 300 square miles for feeding, and, in some even more desolate areas, they probably could not exist" – *Encyclopaedia Britannica*.

Iviagiknak [*Canadian Inuktitut*: "like the breast of a woman"] A sandy place at the mouth of the **Coppermine River** where Franklin's second expedition camped on the nights of 18–20 July 1821.

Kalâtdit Nunât [*Canadian Inuktitut*: "Land of the People"] Greenland. (Greenlandic: *Kalaallit Nunaat*.)

Kikertak [*Canadian Inuktitut*: "The Island"] King William Island. The Inuit who live there call themselves the Kikertarmiut, or Island Dwellers. They are a subgroup of the Netsiliks (see Glossary 2: "Inuit"). It was on this island, which lies just off the northern coast of our continent, a little west of the Boothia Peninsula, that Ross located the **North Magnetic Pole** in 1832. The final Franklin Expedition was fatally beset by ice there (in Victoria Strait, off the northwest coast) in 1846–8. Kikertak was originally a territory of an Inuit group called the Ugjulirmiut. The Netsiliks lived eastward of them. "When the Ugjulirmiut obtained an enormous stock of metals and wood by the destruction of Franklin's ships, the Netchillirmiut commenced to visit King William Land, in order to partake of these riches. Thus they . . . intermingled with the Ugjulirmiut" – Boas.

King William Island [*English*] See **Kikertak**.

Kuujjuarapik [*Canadian Inuktitut*] See **Great Whale River**.

Labrador [*Latin*] "Labrador – *Laboratoris Terra* – is so called from the circumstance that Cortoreal in the year 1500 stole thence a cargo of Indians for slaves" – Parkman. Prof. Bruce Trigger adds: "Named after him because he was a farmer (*labrada*)."

North Magnetic Pole This is the point to which the compass needle points, as opposed to the northernmost point of the earth's axis, which we call the True North Pole. The Magnetic Pole is migrating in a northwesterly direction. When first discovered by Ross in 1831, it lay on the Boothia Peninsula of the North American mainland. In the mid-1980s it had reached Bathurst Island; by 1991 it was on the northern tip of King Christian Island, not far from **Isachsen**.

Northwest Passage This "Arctic Grail," as it has been called, was simply a hoped-for waterway connecting Europe with Asia across North America. When the North American mainland failed to answer, explorers began to search out the Canadian Arctic archipelago as early as the late sixteenth century. Sir John Franklin (see Glossary 1) and 129 men were lost in 1845–8 on an expedition to complete the Passage. According to some reckoners, the dying Franklin men did "forge the last link with their lives" when they reached **Starvation Cove**. Others credit their would-be rescuer McClure (1854). Amundsen (1906) was the first to sail the Passage's entire length.

Nunavik [*Canadian Inuktitut*] Aboriginal name of the Inuit homeland in Nouveau-Québec (the northern part of the province, which includes **Inukjuak** and **POV**). This name has now been officially recognized by the Canadian government.

Nunavut [*Canadian Inuktitut*: "Our Land"] The Arctic of the Canadian Inuit. Some Inuit groups would like the northern half of the Northwest Territories to become a province under their control, called Nunavut. (The other half would become the territory of the *Dineh*, or Indians.) In 1992 the Inuit Tapirisat of Canada (see Glossary 2) and other groups signed an agreement with the government which seems to recognize the existence of Nunavut. At this writing it is too early to say what the reality will be.

Pond Inlet [*English*] Name given by John Ross in 1888 to honor John Pond, Astronomer Royal. (On the old Franklin maps the place is called Pond's Bay.) According to Boas, its original inhabitants, a group called the Tununirmiut, summered there. A permanent settlement did not exist until this century. Mittimatalik (the native name) is a beautiful Inuit town on the north coast of Baffin Island. "Possibly named after Mittima, the Inuk who ran the Sabellum Company trading post at Singiyok in the 1930s" – Indian and Northern Affairs Canada, *The Inuit* (pamphlet). Some people were relocated from here to Resolute; one man shot himself rather than go. In 1988 the population was 943. According to the local tourism brochure, "wage employment is higher than [in] most Arctic communities owing to the Strathcona Sound lead-zinc development and to oil exploration in the High Arctic Islands."

Port Harrison See **Inukjuak**.

POV [*Canadian Inuktitut, abbr.*] **Povungnituk**.

Povungnituk [*Canadian Inuktitut*: "The Place That Smells Like Rotten Meat"] A town on eastern Hudson Bay, a little north of **Inukjuak**. One explanation for the name is that "since so many belugas used to be taken and butchered there, the place, in time, began to reek of them" (Zebedee Nungak and Eugene Arima). Another Inuk says that many people starved to death here, and the stink of their decomposing bodies inspired the name.

Resolute Bay [*English*] Name for Qasuittaq, a settlement of relocated Inuit on the south coast of Cornwallis Island. "Resolute Bay and **Grise Fiord** . . . were not the creations of Inuit community life but instead were artificially created by government . . . Resolute was formed in 1947 as a meteorological station for a joint Canadian-American expedition known as Arctops. In fact, a different site was intended for this base but bad ice conditions and a late arrival of ships made Resolute Bay the only alternative site" – Position paper by Makivik Corporation, Inuit Tapirisat of Canada and the Kativik Regional Government.

Resolution Island [*English*] Island just east of Meta Incognita Peninsula, Baffin Island, where the flagship in Franklin's first Arctic expedition was almost wrecked in 1819.

Starvation Cove [*English*] An inlet on the north coast of our continent, separated by

Simpson Strait from **Kikertak**. It was here that the dying men of the last Franklin Expedition reached their "farthest south" before succumbing to hunger.

Tudjaat [*Canadian Inuktitut*]   Another name for **Resolute Bay**, Cornwallis Island.

Uktuk Lake [*Canadian Inuktitut*: "Cunt Lake"]   A narrow cliff-lipped body of water a few miles southwest of **Pond Inlet**, Baffin Island.

Van Diemen's Land [*English*]   Tasmania. Sir John Franklin (see Glossary 1) was Governor there until the year before his final Arctic voyage. It was often referred to as "V.D. Land."

Vinland [*Norse*: "Vine-Land" or "Wine-Land"]   North America.

4
General Glossary

Airaq [*Canadian Inuktitut*] "Roots that we eat. It's so good when you cook it with Crisco oil" – Hannah Panipakoocho, Pond Inlet, Baffin Island (1989).

Aputik [*Canadian Inuktitut*] Snow.

Armauti [*Canadian Inuktitut*; lit., "to carry"] The pouch between a woman's hood and her body where she carries her baby. (Also: *armaouti, armautik, amouti*.)

Atsiaq [*Ungava Inuktitut*] Diminutive for animal names.

Aya-aya songs [*Canadian and Greenlandic Inuktitut*] These songs, often accompanied by drumbeats, contain the word *aya* (var.: *ayaiya, ajaja*, etc.), either as a refrain in a story-song equivalent to a ballad, or else as the only word in the song, sung repeatedly.

Inukpo [*Resolute Bay Inuktitut*] Liquid seal fat, used as a dip for meat.

Inukshuk [*Canadian Inuktitut*] A man-shaped "statue" made of stones, used to scare caribou in the direction wanted by the hunters.

Kamiks [*Anglicized Canadian Inuktitut*; the actual plural for *kamik* is *kamiit*] Boots; outer footwear. In this book the kamiks referred to are usually handmade from animal skins by a *kamiliurpuq* (= "she makes boots"), although factory-made army boots, for instance, would also qualify as kamiks. Polar bear kamiks are warm and beautiful but very scarce. Sealskin kamiks are the most common; they are waterproof, but thin, and wear out easily. They are sometimes soled with walrus hide, which makes them incredibly tough, but the *kamiliurpuq* who does this will want good compensation, since she must chew the walrus hide for a long time. Caribou-skin kamiks are very warm and therefore a good choice for winter, but they are not as waterproof as the sealskin variety.

Komatik [*Canadian Inuktitut*] Native long-runnered sled. (I have usually seen it spelled this way; variants include *qamutiik, qamotik, kamatik*, etc.)

Kulawak [*Canadian Inuktitut*] A good hunter who follows the laws which dictate which caribou are proper to kill at a given time.

Manulik [*Canadian Inuktitut*] Frost that forms on the fur ruff of someone's hood from his breath.

Mattaq [*Canadian Inuktitut*] Skin of narwhals (and sometimes other whales, especially white whales). A delicious food. (Common variants: *maktaq, muktuk*.)

Nadlak [*Canadian Inuktitut*] Caribou crossing.

Nanoq [*Canadian Inuktitut*]   Polar bear.

Pirruqsiat [*Pond Inlet Inuktitut*]   Flowers.

Piujukuluk [*Canadian Inuktitut*]   Dear little good thing.

Qakiuti [*Canadian Inuktitut*]   Rifle.

Qilaujjauti [*Pond Inlet Inuktitut*]   Drum of white sealskin; used for **aya-aya songs**.

Quki utikuluk [*Canadian Inuktitut*]   Nice gun.

Qungaliit [*Canadian Inuktitut*]   Sorrel.

Savik [*Canadian Inuktitut*]   Small kitchen or pocket knife, as opposed to the broad snow knife or the **ulu**.

Secret [*Reepah's English*]   Cigarette.

Skidoo [*English and Inuktitut*]   Motorized sled.

Suluk [*Canadian Inuktitut*]   Wing.

Suluk [*Yupik*]   Bird.

Tripe de roche [*French*]   Rock-tripe. Black lichen used by Arctic explorers to fend off starvation.

Ujarok [*Canadian Inuktitut*]   Rock.

Uktuk [*Canadian Inuktitut*]   Cunt. (Also: *utuk*.)

Ulu [*Canadian, Greenlandic Inuktitut*]   Crescent-shaped woman's knife used for flensing skins, dicing, etc. There is a drawing of a Greenlandic *ulo* (common variant spelling) in *The Ice-Shirt*.

Umiak [*Canadian Inuktitut*]   "Seal skin boat [u]sed during seasonal migrations [;] it could contain as many as twenty persons, their gear, sails and paddles (a family boat, it was considered a 'women's' boat in Greenland and was rowed (not paddled) by women exclusively there; custom allowed males to paddle the *umiaq* in Ungava[)] . . ." – Lucien Schneider.

A Chronology of the Sixth Age of Wineland

The Age of the Rifles

??	In Baffinland, SEDNA becomes a Power of plenty.
?30,000 BC	Siberian hunters cross the Bering Strait land-bridge to the northern Yukon.
?10,000 BC	Bering Strait land-bridge submerged.
?2000 BC	Independence I culture present in northern Greenland, Ellesmere Island, Devon Island and Cornwallis Island.
	Arctic Small Tool culture present in Alaska, Canada, Greenland.
?1700 BC	Pre-Dorset culture present in Low Arctic.
?1000–500 BC	Independence II culture supplants Independence I.
?500 BC–?AD 1000	Dorset culture dominant in Arctic.
?900–?1200	Thule Inuit migrate east from Alaska, reaching Greenland.
?985	Eirik the Red establishes a Norse settlement in Greenland.
?1200	Commencement of Little Ice Age.
1284	Roger Bacon describes gunpowder.
ca. 1400	First known use of rifled gunbarrels.
?1500	The Norsemen are now extinct in Greenland.
1515	In Germany, Johann Kiefuss invents the wheel lock musket.
1554	First guns cast in England.
1576	First voyage of Martin Frobisher to the Arctic.

1577	On his second voyage, Frobisher visits the Greenland Inuit.
1585	First bomb invented.
1587	John Davis sails to the Arctic in hopes of finding a Northwest Passage.
1595	The English army stops using the bow.
?1600	Modern Inuit culture present in the Arctic.
1605	Captain Gotske Lindenau begins kidnapping Inuit.
1616	William Baffin searches for the Northwest Passage.
1621	Lead smelting and mining begins in Virginia.
1680s	The Cree Indians, armed by traders, begin to displace the Chipewyan.
1700	The caribou population in Athabascan Indian territory is approximately 2,400,000. (See entries for 1950 and 1960.)
1716	One-third of the Indians returning from York Factory die of starvation, due to being given insufficient powder and shot.
1719	Trade beads available to the Inuit at Fort Churchill.
1721	Hans Egede sails to Greenland and begins converting the Inuit.
1741	The Russians discover the Aleutian Islands. They enslave, pillage, rape and murder the native people.
1743	The Hudson's Bay Company establishes its first inland trade post, Henley House on the Albany River.
1745	An Act of Parliament offers £20,000 to any British subject discovering the Northwest Passage by means of Hudson Strait.
1760–4	The Chipewyan begin to become dependent on firearms.
1760s	The Chipewyan, Beaver, Slave and Cree Nations make peace.
1760–1860	The Kutchin Indians lose 80 percent of their population.

1774		The Hudson's Bay Company establishes Cumberland House.
		The trader Graham teaches 40 Inuit men how to use guns.
1776		The Hudson Strait qualification of the British Act is repealed.
1784		The rival Northwest Company enters the field.
1786	Sir John Franklin born.	
1789		Mackenzie Inuit known to be trading for iron (through native middlemen) with Russians.
1792		Northwest Company traders seize Chipewyan women whose relations owe debts, and sell them to their employees as sex slaves.
1795		Beaver populations begin to decline west of Hudson Bay, thanks to steel traps.
1800–21		Violent trade war between the fur companies.
1800–1900		Canadian Athabascans practice preferential female infanticide, since, says a Slavey Indian, "women are only an encumbrance, useless in time of war and exceedingly voracious in time of want" (Yerbury).
1805	Franklin helps survey the coast of Australia.	
1807		In Scotland, the clergyman Alexander Forsyth patents a percussion gunlock.
1812–13		Slavey and Dog-Rib Indians murder white families at Fort Nelson, probably on account of starvation for lack of ammunition.
1814	Franklin wounded in the Battle of New Orleans.	
1815		In the USA, Joshua Shaw invents the percussion cap.
1817		In Hudson Strait, one bullet is worth one wooden eye-shade in trade.
1818	Franklin sails with the Buchan Expedition to Spitzbergen as second in command.	

1819–22	Franklin commands an expedition from Hudson's Bay to the Polar Sea. Ten men die of starvation and exposure. One of them is Hood, Greenstockings's lover.	
1823	Franklin marries Eleanor Porden, who dies shortly afterward, leaving a daughter, Eleanor.	A band of Indians at Fort Simpson trades furs for food – a new and very ominous trend. The Indians here are now becoming dependent on the traders for survival.
1823–4		The Yellowknife go to war with the Dog-Rib and other Nations over access to trapping areas.
1825–7	Franklin commands a second expedition to the Polar Sea, this time exploring west to Alaska. Upon his return he is knighted.	
1828		The Acts of Parliament offering a reward for discovery of the Northwest Passage are repealed.
1829		William Edward Parry is knighted for his four Arctic voyages.
1830		The Hudson's Bay Company remarks on "a general Complaint of Want of animals and dearth of Provisions" in the Mackenzie District.
1831		James Clark Ross locates the North Magnetic Pole.
1833	George Back goes on an expedition to find and relieve Ross. Finding Ross to be safe, he descends and maps the Great Fish River instead.	Caribou become scarcer in the Mackenzie District.
1836	Back, now promoted to Captain, takes the *Terror* to Repulse Bay, where he's caught in ice and almost crushed.	
1840–2		Starvation and cannibalism are common among the Indians in the Mackenzie District. "For the majority [of the Indians], only trapping could provide the furs necessary to obtain trade goods, and these goods, especially ammunition, had become indispensable for survival" (Yerbury).

1845	Sir John Franklin commands an expedition to complete the Northwest Passage.	Christian Schoenbein invents guncotton.
1845–6		Caribou return to the Mackenzie District.
1846		The Americans begin whaling in the eastern Arctic.
1846–7		The Inuit south of Rankin Inlet own firearms.
1847	Sir John Franklin dies of unknown causes.	.44 caliber "Walker" Colt handgun adopted by the US Army.
1848	The last Franklin Expedition survivors die of scurvy and starvation en route to Back's Great Fish River.	
1849		In France, Claude-Étienne Minié invents an expanding projectile to make better use of rifling.
1850	The British government offers a £20,000 reward to anyone who relieves the Franklin Expedition.	
	First three graves found on Beechey Island.	
1851		Colt Navy model introduced.
1854	Robert McClure's expedition completes the Northwest Passage.	
	John Rae learns from Pelly Bay Inuit that a party of Caucasians is known to have starved to death in the west.	
	Franklin and his men are officially declared dead.	
1857		Smith & Wesson introduces the first metallic cartridge gun, the "Number 1" .22 revolver.
1858		Remington introduces a revolver with a solid frame.
1859	Francis Leopold M'Clintock discovers a skeleton in a steward's uniform on a gravel ridge on King William Island. His second in command, Lt. William Robert Hobson, finds a lifeboat with two skeletons.	
1860		US Army agrees to issue the Colt revolver to mounted troops.

		Major E. Schultze of the Prussian Army invents a nitrocellulose propellant suitable for shotguns.
		The Hudson's Bay Company upgrades its trade guns from muzzle-loaders to percussion-cap firearms. But the Inuit continue to prefer muzzle-loaders for some time, due to the difficulty of getting caps.
1860–1		Whalers at Winchester Inlet trade with the Inuit: powder and shot for musk-ox meat.
1860–1915		Greatest number of whaling voyages into Hudson Bay.
1866–7		The Hudson Bay Company commences the fur trade with Inuit at Marble Island.
1867		Venereal disease arrives at Marble Island.
1869	Charles Francis Hall discovers the skeleton of Lt. Henry LeVesconte.	
1870		Smith & Wesson introduces the .44 caliber rimfire "Model Number 3" handgun with top-break design to clear all chambers simultaneously.
		Whalers get into the fur trade in Hudson Bay.
		Beginning of the transcontinental railway in Canada.
1871		First reported use of a whaleboat by Inuit at Marble Island.
1872		Smith & Wesson tries unsuccessfully to sell a double-action handgun to the Russian Imperial Army.
1872–3		Trade with the Inuit accounts for 0.9 percent of the profits of the whaler *Abbie Bradford* (see also entry for 1886–8).
1873		Colt produces the single-action .45 revolver with a metallic cartridge.
1877		Colt introduces the first double-action revolver.
1878		Lt. Frederick Schwatka discovers a Winchester rifle among the Inuit at Depot Island.
1879	Lt. Frederick Schwatka discovers the grave of John Irving.	

1880		Britain transfers sovereignty of the Arctic archipelago to Canada.
1883		In Europe, Sir Hiram Stevens Maxim invents his eponymous machine gun.
1884		In France, Paul Vieille makes the first true smokeless powder.
1884–5		The whaler *Abbie Bradford* takes on 15,582 lbs of caribou in trade with Hudson Bay Inuit.
1885		Completion of the Canadian Pacific Railroad.
1886–8		Trade with the Inuit accounts for 23.9 percent of the profits of the *Abbie Bradford* (see also entry for 1872–3).
1887		Nobel invents Ballistite, a smokeless powder.
1888		Inuit on the south shore of Hudson Strait begin to give up the use of the bow and arrow.
		Sir John Ross names Pond Inlet.
1889		Colt introduces a swing-out cylinder double-action revolver of improved design.
1889–1911		Almost half the children born at Cape Fullerton are mixed-bloods.
1890		The bison are now almost exterminated on the western plains.
1892		In Austria, Joseph Laumann produces the first true auto-loading pistol to use smokeless powder.
1893		Hugo Borchardt develops a recoil-operated pistol.
1894	The syllabic script is introduced by missionaries on Baffin Island.	
1896		Paul and Peter Mauser begin manufacturing their recoil-operated pistols.
1899		Scottish whalers establish a station on Southampton Island. Within three years, all but 5 of the local population are dead of disease.
1900		George Luger redesigns Borchardt's pistol into the Luger; Deutsche Waffen und Munitionsfabriken begins regular production.

		Firearms are in common use along Hudson Strait and northwest Hudson Bay.
		Steel foxtraps introduced into the western Arctic.
		Caribou populations decrease noticeably in the western Arctic.
		Colt puts John Browning's .38 auto-loader pistol into production.
1903		The United States buys Alaska from Russia.
		The musk-oxen population is so depleted around Hudson Bay that the Superintendent bans the export of their hides.
1903–6		Amundsen becomes the first to sail the Northwest Passage.
1908		Colt refines the 1889 revolver into the Army Special Model, whose design remains stable until the 1960s.
1909		DuPont introduces smokeless powder propellants into the USA.
		The Hudson's Bay Company establishes its first permanent post in northern Québec.
1911		Browning produces the superb M1911 auto pistol.
1917		Submachine gun first deployed.
1920s	Boom in the fur market.	
1921		The RCMP establishes a detachment at Pond Inlet.
1926		John Browning dies.
1929		In Germany, Fritz Walther introduces the Polizei Pistole (PP).
1930	Drastic drop in the fur market.	
1931		Walther introduces the Polizei Pistole Kriminal (PPK).
1934–5	Mass starvation in the central Arctic.	
1935		.357 magnum handgun cartridge introduced.
		Browning Hi-Power introduced by Fabrique Nationale in Belgium.
1938		Trapping by non-Inuit becomes legally restricted.

1947		The Soviets introduce the AK–47 (Kalashnikov) assault rifle.
1950		The caribou population in Athabascan Indian territory is approximately 700,000. (See entries for 1700 and 1960.)
1950s	The Ihalmiut (Caribou Inuit) suffer mass starvation, possibly because abuse of repeating rifles disturbs the caribou migrations. Mowat writes: "Where, *during my own lifetime*, there had been as many as a million caribou, there were now only pathetic and scattered remnants of a species that biologists now fear may be doomed to extinction." – "I'm not sure that you can blame the repeating rifles on the Ihalmiut's problems in the early 1950s," writes Prof. Frank J. Tester (see source-note to p. 123). "The historical record shows that the Inuit had always experienced periods of starvation when caribou changed migration routes and when their populations fluctuated . . . There had been no change in hunting practices . . . I think we are terribly arrogant in thinking we understand such things."	
1953	First Inuit families relocated from Inukjuak (Port Harrison), Québec, to Resolute Bay, Cornwallis Island and to Craig Harbour (near Grise Fiord), Ellesmere Island. "There were already Inuit families living with the RCMP at Alexander Fiord [farther north on Ellesmere] prior to the 1953 relocation" – Prof. Frank J. Tester.	
1955	Levi Nungaq, Minnie Allakariallak and their families are relocated to Resolute.	
1953–7	Nineteen Inuit families relocated from Inukjuak to Resolute and to Grise Fiord, Ellesmere Island.	
1956		.44 magnum handgun cartridge introduced.

1960		The caribou population in Athabascan Indian territory is approximately 200,000. (See entries for 1700 and 1950.)
1960s	Most Canadian Inuit move into permanent settlements. Says Tester, "they moved because of government policy. They had to send their kids to school and families were not willing to leave their kids in settlements in the hands of priests and nuns while they were living out on the land . . . Who the hell would live in a cold igloo in the middle of nowhere, with minimal goods and services[,] when within travelling distance there was fuel, light, food, warm buildings, radio[,] etc.[?]"	
1962		Inuit gain the federal vote in Canada.
1968		Oil is discovered at Prudhoe Bay, Alaska.
1969		Committee for Original Peoples' Entitlement formed.
1971		Inuit Tapirisat of Canada formed (see Glossary 2).
1975		Inuit and Cree sign the James Bay and Northern Québec Agreement, abandoning claim to 981,610 sq. km. in exchange for other hunting, fishing, political and language rights.
1979		Inuit Committee on National Issues formed.
1981		More than 17 percent of Inuit houses are in need of major repairs (1981 census data).
1984		Extra water released through the spillway of the Hydro-Québec Dam drowns 10,000 caribou during their attempted crossing of the Caniapiscu River in northern Québec.
		The Inuvialiut of western Arctic Canada sign an agreement analogous to the one of 1975.
1988		Hunting and trapping account for 58 percent of family income among northern native groups in the USSR.

		Native people make up 6 percent of the general population in Canada and 46 percent of the prison population.
		Hundreds of thousands of hungry harp seals leave their usual summer feeding ground in the Barents Sea and come to northern Norway – a sign of ecological crisis in the Arctic. Simultaneous drastic declines in Arctic sea-bird populations are reported.
		Polychlorinated biphenyl contamination is confirmed at Yellowknife.
1989		Serious damage to the ozone layer is reported over the North Pole.
1990	A resolution to apologize to and compensate the Inuit who were relocated to Resolute and Grise Fiord is rejected.	
1992	Canadian Inuit vote in favor of Nunavut land claims agreement.	

Sources

And a few notes

T aken by itself, the vast mass of open source information is as useless as an uncompleted bridge that takes us not quite across a river . . .

ROY GODSON, ed., *Clandestine Collection* (1982)

Note

It may be of interest to the reader to know what use I have made of my sources. My aim in *Seven Dreams* has been to create a "Symbolic History" – that is to say, an account of origins and metamorphoses which is often untrue based on the literal facts as we know them, but whose untruths further a deeper sense of truth. Here one walks the proverbial tightrope, on one side of which lies slavish literalism; on the other, self-indulgence. Given these dangers, it seemed wise to have this source-list, so as to provide those who desire with easy means of corroborating or refuting my imagined versions of things, to monitor my originality,★ and to give leads to primary sources and other useful texts for interested non-specialists such as myself.

In a way this Dream is a companion to the first volume of *Seven Dreams*, *The Ice-Shirt*, and some of the information herein was obtained on my first trip to Greenland and Baffin Island in 1987, as noted below. I have never been to King William Island, where so many survivors of the Franklin Expedition perished in the summer of 1848. It is one of the book's gimmicks that most King William Island landscapes are actually Cornwallis Island landscapes, for reasons that will be clear to any careful reader. In this Dream, as with the others, I have mixed my colors not only from the palate of times, but also from the palate of places.

★ For two explanatory cases, see my examples in the Source-List for volume 1, *The Ice-Shirt*.

The Rifles

page xiv   Epigraph against killing – Barnabas Piryuaq, "Life As It Was" in *Inuktitut* magazine (fall 1986, no. 64), p. 16. But see below, section II (Pond Inlet), note to p. 39: "wasteful killing of animals."

page xiv   Epigraph in favor of killing – Jan Welzl, *The Quest for Polar Treasures*, trans. M. and R. Weatherall (London: Allen and Unwin, 1933), p. 268.

RIFLE-TEXT

page 3   Descriptions of Cornwallis Island – from a visit from 16–25 August 1988, and another from 15–21 September 1988.

page 7   Interview with Levi Nungaq – in Minnie Allakariallak's house, Resolute Bay, Cornwallis Island, 19 September 1988; Elizabeth Allakariallak interpreting. Mr. Nungaq's account is a relatively mild one. One Inuk lady in Resolute told me (BBC interview, October 1991): "When we arrived here it was dark and cold. I remember having to stay in a shed where we were living for a whole month. I was unable to go out of the house, and I was with . . . my child whom I wasn't too sure how to take care of. I hadn't eaten for a whole month, and I was starving . . . My child was really skinny from starving." Her husband, a master of sad details, said: "We were used to eating mussels, clams, birds, all sorts of birds, berries, berries growing. There was no moss here, so there was not a berry." He said that in Churchill some whites had tried to buy an Inuk baby for $200. People there gave the Inuit 25¢ to take their photographs, and he found this helpful . . . Listening to these stories was almost unbearably painful.

page 9   Voluntary *vs.* involuntary relocation – The story of Resolute is not a happy one. What makes it even sadder is that in the 1960s almost all the Canadian Inuit moved into towns anyway. According to some authorities, the number of game animals had been so reduced by then that people could not live on them anymore. A book tells it blandly enough: "As it became more difficult for the Inuit to support themselves in the outlying trapping camps, families gradually moved into the settlements, first on a seasonal basis and then permanently" – Martina Magenau Jacobs and James B. Richardson III, ed., *Arctic Life: Challenge to Survive* (Pittsburgh: Carnegie Museum of Natural History, 1983), p. 150. However, this claim has been disputed. Other authorities say that the game supply continued to be perfectly adequate, but that people wanted access to medical care and especially to schools for their children. This seems equally plausible. One Inuk in Resolute, Tony Maniq, told me (BBC interview, October 1991) that he hunted only on weekends but succeeded in bringing back fifty percent of the food that his family consumed. I asked him whether in that case he could live life the old way. He said that it would certainly be possible – food, shelter, heat and clothing would be no problem – but his family wouldn't go for it. Another very old man told me that he could very easily live as he used to, but his grandchildren weren't tough enough. He would never want to go back to the old life because he'd feel sorry for them.

page 15   Welzl on devil-fish, meteor, Kaminerorov Expedition – op. cit., pp. 286, 195, 250. Devil-fish do exist but Welzl has exaggerated their attributes a little.

page 18   Walrus epigraph – R. N. Rudnose Brown, DSC, *A Naturalist at the Poles: The Life, Work and Voyages of Dr. W. S. Bruce, the Polar Explorer* (London: Seeley, Service & Co., 1923).

page 18   Whale epigraph – Franz Boas, *The Central Eskimo* (Lincoln: University of Nebraska Press [Bison], 1964 repr. of 1888 ed.).

I
KING WILLIAM ISLAND

page 21   Epigraph on pain – Yukio Mishima, *Sun and Steel*, trans. John Bester (New York: Grove Press, 1970), p. 39.

page 21   Description of seal hunting – from an Inuktitut video shot in Grise Fiord, Ellesmere Island.

page 22   Starving man's landscape – Eureka Sound, Ellesmere Island, September 1988.

II
POND INLET

page 25   Epigraph – Jacob Dickinson, letter to author, 1 September 1986.

page 26   Descriptions of Pond Inlet – from a visit in July–August 1989.

page 27   Resolute where the stewardess thought "they played cards and stabbed the loser in the back just for fun" – This fabrication is typical of Resolute's bad reputation in some other communities, especially among whites.

page 28   Three-wheelers – These are now illegal in the North due to their high accident rate. People usually drive four-wheelers (Hondas).

page 29   The "match-box" houses – I will always remember the white woman I met at Pond Inlet who was there to involve the Inuit in mortgages. Of course it would not work very well, since the Inuit did not usually save money, but she said: "I'm here to soften the blow. Of course we're shoveling another layer of earth on the grave of their culture, but at least I can do it with sensitivity."

page 35　Old lady interviewed – Mary Innualuk.

page 37　Death of the dog-teams – Mary Innualuk added: "The government doesn't want animals to be killed to feed our dog-teams. That's why we have skidoos. The people used to look after their own teams well. But nowadays the whole town seems to take care of the few teams here. Whenever someone wants to throw away an old carcass, they bring it to the hunters."

page 39　Wasteful killing of animals – According to Mr. Glenn Johnson, who was then (1989) the manager of the Hudson Bay store at Pond Inlet, seal hunting in particular suffers from these practices. Since the seal market is depressed, the Inuit cannot sell the skins anymore and therefore fail to make back their hunting costs. Big seals don't taste good, and the head of a seal seen in the water gives little clue to its size. For this reason seals are often shot on sight in summer, and if they are discovered to be big the hunters leave them to sink, as it is no longer worth their trouble to skin them. The dog-teams are much fewer and smaller these days, since so many dogs have died of distemper, so it isn't worth the hunters' while to bring back the carcasses for dogfood, either. But there may be a more general explanation. The ethnographer Richard K. Nelson draws the following distinction between Kutchin (Alaskan Athabascan Indians) and Alaskan Inuit: "The Kutchin have a well-developed conservation ethic, whereas the Eskimos do not share this adaptive characteristic. Indians rarely kill an animal without reason. Either they want the meat for food or the hide for sale, or they kill the animal to get rid of it (in the case of grizzly bears and ravens). The Eskimos, on the other hand, sometimes engage in purposeless killing . . . The Kutchin hunt as a means to an end . . . The Eskimo, on the other hand, hunts as an end in itself; he hunts in order to eat, of course, but above all he hunts in order to be an Eskimo. The ultimate compliment is to be told, 'You're a hunter!' or 'You're a man!' Being a hunter and being a man are inseparable. Part of the Eskimos' great adaptive success certainly relates to the fact that they live to hunt rather than merely hunt to live" – *Hunters of the Northern Forest: Designs for Survival among the Alaskan Kutchin* (Chicago: The University of Chicago Press, 1973), pp. 311–12.

Wayne Spencer notes that in the eastern Arctic, where whales are wounded with rifles before the kill, rather than being harpooned, "the problem of wastage is serious. As many as half the whales struck are not landed, and of those which are, the meat is rarely utilized. The muktuk is a delicacy but even that is not saved." However, Spencer believes that this problem is soluble by establishing monitors to log kills, insure that the proper equipment is used, and verify that an experienced man leads each party. "In the 4 years which the author spent in Inuvik, each summer accompanying whalers based at Kendall Island, not only was wastage non-existent, but the authority and wise direction of the headman was clearly evident. One of the instructions most strongly impressed on whaling parties was the necessity of harpooning the whales before shooting them" – "Arctic Wildlife Sketches: Whales of the Northwest Territories" (Pond Inlet: Northwest Territories Renewable Resources pamphlet, ISBN 0–7708–7130). To me this makes eminent sense. Rifles can be either good or evil.

page 46   Hearne footnote – from Farley Mowat, ed., *Tundra: Selections from the Great Accounts of Arctic Land Voyages* (vol. 3 of the "Top of the World" trilogy) (Toronto: McClelland & Stewart, 1973), p. 45.★

page 48   "Our own misery had stolen on us by degrees . . ." – ibid., p. 182.

page 50   ". . . after halting an hour . . ." – ibid., p. 168.

page 50   "His life was not completed" – cf. Taivitialuk Alaasuaq, "Aliakammiq's Kayak Drowning," in Zebedee Nungak and Eugene Arima, *Inuit Stories: Povungnituk* (Hull, Québec: Canadian Museum of Civilization/National Museums of Canada, 1988), p. 95.

page 51   Caribou epigraph – Information sheet: *Fauna of Auyuittuq National Park Reserve and Proximity (ca. 1976)*, p. 1.

III
RESOLUTE BAY

page 55   Tennyson's epitaph for Franklin – on the cenotaph in Westminster Abbey. Reprinted in *The Poetical Works of Alfred, Lord Tennyson (Poet Laureate), Complete Edition from the Author's Text* (New York: Thomas Y. Crowell & Co., 1885), p. 598.

page 56   Rules on preparing and using caribou skins – based on Jill Oakes, *Inuit Amuraangit/Our Clothes: A Travelling Exhibition of Inuit Clothing* (University of Manitoba, Dept. of Clothing and Textiles, 1987?).

page 57   New rules – "As would be expected, Inuit social life has undergone dramatic change as a result of population concentration, the availability of government housing and social assistance, construction of community halls and recreation centers, and the introduction of newspapers, radios and televisions. Along with these social and economic changes, traditional practices such as infanticide, senilicide and spouse exchange, which arose as functional social adaptations to the harsh arctic climate, have disappeared" (Jacobs and Richardson, p. 163). An article in the *Nunatsiaq News* (8 March 1991, Year 19, No. 7, p. 1), is more to the point: "Fully one-third of the NWT population has been profoundly affected by someone who has tried or managed to commit suicide" (Matthew Spence, "Suicide: learning to grieve part of the process").

According to Buster Welsh, a scientist at Resolute (1988), fishes in that area are now so contaminated with lead that it's necessary to sell smaller fish along with any 25–30-year-old lake trout, in order to bring the average concentration down to legal levels.

IV
INUKJUAK

page 61   First caribou epigraph – Secrétariat des activités gouvernementales en milieu amérindien et inuit, *Native Peoples of Quebec* (1984), "The Montagnais" (p. 120).

★ I have sourced Mowat's three volumes of reprinted selections, the "Top of the World trilogy" (*Ordeal by Ice*, *The Polar Passion* and *Tundra*) in place of the originals whenever possible, because the trilogy is in print and the originals are not.

page 61   Second caribou epitaph – *Encyclopaedia Britannica*, vol. 6, entry for "Northwest Territories" (p. 261).

page 65   Descriptions of Inukjuak – from a visit in August 1990.

page 67   "I have undertaken with the advice of the Executive Council . . ." – Sir John Franklin to Lady Franklin, 26 April 1839, in George Mackaness, ORE, MA, Litt. D, DLitt., FRAHS, *Some Private Correspondence of Sir John and Lady Franklin (Tasmania 1837–45)* (Sydney: D. S. Ford, Printers, 1947), p. 65.

page 78   Syphilis epigraph – Franz Boas, op. cit., p. 18.

page 89   Bone epigraph – Owen Beattie and John Geiger, *Frozen in Time: Unlocking the Secrets of the Franklin Expedition* (Saskatoon, Saskatchewan: Western Producer Books, 1987), p. 55.

page 96   Relocation epigraph – Northwest Territories Legislative Assembly brochure (*ca.* 1987), p. 5.

page 97   Firearms epigraph – William Byrd's *Histories of the Dividing Line betwixt Virginia and North Carolina* (New York: Dover Books, 1976). Some might wonder why I quote Byrd here, when he might be more apposite in Dream 3, which concerned itself with Virginia. The reason is that the introduction of firearms among native American populations seems always to have produced the same effects: dependency, decimation of game, and resultant loss of liberty and/or life. See Dream 2 for a more detailed study of this melancholy phenomenon.

V
NORTHWEST PASSAGES

page 101   Murchison's accolade for Franklin – as quoted in Beattie and Geiger, op. cit., p. 16.

page 101   "No, no, my dear Franklin . . ." – Captain Beaufort to Sir John Franklin, 10 June 1840, in Mackaness, op. cit., pp. 98–9.

page 102   Lady Jane's speech patterns – based on her letters and diaries, of which a number of samples are given in Willingham Franklin Rannsley, *The Life, Diaries and Correspondence of Lady Jane Franklin 1792–1875* (London: Erskine Macdonald, 1973).

page 108   Phaeton's epitaph – Ovid, *Metamorphoses*, trans. Frank Justus Miller, rev. G. P. Goold (Cambridge: Harvard University Press: Loeb Classical Library, 1977), p. 82. Miller's translation of the Latin (p. 83) is: "Here Phaeton lies: in Phoebus' car he fared,/and though he greatly failed, more greatly dared."

page 109   Death and disappointment epigraph – William Tecumseh Sherman, *Memoirs* (New York: Library of America, 1990 repr of 1886 ed.), p. 870.

page 109   Description of the streets and airport of Stromness – actually of Resolute, September 1988.

page 110   Franklin's words to Jane on the phone – in part based on his last letter to her from Greenland.

page 112   Greenland ice epigraph – Danish Tourist Board pamphlet (*ca.* 1987), p. 1.

page 113   ". . . the island seems to be in a most flourishing condition . . ." – in Mackaness, op. cit., p. 12.

page 114   From here onward I am sporadically indebted to the fact-marshaling and cautiously informed speculations of Richard J. Cyriax's *Sir John Franklin's Last Expedition: A Chapter in the History of the Royal Navy* (London: Methuen and Co., 1939). I highly recommend this book to those who wish a more literal discussion of the final Franklin Expedition, and how its fate was determined by the preparations and assumptions made, the geography of the region, etc. I wonder whether we do have the final word on the cause of the disaster. Beattie and Geiger are certain that they have proved lead poisoning to be a principal circumstance, no doubt because they were the first to apply the techniques of modern forensic science to the evidence (an earlier autopsy notwithstanding). Cyriax is equally certain that it had to do with scurvy, no doubt because in *his* time the existence of Vitamin C had just been proved. To me it seems that the simple fact of being beset by ice for so long was fatal, and that the two ancillary causes mentioned were just that. In any event, Geiger grants that "there is no single reason why the expedition failed" (p. 161).

page 115   Stefansson epigraph – Mowat, *Tundra*, op. cit., p. 317.

page 116   "Are you cold? . . . Because you're a nice little white man" – P. E. Spalding, *Salliq: An Eskimo Grammar* (Ottawa: Educational Branch, Department of Indian Affairs and Northern Development, 1969), p. 11.

page 117   "We are accustomed to starvation . . ." – Franklin, *Narrative of a Journey to the Shores of the Polar Sea in the Years 1819, 20, 21, and 22* (New York: Greenwood Press, 1969 repr. of 1823 ed.), p. 271.

page 123   Cheap and readable epigraph – B. Gilbert, intr., *Thirty Years in the Arctic Regions* (New York: H. Drayton, 1859), p. 5.

page 123   Rifles and starvation – The following remarks by Boas (op. cit.) are relevant: "That the mode of life of the Eskimo depends wholly on the distribution of these animals will therefore be apparent" (p. 11). But "the opinion that the Eskimos are dying out on account of an insufficient supply of food is erroneous, for, even though the natives slaughter the seals without discrimination or forethought, they do not kill enough to cause any considerable diminution in numbers" (pp. 18–19). In his time (the 1880s) the "diminution" was evidently not considerable enough for him to notice it. (Even now, I've never been told by anyone that seals are endangered in the Canadian Arctic.) The causes of starvation which he recognized were: late ice formation in the fall, which restricted access to seals, storms in winter, and unfamiliarity with a specific stretch of country. It was not for another twenty to thirty years that the damage done began to be noticeable. (Jacobs and Richardson [p. 139] set the difficult period in the 1930s, when fur prices collapsed simultaneously with the decimation of large game and fur-bearing creatures.) If even an intelligent observer such as Boas could fail to see what was happening, we surely have no cause to tout the acuity of hindsight. The rifles were not evil in and of themselves; nor were the white men who introduced them evil men. How inconvenient, that there are no villains in this tragedy!

page 123   Rifles and starvation reconsidered – "I'm not sure you can blame the repeating
rifle on the Ihalmiut's problems in the early 1950s," writes Prof. Frank J. Tester (letter
to author, 27 August 1991: Tester has been studying sociological conditions at Resolute
and Grise Fiord). "The historical record shows that the Inuit had always experienced
periods of starvation when caribou changed migration routes and when their populations fluctuated as part of natural cycles. Caribou biologists are fascinating to listen to
on such matters. They know everything – and nothing at the same time. They blame
overhunting for declining numbers (but in the case of the Kaminuriak herd, the number
soared right after one biologist who participated in [a] hearing I held in the late 1970s
into [the] possible impact of pipeline construction on the Keewatin region, finished
predicting disaster and possible elimination of the herd due to overhunting). There had
been no change in hunting practices in the period of the few years over which this
change occurred. I think we are terribly arrogant in thinking we understand such
things. I've seen biologists present population data which had margins of error almost
as big as the populations themselves – and do it with a poker face!"

page 124   Footnote – Karl O. Brauer, *Handbook of Pyrotechnics* (New York: Chemical
Publishing Company, Inc., 1974), pp. 3–4.

page 124   Codex with Hussite war wagons – MS Codex 3062 (1432), courtesy of the
National Library of Vienna, in M. L. Brown, *Firearms in Colonial America: The Impact
on History and Technology 1492–1792* (Washington: Smithsonian Institution Press, 1980),
p. 16.

page 126   For an excellent and concise description of repeaters on the battlefield, see
Tom Wintringham and John Blashford-Snell, *Weapons and Tactics* (New York: Penguin,
1983), pp. 147–55.

page 126   J. Colin Yerbury writes that between 1650 and 1850, "the theoretical effective-
ness of musket fire was about 40 to 53 percent at 100 yards and 18 to 30 percent at 200
yards. The higher percentage represented trained soldiers . . . This single shot weapon
was capable of two or three shots a minute, and it is estimated that in the Subarctic
between 25 and 35 percent of the shots misfired, compared to 15 percent and 25 percent
under dry conditions" (*The Subarctic Indians and the Fur Trade 1680–1860* [Vancouver:
University of British Columbia Press, 1986], pp. 49–50). Yerbury notes that the
English had begun to trade guns to the Cree at York Fort as early as the 1680s; the
Cree used these guns not only for hunting but also for warfare (pp. 19–20, 22–3).

page 127   Sea-unicorns were probably narwhals.

page 128   Heinrich Klutschak, *Overland to Starvation Cove: With the Inuit in Search of
Franklin 1878–1880*, ed. and trans. William Barr (Buffalo: University of Toronto Press,
1987), p. 118. The original date of publication was 1881 (*Als Eskimo unter den Eskimos:
Eine Schilderung der Erlebnisse der Schwatka'schen Franklin-Aufsuchungs-Expedition in den
Jahren 1878–1880* (Vienna: Hartleben Verlag). The 1987 University of Toronto Press
version is the first printing in English.

page 129   Ross – in Mowat, *Ordeal by Ice* (Salt Lake City: Peregrine Smith Books, 1973),
p. 208.

page 129   Boas – op. cit., p. 102.

page 129   Superintendent Moodie – quoted in W. Gilles Ross, *Whaling and Eskimos: Hudson Bay 1860–1915* (Ottawa: National Museums of Canada, Museum of Man, publications in ethnology, no. 10, 1975), p. 109. Ross sources the *Report of the Royal Northwest Mounted Police* (Ottawa: King's Printer, 1905).

page 129   Jeannie Mippigaq, *Memories from Kuujjuarapik* (Inukjuak, Nunavik (Québec): Avataq Cultural Institute Inc., 1990), p. 32.

page 129   Richard K. Nelson, *Hunters of the Northern Ice* (Chicago: University of Chicago Press, 1969), pp. 302, 213, 308, 233–5.

page 130   Vilhjalmur Stefansson, *Hunters of the Great North* (New York: Paragon House, 1990), pp. 65–6.

page 131   Farley Mowat, *People of the Deer* (Toronto: Seal Books/McClellan and Stewart, 1975), pp. 64–5.

page 131   Minnie Takai – Avataq Cultural Institute Inc., *Northern Quebec Inuit Elders Conference, Povungnituk, Quebec, September 18–October 5, 1982* (Inukjuak, Nunavik (Québec): Avataq Cultural Institute Inc., 1983), p. 38.

page 131   Moesie Maqu – ibid., p. 76.

page 131   Monsieur Nicholas Jérémie – quoted in Yerbury, op. cit., p. 21.

page 131   Gontran de Poncins, *Kabloona* (New York: Time Incorporated, 1965), p. 317.

page 131   Levi Nungaq – interviewed by author.

page 132   Hugh Brody, *Living Arctic: Hunters of the Canadian North* (Toronto: Douglas & McIntyre, 1987), p. 189. For further remarks on today's hunting with rifles and snowmobiles, see Jacobs and Richardson, op. cit., p. 157.

page 132   RCMP Inspector Denny La Nauze, on the Coppermine Inuit (1914), in Mowat, *Tundra*, op. cit., p. 285.

page 133   Franklin on the Crees – ibid., p. 123.

page 134   Welzl epigraph – op. cit., p. 75.

page 135   "Our unfortunate deaths are the only drawback . . ." – This sentence is stolen verbatim from Franklin, op. cit., p. xiv, except that in Franklin's original the sentence begins "The unfortunate death of Mr. Hood is the only drawback . . ."

page 136   Seeds epigraph – In-Cho Chung, *The Arctic and the Rockies as Seen by a Botanist: Pictorial* (Seoul, Korea: Samhwa Printing Co. Ltd., 1984), p. 29.

page 137   Description of *Terror* and *Erebus* "sailing in the blue" – after a painting by Robert Hood, "The Hudson's Bay Fleet 31 July 1819 by Cape Farewell," appended to his *Narrative of the Proceedings of an Expedition of Discovery in North America Under the Command of Lieutenant Franklin, R.N.*, in C. Stuart Houston, ed., *To the Arctic by Canoe 1819–21: The Journal and Paintings of Robert Hood* (Montréal: The Arctic Institute of North America/McGill–Queen's University Press, 1974), plate 2.

page 139   Description of the whale-butchering – I saw this in Nuuk Harbor, Greenland, in 1987.

page 139   Enthusiasm of the men – so one imagines. But it is also possible to suppose that the men were discontented and would rather have gone to Pangnirtung where there is now a very reasonable bed and breakfast and other attractions, because they'd heard the saying that rang all over Baffin Island: Go to Pang, get a bang.

page 144   Description of Franklin at dinner – after an engraving in Houston, op. cit., p. 190.

page 145   "The ships are now being swung . . ." – Franklin's last dispatch, in Cyriax, op. cit., pp. 62–3.

page 147   "He conceived that the greatest impediments from ice . . ." – after a letter by Franklin, 24 January 1845, in ibid., p. 24.

page 148   Epigraph on Outsiders – Nelson, *Hunters of the Northern Forest*, op. cit., p. 307.

page 149   Clyde River and Pond Inlet – There is no indication that Franklin did or did not visit these places. Most likely he would not have; the former was very much out of his way; the latter a little so; it is conceivable that ice-vagaries compelled him there. Forty-odd years later, Boas (op. cit., p. 34) wrote that "River Clyde . . . [is] not always inhabited, but . . . visited at irregular intervals by the Akudnirmiut," an Inuit tribe which was more or less nomadic, like all of the people in Baffin-Land at that period who did not have some connection with the whalers. In the same place, Boas mentions Pond Bay as being a summer residence of the Tununirmiut, a subtribe of the Aggomiut. These latter people hunted narwhals and belugas as their descendants do today.

page 151   Extract on lead psychosis – Donald B. Louria, "Trace Metal Poisoning," in James B. Wyngaarden, MD and Lloyd H. Smith, Jr., MD, *Cecil Textbook of Medicine*, 17th ed. (Philadelphia: W. B. Saunders Co., 1985), pp. 2308–9.

page 152   SEDNA and the FULMAR – Boas, op. cit., pp. 175–83.

page 154   Raw ptarmigan – tastes much like yellowtail sashimi.

page 167   Description of Wellington Channel – after a watercolor of Wellington Channel, Beechey Island, by James Hamilton, *ca.* 1852 (Glenbow Museum, Calgary).

page 168   Princely wage epigraph – Martin Lindsay (Royal Scots Fusiliers), *Those Greenland Days* (London: Blackwood, 1932), p. 111.

page 168   Description of the ships in winter – partly based on Sherard Osborn's *Stray Leaves from an Arctic Journal* (1852), in Mowat, *Ordeal by Ice*, op. cit., pp. 270–1. Osborn was one of the men sent to search for Franklin.

page 174   Descriptions of Cornwallis Island – from a visit in March 1991.

page 176   The first overland expedition – "These naval men were sent to carry out a difficult task with totally inadequate resources. In accepting the leadership of the expedition, Franklin perhaps too readily succumbed to the temptation of fame and career advancement. As commanding officer he should have recognized that the Admiralty was attempting to promote this first visit by white men along the northern coast of North America 'on the cheap.' A navy man, Franklin was unfairly given an overland assignment inappropriate to his training and previous experience" – C. Stuart Houston, *Arctic Ordeal: The Journal of John Richardson, Surgeon-Naturalist with Franklin 1820–22* (Montréal: McGill–Queen's University Press, 1984, p. xxiv). Mowat is even more openly critical: "Franklin's bull-headed conviction, that an officer of the Royal Navy knew more about local conditions than any inhabitant, would undoubtedly have led to the destruction of his party – as Akaitcho prophesied – had the Chipewyan chief not forced him to give up the attempt to go on to the coast that autumn. But Franklin did not learn anything from this lesson, as the tragic course of the famous Franklin Expedition of 1845 demonstrated . . ." (*Tundra*, op. cit., p. 135 fn.)

page 176 In light of the central metaphor of my first Dream, it may be worth making reference to an observation in Franklin (op. cit., pp. 293–4) that several Chipewyan tribes believed that they came from a place "where there was no winter, which produced trees, and large fruits, now unknown to them . . . the sea has since frozen, and they have never been able to return."

page 179 Simpson's remarks to Back – actually confided only to his journal, which is quoted in Houston, *To the Arctic by Canoe*, op. cit., p. xxvii.

page 179 Events of the first overland expedition mentioned here, from Fort Enterprise to Bloody Falls – Houston, *Arctic Ordeal*, op. cit., Wednesday, 13 September 1820 (p. 10), Thursday, 14 September (p. 11), Wednesday, 9 October (pp. 17–18), Monday, 19 October (p. 19), Friday, 1 December (p. 22), Friday, 5 January 1822 (p. 25), Wednesday, 14 February (p. 29), 22 May (pp. 39–41), Friday, 15 June (p. 51: "Dr Richardson was obliged to refuse . . . only in proportion to the deer brought in" – this sentence almost verbatim), Saturday, 7 July (p. 68), Sunday, 8 July (p. 68), Thursday, 12 July (p. 75), Sunday, 15 July (p. 77).

page 183 Impressing Akaicho with the eclipse – Franklin, op. cit., pp. 228–9. For dramatic purposes I have altered the chronology of this eclipse in the narrative. It actually occurred before the Coppermine journey.

page 183 Hearne on the murder of the young Inuk woman – *A Journey from Prince of Wales's Fort to the Northern Ocean* (1772), excerpted in Mowat, *Tundra*, op. cit., p. 60.

page 183 Events of the first overland expedition mentioned here, from the mouth of the Coppermine to Point Turnagain and then back to Fort Enterprise and Fort Providence – Houston, op. cit., Wednesday, 18 July (p. 82), Thursday, 19 July (p. 83: Richardson's diary entry about the terror of the voyageurs is quoted from here), Saturday, 18 August (p. 114), Monday, 20 August (p. 115), Wednesday, 22 August (loc. cit.), Thursday, 23 August (p. 116), Friday, 24 August (p. 118), Saturday, 25 August (p. 119: Richardson's diary entry about the joy of the voyageurs at landing is quoted from here), Friday, 7 September (pp. 126–7), Saturday, 8 September (p. 127), Monday, 10 September (pp. 129–30), Friday, 14 September (p. 133), Monday, 17 September (p. 136), Sunday, 23 September (p. 138), Tuesday, 25 September (p. 139), Thursday, 27 September (p. 141), Saturday, 6 October (pp. 146–7), 11 October★ (pp. 150–1), 20 October (pp. 154–5), 23 October (p. 156), Monday, 29 October (p. 161), Tuesday, 30 October (p. 162), Thursday, 1 November (p. 163), Wednesday, 7 November (pp. 164–5), Friday, 9 November (p. 165), Friday, 16 November (p. 167), Saturday, 17 November (pp. 167–8), Friday, 14 December (p. 178: Akaicho's words verbatim aside from some modernized punctuation).

★ Richardson does not consistently supply weekday names for his dates.

Yerbury remarks: ". . . subsistence in the northwestern transition boreal forest and the Mackenzie drainage system was a high-risk, low-return activity, especially after overexploitation resulting from the population movements into the area and the lack of conservation practices in hunting and trapping" (op. cit., p. 146).

page 195   Michel, Hood, Hepburn and Richardson – Mowat argues in *Tundra* that there is no evidence that Michel killed the first two voyageurs for food, only that he ate them. "It can be assumed that Michel's corpse did not go to waste after he was 'executed.' Hepburn and Richardson were in comparatively good condition when they reached the Fort . . ." – op. cit., p. 183.

page 195   Hood's silhouette – It appears in the frontispiece of Houston, *To the Arctic by Canoe*, op. cit.

page 195   Greenstockings's clothing – Typical Chipewyan women's garb is described in ibid., pp. 72–3.

page 196   In light of the events narrated here, it is interesting that Franklin mentions, deadpan, that the Crees "speak of Weettako, a kind of vampyre or devil, into which those who have fed on human flesh are transformed" (ibid., p. 77).

page 197   Franklin sees more than 2,000 caribou – Franklin, op. cit., p. 240.

page 199   Survival epigraph – Willie Cooper, ᑦᕐᐊᑎᐅᑦ ᐊᐅᑳᕈᔭᖕᒋᑦ/*Memories of a Kuujjuamiuq* (Inukjuak, Québec: Avataq Cultural Institute Inc., Publication of the Documentary Center on Inuit History No. 1, 1989), p. 5.

page 199   Description of fishing – from a visit to Pond Inlet in 1989.

page 200   Fishing epigraph – Saali Arngnaituq, "The Giant and the Man," in Nungak and Arima, op. cit., p. 23.

page 200   Crozier on tinned meats in the Antarctic with Sir James – after Captain Sir James Clark Ross, *A Voyage of Discovery and Research in the Southern and Antarctic Regions During the Years 1839–43* (1847) (New York: August McKelley, 1969), p. xx. Even though this book was not published until after Franklin's departure, Franklin would certainly have had the benefit of Crozier's experience.

page 200   According to Cyriax (p. 112), "Goldner's processes are free from any suspicion of deliberate fraud." Cyriax does not believe the number of tins found by the search expeditions who reached Beechey Island to be excessive. Sir James Ross, however, did believe that some of the meat had putrefied. For a full discussion, see Cyriax, op. cit., pp. 109–17. Beattie and Geiger suggest (op. cit., pp. 156–8) that the end seams of some cans were incompletely sealed, which would have led to spoilage, and that the lead solder itself "played an important role in the declining health of the entire crews of the *Erebus* and *Terror*, not only in the loss of physical energy but increasingly in the mind's despair . . . even very subtle effects of low lead exposure could have had significant impact on the decision-making processes of the men, particularly the officers" (p. 161).

page 203   Hood on danger – Houston, *To the Arctic by Canoe*, op. cit., p. 13. I have slightly altered this extract for clarity.

page 205   Cumulative effects of lead poisoning – see, e.g., Louria, in Wyngaarden and Smith, op. cit., pp. 2308–9. Three treatment agents for lead poisoning do exist (dimercaprol, calcium disodium edetate and D-penicillamine), but these are themselves dangerous.

page 211   The Finnlander Kid's skull – after an Okvik figurine of walrus ivory dug up from Panuk Island, Alaska, as photographed in Allen Wardwell, *Ancient Eskimo Ivories of the Bering Strait* (New York: Hudson Hills Press, 1986), p. 46, # 23.

page 212   Franklin's choice of direction – "The expedition was foredoomed to failure by [Sir James] Ross's error in closing the eastern channel [east of King William's Land]; chance then took a hand to make the catastrophe complete." Thus Leslie H. Neatby, *The Search for Franklin* (London: Arthur Barker Ltd., 1970), p. 267.

VI
PEEL SOUND

page 216   Landscape description – actually recorded a few miles east of Eureka, Ellesmere Island (September 1988).

page 216   The weather station at Eureka, by the way, offered good examples of the contradictions brought by the rifles. (1) Inside the station everything was warm, clean, abundant, wasteful. My friend Ben said that he could have made three meals out of every pail of dinner slops. (2) The station personnel knew far less than we did of the surrounding area. (3) Some of them would walk through knee-deep drifts without gloves or good boots, because they could count on the station's being there. In five to ten minutes they'd be freezing, and need to return to a heated vehicle.

page 221   The ship's fittings – "Memorandum of the fittings of Her Majesty's ship *Erebus*, by Mr. Rice, of Chatham Dockyard," in Sir James Ross, op. cit., vol. 1, Appendix 1, pp. 327–8. The two ships were refitted with yet more armor (such as the iron sheeting) after the Antarctic expedition described here by Sir James.

page 225   Franklin on the Dog-Rib Indians – Gilbert, op. cit., p. 393.

page 226   Episode of the pillaging "Esquimaux" – ibid., pp. 415–22.

page 226   *Teyma, teyma!* – In present-day Resolute Bay Inuktitut this means: "Stop, stop!" (According to the dictionary of Schneider, *taima* can also mean, "It is ready." Since this encounter took place close to two centuries ago and a considerable distance to the west, where other dialects might have held sway, it is possible that the word meant something else. However, the Resolute Bay meaning seems as likely as any.)

page 226   Warning of the Inuit against the ice – ibid., p. 429.

page 226   The near-shipwreck by Point Sabine – ibid., pp. 438–9.

page 230   Skeleton epigraph – Mircea Eliade, *Shamanism: Archaic Techniques of Ecstasy* (Princeton: Princeton University Press, Bollingen Series LXXVI, rev. ed., 1971), p. 62.

page 234   Hood on Inuit women's breasts – Houston, *To the Arctic by Canoe*, op. cit., p. 14.

page 238   Dismemberment and renewal epigraph – Eliade, op. cit., p. 44.

page 239   The Admiralty paper signed by Gore and Des Voeux – after a facsimile in Beattie and Geiger, op. cit., p. 36.

page 241   'I thank Thee, FATHER . . ." – Luke 10.21.

page 250   Franklin imagines his death – after a depiction of his burial on his monument at Waterloo Place, London.

page 266   Description of Isachsen – from a visit in March 1991.

page 270   Failure of the sleeping bag – I am still not certain what happened. I don't think that the manufacturer intentionally cut any corners. However, when I received the bag I was concerned by how thin the down seemed to be, and called the company. They reassured me. There was no way I could afford to go north to test the sleeping bag before relying on it, so I took the company at its word. The down was not thick enough. My best guess as to the *primary* cause of the failure is that the vapor barrier liner inside the sleeping bag did not work. This allowed body vapor to diffuse into the down itself. Had the VBL done its job, there might have been frost on the inside of the bag, and maybe on the outside from my breath. But what I distinctly felt was that the clumps of down themselves froze into hard lumps. I very much like this sleeping bag in the abstract. It may well do its job in moderately cold temperatures. However, for extreme temperatures I cannot recommend it. I have just purchased a Woods sleeping bag, which weighs 25 lbs and comes with a wool liner. As my friend David in Resolute said, "Survivability excludes portability."

page 293   Penguin epigraph – Rudnose Brown, op. cit., pp. 50–1.

page 295   Diminished success of hunting epigraph – *The Inuit* (Canadian government pamphlet) (1990), p. 53.

page 301   Epigraph – Edward Pellham, *Gods Power and Providence; Shewn, IN THE MIRACVLOVS Preservation and Deliverance of eight Englishmen, left by mischance in Greenland, Anno 1626, nine moneths and twelve dayes* (London: R.Y./John Partridge, 1631).

page 305   For another useful if somewhat overpopular and hypothetical description of the Franklin Expedition's probable movements on King William Island, see Paul Fenimore Cooper, *Island of the Lost* (New York: Putnam, 1961). Neatby and Cyriax are more thorough, and trace out the final movements of Franklin's men in some detail. It seems that many of the weaker men encamped at Terror Bay (south of Cape Crozier) and died there. The remainder rounded Cape Herschel (where they could have completed the Northwest Passage in the ships had there been no ice), and then continued east, some dying on the way. The remnant crossed Simpson Strait to Starvation Cove.

page 308   Cyriax proposes another explanation for the fact that the Inuit did not stay to help the white men: they saw that they simply could not feed all of them.

VII
KING WILLIAM ISLAND

page 311   Meat epigraph – Heinrich Klutschak, op. cit., p. 23.

page 311   Descriptions of King William Island – actually, of Cornwallis Island and Ellesmere Island (August–September 1988).

page 315   "Cannibalizing the trunk of the body . . ." – Beattie and Geiger, op. cit.,
    p. 62.

page 315   Stefansson on meat – op. cit., p. 69.

page 320   Schwatka's men and the Caucasian skull – Klutschak, op. cit., p. 116.

page 320   Use of ship timbers for tools and fuel – ibid., pp. 112–13.

page 320   Eskimo Joe's finds – ibid., p. 110.

page 324   Most likely some of the men lived through June. A few survivors seem to
    have returned to one or both of the ships to eke out a fifth winter, according to Inuit
    reports and the discovery by one of the searchers of some equipment discarded en route
    north to the ships. Perhaps one or two might have even made it to Back's River before
    they too perished.

STRAIGHT SHOTS

page 327   Sarah Bacon epigraph – Avataq Cultural Institute Inc., op. cit., p. 121.

page 328   "Greenpeace knocked out the selling of seal skins . . ." – The problem caused
    by these do-gooders is not confined to Greenland. "Until recently, money earned from
    selling sealskins provided valuable monetary support for many Inuit families. But
    adverse publicity from groups involved in the 20-year-old international anti-sealing
    campaign has destroyed virtually the entire seal fur market and brought hardship to
    many Inuit families" – Indian and Northern Affairs Canada, *The Inuit* (Ottawa:
    Minister of Supplies and Services Canada, 1990), p. 52.

page 329   Description of Ameralik Fjord – from a visit in July 1987.

page 330   Story of the caribou hunt – I heard this from an Inuk in Iqaluit in 1988.

page 331   As with the problem caused by the sealskin ban, the problem of inexperienced
    hunters is ubiquitous. Writing almost thirty years ago about a town in Alaska, Richard
    Nelson noted: "The last twenty years . . . have seen a great decline in the importance
    of hunting . . . Today, some of the young boys probably have not seen their first
    caribou by the time they become teenagers . . . In the next few years we must put
    forth a maximum effort to live with the people and learn from them whatever we still
    can, before it is lost forever in the icy graves of the old men" (op. cit., pp. 384–7).

page 333   Party line epigraph – Manès Sperber, *The Burned Bramble*, trans. Constantine
    Fitzgibbon (New York: Holmes and Meier, 1988), p. 198.

page 334   Testimony and comment for Scene I – *House of Commons Issue No. 22, Monday,*
    19 March 1990, Minutes of Proceedings and Evidence of the Standing Committee on Aboriginal
    Affairs, respecting: In accordance with its mandate under Standing Order 108(2), to obtain the
    latest information on current matters, relating to aboriginal affairs; Second Session of the Thirty-
    Fourth Parliament, 1989–90 (Ottawa: Queen's Printer for Canada), pp. 8, 10–12, 14–15,
    19, 22–3. I have often abridged testimony, interleaved the testimony of various
    witnesses, and changed the order of testimony.

page 334   Alleged forced prostitution – A friend in Resolute sent me a letter dryly
    describing that epoch: "The store in the early days of Grise Fiord and Resolute, was a

government store. The goods, often unsuitable for northern use[,] were bought with a loan from the 'Eskimo Loan Fund' (government), were offered for trade for furs, and in the case of Grise Fiord only after the RCMP officer slept with your wife. Funds were recorded by the RCMP; wages, if any, earned by the people by working for other government agencies were also recorded in the book, the first cashless society. I have not been able to find out how welfare was issued if at all."

page 336   An attached annex to the testimony in Issue No. 22 (Annex 4) is a report by an independent contractor acceptable both to Makivik, the Inuit corporation, and to Indian and Northern Affairs Canada. The report finds that the Pond Inlet Inuit involved in the relocation were promised that they could return home if they were unhappy, and the Inukjuak Inuit had grounds for believing that the promise applied to them also, whether it was made to them or not, and that that promise was not kept.

page 336   Pilot's testimony and comment (Scene II) – *House of Commons Issue No. 40, Monday, 18 June 1990, Minutes of Proceedings and Evidence of the Standing Committee on Aboriginal Affairs, respecting: In accordance with its mandate under Standing Order 108(2), a study on literacy; respecting: Follow-up on Grise Fiord Issue; including: Third Report to the House (on Grise Fiord); Second Session of the Thirty-Fourth Parliament, 1989–90* (Ottawa: Queen's Printer for Canada), pp. 40, 42–5, 47–9, 51, 60. Again, I have abridged and changed the order of testimony – without (I honestly believe) doing violence to the sense. Perhaps I should add that Pilot testified voluntarily.

page 338   Rationale for rejecting the resolution – see the report by the Hickling Corporation of September 1990, *Assessment of the Factual Basis of Certain Allegations Made Before the Standing Committee on Aboriginal Affairs Concerning the Relocation of Inukjuak Inuit Families in the 1950s,* submitted to the DIAND Northern Program. By and large, this is a cowardly document. It deals with allegations of slave labor, theft of mail, forced prostitution, etc., in one elegant sweep: "It was understood that the contractor would not be expected to deal with allegations that might be considered to fall under the Criminal Code" (pp. 2–3). As to the question of whether the relocation was voluntary, as the government claims, or essentially involuntary, as the Inuit claim, saying that they felt they had to do what white people told them, "it was not possible for us to reach conclusions . . . We uncovered no direct evidence that would support this assertion" (p. 9). Nor (to judge from the questions which they asked the Inuit) did they look for it. Having conveniently limited its scope, the Hickling report does not limit its recommendations. "The evidence that we have examined does not support the allegation that the Government committed wrongdoing in the planning and conduct of this project. The material we examined leads us to a different conclusion, namely that the project was conscientiously planned, was carried out in a reasonably effective manner and that the Inuit participated in it voluntarily, in their own search for a better life, and benefited from the experience . . . In our view, to apologize for a wrongdoing it did not commit would constitute deception on the part of the Government" (p. 6). This strikes me as coldbloodedly mendacious. On a few points, however, it is possible to give the Government the benefit of the doubt. The Inuit maintain that the real purpose of the relocation was to prove sovereignty over the Arctic islands, and that the supposed concern over the scarcity of game in Inukjuak was a mere smokescreen. This may be true, and it may not be. The Hickling report, needless to say, says that it isn't. Based on the limited amount of evidence available to me, it was difficult for me to make a determination about this. But it doesn't matter. The Canadian government could have been suffused with intentions of the utmost benignity. Once the Inuit wanted to return, however, it was in the wrong to refuse to assist them to do so.

For further information on the relocation allegations, please see the exchange of letters immediately following this Sources section.

page 339   Black bear epigraph – Government of Newfoundland and Labrador, *Newfoundland and Labrador: Hunting and Fishing Just Waiting for You* (Saint Johns: Department of Development and Tourism, Tourism Branch, 1986), pp. 5–6.

page 341   Hall epigraph – quoted in Chauncey C. Loomis, *Weird and Tragic Shores: The Story of Charles Francis Hall, Explorer* (Lincoln, Nebraska: University of Nebraska Press/Bison, 1991), p. 193.

page 342   Epitaph: "Scattered throughout Arctic America . . ." – National Geographic Society, *The World of the American Indian* (Washington, D.C., 1974), p. 84.

GLOSSARIES

page 347   Akaicho quotation – Franklin, op. cit., p. 251.

page 348   Franklin quotation – Houston, *Arctic Ordeal*, op. cit., p. xxii.

page 348   Greenstockings quotation – Franklin, op. cit., p. 254.

page 350   Tattannoeuck quotation – George Back, *Narrative of the Arctic Land Expedition to the Mouth of the Great Fish River* (London: J. Murray, 1836).

page 351   Copper Indians quotations – Franklin, op. cit., p. 287; Yerbury, op. cit., p. 153.

page 354   Back's Great Fish River quotation – Back quoted in Cyriax, op. cit., p. 145.

page 354   Beechey Island quotation – Beattie and Geiger, op. cit., p. 92.

page 355   Inukjuak quotation – Secrétariat des activités gouvernementales en milieu amérindien et inuit, *Native Peoples of Quebec* (1984), p. 163.

page 356   Kikertak quotation – Boas, op. cit., p. 48.

page 356   Labrador quotation – Francis Parkman, *Pioneers of France in the New World* (1865), in *France and England in North America*, vol. 1 (New York: The Library of America, 1983), p. 165 fn. Trigger's addendum: personal note to the author, 1989.

page 357   Povungnituk quotation – Nungak and Arima, op. cit., p. 13.

page 359   Umiak quotation – Lucien Schneider, osu, *Ulirnaisígutit: An Inuktitut–English Dictionary of Northern Quebec, Labrador and Eastern Arctic Canada* (Québec: Les Presses de l'Université Laval, 1985).

CHRONOLOGY

page 365 1800–1900 – Yerbury, op. cit., p. 157.
page 366 1840–2 – ibid., p. 125.
page 371 1950s – Mowat on caribou: *Tundra*, op. cit., p. 396.
page 371 1950s – Tester on caribou: letter to author, 1991.

SOURCES

page 376 Epigraph – Roy Godson, ed., *Intelligence Requirements for the 1980s:* no. 5, *Clandestine Collection* (Washington, D.C.: National Strategy Information Center, Inc., 1982), p. 200.

ILLUSTRATIONS

Pencil drawings of rifles (pages 129–31) and ceremonial mask (page 249) – sketched with reference to photographs in the following sources: Northwest Company trade fusil from Brown, p. 285. Brown in turn sources the Museum of the Fur Trade, Chadron, Nebraska. BAR grade 1 from the 1990 Browning catalog, pp. 28–9. Ruger "All-Weather" rifle from that company's 1989 catalog, p. 10. Sealskin mask from Betty Issenman and Catherine Rankin, *Ivalu: Traditions of Inuit Clothing* (Montréal: McCord Museum of Canadian History, 1988), p. 88 (photo; item # 30) and p. 97 (catalogue description, item # 30).

Ballpoint drawings (pages 158 and 241) – made for me by Jamie T. and by Annie Atagootak, respectively, in Pond Inlet in 1989. Many other Inuit children contributed drawings, and I would like to thank them one and all.

MAPS

The outlines of landforms on many of the maps in this book are traced, at least in places. I have made use of a number of sources, including a map entitled "The Inuit North," reproduced on the back cover of *Inuktitut* magazine (summer 1986); a map entitled "Indian and Inuit Communities and Languages," which is a sheet in *The National Atlas of Canada* (fifth ed.); the maps which appear in Klutschak and in Beattie and Geiger; various maps of the world, Canada and the polar regions in *The Times Atlas of the World* (seventh ed.); and, last and most, a variety of topographic maps issued by the Canada Map Office, Department of Energy, Mines, and Resources (Ottawa). The specific maps to which I referred in preparing my own copies varied in scale. Among them were maps of: Belcher Channel, Ellef Ringnes Island, Eureka, Inukjuak, Isachsen, Lancaster Sound, Pond Inlet, and Resolute. I have also made use of my own sketch-maps of various places whenever I could (I have never been to eastern Greenland, King William Island, Beechey Island or the Coppermine).

Exchange of Letters on the Relocation Allegations

I
ROYAL CANADIAN MOUNTED POLICE

RCMP Headquarters
1200 Alta Vista Drive
Ottawa, Ontario K1A 0R2   *23 May 1991*

Ladies and Gentlemen:

I have just completed a book which is partially concerned with the relocation of Inuit families from Inukjuak, Québec and Pond Inlet, Baffin Island, to Resolute Bay and Grise Fiord in the 1950s. I have visited each of these places except for Grise Fiord. I have interviewed a few people and read the Standing Committee hearings and some other relevant documents. At this time I feel that I understand the Inuit point of view on this issue fairly well. Doubtless you are aware that it does not put the RCMP in an entirely favorable light. In the interest of fairness I would very much like to have you comment on the appropriate sections of my manuscript, here subjoined. In this book I tell the story as I see it. But I have no axe to grind; in fact, I'd be delighted if you could convince me that some or all of the allegations made by the Inuit were exaggerated. If you can show me that my conclusions are wrong, I'll change them. Any remarks you care to make will be incorporated into my text or notes whenever possible.

. . . Thank you very much for your help.

Yours truly,
WILLIAM T. VOLLMANN

Dear Mr. Vollmann:

Like yourself I have conducted a limited amount of research on the relocation of Inuit families in the 1950s. As you have surmised I do not feel that you have accurately portrayed these events in your manuscript. But as you say this is the story as you see it. I can see no purpose in trying to dispute your account point by point. Instead I enclose copies of reports which give a much different version of what took place. And if you come to Ottawa, I understand that there are other relevant sources at the National Archives of Canada.

Yours truly,
DR. WILLIAM BEAHEN
A/IC RCMP Historical Section

Dr. William Beahen A/IC RCMP Historical Section
RCMP Headquarters
1200 Alta Vista Drive
Ottawa, Ontario K1A 0R2   *23 May 1991* [mis-dated]

Dear Dr. Beahen:

Thank you for your prompt and helpful reply to my letter. I have now read the materials you enclosed (or reread in the case of the Hammond Report). It is a bit strange for me as an outsider to see each of the two sides painting such a completely different picture. I hope you'll forgive me for raising specific points, which you forbore to do after reading my ms. I will of course be taking the same approach with Makivik if and when I hear from them.

A.   *RCMP Quarterly* article, volume 20 # 2 (n.d., but I assume Feb. 1954 from the ref. given on p. 142)

This certainly does suggest, as do many other sources, that the relocation was undertaken with the best of intentions. Cst. Fryer's account of life at Craig Harbour is positive and believable. I was particularly interested in the mention on p. 139 that relocated Inuit from Inukjuak had not ever shot walrus or caribou before. That indicates that they were being empowered to become self-reliant in an appropriately traditional way, and I can't imagine anything better than that.

P. 141 confirms, however, what Mr. Bob Pilot mentioned in his testimony to the Standing Committee on Aboriginal Affairs – namely, that the Inuit and the RCMP were apart for much or most of the time. The RCMP's impressions of the relocatees' happiness and well-being, therefore, might not always have been accurate. This is the only way I can account for the shocking discrepancy between Pilot's testimony and that of the Inuit witnesses in the earlier hearing.

(By the way, it was not always clear to me whether the witnesses were speaking of Craig Harbour/Grise Fiord or of Resolute. But it really doesn't matter. The *RCMP Quarterly* article could be entirely right about conditions at Craig Harbour; Pilot himself says in his testimony that "you are talking about Resolute Bay. There were two different situations here." If either of these places suffered from the conditions that the Inuit witnesses mention, then the *Quarterly's* account is irrelevant.)

Regarding the absolute clash between the idyllic claims of the article and the bitter claim of the Inuit witnesses, one of the following must be true:

1. The Inuit witnesses were maliciously lying, in order to gain financial compensation and/or defame the Canadian government. (An analogy in my country might be the Tawana Brawley case.)

2. The Inuit witnesses and the RCMP had different understandings and perceptions of events. For instance, what they thought of as forced prostitution might have occurred episodically, the white men believing that the Inuit women they propositioned submitted voluntarily, and the Inuit women believing that they were required to submit. Such interpretations of other testimony, such as theft of money from letters, become more far-fetched, but possible, I suppose. And it seems to me not improbable that different understandings could have existed over what the Inuit call forced labor. The RCMP might well have felt that they were doing the Inuit a favor and one way in which the Inuit might repay the government's efforts would be to provide free labor, etc., etc.

3. The RCMP was unaware of or deliberately covered up the corruption of its own officials. In other words, at least some of the Inuit allegations are true.

I find it very odd that the most extreme charges against the RCMP do not appear in the Makivik Report. This makes me want to give them less credence. I have written to Makivik about this and other matters, but so far haven't heard from them since my Québec City address was no longer current and I had to re-post the letter to Kuujjuaq.

On the other hand, the Inuit interviews which I conducted and quoted from in the text that I sent to you give an awfully negative view of the relocation. This makes me more skeptical about the article.

What is your own opinion of the Inuit witnesses' allegations, and which of my three propositions would you pick to reconcile the discrepancies between the two perspectives?

B.   Marc M. Hammond's report of findings, 3 August 1984

Hammond's findings (his p. 1) suggest that at least one very important aspect of the relocation was mishandled, judged both by our standards and by the standards of the time. This is the business about the Inukjuak Inuit believing that they would be returned home gratis if they desired it. And they weren't.

Or am I misreading something? How would you address the complaints about this in the two interviews of my text?

By the way, it is inexplicable to me why Hammond did not consult Inuit for their version (see his list of persons, p. 21).

The sovereignty thing (p. 3, extract # 3) I personally find a red herring, and don't see why the Inuit make it into such an issue. What's the difference why they were relocated if it was voluntary and they benefited (assuming, of course, that it *was* voluntary and they did benefit)? There was nothing wrong with Canada's asserting its claim to the archipelago by encouraging settlement there. What's your opinion of Levi Nungaq's statement? (*Levi didn't really wanna come here; my parents didn't really wanna come here, but because his brother was stuck here and he couldn't leave him, they had to come here. At that time, one of the difficulties they had, they assumed anytime a white guy told them what to do, they thought they had to do it.*★ *So, RCMP got those people. In 'fifty-five his family moved in here. They didn't really hesitate to do that; they thought they'd be back in two years.*) That's the heart of the matter.

In Pond Inlet, as my ms. notes, I was told of a man who committed suicide rather than be relocated. In Resolute they knew immediately who he was, and gave me the name of a relative of his who lives there. The fact that the story would be repeated in two separate communities makes me inclined to believe it, despite para. 4 on p. 14 of Hammond's Appendix C. Again, it is highly unfortunate that no Inuit are sourced in the Hammond Report.

What have your researches turned up about the dates and frequency of Inuit requests to return from 1956 onwards? Obviously if there are none or not many (and if there's no reason to think that records have been lost) this weakens the Inuit case.

In Appendix A, p. 5, where did the 60 caribou skins at the HBC posts at Inukjuak come from, if the Inuit there had never shot any, as stated in the *RCMP Quarterly* article? Were these skins brought in from elsewhere, or was it simply that the relocatees hadn't shot caribou, but other locals had?

On p. 10 of the same Appendix, prices for ammunition at Iqaluit at the time are listed. They seem reasonable. In your opinion, is Levi Nungaq's claim that a single bullet cost two sealskins at Resolute inaccurate?

★ This might be the same thing as Reuben Ploughman's claim (Hammond, p. 14) that the Inukjuak Inuit were "extremely trusting of Government."

Appendix C, p. 8, describes the "excellent appearance" of the Resolute settlement. Do you think that the Inuit witnesses are simply looking back with unfair hindsight?

In Appendix D–2, pp. 2, 3 and 5, Mr. C. J. Marshall's objections (points 2, 5, 9h and 10) do seem serious to me, and while Mr. Cantley's replies generally explain the circumstances satisfactorily, they don't say how the difficulties mentioned are to be overcome. (Unfortunately, the report from Cst. Gibson referred to on p. 6, which says that there aren't any serious problems at Resolute, is not attached.) Would you agree that the first winter at Resolute was more difficult than it should have been, or would you be more inclined to say that hardship and uncertainty was simply more common then and so once more hindsight is rearing its ugly head?

Thank you very much for wading through all these queries. I look forward to hearing from you again, if you're not too sick of me.

Yours sincerely,
WILLIAM T. VOLLMANN

24 July 1991

Dear Mr Vollmann:

This is in reply to your letter dated 23 May 1991, which oddly enough was not received at this office until 10 July.

I hasten to assure you that I am not sick of you but I am sorry to say that I must disappoint you. While your research project is most interesting, I am afraid that I cannot do more to assist you than the material I have already provided. Besides many other duties, our two-person historical research staff receives an average of 85 inquiries like yours each month. It is impossible for me to devote enough time to help you sort out the research anomalies that you have encountered. I am afraid I can only offer you my best wishes for a successful conclusion of your project.

Yours truly,
DR. WILLIAM BEAHEN
A/IC RCMP Historical Section

2
MAKIVIK CORPORATION

Makivik Corporation
4898 de Maisonneuve West
Westmount, Québec H3Z 1M7   *24 May 1991*

Ladies and Gentlemen:

I have just completed a book which is partially concerned with the relocation of Inuit families from Inukjuak, Québec and Pond Inlet, Baffin Island, to Resolute Bay and Grise Fiord in the 1950s. I have visited each of these places except for Grise Fiord. I have interviewed a few people and read the Standing Committee hearings and some other relevant documents, including your report. In the interest of fairness I would very much like to have you comment on the appropriate sections of my manuscript, here subjoined. (Another copy of the same sections will be sent to the RCMP for their version.) In this book I tell the story as I see it, and I basically uphold your point of view. But I have no axe to grind about the RCMP; if they can somehow convince me (which I doubt) that my conclusions are wrong, I'll change them. Any remarks you care to make will be incorporated into my text or notes whenever possible.

I am especially interested to learn why the Makivik Report did not raise the issue of sexual abuse at all, when this was such an explosive topic. But I would welcome any and all comments from you.

The basic theme of my book is one that you might disagree with as being too gloomy: that non-Inuit are rapidly and irrevocably destroying most Inuit lifeways, leaving in their wake welfare dependency, alcoholism, violence, gasoline sniffing, and an unbridgeable gap between older and younger people, and that within the next 20 years the Canadian Arctic will become so ecologically damaged (by, say, oil spills in Lancaster Sound, mining, bulldozing, etc.) as to finish the job. This is how things seem to me, and obviously I do not want to believe that I am right. In my view the relocation is a typical example of non-Inuits' wanton disregard of Inuit life and priorities. I would be interested in your thoughts on this. Tell me if there is anything that can be done, anything that you are doing, that has hope of addressing these longterm problems, and if there is anything that my readers (by and large, US and British people of average decency, without much real knowledge of the Inuit) can learn from you, do with you, or help you with. As a US citizen I have a great envy of and respect for your heritage. I go to the Arctic whenever I can, and want nothing better than that it be preserved for itself and for your use . . .

Yours sincerely,
WILLIAM T. VOLLMANN

No reply received.

3
INUIT TAPIRISAT OF CANADA

Elizabeth Qulaut and John Bennett
Editors, Inuktitut Magazine
Inuit Tapirisat of Canada
170 Laurier Avenue West
Suite 510
Ottawa, ON   K1P 5V5   *24 August 1991*

Dear Ms. Qulaut and Mr. Bennett:

   . . . I have just finished writing a book called *The Rifles*, which deals in part with the 1950s relocations from Inukjuak and Pond Inlet to Resolute and Craig Harbour/Grise Fiord. One of my main purposes is to increase awareness of and respect for Canada's Inuit in these very difficult times when the Arctic seems about to be overrun. This book will probably be distributed reasonably widely in the US, the UK, and (I hope) Canada. So it's absolutely necessary for any allegations, etc. which it makes to be substantiated.

   At the very end of my book I quote at some length from the *House of Commons Issue No. 22, Monday, 19 March 1990, Minutes of Proceedings and Evidence of the Standing Committee on Aboriginal Affairs, respecting: In accordance with its mandate under Standing Order 108(2), to obtain the latest information on current matters, relating to aboriginal affairs; Second Session of the Thirty-Fourth Parliament, 1989–90* (Ottawa, Queen's Printer for Canada), pp. 8, 10–12, 14–15, 19, 22–3. No doubt you are familiar with this document. In it, a number of ITC witnesses give testimony on the relocations. The ITC witnesses whom I quote in my book are Mr. Samwillie Elijasialuk, Mr. Andrew Iqaluk, Mr. Allie Saaluviniq, Mr. John Amagoalik, and Ms. Martha Flaherty. These people make allegations concerning forced prostitution, forced labor, theft of mail, etc.

   From talking with people in Pond and in Resolute, I'm satisfied that these claims are probably true. I've written to the historical section of the RCMP, and they made no effort to refute the allegations point by point.

   One thing that baffles me is that the Makivik Report (Annex 4 to the Standing Committee minutes) does not raise the same allegations that your witnesses did. Their assessment of the relocations was also of course negative, but they did not raise the same serious charges which the ITC witnesses did.

   I want very much to help, and to help I need to understand this discrepancy. Can you explain it? Is there any additional information about the allegations which you can give me? Are there any other Inuit groups which make the same charges?

   I have written twice to Makivik, once to their Québec City address, which seems no longer good, and once to their Kuujjuaq address. (I enclose a copy of that letter for your information.) I got no reply.

Any statement from you will appear (or, if more than a few pages, be excerpted from) in an Appendix to my book . . .

Yours sincerely

WILLIAM T. VOLLMANN

I received a nice note from Bennett (who has helped me before) telling me that my note had been referred to Mr. Jack Hicks of ITC. When I visited Hicks in Ottawa, he refused to give any official response. I support what the ITC is doing and have no quarrel with them. My conclusion on the relocation matter is that, as usual, people are far better sources of information than organizations.

4

PROF. FRANK J. TESTER, UBC

School of Social Work
University of British Columbia

[Tester to Vollmann: Extracts]   *27 August 1991*

There is currently considerable controversy about whether or not people were relocated for purposes of the Canadian government securing sovereignty over the arctic islands. The idea of people being used for such a purpose has a certain dramatic appeal and certainly is the stuff which lawyers love to pursue as it conjures up possibilities of making a huge human rights case, comparison with Nuremberg trials etc. The possibility of getting compensation from the Canadian government with comparisons to the forced relocation of the Japanese Canadians on the west coast during WW II etc. also fuels the whole thing. I'm not a lawyer and have little respect for most of them – including some of those who would like to profit from preparing such seemingly humanitarian cases . . .

Yes, sovereignty was a relevant consideration in the movement of people. No, it was not the only – or even the main reason. At the time, the concern for sovereignty – at least among the lower level civil servants who conceived of the idea – didn't appear to have been as "big a deal" as it is for people now. I think what happened was the government was starting to panic about welfare and related matters and had some problems in arctic Quebec related to relief and welfare considerations. I'm not sure these were any worse than elsewhere at the time, but the idea developed to see if relocations would work as a way of solving the problem of people becoming dependent on the state for sustenance and support.

The then head of the arctic division of the RCMP – a bit of a romanticist who wanted to preserve Inuit culture as it had been when he sailed the St. Roch through the northwest passage in 1942 – was part of the scheme to relocate people to the high arctic to see if they could "make a go of it" in an area that apparently had adequate game populations to support human communities. This was surmised because the Greenland Inuit were travelling to Ellesmere Island to hunt (and hence there was some concern for the sovereignty issue . . .).

In other words, it was not part of a conscious diabolical plot to use human beings to enforce Canadian sovereignty . . . The language used in the government documents is, however, rather horrifying. The bureaucrats talk about a "human experiment" . . .

I am convinced – in fact the records prove – that they were prepared to make other such relocations . . . I think the publication of Farley Mowat's *People of the Deer* in 1951 had a lot to do with the pressure and fears that developed within the bureaucracy. His book – which is mostly fabrication I'm afraid – put a lot of pressure on the government to make sure that no more Inuit died of starvation in this country. You can understand – in a modern western nation like Canada, trying to play a role on the international stage – this sort of thing just doesn't look good.

I suspect that officials over-reacted. I don't think conditions in arctic Quebec – while bad – were as bad as officials believed . . .

There is no doubt in my mind that the conditions under which people lived in Resolute Bay and in Grise Fiord were pretty terrible, that the whole operation was badly planned and badly executed and that people suffered. Supplies that were supposed to have been sent went missing, people had inadequate tents and equipment and even inadequate ammunition for their rifles. I have no reason to doubt the charges of sexual abuse, but doubt that such charges will ever be proven.

Equipment List for
Isachsen Trip

T he visit to Isachsen was no stellar accomplishment, a fact for which my gear can be partly credited. All the more reason to save others from reinventing various wheels. No outfitting company sponsored me, so I have the luxury of listing brand names with positive and negative remarks. Here, then, for what it is worth, is what I took with me in March 1991, on a solo trip, which required some backup, but to an abandoned weather station, which I knew would shelter me from the wind, so that there was no need to bring tents and appurtenances. The lowest temperature which I expected to find was about −40° to −45°C.

CLOTHING

Marmot "8,000 meter" baffled down parka. Excellent for about a week. Then the absorbed water vapor began to freeze noticeably.

Feathered Friends "40° below" baffled down pants. Ditto.

"Davco Drywall" (Tulsa, Oklahoma) red baseball cap. Useless but it amused me.

Patagonia capilene balaclava. Excellent.

Patagonia capilene facemask, with fur ruff added around the mouth and nose. Fur ruff was a hindrance when it froze (I used coyote; should have tried wolverine). Otherwise excellent. I wish I'd had a spare.

Eddie Bauer down facemask. Good wind protection, but quickly froze into an iron deathmask.

Wild Things custom Thermax/Thermoloft-lined climbing suit with fur ruff added to the hood. Fur ruff irritating as above. Insulation inadequate when staying still. Zippers maddening. Very difficult to defecate and to dry sweat from the middle of my back. However, a reasonably warm layer. It was my fault I didn't have more layers.

Wild Things custom VBL suit.   Ditto.

Patagonia expedition-weight capilene top.   Excellent. Had a tendency to work up under jumpsuit, which was irritating, but that was the fault of the jumpsuit. Perhaps I should have had an inner capilene jumpsuit.

Patagonia expedition-weight capilene bottoms.   Excellent.

Steger Designs fur-ruffed leather expedition mitts.   Excellent for about a week. Much thicker and warmer than the Chouinards. Inuit acquaintances were not impressed by them, preferring sealskin, or, for maximum warmth, caribou skin. Someone told me that Steger himself did not take these to the Pole at all, but wore beaver-fur mitts. I have not spoken with Steger and cannot verify whether this is true.

Chouinard nylon shell expedition mitts with PolarPlus liners.   Very good. These were essential to have once the Steger mitts iced up inside. Good only for backup, however.

Gore-Tex ski gloves.   Not warm enough; hard to put on with numb fingers.

lightweight capilene gloves.   Excellent.

lightweight polypropylene gloves.   Excellent.

Stephenson Warmlite VBL gloves (2 pair).   Excellent during periods of activity; quite dangerous otherwise. Under the capilene or polypro gloves alone, in the sleeping bag, the moisture in these would freeze against my fingers.

Stephenson Warmlite VBL socks (2 pair).   Excellent.

Hollofill socks.   Excellent.

wool socks (2 pair).   Excellent.

Thermoloft-lined socks.   Excellent.

Steger Designs "Arctic blues" rubberized "shoe-pac" type mukluks with wool insoles and spare liners.   Useless to me. In the cold these shrank so much that I could never get my feet into them. However, if my sleeping bag had worked better I could have warmed them inside it at night and they might have worked, so I can't pass judgment.

Sorel "Dominator" rubberized "shoe-pac" type boots with neoprene insoles.   Excellent for a week. One is supposed to change the felt liners after each use, but this is not easy with numb fingers since they fit very tightly. The VBL socks saved me from having to do this. After a week, however, the liners had absorbed sufficient moisture to freeze to the leather, and became disagreeable to put on, although they would thaw after I walked half a mile or so. I find the leather of the uppers to be too soft; they wrinkle and tend to drag socks down, so before this trip I sewed some long thin strips of leather inside them to make them a little more rigid; this worked very well.

Sherpa "Snow-Claw" snowshoes, sufficient for my weight without a full pack, with a short-toothed "recreational" binding. The snow was so hard that these were unnecessary.

EQUIPMENT

Stephenson Warmlite "Triple" sleeping bag with X Thick "SSSS" top and integral foam pad. Despite the manufacturer's claim, this is not good to −40°. There is not enough down to keep a person warm. The integral pad works well, though it is bulky. The many tiny zippers are quite horrible to work. I cannot recommend this bag for winter Arctic use.

bivvy sack for the same, made slightly oversize to accommodate my down parka and pants if so needed for extra warmth. Good.

ground cloth (to wrap around sleeping bag if needed). Adequate.

oversize Chouinard stuffsack for all these. Being nylon, it became very brittle and tore, although it lasted the trip. Not worth the expense.

North Face "Snow Leopard HC" backpack (9,000 cubic inches capacity). Despite the manufacturer's assurances, the plastic hip belt buckle shattered immediately.

homemade broomhandle walking stick with attached ski pole basket and screw-nail point. Excellent.

Mossberg 500 12-gauge pump shotgun with 50 rounds of rifled slugs. Excellent. I took off the wooden stock for compactness. When degreased and sprayed with Synco Teflon Super-Lube, the action moved smoothly until the very last day.

MSR XGK II stove. Plastic pump shattered the first night. Otherwise excellent.

MSR XGK stove as a backup. Adequate. This stove was old and had a "heart murmur."

MSR XPD cookset with heat exchanger. Excellent.

small foam pad square to insulate base of stove. Unnecessary indoors.

measuring cup

spoon

fuel cans, windproof matches, etc.   Hurricane matches rarely work well. I should have brought three times as many matches as for a summer trip.

Nissan stainless 1-liter thermos.   Would keep boiling water from freezing for about 13 to 14 hours with temperatures in the −30s. Cap had to be tapped with a hammer before it would open. Conduction to the cold metal made handling this item a very unpleasant experience. I should have insulated this in a sealskin.

hammer with fiberglass handle.   Adequate.

saw to cut snow blocks.   Confiscated by the airline, so I never got to try it.

plastic siphon for Arctic A diesel.   Shattered right away.

"Life-Link" 2-piece Lexan shovel.   Adequate.

lightweight rope and parachute cord

duct tape

knife

extra baggies (polyethylene OK to −100°F).   Adequate.

FOOD

BREAKFAST

homemade muesli with dried fruit and chocolate @ 1 cup per day

powdered milk @ ¼ cup/breakfast

LUNCH

homemade fruit-nut pemmican (1 bag, or about 10 cups)

homemade beef jerky (1 bag)

various instant soups, with soy flour and oil for thickness, and hard sausage and cheese added

DINNER

instant mashed potatoes

home-dried vegetables, spiced to taste

homemade and -dried meat-onion sauce (from 5 lbs ground beef and 5 lbs chicken)

pasta (1 bag)

cheese (2 lbs − this includes the cheese used in the soups for lunch). The food was fine except for this, which froze as described in the text.

OTHER
> chocolate bars @ 1/day
> Tang and instant cocoa

Although I planned a trip of only 10 days, I brought provisions for 20, in case my return should be delayed by bad weather or if my metabolism simply needed more.

MEDICAL SUPPLIES

ibuprofen (for sore muscles and as a possible aid for frostbite).   Not used.

ace bandage.   Not used.

band aids.   Not used.

vaseline to grease face and extremities as needed.   Excellent.

Desenex athlete's foot ointment, as needed with long use of VBL socks.   Froze
> solid.

OBSERVATION AIDS

Peet pocket barometer.   Excellent.

Ertco Pentane thermometer (range −100° to +50°C).   Excellent, until it broke.

"Wind Wizard" windspeed indicator.   Adequate.

Brunton compass (mainly to watch the foolish play of the needle).   Adequate.

topographic maps.   Adequate.

EFFETE PURSUITS

Notebook

Franklin's *Narrative of a Journey to the Shores of the Polar Sea*

Paper and pencils for sketching at −30°C.   Excellent.

Acknowledgements

CANADA

Like other Dreams in the series, this book straddles the gap between fiction and documentary history. I owe a lot to the shade of poor Franklin, a decent inoffensive soul with whom I have taken gross liberties. I owe still more to people I've actually met. In Resolute Bay, Cornwallis Island, I want to thank Mr. Levi Nungaq for sharing with me his memories of being relocated from Inukjuak. I am indebted to Ms. Elizabeth Allakariallak (1988), who took the trouble to act as interpreter during the interview, and once again during another interview conducted for the BBC in 1991 under trying circumstances. Mr. David Roberts arranged excellent lodging at a time when provisions were low and the plane home had been delayed half a week. David also first showed me the standing parliamentary hearings on the relocation. Both David and Elizabeth put me up on my visit to Resolute in 1991, and loaned me extra gear which made a big difference at Isachsen. They've cooked me meals, driven me around, introduced me to people, and I sincerely appreciate it. They have been better friends than I deserve. Ms. Minnie Allakariallak let me try Inuit-style food (I had a field day whacking frozen meat with her axe) and baked the best bannock I have ever eaten. I have stayed with her twice now and feel that I've learned a lot from her. Mr. Claude Paquet and Ms. Jacinthe Saint Laurent, the two radio operators for the Coast Guard at Resolute, sent messages for me in 1988 and were always hospitable; it was pleasant to come out of the wind for a half-hour now and then to chat with them. Mr. Buster Welsh of the Department of Fisheries educated me about the state of lead contamination in Arctic char. Corporal Jim O'Neill of the Royal Canadian Mounted Police gave me information on polar bear safety (likewise the Polar Bear Watch Officer in Inuvik and Mr. Bob Gamble of Parks Canada – Yellowknife).

I would like to thank Mr. Dennis Stossell of Atmospheric Environmental Services (Environment Canada) in Winnipeg for his kind assistance in transportation from Resolute to Eureka, Ellesmere Island, where AES operates a weather station, and also in arranging for me to visit the decommissioned station at Isachsen, Ellef Ringnes Island. His advice and encouragement went beyond the bounds of duty. Whenever I had a question, Dennis was able either to answer it or to introduce me to someone who could. Marv Lassi, inspector of auto stations, gave me a key to the shed that he built at Isachsen, explained the layout of the station, showed me how to use the propane heater, which was literally a lifesaver. I am sorry that I left the place in worse shape than I found it. Thanks also to the AES people in Resolute for their help with these charter flights. Ivan was especially kind.

At Eureka, Mr. John Paten, handyman, was official chauffeur on slops trips to the dump to visit the Arctic wolves and one very greedy seagull. He also gave me a much-needed beer. Ms. Kelly Jane Phineuf, weather balloon operator, ran the Skull Point Ride-Along Service. I don't know which I enjoyed more: the scenery, the warmth of Kelly's personality, or the warmth of the van, which gave my frozen boots a chance of thawing for a few minutes. Mr. Wayne Emond, Officer-in-Charge, let my friend Ben and me camp in close proximity to the station and fill up my water bottle inside as often as I liked, which I greatly appreciated once the rivers froze. Wayne also invited us in for dinner on the last day. Speaking of dinner, I must mention the cook, Mr. Robert Bougard, who also gave me dinner on my return from the Sawtooth Range. The food was hot, the meat succulent with little bits of fat. May Robert live forever. Most of all on that trip I'd like to thank the above-mentioned Ben, that is to say Mr. Ben Pax of San Francisco, who, putting aside common sense, bore with me for thirty-four days of wind, fog, snow, loneliness and frozen shoes. He has been a fine companion, partner and friend.

In Pond Inlet, I am grateful to Mr. and Mrs. Glenn and Elisapi Johnson, to Mr. John Henderson and his wife Mrs. Carmen Kayak, to Ms. Peggy Richardson for a wonderful thirtieth birthday party, to Mr. Joannie Mucktar, to Ellen and Pakkuk, to Ms. Lily Tongak, Mr. Ray Stubbert and his family, and to Mr. Seth Pilsk for accompanying me on that first visit. I would also like to thank Ms. Hannah Paniapakoocho, Ms. Jolene Lightstone, and everyone else in that crew.

In Ottawa, Mr. David Webster, editor of *Inuktitut* magazine, very kindly gave me permission to reproduce a map of the Canadian Arctic archipelago in the first publication of the Textual Note to this volume. Mr. Webster also sent me an Inuktitut–English dictionary and a list of helpful contacts. I thank him. Ms. Megan Williams of the Canada Arts Council gave me access to the Arctic research transportation schedule for 1991, which assisted my travel plans – no thanks to Polar Continental Shelf. My thanks also to Mr. Brian Hannah of Weatherhaven.

UNITED STATES

Esquire magazine gave me $5,000 of the $12,000 that I required to visit Isachsen in spring 1991. I especially want to thank Mr. Will Blythe for making this happen. It was the first of many kindnesses he has done me. My friend and former teacher, Dr. John E. Mawby, introduced me to Dr. Howard Hutchison of the University of California Museum of Paleontology, Berkeley, who gave me useful suggestions on travel in Ellesmere Island. I would also like to thank Mr. Jim Fife of Mountain Safety Research for his advice on the use of MSR stoves in extreme conditions. My parents wrote me a long letter about my plans to go to Isachsen, concluding: "You will surely freeze to death." But when I persisted in my folly, they paid for the backup stove, the snowshoes, and a variety of other items which I was glad to have. Ms. Helen Epstein, Mr. Seth Pilsk, Mr. Paul Foster and Mr. Michael Jacobson kindly read and commented on the manuscript. Mr. Paul Slovak at Viking continued to help me with patience, friendship and encouragement.

ENGLAND

As ever, I am grateful to my friends Esther Whitby and Howard Davies for their care on this manuscript. I hope that circumstances will allow us to continue working together.

ᐅᐊ ᕝᑦ

SIBERIA

Grise Fiord

BERING STRAIT

Resolute

ALASKA

CANADA

King William Island

Coppermine

HUD BA

Churchill

o Winnipeg

UNITED STATES

	A	B	C	D
1	◁	△	▷
2	ᘁ	ᐸ	ᐱ	ᐳ
3	ᘁᖯ	ᐸᖯ	ᐱᑊ	ᐳᑊ
4	ᖯ	ᖯ	ᑊ	ᑐ
5	ᒐ	ᒐ	ᒉ	ᒍ
6	ᒐ	ᒐ	ᒉ	ᒍ
7	ᒐ	ᒐ	ᒉ	ᒍ
8	ᔭ	ᔭ	ᕂ	ᔨ
9	ᐸ	ᐳ	ᐯ	ᔭ
10	ᕐ	ᕐ	ᕌ	ᔭ
11	ᕈ	ᕋ	ᕆ	ᕇ
12	ᖊ	ᖊ	ᖏ	ᖏ
13	ᖊᖯ	ᖊᖯ	ᖏᑊ	ᖏᑊ
14	ᙯ	ᙯ	ᙰ	ᙰ

S Y L L -

ᒋᒍᕐ ᐅᑎᒉ ᖅᑕ ᑐᖅ

he never sto

ᐅᐃᑕᒉᙯ (uit

takes him as

husband

ᔨᐸᑎᖅ

0

650   SCALE OF MILES